The Ghosts
Of Bayou Potomac

Louis Tridico

This is a work of fiction. All characters, events, organizations
and some of the locations portrayed in this novel
are products of the author's imagination.

THE GHOSTS OF BAYOU POTOMAC
Copyright 2013 by Louis Tridico
Duke Street Press

ISBN-10: 0615856497
EAN-13: 9780615856490

For Casey, who always loved a good ghost story

Table of Contents

Chapter 1

The White House press conference looked like any other press conference in the James S. Brady Press Briefing Room: the seated press corps, the cameras, the lights, the presidential podium, with assorted presidential advisors off to one side. But there was one big difference that day. There were two presidents in the room. One very much engaged. And one who was very, very dead.

President Beau Bergeron was the president who was very much engaged. One year into his first term and the shit had finally hit the fan. He, of course, was the fan.

"Mr. President, some would say sending the *George Washington's* carrier task force toward the South China Sea is too provocative at this time."

Beau looked at the NBC correspondent and gave him his most thoughtful look. *What an asshole,* he thought. *What the guy really meant was, he thought sending the task force was too provocative.* "Good question, Steve, if there had been a question mark at the end of that statement," Beau said. There were some mild chuckles from the room. "The Seventh Fleet has operated in the those waters long before I got here. Its deployment is routine, as is how we position our forces in the area. There is no provocation."

The room erupted into questions.

"Cathy," Beau said, and pointed at a thirty-something blonde from some Christian magazine whose name he couldn't remember. But he could remember Cathy. She looked like some hot country singer from Nashville. Big hair. Big boobs. Big blue eyes.

She stood up, wiped her bangs from her eyes and smiled at Beau. "Mr. President, since the National People's Congress has yet to elect a new president, do you feel this is a power play by the chairman of the Central Military Commission to make a move on that position and bring the military hardliners into power?"

Beau nodded and thought to himself, *"Definitely a C-cup. Maybe a 37."* The First Lady sported an impressive rack, so he had something to compare it to. "Ah. *There's* a question," he said. Again, a few chuckles. Mike from NBC didn't look happy. "The National People's Congress is taking a prudent approach to selecting their next leader. I applaud that. President Lu's untimely death caught everyone by surprise. They're just trying to get a handle on the thing and do what's best for China."

Lu's "untimely death" had been a big surprise, most certainly for Lu, who was only 58 years old and in perfect health. Beau and the rest of the world had been told it was an aneurysm in the brain. The CIA wasn't so sure. Intel coming out of Beijing pointed to some other possibilities. They were still looking into that. Beau had never met the man, but there had been plans in the works for Lu to visit Washington. *Scratch that party.*

Beau, of course, couldn't reveal what he *really* knew was going on over there. China's new aircraft carrier and its support ships had quietly moved into the South China Sea, international waters that the Communist regime had always claimed as their own. Most of the tension over the years had been between Chinese fishing fleets and the local Coast Guards of South Korea, Taiwan, Vietnam, Malaysia and the Philippines. Nothing for anyone to get overly excited about. But these were rich fishing areas, and the economics were tremendous. Beau knew it wasn't so much the fish, though, as the *oil*. Some estimates had over 200 billion barrels of oil under the South China Sea. Basically 80% of Saudi Arabia's reserves. It looked liked the Chinese were finally going to put a stake in the ground, or a buoy in the water, or a drilling rig, or whatever, and make it official. They wanted the oil all to themselves.

Before becoming president, and before serving two terms as Louisiana's governor, Beau had been a successful attorney specializing in the oil business. There was a lot of shit he didn't know anything about, but oil wasn't one of them. There was a ton of money to be made by somebody out there.

The Chinese navy's movements were known to everyone in this room. What they didn't know, and Beau did, was that the hardliners really were running the place over there, and they were going for the oil grab. Or so the CIA said.

This constituted the "shit" part of "hitting the fan." And while Beau Bergeron had plenty of shit thrown his way during his political career, this kind of shit he could do without. The Chinese had been flexing their economic muscle for years, even though some of their domestic policies and human rights records were abysmal. Still, their military buildup had been relatively passive, although steady. It had been watched with concern by America and her Pacific allies, but until now, nothing appeared overly aggressive. *Until now,* he thought.

Beau's first year in office had been relatively tame. No big initiatives were launched. This was all by design, part of his "Small, Medium and Large" strategy that had made his two terms as Louisiana's governor so successful. It went something like this: introduce small, winnable programs at first. A couple of quick wins to get some positive vibe and attract the bandwagon crowd. Then move on to one or two slightly more ambitious things and knock them down. Now the bandwagon was getting full. Everybody wanted to be on board, and even his detractors wanted to join the success. Finally, with allies on both sides of the aisles, he'd go for the big win. The defining program. In the case of Louisiana, it had been dramatic education reform that had vaulted the state from near last in the country to somewhere in the middle in teacher pay, student scores and assistance for the poor.

Small, Medium, Large. His statewide success had gotten the attention of the national media and the party machine. If he could fix Louisiana, they thought, hell, he could fix anything. His inner circle had pushed him to consider a run for president. Or V.P. if it was offered. Make a strong run in the primaries and see what happens, they said. He had been reluctant, but the polls bolstered their point and soon he was a legitimate contender. He was in his mid forties, six-one, handsome, lean, with a full head of black hair and a little gray around the temples. His dark features, warm demeanor and Cajun accent made him stand out, especially among women. He was very comfortable in his skin, affable, and a great storyteller. The camera loved him. And men labeled him a "guy's guy." Somebody they could hunt or fish with, or sit at a poker table with and knock back a few beers.

Before he knew it, he was standing in front of the Capitol building on a clear, cold January morning with one hand raised as he took the oath of office. The first Cajun President. *Crawfish boils in the Rose Garden*, late-night comics proclaimed. The pundits now called D.C. and the White House "Bayou Potomac."

The rest had been a blur. Moving his wife and three teenage kids into the White House. Getting his team in place. Trying not to make an idiot out of himself, because he knew the media who had loved him before, who had put him in office, would now turn on him at the drop of a hat.

One year in, and he was still in the *Small* phase of the plan. A couple of easy wins. By this time, he wanted to be into the *Medium* stuff, but Washington was proving to be a little savvier about President Beau Bergeron's strategy. The game was on.

Now this shit, he thought.

"Carl," Beau said with a nod to an older gentleman in the front row. This would be Carl Keegan with *The New York Times.* He was an ancient warrior who'd parried with at least five presidents. Beau always thought he looked a little like a nice grandfather type, but he knew Keegan was far from it. He was a boozy Darth Vader with a pen instead of a light saber.

"What if the hardliners are already in place in the Chinese government? Is your administration, just one year on the job, prepared to assert America's position in the Asian-Pacific region?"

Beau again nodded. The old bastard knew what was up and was baiting him. Keegan had sources all over town, including Langley. He'd have to be careful here, because he knew the truth would be out in a few days, if not tomorrow.

"Well, Carl, we'll know soon enough who's in charge over there. When that happens, we'll continue our ongoing dialogue with Beijing on issues relevant to both our countries: fair trade, a strong global economy and stability in the region, to name a few. I'll have him or her over for some good jambalaya and a few cold beers. Friendship starts with a full stomach, my grandmother always said." He gave Keegan, and the cameras, a slight smile. He could have sworn the old journalist rolled his eyes, but Beau was already looking toward the back to answer another question.

And that's when he saw him. Off to the right, standing next to a CNN cameraman. A distinguished looking gentleman with a full head of gray hair, parted on the left in a bit of an early comb-over. He wore what Beau could only describe as a period costume: a dark coat with vest, a high-collared shirt with a black silk neck cloth tied in a bow. He looked to be about six feet tall. He was paying rapt attention to the press conference, and in particular, the cameras and lights. Stranger still, he was eating from a bag of potato chips. Beau was never much on decorum, but attending a presidential press conference while eating a bag of chips was kind of pushing it. No one seemed to be paying the guy much mind, either, despite the archaic clothes and crunchy potato chips. Beau's initial thought was that the guy was part of some kind of historical re-enactment, or tour of the White House. An actor playing a part.

Beau caught himself staring, and then turned back to the shouting reporters, finally choosing the reporter from the Associated Press, a rumpled middle-aged man with horn-rimmed glasses. "Mr. President, is it true the Chinese ambassador has been summoned to the White House, and you'll be speaking to him later today?"

Crap, Beau thought. *Who the hell let that out of the bag?* He continued to be amazed at how much access these White House correspondents had to inside information. He went for it. "Yes, the ambassador is scheduled for a meeting later today. Part of our ongoing discussion of the Chinese government's transition. I find these meetings to be very informative, and we get real-time answers to our questions."

"Thank you, Mr. President," Carl Keegan said loudly. As senior reporter in the room, it was his job to end the press conference.

"Thank you, everyone," Beau said and nodded to the still-shouting press corps. He took one last look at the costumed gentleman on the right, whose head swiveled around the room, watching the press conference end. Beau stepped off the stage and was greeted by his Chief of Staff, Terry Melancon.

"Good job," Terry said.

"Who the hell is that guy with the costume on?" Beau said, pointing toward the odd gentleman.

Terry looked that way and back at Beau. "What guy?"

Chapter 2

Beau, Terry and press secretary Cindy Walker stepped out of the press briefing room, down the hall past the Cabinet Room and into the Oval Office. Walker was a plain but attractive woman of 40, with auburn hair and stylish glasses. Terry, a lifelong friend of Beau's, was just under six feet, stocky, with short, thinning blonde hair and pale blue eyes.

"Keegan will probably lead with the hardliner angle," Walker said. She shut the door behind her and stood with her arms folded. Beau plopped down on the sofa. Terry paced near the president's desk.

"Broke-dick asshole is in tight at the CIA," Terry said. "Pisses me off."

"I don't want it to look like we're clueless about what's going on over there," Beau said. "We still know more than the press. I think." He stared at Walker. "Please don't quote Terry's 'broke-dick' comment."

"Not a chance," Walker said. "Since they know the ambassador is headed over today, let's use that."

"How so?" Terry stopped pacing a moment.

"After the meeting, we'll leak that we've gained some new information that points to a power grab by the military boys," she replied. "Steal some of Keegan's thunder, looks like we're ahead of this thing."

Beau closed his eyes and ran his hand through his thick hair. "Let me think about it. Anything new from David?" he asked.

Terry looked at his watch. "Briefing in 15 minutes," he said. David Cassidy was Beau's National Security Advisor, a former Special Forces soldier with a mind like a computer with a steel trap inside.

Beau stood up and looked at Walker. "Thanks, Cindy. Can you give Terry and I a minute? And tell Mrs. Foster, too?"

"Sure thing, Mr. President," she said and left the Oval Office.

Beau sighed. "Got a really bad feeling about this, Terry. I think the Chinese, or at least some of them, have been waiting for a stare-down with us for a long time. This might be their coming-out party after all."

"Dangerous," Terry said. "They're betting we don't have the stomach for a knife fight."

"You think that's all they want? A couple of quick, bloody blows directed our way, then step back?"

Terry rubbed his eyes and sat down. "I think so. They know this won't be war. And they don't technically have to *win* anything. They'll take out one of our ships, or a few planes, we'll reciprocate and everybody will call time out. A draw is a victory for them on the world stage. It shows they mean business, that they stood up to the world's largest navy and took their shots."

"All they want is parity, then?" Beau said.

"Pretty much."

"I worry it won't end in just one round, though," Beau said. "Being in their backyard, they might want to play up the home-field advantage."

"Could be," Terry said. He pulled out his phone and tapped in a couple of lines of text to his assistant. Then said without looking up, "What guy?"

"Huh?' Beau replied. "Oh. That old dude dressed like he stepped out of the 19th century, with the costume on. He was standing in the back on the right. Eating a bag of chips."

Terry looked up. "I didn't see him. You sure?"

"Yeah. Weird. Nobody even looked at him. You'd think those reporters would have been all over him."

"There wasn't any guy there."

"Yeah, there was."

"Okay, you're the President. You win."

Beau walked back to his desk. "You know what else was weird? He looked familiar. I've seen that guy before."

Terry put his phone away. "Yeah, whatever. You got a few minutes before David and his team briefs you on the latest. Anything else on your mind?"

Beau sat down behind his desk. Like many presidents before him, he used the famous *Resolute* desk. It was made from the wood of the *HMS Resolute*, an abandoned British ship discovered by an American vessel and returned to England. After the ship was retired, Queen Victoria had the desk made from the timber and it was given to President Rutherford Hayes in 1880. Most Americans knew it as the desk President Kennedy had in that famous picture of his son, John Jr., peeking out of the kneehole panel.

"When's Marissa getting back again?" Beau said. Marissa Bergeron, the First Lady, had been on a weeklong multi-city tour of urban schools.

Terry scrunched his face. "Uh, tomorrow, mid afternoon maybe? I'll double check."

"Good."

"You worried about the Chinese?"

"What, me? Worried?" Beau said.

Terry left and started to walk to his office in the other corner of the West Wing from the Oval Office, but turned instead and walked to the press secretary's office. He stuck his head in the door. Cindy Walker was on the phone. She saw him, held up a finger and wrapped it up.

"Everything okay?" she said after hanging up.

"Yeah. Got a question. You still tape the press conferences?"

"Yep. I wish he'd watch some film like he used to. Help his game some." At the beginning of Beau's term in office, his press conferences were taped, and he, Walker, Melancon and others would grade his performance and hone his skills dealing with the predatory White House press corps.

"Multi cameras?" Terry said.

Walker nodded. "Yeah. Remember how we used to look at the press's eyes while he was answering a question. Body language, stuff like that. Helped me put a playbook together, which I wish he'd still read now and then."

"Good. Can you get one of your people to send me the whole thing? Every camera angle?"

"Sure. Why?"

Terry shrugged. "He's gonna be up there a lot in the next week or so. People are going to be getting nervous. And our adversaries will be watching. Just want to make sure he's sharp."

"Okay. QuickTime all right? Watch it on your computer?"

"Perfect. And ASAP if you could."

"We're on it."

Terry walked out and headed to his office. Truth be told, Beau had been excellent at the podium. It was his sighting of the mysterious guy in costume that had bothered Terry. He was 100% sure no one like that had been in the room. He had been watching the press with an eagle eye throughout the whole thing. If somebody like that had been in the room, he would have seen him. But the President had. Or thought he had. Or imagined it.

And *that's* what really bothered Terry.

Beau stood over the toilet and took a leak. A presidential leak. He smiled at that thought. He always half expected some aide would hold his johnson for him, lest the presidential hand touch the presidential privates during this most basic of human duties. *Did presidents Andrew Johnson and Lyndon Johnson call their johnsons "johnsons?" Hmmm.* He snapped out of this train of useless thought. No, he had the small lavatory to himself. He enjoyed these moments, the rare time he was actually alone. He'd close his eyes and imagine himself somewhere else. Maybe back in Houma, Louisiana, his hometown. At his family's camp on Bayou

Dularge, getting ready to head out and catch some specks or reds. Man, he'd love to be there right now. This job was ridiculous, and half the time he regretted winning the election. And he was only one year in to his first term. *Crap,* he thought. *That was sobering.*

The fucking Chinese weren't just testing America. They were testing *him.* A young president with no foreign policy experience, one year in, with his mind on all kinds of domestic issues. He smiled at that thought. *Domestic issues.* His real domestic issues were three teenagers, living in this nuthouse. Raising wild animals like that is hard under any circumstances. But here? With the whole world watching? There was Beau, Jr. 18 years old, enjoying his senior year of high school. Nina, 15, who looked just like her mother and was the definition of jailbait. And Marie, a bookish 13-year-old who asked way too many questions. Not bad kids. Not great kids. But each one a handful. A frightening, fantastic, train-wreck of a media story waiting to happen, each and every one of them.

Beau finished up and washed his hands. He took a hard look at himself in the mirror. The hair was still mostly black. A little gray here and there and some by the ears, but he had that coming in. He'd seen pictures of how quickly presidents aged in this job. If he stayed for two terms, he knew he'd probably walk out of here completely gray. Might be the job. More likely the teenagers. Especially the girls. They'd probably kill him before all was said and done. Could he get the Secret Service guys to protect him from his crazy daughters? *Hmmm. There's a nice thought.*

He walked back into the Oval Office and saw his secretary standing by the outside door, blocking it. Mrs. Foster had been with him since his days in Baton Rouge. Late sixties, steel gray hair, tall and imposing. An elegant woman who had grown up with his mother down in Terrebonne Parish. She had taught him English I and II in high school early in her career, retired and did some local clerical work for a Houma attorney and supporter. It was her ninth year with him. Not counting the couple of years of English I and II.

She heard Beau come in and turned toward him. "Mr. Cassidy and his people are waiting, Mr. President."

"Thanks, Mrs. Foster. Send them on in," he said. He dropped into his desk chair, leaned back and crossed his legs.

Before she let them in, she took a step toward Beau. "And, uh, T-Ron, Jimmy and Big Mike are in the building."

Beau sat up. "Oh boy."

"Yeah, and they parked their bass boats out back."

"Well, that should give the news media something else to talk about tonight," he said. "Are they on my calendar?"

"After the Chinese ambassador, sir."

Beau rubbed the bridge of his nose. "Okay." He smiled. "Send in Mr. Cassidy, please."

David Cassidy looked nothing like his Sixties heart-throb namesake. He was about forty, lean and wiry, just barely five-foot ten, with short brown hair and dark eyes. He moved easily into the room and stood before the president's desk. Beau had read the man's top-secret background.

Ex-Delta Force. One of the first Special Ops guys dropped into Afghanistan back in the fall of 2001. Organized the Northern Alliance fighters. Blew shit up. Guided in the bombers. In one instance, he slipped into a Taliban camp in the middle of the night and killed six of them with just a knife. Scary little bastard. Looking at him, you'd never know it. Kind of small, thoughtful. No swagger or bullshit. A real, honest-to-God snake eater, though. And smart. He later got moved back to the Pentagon, served as an assistant to the Army's Chief of Staff. Impressed a lot of people. Got a White House post in the last administration. Impressed Beau's predecessor a lot. Now he was his National Security Advisor. Two young men in their thirties followed Cassidy in. One a little chubby with thinning red hair and glasses, the other a tall, muscular type with blonde hair and a strong jaw. *Military bearing,* Beau thought. Trailing them was Terry Melancon.

"Morning, Mr. President," Cassidy said. "You remember Todd and Kurt."

"Absolutely," Beau said. He didn't. He got up and led the men to the sofas and everyone sat down. "Okay, what do you have?" he said.

"Looks like they're setting up a blockade, sir," Cassidy said. They're deploying their carrier battle group along the northern entrance to the South China Sea. It's the proverbial line in the sand."

"They haven't said that," Terry said.

"Not yet," Cassidy said. "We think they're waiting until they're in position."

"Which will be when?" Beau said.

Todd, the redhead with glasses, said, "In the next six hours, sir. Max."

Beau looked to Cassidy, who nodded in the affirmative.

Kurt, the tall military type, added, "They've begun to launch sorties from the carrier, out at least 200 miles."

"They know we're coming?" Beau said.

Cassidy gave a quick nod. "No doubt."

"This line? How soon till we cross it?"

"48 hours, Mr. President," Cassidy said. "Our planes a lot sooner."

"Shit," Beau said. "Our planes will be mixing it up with them by tomorrow, at least flying close to theirs."

"Admiral Lear has specific rules of engagement," Cassidy continued. "Just normal flight ops, out and back. No low-level stuff. Nothing aggressive."

"And what happens when some Chinese jet jockey starts playing chicken with one of our guys, or gets too close to the *Washington*?" Terry said.

"Assertive, just not aggressive, is what I think Admiral Lear said," Cassidy replied.

"I'm gonna need to talk to Lear personally, David," Beau said. "Set that up."

"Sure, but Admiral Winston will want to be present." Winston was the Navy's top guy on the Joint Chiefs of Staff.

"Fine," Bergeron said. He looked at Cassidy for a second. "What's their mood, though, David? You think they want to go a round or two?"

Cassidy sighed. "Afraid so, sir. This might go hot."

"Fuck," Terry said.

Beau rubbed the back of his head and frowned. "Anybody at the Pentagon got a plan ready in case it does?"

Kurt chimed in. "Yes sir, one exists. They're making some adjustments to it now. We want to make it so costly to the Chinese they won't want to take the risk."

"Uh huh," Beau said. "But how much will it cost *me?*"

Chapter 3

The Chinese aircraft carrier *Liaoning,* a remodeled Soviet-era vessel they picked up at a garage sale in the Ukraine back in 1998, cruised at a steady 15 knots in the South China Sea. Originally purchased for "research and training," the Chinese moved on from that phase and made the conventional-powered ship fully armed and operational. Its distinctive upwardly sloping bow cut a sleek profile on this bright, clear night.

Admiral Yang Jinping stared out into the darkness. His thumb and forefinger squeezed his bottom lip together. Short, slight, with a hint of a pudge, the 52-year-old officer was China's top carrier strategist. He had no combat experience, but he had read a lot of books. His bridge crew sat at their stations, monitoring radar and ship communications, maintaining their course now that the last of the fighters had returned. He could feel their tension. This was no routine training exercise, they knew. Word had spread they were going to poke a stick at the American navy and see what happened. Yang knew that wasn't quite the truth. In fact, they were going to seal off the South China Sea for good. It was their backyard. How would the Americans feel if the Chinese fleet regularly parked their ships in the Gulf of Mexico?

He paced the bridge, peppering the crew with questions and requests for reports. He needed these young men fully alert. Things would get really interesting in a few days. He was pretty certain he'd be getting that combat experience he always wished for. Maybe he'd write a book after it was over. How the hero of the new Chinese navy had taken on the powerful American navy and defeated them with superior tactics. A movie might even be made. That would be pretty cool.

Yang knew the American carrier *U.S.S. George Washington* and her battle group were headed this way. Not that he had any great intelligence operation going. He just had the TV tuned to CNN. Pretty comprehensive report. The cute blonde reporter made it even better. Its planes would be flying nearby probably tomorrow. That's when the fun would begin. The *Liaoning,* along with her cruisers and destroyers, had created a long, gray steel wall that the Americans wouldn't dare try to penetrate. He liked that it would be just his carrier group against the American group. One on one.

He smiled slightly. The military boys back in Beijing were finally going to be running things. That would be a plus for his career. Do good out here, and he was fast-tracked for leadership in the capital. He was still a relatively young man, so a stint in politics was easily in his future. Screw up, though, and he was done. Better to die out here than go back home and face the wrath of those old bastards. But he had no intention of dying, and if things played out right, there wouldn't be any shooting at all. The Americans would just quietly turn around and sail back out to the Pacific.

Well, that was what the old guys were planning on, anyway. He had other plans.

Beau had a 10-minute photo op with business leaders in the Red Room over in the Residence. It was a bi-partisan thing about creating jobs by helping small businesses, so no big whoop. A couple of words of encouragement, some handshakes and pictures. Press would be there, but there'd be no questions. He made the walk over from the Oval Office with his security detail and his aides, a few who whispered some pre-game info into his ear about the people he was about to meet. The spring day was nice, so they walked outside along the West Colonnade that ran past the Rose Garden. A gardener was on his knees, tending to some recently planted flowers. There was the faint smell of freshly mowed grass in the air. It made Beau think of home for some reason.

The group entered the Palm Room and walked past its large oval image of Lady Liberty on the wall. They entered the Residence, what many think of as the actual "White House" seen in pictures, and walked down the long Center Hall to the stairs that led up to the Residence's first floor. Beau liked to take the stairs if nothing more than to stretch his legs. Once on the first floor, they took a right and headed down the Cross Hall, a wide, long room that connected all the key rooms on the first floor. Beau noticed a few staff members and other White House butlers and cleaning people moving about. He also saw a gaggle of twenty-somethings outside the door to the Red Room, probably assistants to some of the congressmen and women inside with the business folk.

Beau stopped outside the Red Room to greet all the aides, many their first chance to meet the President of the United States. Before entering the Red Room, he looked back the way he had just come. Farther down the hall, standing near the entrance to the East Room, was that guy again. The one he had seen at the press conference. He wore the same period costume. The gray-haired gentleman walked alone with his hands behind his back, admiring the furnishings and architectural details as if he were about to move into the place. He stopped and looked up at a painting on the wall. Beau couldn't remember the subject matter. He had passed it many times going into the huge East Room for various functions. He stared intently at the man. His aides followed suit and looked that way. They followed his line of sight, looked at each other, and back at the President. He continued to stare at the man.

"Cary, who's that man down there?" Beau said. He was addressing his personal assistant, 26-year-old Cary Guidry, a cute, petite brunette who cradled an iPad in her arm. She looked down at the end of the hall, stood on her tiptoes to see over a few other people and turned back to her boss.

"Sir? You mean Mr. Warren? The one who just walked into the Green Room? He's one of the butlers, sir."

Beau frowned and shook his head. "No, not him. The other guy down by the door to the East Room." Just as he said that, the man turned toward Beau, smiled slightly and made an elegant bow.

Cary stepped through the group of aides for a better view. She stared and moved her head from side to side. "What guy? There's nobody there."

Beau stared down at Cary. "Looking at the painting." He looked back up toward the guy. He was gone.

"Sir? Don't see him. I can walk down there if you like."

Beau wanted to walk down there himself, but shook his head. "Never mind, he must have left. Looked familiar."

His aides looked down there again and back at the President. They shot each other glances. Beau adjusted his tie, but continued to stare down the hall. "Okay, let's do this," he said, and walked into the Red Room.

"Angler in the Red Room," he heard someone say behind him. That would be Steve Olson, his top Secret Service guy talking into his wrist microphone. "Angler" was Bergeron's code name the Secret Service liked to use. He kind of liked it, a reference to his love of fishing. Beats something stupid, like "Horn Dog" or "Crawfish."

Inside were a few senators and congressmen, from both parties, along with five men and women in sensible suits and shoes. Beau smiled and waded into the group, shaking hands and making nice. He tossed out a few jokes, got the obligatory laughs and posed with everyone. After some photos, he hung around a few minutes longer than necessary. It was an old trick he used back in Louisiana. Everyone expected you to blow into and out of these things like a high-priced doctor who saw you for two minutes and then walked out of the examination room. He learned to make the moment feel special and intimate to his visitors by going off the script a little for a private conversation or two. He took great pains to prepare for these, so he knew names and anecdotes and used them wisely. Every moment counted in politics.

Beau wrapped it up and begged forgiveness for having to run, which sounded sincere, and then headed out the door with his people. He turned right to head back to the stairs and the West Wing, but stopped and stared toward the East Room. The guy was back, now framed in the doorway to the big room. He was looking right at Beau and gestured with his head for the President to follow him down the stairs.

Beau saw him. "Let's go, guys," he said. He picked up the pace so fast that everyone fell behind him. Before turning to walk down the stairs, he peeked into the large empty East Room. A lone worker vacuumed a huge rug. The man looked up and smiled at the President. He turned off the vacuum and stood at attention.

Beau smiled at the man and waved to continue. He turned and hurried down the stairs, the footsteps of the herd behind him echoing off the walls. In a moment, he was back on the ground floor and looked right back towards the West Wing. No sign of the old guy. He then turned left and saw him, at the entrance to the Visitor's Foyer. The man smiled, and waved for Beau to follow him. He stepped into the Foyer.

Beau picked up his pace even more and almost trotted to the Visitors Foyer. He slowed as he entered the large room with its pink-and-white checker-boarded marble floor. The walls were adorned with presidential portraits. A uniformed Secret Service agent was standing inside. No one else was around. He looked at the agent.

"Did you just see an old gray-haired guy in a dark period costume walk in here?"

The agent looked left and right. "No sir."

"Just now. Full head of gray hair."

"No one like that, sir." The agent shot a glance at Steve Olson, who had just entered the room.

Huh, Beau thought. He took a deep breath and looked around.

That's when he saw it. One of the paintings on the wall. A huge thing about six feet tall. For a moment, he felt a little dizzy and blinked his eyes. The man in the painting was the 13th president of the United States. 1850-1853. Millard Fillmore. *The same guy who had led me here*, he thought. *The same guy I saw at the press conference earlier. Same gray hair. Same clothes.*

What the hell? He looked back the way he had come. Stole a glance over to the agent. Then back to his aides, who were now gathered in the Center Hall. Beau walked back to the group, a little shaken.

"What next, Cary?" he said.

"Mr. Melancon is waiting for you in your office. Prep for the Chinese ambassador. You okay, sir?"

"Uh, yeah, fine. Okay. Uh...Cary, is there some kind of play, or historical re-enactment going on today?"

She looked down at her iPad as they walked back toward the West Wing, swiping her finger across the device a few times. "No, nothing I see."

"No 'living tours' where guides dress up like past presidents, something like that?"

"No, sir. Why do you ask?"

He looked back from where they had come. "I don't know, thought I saw a guy dressed up in a costume back there."

"Like one of the presidents?" she asked.

"Yeah. Millard Fillmore to be exact."

"Millard Fillmore? I wouldn't recognize him if I tripped over him," she said with a smile. "Washington, Lincoln, Jefferson, Teddy Roosevelt, maybe. But Fillmore? You've got a better sense of history than I do."

Beau nodded and thought for a second. "I'm part of the club. I had to take a test." He winked at her and slapped her back slightly.

"Probably just a ghost," she said.

"Funny," he replied. A slight tingle ran up and down his spine.

Beau found his Chief of Staff sitting on one of the sofas in the Oval Office, laptop propped on the coffee table. He was tapping a few keys. "How'd it go?" he said without looking up.

Beau took off his jacket and hung it on a rack near his desk. He loosened his tie slightly and sat across from Terry. "Fine. Saw my phantom again, though."

Terry looked up. "What?"

"The guy I saw at the press conference, in the old clothes. Saw him standing by the East Room, then he led me to the Visitors Foyer."

"Led you?"

"Yep. That's when I saw it. The painting of Millard Fillmore down there? It was the same guy. Same clothes. Same hair. Everything. The guy who led me down there looked *exactly* like Fillmore in the painting."

"Where'd he go?"

"Vanished," said Beau. He sat forward and whispered, "And get this, the guard in there never saw anybody come into that room. And I'm telling you, it was the same guy I saw at the press conference."

"Yeah, about that. Got some video. I've looked at it from every angle, the whole thing. Don't see anybody like that."

"That's crazy, he was there," Beau said.

"Find him," Terry replied and turned the laptop around to face the President. He got up and sat down next to Beau. "Go ahead."

Beau looked at him and back down at the laptop. Terry had the QuickTime movie up on the screen. Beau scanned through the press conference, back and forth. There were angles where the camera was on him. Others, the questioning news media. He concentrated on the camera that captured a wide shot of the room, from his perspective on the podium. There was no sign of his mysterious visitor. "I don't see him," he said.

"Yeah, neither do I. At what point did you spot him?"

Beau thought a second. "Right after I answered Keegan's question, I went to the AP guy. That's when I saw him."

Terry nodded and reached over to the laptop. He scanned to that spot in the press conference. The first camera was on Beau.

"Okay, okay!" Beau said. "See, right there. Watch as I call the AP reporter. See how I glance to the right for a second and squint slightly? That's when I saw him."

Terry said nothing, but scanned to another camera. "All right, same moment, but from your perspective. Hear your question? This is when you would have been looking at your guy. Notice anything? There's nobody like that standing there."

Beau leaned down for a closer look at the screen. "I'll be damned," he said. "I swear, Terry, I saw him. He was *there.*"

"Hey, those lights can be tricky, you know."

"My vision was fine."

"And you saw him again, just now?"

Beau got up and paced a bit. "Yeah. Same guy, except now I know who he is. Uh, who he *looks* like."

"Sure it *wasn't* the painting you saw?"

Beau shook his head.

Terry sat back. "Okay, not sure where to go with this. Maybe you need some more sleep? Marissa gets back tomorrow. Maybe we get you laid. Or just get your eyes checked. Or do we call the Ghostbusters?" He managed a slight grin.

"Let's just keep this to ourselves," Beau said. "Is it too early for a drink?"

Chapter 4

One Scotch and 45 minutes later, Beau Bergeron sat stone faced as the Chinese ambassador went on and on about his country's peaceful intentions and earnest effort to pick a new leader. The squat little man with chubby cheeks and squinty eyes appeared a little sweaty and a lot nervous. His translator was a lot calmer. She was a young woman of about 30 with librarian glasses and delicate features. She was also a spy for the Chinese intelligence agency, the Ministry of State Security. Beau knew this, thanks to those wonderful folks over at the CIA.

Joining them was Frances Gottleib, Beau's Secretary of State, a slender woman of 60 with shoulder-length gray hair, a broad face and big gray-blue eyes. She wore a navy-blue suit dress. Across from her was National Security Advisor Cassidy, and next to him was Terry Melancon.

What had Beau stone faced was not his legendary poker skills, but the other person in the room. President Millard Fillmore, now seated across the Oval Office in Bergeron's chair with his feet on the desk. He was listening intently to the proceedings. He appeared just a few minutes after the meeting started. Beau had simply looked at the ambassador for a moment and then looked over to his desk and Fillmore was there. No door had opened. No one had walked in. He just *appeared.*

Beau's heart was beating way too fast. No one else in the room saw Fillmore. Just him. So Beau had played it cool, keeping one eye on the business at hand and the other on the man, or ghost, now occupying his desk chair. To anyone there, it looked like Bergeron was simply staring out the window.

Secretary of State Gottleib pressed the ambassador for details about his government's transition and timeline. She was firm but calm. Beau knew the next to speak would be Cassidy, with pointed questions about the Chinese Navy's "exercises" in the South China Sea. They had rehearsed the whole meeting, mainly for the spy's benefit, since she would be reporting right up the chain the moment she was back at the Chinese embassy. Beau would speak later with a few well-chosen words meant to send a clear signal back to Beijing.

Man, I could use another Scotch, Beau thought. The guy, Fillmore, seated in his desk chair, made eye contact with him and shook his head *no*, and then stared back at the Chinese ambassador. Beau directed his attention at the ambassador as he rattled on in Chinese. He waited for the translation from Mata Hari, who spoke flawless English. She said, "Madame Secretary, we are quite confident that in the next 72 hours a new leader will be chosen. There is no fight for power. Surely you can understand, as in your politics, there are varying opinions and allegiances that must be worked out."

Beau knew the nerds at the State Department would pick apart every noun, verb, adjective and adverb these two were spouting to pick up little "tells" that might be useful later. It was beyond him.

Now it was Cassidy's turn, and the real reason for this little chat. Since he was not a diplomat, but a former combat soldier, he went right for it and asked the man what his country's intentions were in the South China Sea.

Beau focused on the man's eyes as this question was translated back to him. If he had been holding cards, Beau would have gone all in. The ambassador had nothing but a pair of deuces, and was lying about it. There were more assurances that nothing was out of the ordinary, but Cassidy continued to press the point. This caused the Millard Fillmore guy to lean forward and rest his elbows on the Resolute desk. Beau thought he was going to say something.

Finally, Beau had enough. "Mr. Ambassador," he said. All eyes turned to him, because he had been quiet the whole time. "I'm pretty sure you understand English, despite your...translator...you have here." He gave her a knowing glance that probably ended her spy career, at least in Washington. "In a few days, our fleet will sail through international waters, waters we and every other seafaring nation have used for years. Your fleet looks suspiciously like it's not going to let us do that. I hope that's not the case. Tell your admirals to be very careful out there."

Beau noticed the man nodded slightly and looked to his translator out of habit. The ambassador had understood every single word. Then, the fun began.

Beau leaned forward a bit and said, "You know, Mr. Ambassador, back in Louisiana, where I'm from, the bayou is full of fishermen trying to make a living. They work hard and there's plenty of fish and crabs to go around. No one owns the bayou. It's for everyone. You'd have to be ate up with the dumbass to try and stake off a part of the water all for yourself. Next thing you know, every Boudreaux and Thibodeaux would be up in your traps. Not really worth it, is it? That'd be a full eight bags of stupid if you ask me."

Terry looked down and flicked a piece of lint off his knee, barely suppressing a smile. The two Chinese nodded politely. The girl did her translation and Beau could see her struggle a bit. The ambassador frowned at her and cocked his head. In any language, it meant *what'd he say?*

Beau glanced back at the apparition, or hallucination, that sat at his desk. The man gave the President a confused look. *What'd you just say?*

Beau turned his attention back to the Chinese. "Make no mistake, and I want to be very, very clear here: under no circumstances will the American Navy be bullied in international waters. Or any waters for that matter. We're not looking for a confrontation, or to make a point. I hope the same is true of your navy, Mr. Ambassador. Are we clear?"

China's crappy-poker-player ambassador shook his head in the affirmative and said, through the translator-spy, "Yes, I understand, Mr. President. I will convey your point to my superiors in Beijing."

"Then we're done here," Beau said. He stood and smoothed his jacket down. All the others stood, hands were shaken, and the Chinese were escorted out of the Oval Office.

"Make sure she's on a plane out of the country tonight," Beau said. "One-way ticket."

Gottleib said, "Yes, sir."

"Or just have a bus hit her," he continued. "Can we still do that? You know, have accidents happen to people?"

Cassidy looked at Terry. "Accidents happen all the time in Washington, Mr. President."

Beau waved a dismissive hand and shook his head. He caught himself, looked up and said a little loudly, "Just kidding. Presidential joke. Please erase that from the tape."

"We're not taping anything, Mr. President," Terry said.

"Right. Video?"

"Nope."

Beau looked over at his hallucination. Then at his watch. "After I meet with the crew, do I have time to run up to the Residence? Want to be there when the girls get home."

Terry stuck his head out the door and said a few words to Mrs. Foster. He looked back at Beau. "That's where they put the guys. You're good for about 45 minutes. We can move some stuff around."

Beau hurried over to the Residence and scampered up the stairs to the second floor. Steve Olson, his Secret Service guy, was right on his heels.

"I got it, Steve. Thanks," he said, and walked into the West Sitting Hall. Olson hung back outside in the Center Hall. Inside were three middle-aged men, seated on the sofa and in one chair. They stood as one.

"Hail to the Chief!" the nearest one yelled. This was Thomas Ronald "T-Ron" Guerin, a beefy Cajun with dark features, a receding hairline and an extending waistline. He wore a blue blazer over a white golf shirt.

"T-Ron," Beau said and shook his hand. T-Ron gave him a bear hug.

"Fuck, don't kiss him, asshole," another man said. Michael "Big Mike" Moreau lived up to his nickname. Six-five, 290, also going a little thick in the middle. He had a big, broad face, graying brown hair and the rough features of a man who worked the land. He wore jeans and an expensive leather jacket over a red flannel shirt.

Smiling broadly behind him was Jimmy Fontenot. Thin, with big brown eyes and curly auburn hair. He was the only one wearing a suit.

Beau greeted them all with handshakes, slaps on backs and one fist-bump. "What're y'all drinking?" he said.

T-Ron looked around. "The good shit. Got any home brew?"

Beau held up a finger, smiled and looked back toward the Center Hall. A butler was in earshot. "Dave, four bottles of Abita Amber, if you could?"

"Yes, sir, Mr. President."

Beau took off his jacket and tie and sat down in a chair. The other men also sat down.

"That your Secret Service dude?" Big Mike said, nodding to Olson standing outside the door.

"Yep. You idiots steal anything and you're dead," Beau said. They all laughed, but noticed Olson was not laughing.

"Right," Jimmy said. "We still on for this weekend?"

Beau sighed. "Think so, but you never know in this job." *Well*, Beau thought, *he did know. This week was sucking big time.* "I can't believe you drove all the way from Louisiana dragging those boats behind you. You'll be on the news tonight, I'm sure. They let you in?"

T-Ron laughed. "Hell, yeah. Your people greased the skids and we were escorted in like the Queen."

"The Queen never showed up pulling a bass boat behind a Ford pickup," Beau said. "Although I'd like to see *that.*"

"Where's that dickhead Melancon?" Jimmy said.

"Running the country while I'm up here talking to you jackasses," Beau said.

"That's a scary thought. Watch the money," Big Mike shot back. "I still say he pilfered the social budget our senior year."

"Yeah, remember his room at the house?" T-Ron added. "The last year it looked like the Ritz. He was getting laid regularly in there. Stocked bar, big TV, that sound system."

"He was running the football cards on fraternity row for that bookie, remember?" Beau said. "Made a killing."

"Asshole," Jimmy said.

The five of them – Beau, Terry Melancon, T-Ron, Big Mike and Jimmy – had all been in the same fraternity at LSU. Phi Gamma Delta. Sometimes called Phi G – the "Phi" pronounced "phee" like the Greeks did. Known by its common nickname, "FIJI."

The bottles arrived in a large ice bucket with frosted mugs. The butler poured each man a beer, with a perfect head of foam on every glass.

Big Mike held up his mug in a toast. The others followed suit. "To big bass and hot ass."

"Big bass and hot ass," they all said, and drank heartily.

Beau said, "Where they got y'all bunked?"

T-Ron said, "I got the Lincoln Bedroom."

Big Mike added, "Uh, they put me in the Queen's Room."

"Figures," Jimmy said.

"Relax," Beau said. "That's where Churchill stayed when he came to visit Roosevelt and Truman."

"I'm in the East Bedroom," Jimmy replied. "What happened in there?"

Beau thought for a second. "President Chester Arthur used to stay in there. I think that was Caroline Kennedy's room, too. And Chelsea Clinton maybe."

"Lincoln's bedroom is top shelf," Big Mike said proudly.

"He didn't really sleep in there," Beau said.

"Isn't it supposed to be haunted?" Jimmy asked.

Beau cleared his throat. "Marissa will be back tomorrow. I know she wants to see y'all."

"So how *is* the First MILF?" T-Ron said, and winked at Big Mike.

"Still smokin' hot," Beau said. "The press loves her. And you should see the stares she gets when other world leaders come by. I caught the French president checking out her ass."

"That is one fine woman," Jimmy added.

Beau laughed. "What are y'all talking about? Between the three of you, you got a cheerleader, a Golden Girl and Kate was on the homecoming court, right?"

"Twice," T-Ron said.

"So there you go," Beau said.

"We all definitely married up," Big Mike said.

Although Beau Bergeron had the sexier resume of the group, the rest had done pretty well for themselves. T-Ron owned south Louisiana's biggest and most successful construction company. Big Mike was a huge landowner and farmer, growing thousands of acres of rice. Not to mention the oil and gas that was under that rice. And Jimmy had a franchised chain of profitable Popeyes's Fried Chicken restaurants all over the Gulf Coast and Midwest.

They yukked it up for a few more minutes, finished their beers and got down to business.

"So what do you know about this D.C. Bassmasters Club?" T-Ron asked.

Beau leaned in. "Local club. Joined it about a month after I got to Washington. They fish the Potomac, Lake Anna, Kerr Lake, pretty much around Virginia, Maryland, North Carolina. Good guys."

"Potomac got any good action?" This from Big Mike.

"Not bad. I pulled some six and seven pounders out of there last summer," Beau said.

"Good. We're gonna give it a ride for a few days. Check out the river, get the what's what. See what they're hittin' on," Jimmy said.

"You really gonna be able to fish?" T-Ron asked. "Been readin' about the Chinese thing."

Beau thought about how to answer that one. These were his friends. They'd been together for years, shared everything from cars to girlfriends. There wasn't much they hid from each other. "Uh, we'll see how that shakes out," he said. "Could go to shit. Probably not. Hope not. If I were you, I'd get my fishing in over the next three days." He shot them a mock serious look and smiled.

"Funny," Big Mike said. "Dark humor from a guy with his finger on the button. Don't fuck it up. I don't like my fish glowing in the dark."

"I promise," Beau said, and held up one hand. He looked at his watch. "Okay, I gotta git. The kids'll be home in a minute. Get settled in and I'll look for you later."

"Already unpacked. We're eating out somewhere tonight. Might be late," Jimmy said.

Beau wished he could go with them. He stood and his buddies followed suit. Hands were shaken again. Beau watched them walk back to their respective bedrooms. He turned to Steve Olson. "Hey, Steve. Gonna stretch out for a couple minutes. Buzz me when the kids get here."

"Yes, sir, Mr. President," the Secret Service agent said.

Beau stepped into the Master Bedroom, whose door was connected to the West Sitting Hall. He shut the doors behind him, walked over to the bed, sat down and removed his shoes. He lay back and put his arm over his eyes and sighed. *Man, I need to work out,* he thought. He'd been going since 7 a.m. and normally he'd still have energy to spare. But not today. And probably not tomorrow, either.

"I used to take two short naps a day," a man's voice said.

For a second, Beau thought it was Steve Olson who might have walked into the room. But a quick glance revealed the double doors were still closed. He sat up with a start and looked toward the fireplace. Seated in one of the chairs was his old ghostly pal of the day, Millard Fillmore.

Chapter 5

Beau closed his eyes quickly and squeezed them so hard it felt like he had pushed them deep into his brain. His heart pounded against his ribcage, trying to get out. He opened his eyes again.

"Still here," Fillmore said.

For a moment, Beau thought about calling out to Steve Olson, dutifully maintaining post just outside the bedroom. Then he remembered how silly he had sounded earlier in the Foyer, asking the uniformed Secret Service agent there if he had seen Fillmore walk into the room.

Beau's first words sounded stupid the moment they left his mouth. "How did you get in here?"

Fillmore chuckled. "I have skills even your very alert guard out there can't overcome. You know, they never gave me a guard. Could've used one now and then. Had a lot of enemies back in the day."

Beau felt a little dizzy, as if all the oxygen had drained from the room. He did the eye trick again to make sure he wasn't dreaming. He quickly slipped his shoes on and stood up, looking at the door, and then back at Fillmore.

"Come on over, Mr. President. Have a seat," Fillmore said, gesturing to a chair across from him by the fireplace.

Beau took a tentative step, stopped, and shakily walked to the chair and sat down.

He led with a really stupid question this time. "Are you…a ghost?"

Fillmore made a face, a kind of "good question" acknowledgement. "Technically, no. If you mean, have I been haunting the White House since my death in…what was it? 1874? No. I broke on through to the other side, as Jim Morrison said. Pretty cool, too, if I might add."

Beau leaned forward. "Jim Morrison? As in *The Doors*? And *cool*? Why are you talking like that? Those are 20th-century song lyrics."

"So what? I haven't been asleep for 140 years. You pick up stuff, you know. Besides, I couldn't think of a Jay Z line."

Beau shook his head. "Okay, buddy, who are you?" He stood up and touched Fillmore on the shoulder. His hand didn't pass through him. He was as solid as Beau.

Fillmore looked at his shoulder where Beau touched him, and then back up. "Millard Fillmore. 13th president of the United States, from 1850 to 1853. Whig party. Signed the Compromise of 1850. You read your history?"

Truth be told, Beau knew the name, but not much else. "Sure, sure. The Compromise of 1850."

"Yep. What a piece-of-crap legislation *that* was. We appeased both sides and let the new states out West have their choice of slavery or not. The Civil War was coming. Nothing we could do to stop it. Maybe if we had more balls."

"Uh, right," Beau said.

"You're a Southerner," Fillmore said, and pointed a finger at Beau. "What do you think?"

"I'm against slavery," Beau said.

"No shit," Fillmore said. "You've already had a Negro president."

"Right."

"We came a long way," Fillmore said.

"Uh huh."

Fillmore eyed Beau for a moment. "I *am* Millard Fillmore, son. Watch this." He disappeared for a few seconds and reappeared standing next to the fireplace. "Pretty cool, huh?"

Beau sat back down. Or pretty much just fell into the chair in a heap. He bit a fingernail. "I'm finally losing it," he muttered.

Fillmore walked over and sat back down across from Beau. "Relax. I'm here. You're here. Nobody's crazy."

Beau looked over at Fillmore. The man appeared to be in his fifties, yet had smooth skin and bright eyes. "Why are you here?" he asked.

"Good question," Fillmore responded. "The short answer: I have no idea."

"Wait a minute, wait a minute," Beau said and sat up. "You don't know why you're here? Where were you? Heaven? God didn't send you?"

Fillmore looked down and thought for a moment. "Well, I was in heaven. I was told I was going on a little journey, and the next thing I know I'm here."

"Told? Like...God? You've seen Him?"

"Sure. Sure. You're what, Catholic, right? I was Unitarian. Now, I'm just...Independent. No Whigs in heaven, either!" He laughed loudly. "Nor Unitarians for that matter. Or Catholics. All previous affiliations, religious or political, seem to vanish away."

"I can't believe I'm having this conversation," Beau said. "So you're just hanging around then?"

"Guess so."

"You were at the press conference earlier. Eating potato chips."

"Yep. Your press today is as big a bunch of assholes as they were in my time. Same idiots. Different clothes."

"Dead guys don't eat potato chips," Beau said. He pointed a finger at Fillmore.

"This one does. Pretty tasty, too."

"Can anybody else see you? I think I'm the only one so far."

"Looks like it for now," Fillmore said. "That could change. Who knows?"

"Are you here to give me advice? Help me somehow?"

Fillmore shrugged his shoulders. "Beats me. Seems this business with the Chinese could get interesting. And me? Advice? If you haven't noticed, my picture's not on any money. Not what you'd call one of the rock-star presidents. I had one term and was kicked out. Hell, my own party didn't re-nominate me."

"That sucks," Beau said.

"Yeah, whatever." He did a little dismissive wave and frowned.

There was a slight knock at the door. "Mr. President, the girls are home." It was Steve Olson.

Beau turned to the door. "Okay, Steve. Be right out." He turned back to Fillmore, but he was gone.

Beau put his face into his hands and rubbed his eyes. "Son of a bitch," he said. He stood up and felt wobbly and a bit nauseous. He went into the bathroom and splashed water on his face, but he didn't dare look in the mirror. He was afraid of a face that just saw a ghost.

Beau collected himself and walked out into the hall and up the stairs to the third floor of the residence, where the children had their rooms. He could hear music from one room and laughter from the Spawn of Satan herself, 15-year-old Nina. She was talking on her cell phone. There was silence from Marie's room. The nerd was probably already doing her homework.

Beau thought he'd tackle the nerd first. He tapped on her door.

"Marie?"

Some shuffling inside, and then the door opened. "Hey, Dad," Marie said. Beau looked at his youngest, a hybrid of himself and her mother. Dark hair pulled into a ponytail, her mother's equally dark eyes, but Bergeron's more angular facial architecture. Medium height. She wore faded jeans and a Sponge Bob T-Shirt. She somehow had avoided the awkward look of a typical 13-year-old girl, like a nose a little too big for the face, or a mouth out of proportion. Dumbo ears. That kind of thing. No, Marie looked like a "pre-woman," with just a few curves still under construction.

"Good day at school?" he said. He walked into her room and sat down at her desk chair. She jumped onto the bed.

"Aced a biology test," she said. "No biggee. The usual stuff. Got an English paper due next week."

"Uh huh," he said. "What about?"

"21st-century American authors. Need to pick one and talk about his or her work and how it reflects today's society, if at all."

"Ah," Beau said. "Got anyone in mind?"

"Not yet."

"Why not James Lee Burke?" he asked. "Louisiana author. Brilliant writer."

"What does he write about?"

"Crime, but very literary. Very well-drawn characters. Good but damaged people."

"Damaged."

"Right."

"Okay, I might check him out. When's Mom get home?"

"Tomorrow. Have you talked to her?"

"I'll try to Skype her tonight. How's that China thing going?"

Beau sighed. He kind of wanted not to talk about it for a while. Clear his head. "Well, they want to challenge us a bit, see if we still care."

"Countries have been doing that to us since day one," she said. "Even after the Revolutionary War, Britain continued to deny the United States its legitimacy. The War of 1812 was just the second act of the Revolution. Jackson's victory at New Orleans put a stamp on it."

"Uh huh," he said. *Jeez, I just wanted to know how her day went,*" he thought. "Look, some of the guys are in town for that fishing tournament, in case you see 'em around. Big Mike, T-Ron and Jimmy."

"Okay, I'll say hi if I see them."

"Great, let me check on your sister." He gave her a little kiss on the forehead, which made her frown. "I'll try to join you for dinner."

Beau pulled the door closed behind her, which is how she liked it when she was doing her homework. He walked down the hall to the source of some hip-hop beat that made the diaphragm in his chest vibrate.

Nina's door was cracked open a bit. No chance homework was being done in there. He heard her infectious laugh over the music. A tap on the door got no response. He looked in, and she was lying on the floor with her feet up on the bed. Her eyes looked up and behind her toward him. "Gotta go," she said and switched off her phone. She rolled over twice on the floor to switch off the music from her sound system.

"Hey, Daddy," she said and stood up. She came over and gave him a hug.

Uh oh, thought Beau. Nina stepped back and smiled at him. *Trouble.* She was a younger version of Marissa. Absolutely gorgeous. Flowing black hair, cat-like eyes, full lips, high cheekbones and a nose a Beverly Hills plastic surgeon would love. She was a high-school-boy's dream and a father's nightmare. She wore too-tight designer jeans and a way-too-tight pink tank top. Beau thought about busting her on the *too tight* thing, but wasn't up for the fight. With the Chinese, yes. With Nina? No way.

"Hey, Sweetie. Just came by to say hi. Okay day?"

"Sucked," she said. 'That bitch Katie Svenson was talking to Zach at lunch. I hate her. She does that to piss me off. I told Dave to shoot her."

Dave Dawson was the head of Nina's Secret Service detail.

Beau frowned. "Seeing as I didn't get briefed today on a federal agent shooting a bitchy teenage girl at school, I take it he refrained from drawing his weapon?"

"This time," she said, and winked at him.

Beau just shook his head and stared at his middle child. He knew she would say nothing about her classes today. Something she learned. A test she had to prepare for. Crap Marie would talk about incessantly. High school was a social world for Nina, with annoying classes and tests to interrupt the day.

"You talk to your brother today?"

"Passed him in the hall. We made eye contact. Whatever," Nina said.

"He's at practice, right?"

"Guess so."

Beau Jr. played lacrosse at school, and was pretty good at it. Beau had gone to a few games, and was just beginning to understand it. Not exactly popular when he was growing up in Louisiana. *A combination of soccer, hockey and basketball*, he thought. Beau Jr. had explained how it was a true American game, played by Native Americans for centuries. There was talk he might get offered a scholarship, which was a bit problematic for Beau. Even if the kid merited the offer, the press would be all over it. Cries of favoritism would be heard. Truth be told, Beau would love to get the kid a full ride somewhere. College was pricey, even if he could afford it. It kind of pissed him off that in a normal world, Beau Jr. would be afforded such an honor, but because of his famous father's status, he probably wouldn't get a scholarship. *Assholes.* Young Beau wanted to go to Georgetown here in D.C., something his mother would love. And Beau would be able to catch more games.

"Dad, could I have a little party over here this weekend? Like small, maybe 10 people?"

"Boys?"

"Uh, *yeah,*" she replied. "The girls would sleep over, the boys would leave."

"Good idea." For a moment, Beau went through every scenario he could think of to squash this plan. He could play his China crisis card. The U.S. could be at war this weekend. Always a good excuse to cancel a teen sleepover. But he wanted things to appear *normal,* and the press getting wind that he cancelled his kid's sleepover party, or his bass fishing outing with the guys, would only raise eyebrows here and abroad.

"Okay with me, but before you tell your friends, clear it with your mother. I don't know what she's got going this weekend."

"Ask her secretary."

"I'm not doing that. Just ask your mother."

Nina didn't so much frown as make a face that a girl did just before turning into a vampire. He could have sworn her eyes turned red. Beau considered calling Steve Olson into the room with some holy water and a stake.

"Okay, I'll call her tonight," she said with high drama in her tone. "Whatever."

"Yeah, whatever," he said, and gave her a peck on the cheek. "Get your homework done."

"Yes, sir, Mr. President," she said. Snark mouth had returned.

Beau ignored that and walked out. The music cranked up again.

Did Millard Fillmore have any girls? he thought.

He almost walked right into Terry Melancon.

"What?"

Terry stepped closer. "A squadron of Chinese bombers just took off from the mainland. Headed for our fleet."

"Fantastic."

"Everyone's waiting in the office," he said. "The *Washington* just launched aircraft to intercept."

Beau sighed and said, "Party time. Let's go."

The two men hurried down the stairs, with Steve Olson leading the way. He said something into his wrist mic. Beau couldn't tell what he said. Probably announcing that *Angler* was on the move again. Or maybe he was telling the rest of the staff to start praying.

Beau hoped it wasn't the latter.

Chapter 6

Beau and Terry stepped into the Oval Office and were greeted by National Security Advisor David Cassidy and Admiral Mark Winston, the Navy's guy on the Joint Chiefs of Staff. He was a compact man, about five-ten, with close-cropped hair the color of a dark-gray battleship. He wore stylish gun-metal-frame glasses. Also present was press secretary Cindy Walker.

"Admiral, good to see you again," Beau said, and shook the man's hand. "Lay it out for me."

"About 30 minutes ago, a squadron of SU-30 Flanker strike bombers took off from the Chinese mainland, headed east, southeast. Right for the *Washington's* battle group."

"What is that, like a big bomber?" Beau said. "I'm not familiar with their planes."

Cassidy chimed in. "Looks like a fighter jet, about that same size. Something like one of our F-15s. Two-seater. Russian-made, actually."

"What kind of weapons?"

Admiral Winston said, "C-802 anti-ship cruise missiles. Similar to our Harpoon. Couple of hundred pounds of explosives in the warhead. Range of a little over 100 miles."

"The Flankers can carry nukes, too, Mr. President," Cassidy added.

"How many in a squadron again?" Beau said.

"It varies, but we're counting 19 aircraft," the Admiral replied.

"How'd we find out?"

"Satellites, backed by some eyes on the ground near the base."

"We have spies near their air force base?" Beau said.

"Yes, sir."

"Huh. So what's the bottom line? How soon until they're close enough to launch those missiles? If that's what their intention is."

"The bombers have a range of about 1,600 nautical miles. With their speed and the weight they're carrying, it'll get dicey in about an hour," Admiral Winston said. "That's when they can effectively launch those missiles at the carrier group."

Beau sat on his desk and rubbed his face. "Okay, so what's standard procedure for our guys in situations like this?"

"Well," Admiral Winston said. "We launch aircraft, some to play defense, some offense. The fleet goes on alert. Our offensive planes will intercept and shadow. Once those bombers get inside our defensive perimeter, we go weapons hot and stay on their ass, but wait till they shoot first. If they do, they're dead."

Beau tapped his finger on the desk. "So are they just playing chicken, or is this the real deal?"

"Chicken," Cassidy said, and looked at Winston, who nodded in the affirmative. "If this were a real move, we'd see other things happening, from other directions. It's too isolated and obvious."

"Man, that's some crazy poker hand to play," Beau said. "Crap like this can get out of hand in a hurry. Bunch of kids out there loaded for bear, full of testosterone and adrenaline."

"Right," the Admiral said. "But well-trained kids, at least ours are. Disciplined. Focused."

"Of course," Beau replied. "Sorry, Admiral. Didn't mean to question their professionalism. But you know what I mean."

Winston smiled. "Yes, I do, sir. Got three boys myself. I know exactly what you mean."

Beau looked at his press secretary. "Cindy, I'll need a statement ready. If this does turn out to be chicken, it's pretty provocative. I want my tone to be anger and surprise. Questioning their lack of good judgment. Now's not the time to be doing anything foolish. I want the moral high ground here. That kind of thing."

"Yes, sir. I'll have it in 30 minutes for you to look at."

Terry said, "And if it's not chicken..."

"Then get a press conference set up almost immediately. I want the country and the world to know we're on top of this," Beau said.

Winston chimed in. "Sir, I recommend you change the Defense Condition."

"Agreed," Cassidy said.

The "Defense Condition," what all the thriller writers knew as "DefCon" was a sliding scale of readiness for American forces worldwide. There were five levels, from the least – DefCon 5, when there was peace and love throughout the world – the Age of Aquarius bullshit -- to the most urgent, DefCon 1, which was basically everyone kissing their asses goodbye. During the Cuban Missile Crisis, it got down to DefCon 2, when nuclear war with the Soviet Union was possible. After the 9/11 attacks, the Defense Condition also went to DefCon 3.

"Where are we now?" Beau said.

"Four, Mr. President," the Admiral said. "I advise we take it to three."

"Where's the Secretary of Defense?"

"In the air, sir," Cassidy replied. "Returning from the Middle East."

"Okay, get him on the phone. And take us to DefCon 3."

Winston and Cassidy went to secure phones to make their calls. Beau pulled Terry aside and said, "You know, I could be home doing some fishing right now. Reading about this shit. But nooooo. You said, 'Hey, Beau, you ought to run for president.'"

Terry put his hands up in defense. "Not now. We need to get down to the Woodshed."

The "Woodshed" is the nickname of the Situation Room, a 5,000-square-foot complex of rooms located on the ground floor of the West Wing. It is here that intelligence, Homeland Security, defense and other key departments assemble to keep an eye on things. When the shit hit the fan, this was the best place in the White House to watch it unfold, and hopefully, do something about it. Many believed it was buried deep below ground in some kind of bunker, but that was not the case. It was originally built in 1961, after President Kennedy got pissed that he couldn't get decent information during the failed Bay of Pigs invasion of Cuba. After that, the entire defense and intelligence community had to feed the Situation Room their collective data so it could be better organized for the president and his advisors.

The Situation Room was completely remodeled in 2006 and brought into the 21st century, with high-tech secure communications, flat-screen TVs and monitors. Over 30 people work there at any given time, and are organized around five watch teams that are on duty 24/7. If it's happening, or about to happen, around the world, it's their job to get the info to the President at a moment's notice.

Beau and Terry walked into the larger conference room, where the energy level was high. Some people were sitting, some standing and talking in small groups. Civilians in suits, military guys in full regalia. When the President walked in, everyone stood, shut up and acknowledged his presence.

"Please, everyone, as you were," Beau said. He sat at the head of the table and looked at the big flat-panel displays. One featured the bridge of the *U.S.S. George Washington.* The other a color radar track that was filled with little triangles, squares and circles, with small type around each one. Some of those objects seemed stationary. Others were moving toward each other. And fast. Since this was a Navy thing at the moment, Admiral Winston, who had followed the President in, started things off.

"Captain, if you will?" he said. He nodded at a trim young woman with Hispanic features. Beau thought she looked great in her Navy whites.

She walked to the monitor with the radar on it and with a firm voice said, "Mr. President, let me explain what you're seeing.

Overall, this is the South China Sea. The Chinese mainland is here. Here is the present position of the Chinese fleet. And here is the *Washington* and her battle group. This track is the squadron of Chinese Flankers, headed southeast toward the *Washington.* Here are our F-18 Hornets moving northwest to intercept the Flankers. These other marks that are closer to the carrier are our combat air patrol fighters and other support aircraft."

"Any change in the Chinese jets' direction since they took off?" Beau said.

"No, sir." "Tracking straight at true. No change in speed or course."

"Any other aircraft launching from that Chinese carrier?"

"Nothing new, sir. They've had some aircraft up for a while. Mostly fighters to protect the ships, but they haven't changed course."

Beau studied the radar image now that he knew what was what. He thought this might be a pretty cool video game he and his son could play. In fact there were thousands of kids his son's age sitting out there with their fingers on the triggers of real weapons. *Another comforting thought.*

"When do we know if this is for real?" he asked the room, and the pretty young captain. This time, the Admiral himself took over. He walked to the monitor and put his finger on the screen.

If they're going to launch those cruise missiles, it will be about here. Max range about 100 miles for those things, but they'll want to get a little closer just to be sure."

A close-up of a man's face appeared on the other screen. He was on the bridge of the *Washington.* He looked to be in his early fifties, a little thick in the chest and stomach, but otherwise in good shape. He had a warm, open face, with a bulbous nose and short brown hair.

"Mr. President, Rear Admiral Lear," the young captain said.

"Good morning, Mr. President," he said with a smile. "Or should I say good evening. Dinnertime where you are, sir. About dawn here."

"Good morning, Admiral," Beau said. *Jeez, the guy looked like he was about to head to the office for another boring day at work. Not like a guy with a squadron of Chinese bombers headed his way. I'd be shitting in my pants about now,* he thought.

"Sir, we're tracking the Chinese bombers and will intercept shortly. We're at general quarters now. Our sailors and aviators are at peak readiness."

"Good to hear, Admiral. "I'm not gonna call the game from the owner's box. You know your job."

"Thank you, Mr. President." He looked away from the monitor for a second, and then back up. "The Chinese have dropped down below 10,000 feet and descending. If they were going for a long-distance shot, they would have done it at a higher altitude. This looks like a close-in engagement. Interesting."

"Okay, Admiral. Get back to work. Just keep us informed," Beau said.

"Yes, sir," he replied and walked out of the frame.

"Another tell," Admiral Winston said. "If this were for real, they would have launched as far out and as high as they could, then gotten the hell out of there."

Beau nodded, unconvinced, but didn't challenge the Admiral.

Carl Keegan sat at his cubicle desk in the newsroom of *The New York Times.* The place was buzzing as deadlines neared to close the paper for the evening. The incessant *click clack* of fingers on keyboards mingled with ringing phones and the voices of reporters jacked up on a full day of caffeine.

He stared at his computer screen, reviewing the last three paragraphs he had written. His phone rang, but it didn't break his concentration. He let it go a few more times. In his experience, the more it rang, the better the information on the other end of the line. He reached over and picked it up without ever taking his eyes off the screen.

"Keegan."

"We just went to Defcon 3."

That got Keegan's attention. He knew the voice, so he ignored the pleasantries. "What were we at before?"

"Four."

"Is this normal with what's going on, or did something happen?"

"Happening," the voice said. "Chinese bombers are headed straight for the *Washington.* Our fighters have been launched to intercept them."

"Shit," Keegan said. "How soon?"

"Minutes."

Keegan look over at some TV monitors that displayed the major news networks. CNN. NBC. ABC. CBS. No sign of breaking news. No alerts in the crawls at the bottom of the screens. The story was his. For the moment.

"Okay, anything else?"

"War, maybe," the voice said. "That enough for ya?"

"Stay in touch," Keegan said and hung up. He dialed Cindy Walker at the White House.

The Situation Room had grown quiet. Everyone was watching the monitors. Beau glanced over at his friend and Chief of Staff. Terry returned the look. They both knew that the course of Beau's presidency could take a big turn in a bad direction in the next few minutes.

A loud burp behind Beau made him jump just a bit. He turned to see who it was. It was Millard Fillmore, standing by the door a few feet behind Beau. He had a beer in his hand and was staring intently at the monitors along with everyone else.

He noticed Beau looking at him. "This looks intense," he said, and took another pull on the longneck.

Beau sat up and stared at the ghost of the dead president behind him. Terry noticed that he was watching something behind him and turned that way also. Finding nothing, he looked back at Beau.

"What?"

Beau just shook his head and resumed watching the monitors. Fillmore walked along the side of the conference table toward the flat screens. Of course, no one could see him but Beau. The dead president turned back his way.

"They're trying to distract you from something," he said. "They want you focused on the wrong thing. A useful strategy I used in the courtroom back in the day. Or back in the century." Fillmore laughed out loud and let out another burp. He walked to the screens and touched one of them, pulling his finger back as if it had shocked him.

"Admiral, you think the Chinese are trying to distract us from something? Get us looking at the wrong... thing?" Beau said.

Everyone at the table turned his way. "Interesting thought, Mr. President," Admiral Winston replied.

Fillmore said, "I think I just said that."

"Intercept in five minutes," the female Navy captain said.

All eyes went back to the screens as the American fighters closed on the Chinese Flankers. The little triangles and squares began to merge.

Rear Admiral Lear's face appeared again on the screen that was linked to the bridge of the *U.S.S. Washington.* "Our fighters have visuals on the Flankers. Now at 3,000 feet. No change in course."

"The F-18s are locking on to the Flankers," Admiral Winston said. "Those Chinese pilots are probably getting blasted by alarms letting them know we've got a weapons lock on them. We'll see what they're made of in a second."

Beau felt like he was made of putty at the moment. The incongruity of the tension on the screen and the ghost of a long-dead president standing there drinking a beer pretty much had him feeling a bit disconnected. He could feel his heart pounding again. A thin layer of sweat was forming at his hairline.

"If the Chinese are going to fire, they'll do it now." This from the very calm Rear Admiral Lear, sitting on his command chair on the *Washington,* calling the events like a football game, rather than a guy who was right in the middle of the bulls eye.

The room went completely silent. Even Fillmore didn't move.

A minute later, there were urgent voices coming from the *Washington*. Lear turned away from the camera and barked out some commands. Bridge officers could be seen moving quickly around their command center. "Splash it, repeat, splash it," everyone heard Lear say with a sense of urgency.

"What is it, Tony?" Admiral Winston said to Lear on the *Washington*.

For a second, it looked like Lear didn't hear the question. He turned back to the camera with a frown.

"One of our Hawkeye pilots picked up something weird on his radar just now. In and out, fuzzy. Then one of our CAP fighters got a visual. Subsonic stealth drone low and to our southeast. Almost on top of us. We vectored some of our guys that way and took it out."

"What's going on, Admiral?" Beau said.

Admiral Winston looked a little chagrined. "Well, Mr. President. Looks like you were right. They were trying to distract us. Had a stealth jet of some kind coming up right behind us. An unmanned drone. Lear had one of his fighters shoot it down. Nice call, sir."

"Flankers changing course," the Navy captain said. "Moving toward the southwest now. Our fighters are staying with them," she said.

"Chicken," Terry said.

"We shot down a Chinese fighter?" Beau said. There was some strain in his voice.

"Drone, sir," Lear said from the TV, overhearing the conversation from the Situation Room. "Unmanned. That thing was at wave-top level, 15 kilometers out, heading straight for us. Way too aggressive."

Admiral Winston looked at Lear on the screen. "Tony, get some boats out there and recover anything you can. I want to see how good their stealth technology is."

"Already on it," he replied. "Judging by how close it got, though, I'd say it's pretty good."

Beau had his head down and rubbed his forehead a few times. "Is this an act of war?" he said. "Shooting down another country's plane?"

"They got too close, Mr. President," Terry said. "They know the rules." He looked at Admiral Winston. "They *do* know the rules?"

Winston shrugged. "We'll see. That was very pro-vocative on their part. Maybe a test for us."

"Looks like the Flankers have done a 180 and are heading back to the mainland," the female captain said. "Our fighters are still on them, but they'll have to turn back soon when they get low on fuel."

Fillmore had a big smile on his face and walked back toward Bergeron. He held out his fist. Without thinking, Bergeron completed the fist bump with his predecessor. Fillmore opened his hand in the "exploding fist" gesture and let out a little explosion sound effect from his mouth. "Boom," he said.

Terry looked at Bergeron. "What are you doing with your hand?"

Beau sheepishly withdrew his fist from the air.

Chapter 7

The President of the United States sat alone in the dining room across the hall from the Master Bedroom on the second floor of the residence. Well, that was not entirely true. At the other end of the table sat the other President of the United States, Millard Fillmore, now on his fourth beer of the night.

"Too bad your girls couldn't join us," he said.

Beau noticed Fillmore's cheeks were a little rosier, and his speech was slightly slurred. *Could a ghost get wasted?* He picked at his roast chicken and just stared at Fillmore. "They're teenagers. They're eating in their rooms."

"Always liked to dine with my daughter Mary after my wife Abigail died, right at the end of my term. Then *she* died a year later." He took another sip of his beer.

"Sorry to hear that," Beau said. He took a longer sip of his Scotch.

"No problem," Fillmore replied. "We're all back together now. Of course, right now I'm kind of away on business." He found this wildly amusing and burst out laughing. Beau cringed and looked around to see if anyone could hear outside the door.

"Are you drinking my beer, or did you get that...?"

Fillmore looked at his bottle of Abita Amber and then over at Beau. "From heaven? Hah! This is *your* beer, Beau."

"But that's a real bottle. Why didn't anyone see it when you were down in the Woodshed? Holding it. They can't see you, but the bottle is real."

"Hell if I know," Fillmore said. "Hey, that was pretty cool down there. Like a naval battle."

"It's only beginning," Beau said and took another drink. "Those two fleets are on a collision course."

"Yes, but we've already bloodied their noses," Fillmore said, shaking his fist. "Bam!"

Beau just stared at the ghost. "Easy for you to say. You're dead, and don't have to run for reelection. As if I want to," he muttered as an aside. The Scotch was starting to go to his head a bit. "How did you know about the drone?"

"I didn't. It just looked like a diversionary tactic. Like I said, courtroom stuff," Fillmore said. "You're a lawyer. Haven't you ever done a little misdirection to keep your opponent off balance?"

Beau looked off a second, and then back at Fillmore. "Yeah, maybe a little. I did oil-and-gas stuff. Not the high-drama litigation thing."

"Still," Fillmore said. "Same thing. Study your opponent more, Beau. Think like the Chinese. Figure out what they really want. They think they know you, but I have a feeling they don't."

"Huh,' Beau said. "I don't know *them*. They don't know me. This is how real wars are started."

Fillmore sighed deeply and belched. "Don't I know it. The Northerners and the Southerners never did really understand each other. Not from the beginning. No one was reasonable. Hell, they *wanted* war, the bastards."

Beau emptied his glass of Scotch and put it down. "Got a question for you...Millard," he said. "How can I say this politely? You're not exactly a war-time president. Could you get some of your buddies from the Great Beyond to stop by? Oh, someone like...Washington. Lincoln. Either of the Roosevelts, maybe. That'd be nice. No offense."

"None taken." Fillmore nodded a bit, thinking this through. "Yeah, those guys have got the resume, that's for sure. Played golf with Lincoln the other day. Pretty good with a 3-iron."

Bergeron eyes went wide. "You played *golf* with Abraham Lincoln? I'm pretty sure Lincoln never played any golf in his lifetime."

"He does in his deathtime," Fillmore said. *"Death time.* Is that a word? That's pretty funny."

"There's a golf course in heaven? Really? That's like the oldest joke cliché ever," Beau said. "You know, 'Did you hear the one about Jesus, St. Peter and God teeing off?' Is this some kind of course just for presidents?"

"No, no. Open to everyone. Just have to be dead. Nice course, too."

"This is ridiculous," Beau said. "I'm having a waking dream. You're not real, but my psychosis is."

Fillmore finished his beer. "Anyway, about some additional help for you. I'll see what I can do. Like I said, I have no idea why I'm here. Those are good guys, though."

"Appreciate it," Beau said. "Get Kennedy, too. Thought he did a good job with the Cuban Missile Crisis thing."

"Kennedy, right. Jack *and* Bobby, or just Jack?"

"Just Jack for now, presidents only, but thanks for asking." Beau couldn't believe he was having this conversation. He was ordering up presidents like cheeseburgers. *A John Kennedy, but hold the Bobby. With a side of Teddy Roosevelt.*

There was a tap on the door. "Mr. President, need anything else?"

Beau's head snapped to the closed door. "Uh, another Scotch, Dave."

Dave Franklin stood outside the Dining Room. "Yes, sir, Mr. President." He turned to Steve Olson, Beau's Secret Service protection, who was seated in a chair across the hall. "Who's in there with him?"

"No one," was Olson's terse reply.

"He's talking to someone."

"No he's not."

Franklin frowned. "Okay. Need anything?"

"Nope."

Franklin hurried off to retrieve the drink. Olson watched the butler walk away, and then turned his attention back to the dining room. He heard the president talking again. He wrestled with the idea of whether or not he should speak to Terry Melancon.

Beau didn't feel like going back down to the Oval Office for the remainder of the evening. Hell, he was President. If he didn't want to go into the office, the office would come to him, wherever he was. And right now, he sat in the living room just off the master bedroom. He was taking his time with the latest Scotch that Dave had brought him, reading a report the Navy had compiled of today's fun and games in the Pacific, including details on the recovery of the Chinese drone. He looked up at the TV and noticed one talking head after another commenting on the events. He had the volume muted. They all sounded like yapping dogs anyway.

Terry sat across from him, reading the scroll at the bottom of the screen.

"Hell, looks like they recovered most of the stealth drone," Beau said, reading the Navy report. "The Pentagon and CIA will be happy about that."

"Yeah, it'll tell them just how good their stealth technology really is. Of course, they stole most of it from us," Terry said, without taking his eyes off the screen. He had a glass of bourbon sitting on the table next to him.

"Anything from the Chinese yet?" Beau asked.

"Nothing," replied Terry. "That's a bit troubling. They should be bitching and moaning about it by now."

The U.S. was taking the position that its ships had to defend themselves from a fast-approaching aircraft that didn't respond to repeated warnings to alter its course. That was a little BS, since no one was piloting the thing anyway, at least no one within 1,000 miles. Since it was unidentified, the Navy would say it decided to shoot first and ask questions later.

"I think they don't want to admit they lost a plane," Beau said. "Especially a stealth one." He looked around the living room, hoping to see his stealthy good buddy Millard hanging around. But the old ghost was nowhere to be seen. Beau wondered if he had a tee time to make in heaven. He swallowed the last of his Scotch and put his glass down and rubbed his eyes. The room spun a little. He was officially wasted.

There was a soft tap on the door. Steve Olson walked in. "Excuse me, Mr. President. Your friends are back and wanted to know if you're free?"

"Hell yeah. Tell 'em to come in, Steve. Thanks."

T-Ron, Big Mike and Jimmy walked in, laughing about something that had begun earlier. They looked a little drunk, too.

"Melancon, you piece of shit. How ya doin', buddy?" Big Mike said.

Terry stood up and did the man-hugs with his old frat brothers from LSU. "How'd you assholes get through security?"

"Cajun Mafia. We got connections," Jimmy said.

Everyone grabbed a chair or sofa. T-Ron looked at the TV. "Get that shit off. Somebody turn on Sports Center."

"Good idea," Beau said. He grabbed the remote and found ESPN's popular sports show.

"Almost called you to throw our bail," Big Mike said. "Thought Jimmy here was gonna get into it with some douche bag maître 'd. He was about to call the cops."

"Asshole told us to wait 30 minutes in the bar while our table was getting ready," Jimmy said. "We had reservations. Total bullshit."

Big Mike eyed Beau and his empty glass. "You been hittin' the sauce, brutha? Shit, the Prez looks a little shit-faced, boys!"

"Y'all want another round?" said Beau. "Of whatever?"

They all nodded, the butler was summoned, and drinks were delivered while they all shot the shit about the day.

"I saw a ghost today," Beau said. His speech was a little slurred, so it sounded like, "Saw a gose t'day."

That got the room's attention. T-Ron said, "Yeah, I heard the White House was haunted," as if this sort of thing was normal. "Who'd you see?"

Beau glanced over at his Chief of Staff and said, "Millard Fillmore." He said it as if he were announcing the man into the room. He did look around to see if ol' Mill was there. He wasn't. Beau noticed Terry wince slightly.

Big Mike sat forward. "Millard *Fillmore*? What the fuck? No Lincoln or Jefferson? Somebody like that?"

"Nope, I got Fillmore. Pretty cool guy, actually. He joined me for dinner tonight."

"That's *so* hilarious, *Mr. President*," Terry said. Beau caught his tone and ignored him.

The boys just stared slack-jawed, and then burst out laughing.

"Good one," T-Ron said.

"No, I'm serious," Beau replied. "Been followin' me around all day. At a press conference. In a couple of meetings. Then at dinner. Been drinkin' my beer, too." He took a gulp from his refreshed glass of Scotch and put the glass down. Terry carefully reached over and moved it behind a lamp.

T-Ron, Big Mike and Jimmy all looked at each other. "You're shittin' us."

"I shit you not."

Terry stood up, himself a little shaky now. "Okay, it's been a looonnng day for everyone. Mr. President, I suggest you turn in. Anything happens, we'll wake you up. Big day tomorrow."

Beau stood up, too. "Yeah, probably so," he said, and almost tripped over the coffee table.

"Good idea," Jimmy said.

"Okay boys, see you in the mañana," Beau said, and staggered back to the Master Bedroom through the adjoining door. Terry was right behind him.

The guys watched them disappear through the door. Big Mike said, "Reminds me of the time he got so shit-faced after the Florida game. Remember? Found him on the roof, butt-naked. His date passed out in his room, also butt-naked."

"That was so awesome," T-Ron said.

"What was her name?" Jimmy asked.

"Forgot. But very hot," added Big Mike.

"Zeta, right?" said Jimmy.

"Yeah," T-Ron said. "The Zetas were so hot that year."

Beau sat on the bed and removed his shoes. Terry stood over him. "You okay, buddy?" he said.

Beau looked up. "Fuckin' A."

"Tense day."

"Yep."

"Probably gonna go to a nine on the Sphincter Scale tomorrow," Terry said.

"Guess so."

"Okay, see you in the morning. I'm gonna hang around tonight some," Terry said. "I could use some coffee."

"Hell, why kill a good buzz?"

"Uhh, maybe just to take the edge off," Terry said.

Beau fell back onto his bed. Terry helped pull him up to the pillows.

"Thanks, dear," Beau said. He closed his eyes.

"Sure thing. And Beau, let's leave the ghost stories alone tomorrow. Don't want that kind of shit to leak out to the press. Especially now, okay?"

"Fuck the press," Beau mumbled.

Terry walked out, thinking, *No, they're probably gonna fuck us.*

He walked back into the living room and found T-Ron, Big Mike and Jimmy cracking up about something. ESPN was showing their top sports bloopers of the week, mostly baseball, but some NBA stuff, too. He shut the door behind him, glanced at the TV a second, grabbed the remote and switched off the TV.

"Hey, dickhead," Big Mike said. "We were watching that."

"His highness is sleeping in the next room," Terry said, and fell into the sofa.

Jimmy looked at Terry. "You look like shit."

Terry just shook his head and leaned back on the sofa. "You have no idea."

With the TV off, the group focused on Terry. His eyes were closed and his head was slowly moving back and forth.

"Bad day, huh?" T-Ron said.

Terry opened his eyes and sat up. "Yeah, kind of getting tense around here. Look, about Beau seeing ghosts…"

Big Mike waved his hands. "Our lips are sealed. Besides, we've got more shit that would sink his presidency than him seeing ghosts. Just in case you forgot our four or five or six or seven years at LSU, and maybe the ten after that."

"I try to."

"So he's seeing things again?" Jimmy said.

"Seeing and talking to," Terry replied. "You heard him. He's not joking. This shit gets out and we're sunk, seriously."

Terry's biggest worry was Beau's state of mind, which would affect his appearance, which would affect what he said when the cameras were rolling. Which could be a total disaster during this crisis. If allies saw him a little shaky, that would be bad. And who knew how the Chinese would see him.

"What are you going to do?" T-Ron said.

Terry shrugged his shoulders. "Who knows? I've known him the longest, since we were kids. You assholes met him when he was 18. He's always been an exceptional guy, prone to lofty achievement and the occasional wheels-off moment. Like his desire to be exceptional needs to be tempered every now and then with a truly stupid act of bad judgment."

"Yeah, we could always count on Beau for one of those," Big Mike said. "Usually women, booze, a little weed…"

Or the occasional ghost," Jimmy said.

"Yeah, that," Terry added. "But I thought all that shit was behind us. Now's he's seeing shit again. Like that time he said he saw the *rougarou*. Swears to this day it was real."

"Maybe he has some kind of gift," T-Ron said.

Terry snorted. "Well, he needs to give it back then."

"Again, what do we do?" Jimmy said. "We're his best friends. Loyal to the last man."

"I don't know," Terry said. "We gotta think of something. You millionaires got any ideas?"

"Not yet," Jimmy replied.

"Well, think fast. We gotta get his head straight, and I mean in a hurry."

"Okay, we'll sleep on it," Big Mike added.

Dave, the butler, and Steve, the Secret Service agent, watched the President's drunk friends stagger back to their rooms. They were laughing their asses off about something.

A moment later, they saw Terry Melancon come out of the Living Room, he also a little wobbly.

"President's down for the night, Steve," he said.

"Yes, sir," Olson said.

"And Dave, the President's probably going to have a massive headache in the morning. Might want to have a pot or two of Community Dark Roast ready." Community

Coffee was a Louisiana company that had been handling Cajun hangovers for over 100 years. They shipped the stuff to Washington by the truckload.

"Yes, sir, Mr. Melancon."

"Night, gents," he said, and walked down the hall.

Dave looked at Olson. "Long day."

"Uh huh," he replied. "Tomorrow's gonna be worse."

Chapter 8

The next morning at Bayou Potomac the air was still and muggy, a preview of the upcoming summer still a few months away. Carl Keegan of *The New York Times* stalked the White House press corps office until he found his office, or more accurately, the *Times'* office. He found Dana Newton already waiting for him. She was a young reporter right out of Vassar, who some said was his protégé. She was a plain girl in her mid twenties, made even plainer by her aversion to makeup. She had a short bob of brown hair and wore a non-descript gray skirt, scuffed, low-heeled shoes and a white blouse.

"Morning, Carl," she said. She stood up in the cramped little room.

"Dana," he said. "Should be interesting today." He tossed his leather bag onto a chair. "Got anything?"

Newton grabbed a small notebook and flipped it open. "Nothing ground shaking," she said. "More of a mood."

Keegan gave her a hard stare. "Mood ain't news."

"True, but there's some interesting scuttlebutt going around."

"That ain't news either, unless you want to work for TMZ."

She ignored his comment and looked at her notes. "Seems the President has been acting funny."

Keegan sat down in his chair and waited for her to continue.

"Yesterday, he kept seeing a guy who wasn't there."

"What the hell does that mean?" Keegan said. He was already bored.

"Seems he interrupted a walk to chase down this guy, who looked familiar. Chased him all the way into the Foyer, but no one was there."

"Uh huh. Anything else?"

"Rumor has it Bergeron was pounding back a few more than usual."

"Okay."

"And three of his redneck buddies came in yesterday from Louisiana. They've got fishing boats of some kind parked behind the White House. I think they're here for that fishing tournament the President signed up for."

Keegan made a pensive face. "I don't think they call them rednecks down in bayou land," he said. "Cajuns. *Coonasses,* I think. I think a Coonass is a Cajun redneck."

She smiled. "I stand corrected, then. His *Coonass* buddies are here. Staying in the Residence. They came in late last night after an evening out, plastered from what I hear."

"Wow. There's a surprise," he deadpanned. "Get somebody back there and get some shots of those boats. Maybe they're our secret naval weapon against the Chinese, just in case things go badly."

"The Cajun Navy?" she said with a smirk. "Oh, the *Coonass* Navy. I like that."

"Right. Get that on the web ASAP. Pictures in tomorrow's paper, too."

"First Lady will be back today," Newton continued as she scanned her notes. "Still think she's a twit. All fashion and style, no substance. Bet she's a real bitch behind the scenes."

"An asset for Bergeron, that's for damn sure," Keegan said. He leaned back with his hands folded behind his head. "You're still trying to get something on her, huh?"

"Not overtly," Newton said. "I think she has undue influence over him. One of *those* kinds of First Ladies."

"She's a wife. Her *job* is to have undue influence. Just ask my last three." Keegan gave out a humorless chuckle. "Let's stay focused on our Chinese friends. Anything new last night?"

Newton tossed her notebook on the desk. "All quiet. No more jets heading toward our fleet as far as I know. Heard it got tense down in the Situation Room."

'I bet," Keegan said. "Our source had any access down there?"

"Not directly. He said he got a feeling after everyone left that something else happened."

"Like what?"

"Didn't get specific. Just a vibe."

"Okay, let's run that down. Any sense our guys are going to pull up and not run the blockade?"

Newton scrunched her nose. "No one's used the 'B' word yet, and no, I don't think we're going to stop short. The fleet is full steam ahead."

"Huh, this might get interesting,' Keegan said. "How much time till we cross the line?"

Newton glanced at her watch. "Conflicting reports. Maybe 36 hours. More if they slow down. Heard the *Washington* has the pedal to the metal."

Keegan looked off down the hall in thought. "Sending those jets right at us was a big statement," he said. "Testing us. Like they're spoiling for a fight. Not good. Especially with Bergeron at the wheel. He's got no foreign experience. No military experience. He's a damn lawyer. A deal maker."

"Meaning?" Newton said.

"Meaning he's going to cut some kind of deal, a compromise, with the Chinese. Probably give us some access to all that oil in exchange for us tacitly ceding those waters to Beijing."

"He's fucked if he does that. He'll lose the Senate next year. Then his own re-election two years after that," she replied. "No matter how much money the oil guys give him."

Keegan nodded. "Probably. On the other hand, that bunch of yahoos he's got around him might push him to get aggressive out there. Do something stupid. Might get nasty."

"Then he's fucked again," Newton said.

Keegan looked up at her. "Then we're *all* fucked."

The sun was setting behind the Chinese aircraft carrier *Liaoning*. Admiral Yang Jinping stood outside the bridge, squinting his eyes into the gathering darkness to the east. A stiff breeze tossed his black hair this way and that. He thought about the day's events. The mock attack from the mainland on the American fleet had gone according to plan. The squadron had flown straight at the Americans, and the Chinese pilots never flinched, even when they were intercepted by the American fighters. His little secret surprise – the carrier-launched stealth drone – had given his counterparts on the American ships some pause as it snuck up on them. Almost made it all the way in before it was lost. At least, that would be his official report. A malfunction that made the aircraft crash into the sea. Of course, the Americans shot it down, somewhat of a surprise to him. Beijing had yet to publicly acknowledge the incident, and if CNN was to be believed, neither had the Americans. That gave *him* some pause. They were eager to pull the trigger out there. *Interesting,* he thought. *What were their orders? Were they going to come barreling through the Chinese fleet, or run up to them and stop, diverting their course elsewhere and risk losing face?*

Yang watched a pair of his fighters fly parallel to the ship, turn and then begin their final approach to land on the deck. He wondered if those young men would finally get to see the action they so deserved. They were well trained, and eager to earn respect from the American navy. With any luck, they would get it in the next few days. He envied them a bit. They would have such great stories to tell friends and family at home after all this was over. He would, too. But in a different way. He would probably get a parade. Cheering crowds. Medals. He allowed his mind to wander a bit and he could see the adulation of the Chinese people, and the grudging respect from the old men back in Beijing. He would be one of them some day. Maybe even the top slot.

"Admiral," someone said from behind him. He turned to see the ship's Executive Officer. "We're about to recover our last two aircraft."

Yang nodded. "And the Americans?"

"Still tracking four aircraft to our southeast. One of their E-2C Hawkeye radar planes and some fighters. Seem to be orbiting above their fleet."

"Very well."

"Our second drone is prepped and ready to launch on your order."

"Excellent. We'll wait until later tonight. No doubt they'll be looking for it. Let's let them spend the evening watching ghosts. Get them tired. Then we'll launch our little spy plane."

"Yes, sir," the officer said, saluted and returned to the bridge.

Yang smiled. This wasn't a classroom anymore. Or a chapter in one of the books he had read. Finally, he was going to *write* a book. Strategies and tactics. He wondered what this battle would be called. *The Battle of the South China Sea?* Naval cadets from around the world would study the famous Admiral Yang's decisions and how they led to the defeat of the American fleet. The movie playing in his head came to an abrupt end, like film spooling out of a projector prematurely. The only image left was of the old men in Beijing. Military men, but without teeth. Their orders were explicit. Do not engage the American fleet. Yes, act somewhat aggressively. Let them know the Chinese navy had arrived. But no fireworks.

Well, like he said, he had other plans.

President Beau Bergeron stared at his image in the bathroom mirror. His eyes were red and puffy, his skin looked a little gray and splotchy. His brain felt like it had grown during the night, but his skull hadn't. He tossed back three Advil and swallowed them down in a loud *gulp*.

Down the hall, he could hear the *thump thump* bass of some crappy hip hop song coming from Nina's room. The rhythm had synced with his pulse so now the pounding in his head matched the pounding of the synth drum of the song. *Fantastic.*

Mercifully, the sound stopped, and he heard his bedroom door open.

"Bye, Daddy," she said. "We're out of here."

"See ya, Dad," Beau, Jr., said. He could hear the *clump clump* of his son's walk down the hall. Beau hadn't seen Beau, Jr. last night, nor this morning. The kid had his own agenda. Their paths seemed to cross at random times now.

"Don't blow up the planet, Mr. President." That was Marie trying to be funny.

He thought about running out there for some eye-to-eye paternal contact. That thought made his head hurt even more. Instead he said loudly, "See y'all tonight." He winced. *Ouch, that hurt.*

Then, wonderful silence.

He thought about putting his tie on, but blew that off immediately. He needed the blood in his head. He walked across the hall to the Residence dining room, where Dave the butler had laid out a breakfast of eggs, sausage, toast, OJ and coffee.

"Good morning, Mr. President," he said. Beau noticed his voice was almost a stage whisper. He knew.

"Morning, Dave. Thanks." He sat down and went right for the coffee. Already poured. Black. The aroma alone began to settle his head.

"I'll be outside if you need anything else. I believe Mr. Melancon will be here in a half hour."

"Great," Beau said with little enthusiasm. He hoped his old buddy's head felt like his. A great hangover should be shared.

The door clicked shut as the butler left.

Beau sipped the wonderful coffee and glanced at *The New York Times* that had been laid in front of him. *"Tensions increase in the South China Sea,"* the headline read above the fold. *"American fleet on collision course with Chinese."*

He didn't bother to read it. He buttered some toast and dug into the eggs and sausage. There was alcohol that needed soaking up.

"Morning, Beau," a voice said.

He glanced up to see Millard Fillmore at the end of the table. Sitting next to him was…a newcomer.

Chapter 9

The new face was a large, rotund older gentleman who wore a dark suit with a more modern bow tie than Fillmore's. He had a full, jowly face, receding hairline and a big brush moustache that curled down around his mouth.

Fillmore said, "Allow me to introduce you to Grover Cleveland, our twenty-second *and* twenty-fourth president. 1885 through 1889 and then 1893 through 1897."

"Mr. President," Cleveland said with a somewhat loud voice. "Good to be back. Again. Third time's the charm, right?" More presidential comedy.

Beau gave him a tight smile and a nod. *Grover Cleveland.* Once again, his history failed him. About all he knew about this guy was the trivia question about him being the only president to serve two non-consecutive terms. After that, nada.

"May I?" Cleveland said, motioning to the coffee. "That smells good." He got up and poured himself some of the hot brew. Beau still couldn't wrap his head around a ghost picking up a real cup and pouring real coffee, not to mention drinking it.

Fillmore grabbed a piece of toast, looked at Bergeron, and motioned to Cleveland. "Got you two for one," he said, and laughed out loud. "Two for one. Get it?"

The pounding in Bergeron's head returned. He rubbed his temples and said, "So, Millard. President Cleveland was available, huh?"

"Please, Grover," Cleveland said.

Fillmore nodded. "Yeah, I asked my guy. He said he'd see what he could do."

"Your guy?"

"Yeah. An angel. His name is Sariel. One of the seven archangels."

"Oh, yeah. Right," Beau replied. Now he squeezed the bridge of his nose and shut his eyes. *I'm pretty sure I can just think this craziness away. This can't be happening. But, damn, it is so real,* he thought.

"Anyway, we got Grover here," Fillmore said.

"Uh huh. Everybody else on the course this morning? Some kind of presidential golf tournament? Everybody booked for the day?"

Fillmore laughed out loud again. "Don't think so. It's not my choice who gets to come here. Remember, even I don't know why I'm here."

"Makes two of us," Beau said. He sipped more of his coffee. He watched Cleveland as he sat back and enjoyed his own cup. "So, Millard. What is it really like up there? In heaven," Beau said. He felt like he was about to die anyway, so a description of the hereafter seemed appropriate.

Fillmore quit chewing on his toast and thought for a second. "Well, that's just it. I can't say."

"You mean you won't tell me?"

Fillmore shook his head. "No, it means I'm incapable of describing it to you. At least while you and I are here. It's like my mind here is all muddy about the hereafter. There is no way I can describe it in human terms while I'm on earth. Maybe like *spiritual amnesia.* Or a block or something. The differences between here and there are infinitely vast. About the only way I can describe it to you is...it's just *perfect.* That's the only word I can use. *Perfect."*

"Perfect," Beau repeated. "The golf course, too, right?"

"Well, yeah, that's right," Fillmore said. "There's maybe another word, too. *Simple.* It's not as complicated as the living try to make it. You know, how people down here try to figure out how people age in heaven. Do they look like they did when they were younger? Do people look like themselves? What do they do all day? That sort of thing. All those mortal manifestations we try to apply to heaven. God's got it all figured out. *Perfectly simple.* That's about all I can say about it."

Beau nodded. "Makes sense, I guess." He looked over at Grover Cleveland. "Grover, you agree?"

Cleveland put his cup down and wiped his mouth with a napkin. "Pretty much. When you're there, it makes such perfect sense. Now, when I'm down here, I just can't find the words. It's like my brain is an amoeba brain or something trying to describe one of Michelangelo's works. Just can't do it. I wouldn't worry about it, though."

"I'll try not to," Beau said.

"Millard here says you've got yourself into a bit of a pickle," Cleveland said. "The Chinese?"

"Right."

"What's worse? The short-term risk or the long-term risk?" Cleveland said.

Beau sat back and thought for a second. "Short term I lose some ships, a lot of our sailors and start a war. Which in the long term will cost the lives of a lot more. I guess the prestige of the U.S is at stake, as is my presidency. Long-term, if we screw this up, we lose all influence in the Asia-Pacific region. We give it to the Chinese. Lots of economics involved. And the fact that they're communist. Not a lot of warm-and-fuzzy human rights with those guys."

"You didn't answer my question."

"It's worse long term," Beau said.

"Well, there you go," Cleveland replied. "Be bold now in the short term. The dividends will pay off in the long term."

"You would think."

Cleveland continued, "You know, back before I was president, I was sheriff of Erie Country, New York. Which also made me the public executioner. I personally hung two men. Did you know that?"

"I missed that one in history class," Beau said.

"Well, I did. Made an example of them. Let people know I meant business. Let any other criminals know it, too. That cut down on the mischief, I can tell you that."

"And…"

"And you might need to make an example of these Chinese."

Outside of the dining room, Terry Melancon stopped at the door and turned to Steve Olson, Bergeron's Secret Service agent. He sat in his chair nearby. Arms folded and alert.

"Who's in there with him?" Terry said.

"No one," Olson replied.

"He's talking to someone."

"Yes, he is."

There was an awkward silence in the hallway. Both men could hear the president speaking inside the dining room. Terry stared at Olson, who just shrugged. He went inside.

"Morning, Mr. President," Terry said. "How's that head?"

"Why, just fabulous, Mr. Melancon," he replied.

"Who are you talking to in here?"

Beau folded both hands under his chin and gave Terry a mischievous smile. "Me? Well, I'm having breakfast with former presidents Millard Fillmore and Grover Cleveland. They were so kind to join me this morning." He gestured down to the other end of the table.

Terry stopped before sitting down. "Funny, Beau."

"Why yes, they are. They're down there at the other end of the table, having coffee." Beau looked that way, and both Fillmore and Cleveland nodded and smiled.

"So they're still here?" Terry said. He grabbed a seat.

"Yep."

Terry poured himself some coffee, and took his time dropping in two Splenda packets. "So how long are you going to be running this bit?" he finally said. "It's about to get squirrelly around here and we'll need your undivided attention."

"Oh, you've got it," Beau said. He turned back to look at the dead presidents but they were now gone. "Crap, you scared my guests away."

Terry stared at the president. "Seriously, Beau, what the hell is going on here?"

"You tell me. They're as real as this table." He knocked on it.

Terry sat back and sighed. "Ghosts."

"Technically, no. They're not restless spirits with some kind of agenda. They were sent down here from heaven for reasons unknown, even to them. Maybe to dole out some advice. Who knows?"

Terry sipped his coffee. "Fillmore. Cleveland. That's who the Big Guy sent? The junior varsity? The B team?"

"Yeah, had that same thought, too. I asked for some guys who had war-time experience, but so far, no luck."

Terry buttered a croissant and took a bite. "Remember that night we went camping when we were kids? Off the bayou? And we started telling stories of the *rougarou*? And we started hearing weird noises? And then you said you saw it?"

The *rougarou* was a legendary creature in Cajun folklore. A shapeshifter that might have the head of an animal, like a wolf, or something else.

Beau nodded. "I did see it."

"Right. You think maybe the *rougarou* has followed you here? Shape-shifting into dead presidents to freak you out?"

"It's not the *rougarou,* Terry."

"Oh, okay, I feel better now," he replied. "Did you sleep last night?"

"No, I passed out."

"Comforting. And now you're having some kind of 'episode.'"

"I'm not having an episode. I see dead presidents. And talk to them."

"Okay, let's leave it at that for now and get back to today's business. You'll get your intel briefing here shortly, and we know what'll be at the top of that list. Our planes and the Chinese's will be mixing it up for sure out there. The goal is to keep everyone's fingers off the triggers. The Navy's supposed to lay out the strategy for the next few days, how they plan to run this blockade, and possible contingencies if this turns to shit."

Beau glanced down at *The New York Times* and sighed. He felt a little queasy. What would tomorrow's headline be? And the day after?

Terry saw what Beau was doing. "You read any of that yet?"

"Nope."

"You should. Says that we're at Defcon 3. I'd love to know what asshole leaked that out last night," he said. "Fucking Keegan. We gotta watch that bastard. I think he's bored and wants to take us down."

"Well, I've got a story for him," Beau said.

"Let's hope not."

"What else is on tap?"

Terry looked at Beau's schedule for the day. "Pretty full, as usual. We're gonna have to shuffle you down to the Woodshed throughout the day in between your regular appointments. Couple of biggies, though. Budget meeting at nine with our delightful opposition on the Hill. Cabinet meeting at two. Mostly for show. Supposed to be a platform for you to talk education and science. NASA screaming for more money. Then, you've got the Secretary of State right after that for some one-on-one time to talk Middle East. After that, the Secretary of Defense to brief you on the real shooting war. He's back from the Sandbox.

"Fun."

"Bunch of softball things between those. Photo ops. A couple of new ambassadors over for a meet and greet, shit like that."

"Fantastic. Jeez. My head hurts." Beau massaged his temples.

Terry glanced back at the day's appointments. "And, of course, the lovely Mrs. Bergeron returns this afternoon. I'll try to squeeze her in."

"I bet you would."

"You want me to schedule some afternoon delight for you?"

"Now there's a thought. How much time can you give me?"

Terry let out a sharp laugh. "Hell, you'll only need about four minutes."

"You crack me up."

"You're already cracked, apparently."

Beau put his napkin next to his plate and leaned back in his chair. He looked at his friend. "Terry, I swear this dead president thing is as real as you sitting there."

"Uh huh."

"Maybe I should talk to someone about this. A professional. Isn't there a presidential shrink somewhere around here?"

Terry folded his arms and shook his head. "You don't need to be talking to anyone about this except me and maybe Marissa."

"The guys know about it now," Beau said.

"Yeah, well, they know worse shit about you. I just need to know you've got your head in the game. Seriously."

"I'm focused," Beau said.

"Okay, then we're good to go with the Chinese. The trouble today is going to be *our* military guys. They're getting pissed off at the Chinese now, and will want to show them a thing or two about messing with us."

"They should," Beau said.

"During the Cuban Missile Crisis, the generals pushed Kennedy to invade Cuba," Terry said. "I mean, they wanted to take Castro out, completely, and throw the Russians out in the process. That would have been a bad thing to do. We would have had Vietnam 90 miles off of our coast, plus the *real* Vietnam a couple of years later."

"I read my history, but thanks, Terry."

"Just a reminder. You and you alone are going to have to make one of those kinds of decisions. Mark my words."

Beau smiled. "Me alone? Hey, don't worry, Terry. I've got Millard and Grover. They've got my back."

Terry buried his face in his hands.

Chapter 10

As the sun rose over Washington, it was setting over the South China Sea. The thousands of sailors and Marines of the *George Washington's* battle group went about their business, most thinking about a hot meal for dinner. Well, that and the Chinese. Word had spread of the showdown and everyone was a little more focused. All were combat vets, having served during the post 9/11 festivities, but this could be their first taste of real naval combat, the kind their grandfathers and great grandfathers encountered during World War Two. Ships shooting at ships. Submarines trying to sink each other and surface ships. Aircraft sinking carriers, a la the Battle of Midway. In other words, some serious shit.

The talk at dinner was about the shoot-down of the drone. It had gotten a little too close for comfort before meeting its end, so now all the officers were a little wound up about that. The jet jockeys who had landed before dinner talked about some close encounters with Chinese fighters. Nothing too crazy, just some sniffing-each-other-out kind of thing. But everyone could tell the Top Gunners were itching for some air-to-air action.

For most of the crew, it reminded them of the day before a big high-school football game with a rival. The hallways buzzed, signs and banners were posted, pep rallies were held, dates were lined up. There were lots of women in the battle group, especially on the *Washington*, but it was a sure bet no one would be hooking up under the bleachers. Well, maybe not a *sure* bet.

Admiral Lear was aware of all this. He sat in his office on the *Washington* sipping some hot coffee. He set his cup down and scanned some spy satellite imagery, some other closer shots taken by a few of his own stealth drones, and other photos collected by his various aircraft in the area. The big game was shaping up, and a quick look at some plots on the map painted a big-time confrontation. On one side of the ball was his own battle group. On the other, the Chinese's group. Each one with a carrier of its own. He knew the Chinese had rushed to get that carrier operational. Not an easy task. But it wasn't just about getting a massive ship launched. It was about training the crew, working out the bugs in the system, and most importantly, being able to choreograph the arming and launching of aircraft. The U.S. Navy had been doing that for the better part of 75 years, in all kinds of weather and combat situations.

He had complete faith in his officers and crew. He had trained them to the razor's edge, putting them through countless drills and exercises. Many of his pilots had combat experience, so they knew what it was like to be shot at. He warned them not to get too cocky. The Chinese pilots, although less experienced, had a lot to prove and would be at their best. Whatever that was. He'd been in the business long enough to grasp the esoterics of warfare, and how inexperienced armies and navies sometimes won the day. Hell, America's military history was filled with such examples, from George Washington to modern times. Of course now, the U.S. was the big dog, and everyone wanted their shot at Number One.

On a personal note, Lear had until now a great career. Solid, methodical, no screw-ups. He knew that if he botched this thing, filled with both military and political consequences, he'd be done. Worse, this failure would be in the history books, and his poor decisions studied by cadets at Annapolis for years to come.

That's just not going to happen, Lear thought.

Although highly trained, his crew's professionalism would be tested. But still. He was going to lose some people. Maybe a ship or two. Never mind that he would take every Chinese ship to the bottom in the process, the prospect of losing any of his pilots and crewmembers did not sit well with him.

Then again, after all that fun was over, the U.S. would be at war with China, and his battle group would be sitting in the enemy's back yard. They would come at him with a vengeance, just like that fake bombing-run stunt they pulled earlier.

If all that happened, there was a good chance he wouldn't have many more days left to live.

Well, that's not going to happen, either, he thought again. He had big plans for he and his wife to retire to their cottage on the Chesapeake. Play with his grandkids and do a little fishing. Teach some classes at Annapolis. Play some golf. Shoot the shit with his buds. That sounded like a pretty good plan.

But first, he had to get through this mess.

The parking lot outside the West Wing was usually full, and on this bright morning, it was no different. Well, maybe a little different. On one end were two bass boats sitting on their trailers, each one taking up almost four spaces each. T-Ron, Jimmy and Big Mike caught scathing glances from people as they drove by looking for a space. Parking in D.C. was a nightmare anywhere you went, and the White House was no different.

"You think the boats are safe here?" T-Ron asked.

"It's the fucking White House," Big Mike said. He was rummaging inside his boat's storage compartment. "It's safe. Probably got a satellite or some shit watching us right now. Maybe one of those Predator drones. Somebody screw with my boat, BAM! Hellfire missile up their ass."

He laughed and got a fist bump from Jimmy. "BAM!"

"Whatever," T-Ron said.

T-Ron hopped into his boat and pulled a tarp from the area in the back. A small cage sat at the bottom. A rooster was inside, eyes alert, head darting this way and that. "How ya doin', boy?" he said to the bird. He stuck his hand into the cage and gave its head a stroke. The bird squawked.

"Quit strokin' your cock," Jimmy said. He cracked up with that one.

"A stroke for luck, every day," T-Ron said, ignoring his friend's comment.

Big Mike looked over. "I can't believe you brought that thing."

"Are you kidding? I don't fish without my lucky cock," T-Ron said. He winked at Jimmy and looked at the rooster. "Ain't that right, Boudreaux?"

"Boudreaux" had been with T-Ron for five years now. The day the rooster was hatched, a gas well on T-Ron's property came in and the good times really started to roll. From that day forward, the rooster was good luck, and T-Ron started to pamper the thing. A year later, he was taking it fishing and hunting with him, and his luck held. That same football season, T-Ron brought the bird in the house and held him throughout LSU's latest national championship run. His wife had even made a little purple-and-gold outfit for the bird to wear on game day. The Tigers had been kicking ass in the SEC since then.

"I hate leaving him out here," T-Ron said. He looked around. "This town's full of crime."

"Ask Beau if he'll keep him in the Oval Office for you. That'll make a nice photo up. You, Boudreaux and the President," Big Mike said.

"Hey, gentlemen."

T-Ron, Big Mike and Jimmy turned to see a young woman standing next to T-Ron's boat. It was Dana Newton of *The New York Times*. "Nice boats," she said and gave them a smile.

"Thanks," Big Mike said. He stepped down from his boat and stood next to Newton. T-Ron stayed inside his boat. Jimmy stepped toward her a bit.

"Dana Newton with *The New York Times*," she said, and shook their hands. They introduced themselves to her. "Heading out today for a little time on the water?"

"Didn't know *The Times* had a fishing reporter," Big Mike said.

Newton laughed. "No, no. I'm with the White House press corps. I just saw your boats. Not often we get a couple of these parked out back."

"Have you had any before?" Jimmy said.

"As a matter of fact, this may be a first," she replied.

"You fish?" Jimmy said.

"Hardly." Newton stepped closer to the boat and ran her hand over it. "So where are you headed?"

T-Ron said, "Down the Potomac somewhere. We're friends of the President's. From Louisiana. We're all in a fishing tournament this weekend. He's supposed to be in it, too."

Newton acted surprised. "Oh wait. I *heard* about that. Sounds like fun."

"It's fishing," Big Mike said.

"Is the President any good?" she asked.

"Yeah," Jimmy said. "Used to be, anyway. Probably out of practice. We should kick his ass this weekend." He laughed.

Newton gave him a thoughtful nod. "Guess he's got his mind on other things, right?" she said.

Boudreaux took that moment to let the world know it was still morning with a Cajun cock-a-doodle-doo. Dana Newton about crapped in her pants.

"What the hell was that?"

"What was what?" T-Ron said.

"Was that a rooster?"

"*That* was Boudreaux *le coq*," Big Mike said. "T-Ron's lucky cock. You wanna touch it?"

Jimmy looked at Mike and then at T-Ron. *Game on.*

T-Ron picked up Boudreaux's cage. He handed it down to Jimmy and then jumped out. He opened the cage and pulled Boudreaux out. He tried to wiggle free but T-Ron held on.

"Whoa, he *is* a big cock," T-Ron said. "Ya need two hands to hold it."

Jimmy looked away and bit his lip.

"Go ahead, touch it," Mike said.

Dana Newton had never seen a live chicken in her life. Much less a lucky cock. She carefully reached out and touched Boudreaux's head.

"He's got a big head as cocks go," T-Ron said with a straight face. Blood was nearly dripping from Jimmy's lip.

"You brought him from Louisiana?" she said.

"Oh sure," T-Ron said. "He fishes with me. Goes wherever I go. Guaranteed to work every time."

Dana nodded slowly. "Does the President have a lucky...cock?"

Big Mike, T-Ron and Jimmy all stole quick glances at each other. Silently, they came to an agreement on who would take this softball.

Big Mike said, "We told him he should have a Presidential Cock. Kind of like the First Cock. You know, like the *First Lady*. Or the *First Dog*. That sort of thing."

Jimmy jumped in. "I think he could use a First Cock right now. I tell you dat." Jimmy was dropping into full

Cajun accent mode. Reserved for times like these. Especially *The New York Times.*

"Hell yeah," T-Ron added. "Dem Chinese would never know they got hit upside the head with a cock."

"A *Presidential* cock," added Big Mike.

All three of them looked earnestly at Newton, who found herself searching for words. She was a pretty good interviewer, always ready with the next question long before the subject had answered the previous one. Not this time. She tried to think of a follow-up, but she was having an out-of-body journalistic experience at the moment.

"You should come with us for the bass tournament," T-Ron said. "I mean, the President will be there. If you want to get close to him, and the real action, you should be in my boat. You could hold my cock for me. For luck."

"That's a very interesting idea," Newton said. "Maybe I'll do that. Join you on the boat."

"It'll be fun," said T-Ron.

Newton took a deep breath and smiled. She stepped back from the three gentlemen from Louisiana. "Okay. Thanks for your time," she said. "I'll be in touch." And with that, she walked back towards the entrance to the West Wing. She gave a look back to the men and shook her head.

Big Mike said, "That was fun."

Jimmy slapped his hip and burst out laughing. "Did you see the look on her face? She tried to keep it professional, you know?"

"Boudreaux is gonna be famous," T-Ron said, and gave his cock a kiss on the head. He put the rooster back in its cage and set it into the boat. "You know, it really wouldn't be a bad idea to sneak Boudreaux into the White House. Beau's gonna need all the help he can get over the next few days."

"That'll be a first," Big Mike deadpanned.

"T-Ron's right," Jimmy said. "Beau's freaking out in there. What was all that about the ghosts of dead presidents? He's seeing ghosts now? Man, that better not get out. That chick would love that story." He watched as Newton walked inside.

"Yeah, good point," Big Mike said. "We might have to keep her off Beau's scent for a few days. She's got that sneaky-shit attitude about her. Bet she was fishing for something just now. Something to get on Beau."

Jimmy folded his arms and stared off in the distance. "That ghost thing worries me. Beau always said he used to see stuff, especially when he was a kid."

"The *rougarou*," said T-Ron. "Heard that story a hundred times."

"And don't forget the ghost of that dead pledge. Remember, the one who died in the house back in the fifties? The actives used to tell that story to every pledge class. How the guy's ghost still haunted the upstairs."

"Total bullshit," Big Mike replied.

"Still, Beau said he saw him," said Jimmy. "I kind of believe him. I believe him about the dead presidents, too."

"What are you getting at?" T-Ron said.

Jimmy looked at his two buddies. "We might have to bring in some outside help for him."

"You mean, like, a shrink?"

Jimmy shook his head. "No. Something much better."

Chapter 11

Beau walked back to the Oval Office. Trailing him was his personal assistant, Cary Guidry, the petite young brunette, iPad in hand. Steve Olson was a few steps behind them.

"When we get to the office, Cary, have Mrs. Foster get Marissa on the line."

"Yes, sir."

"And Cary, could you get someone to put together a brief history of President Fillmore's and President Cleveland's lives and administrations?"

"Uh, yes, sir."

"Not a hundred-page biography. Just the key stuff. Successes and failures. Decision-making. That sort of thing."

"Got it."

Beau stopped and looked at her. "You could probably do it. On second thought, why don't you handle it personally?"

"Be happy to, sir." She stared up at him, searching for a clue as to why he would have such a crazy request. She got nothing but a pair of bloodshot eyes staring down at her. *Probably some homework assignment for one of the kids,* she thought.

"Can I get something today?" he said.

"Absolutely, sir. How's noon sound?"

"Perfect."

"Hard copy, or you want it on your iPad?"

"The iPad is fine."

"Okay, then. Consider it done." She smiled at him.

"Great." Beau started walking again, acknowledging other staff members as he passed them. He noticed everyone looked a little tense. Some looked like they hadn't slept. *Oh yeah, that China thing,* he thought, trying to make light of what could be a very shitty day. They finally made it to the Oval Office, where Mrs. Foster was waiting with a full cup of fresh coffee. She handed it to him as he walked past her desk.

"Thanks, Mrs. Foster," he said.

"Everyone's in there waiting for you," she said as he breezed past. "Terry, Mr. Cassidy and the Secretary of Defense. Admiral Winston, too."

"Fabulous," he said, and walked into the world's most famous home office. The men inside weren't just sitting making small talk until the meeting started. Admiral Winston was on the phone, and he didn't look happy. David Cassidy, Beau's National Security Advisor, was looking at satellite photos with Secretary of Defense Mark Severs. Severs had arrived from the Middle East late last night, but he looked fresh and ready to go. He was 52, kind of burly, with a barrel chest, unruly salt-and-pepper curly hair and a dark brow. Reading glasses sat perched on his nose. His navy-blue suit was pressed to perfection.

"Morning, everyone," Beau said. They all turned and watched the President head to his desk chair, coffee in hand. He sat down and looked at his schedule that Mrs. Foster had placed there earlier in the morning. His guests waited patiently for him to look up. He said, "I take it we're not shooting at anyone yet?"

Severs said, "Not yet, Mr. President."

Beau looked up. "Wow. That sounded optimistic."

"Sir, we'll have to firm up our ROE's today," Admiral Winston said.

"The what?"

"Rules of Engagement," Severs said.

"When our guys can shoot and when they can't," Cassidy, ever the pragmatist, explained.

Beau sensed something behind him. His first impression was that a gardener was outside the window. He turned to see Grover Cleveland behind him to his right. Beau looked left and found old pal Millard Fillmore standing there, eating a banana.

He turned back to his guests. Cassidy, Melancon, Severs and Winston all had their eyes on him. Beau noticed Terry Melancon's eyes dart right and left in an effort to see what had made him look back there. He could have sworn he heard Terry's thoughts. *What do you see back there? Your old presidential buddies?*

The two ghosts walked around his desk and sat down on the sofas. Cleveland pulled out a candy bar, unwrapped it, and chowed down. Looked like a Baby Ruth. *Weird*, Beau thought. *As opposed to seeing a ghost, which now had become commonplace.*

"How close are we to the Chinese now?" Beau said.

Admiral Winston walked over to a map of the area set up on an easel. Very low tech compared to the wizardry down in the Woodshed. "Okay, just to get everyone's bearings," the Admiral said. "Up here is Mainland China. To the left is Vietnam. The Philippines to the right. Down here are Malaysia to the southeast, Indonesia and Brunei. Connecting them, of course, is this big body of water in the middle of them all, the South China Sea. One point five million square miles of water. Most of which China wants to claim as their own."

Fillmore and Cleveland were paying rapt attention. Beau took a hit off the coffee.

The Admiral continued. "Up at the northern entrance to the sea are the Paracels Islands here in the west, and Scarbrough Shoal to the east. The Chinese task force is strung between them. Farther south here are the Spratlys, islands the Chinese claim for themselves. Their neighbors and most of the world disagree."

"Remember, Mr. President, back in 1988? About 60 Vietnamese soldiers died trying to defend it from the Chinese," said Severs, the Secretary of Defense.

Beau nodded. In no way in hell did he remember that fact. He thought, *Weren't the Chinese and Vietnamese friends? What the hell is going on? Shit, I gotta bone up on this stuff. I wonder if the fishing is good around there?*

Winston looked at Severs. He didn't like being interrupted, even by his boss. He continued. "Anyway, here, just northeast of all that, is the *George Washington* and her group, steaming southwest right for them. Distance from the Chinese fleet is approximately 400 miles. The distance between here and say...Cleveland."

"I'm sure Admiral Lear would prefer to be sailing toward Cleveland," Beau said, and chuckled to himself.

Winston forced a tight smile.

Hey, guys. Let's try to keep it light, here, Beau thought.

Admiral Winston plowed ahead. "We're going to do a few things with how our ships are arrayed as we approach the Chinese. Some tactical stuff. The two subs attached to the fleet, the *Mobile* and the *St. Louis*, will push ahead of our fleet and sniff out any Chinese subs."

Beau set his cup down. "Admiral, just how many ships do we have?"

"Well, besides the *Washington,* we've got one guided missile cruiser, two guided missile destroyers, the two subs and a supply ship."

Beau frowned. "Seems kind of lean."

"Lean and dangerous," Winston said. "That's a lot of firepower."

"And the Chinese?

"Their carrier group is normally about the same as ours, but they've got four destroyers to our two and an extra cruiser, but kind of old. Not sure about their sub situation. That's why our subs are getting out there to see what they can find. If they detect a Chinese sub, they'll tag it and track it."

Cleveland and Fillmore didn't look happy. Fillmore said, "Kind of outnumbered, aren't we?"

"Admiral, I have total confidence in our sailors and aviators, and in our technology, but still…" Beau said. He didn't like the look of this.

Winston put up his hands. "I understand your concern, Mr. President. That's why we'll stack the deck a bit. We've got land-based air assets in the Philippines and over here in Japan. They're spooled up and ready. We can put a world of hurt on that Chinese fleet."

"Uh huh."

The Secretary of Defense spoke up. "And we'll have some B-2's loitering nearby. They can launch some ship-killer cruise missiles at the drop of a hat."

"B-2's?" Beau said. "Those are the big stealth bombers? The flying wing things?"

"Yes, sir," Severs continued. "They're based in Missouri, but we got them airborne yesterday and have a few always in the vicinity in case we need them."

"That's a long flight."

"Yes, sir. Lot of mid-air refueling. But we have experience with this. Iraq and Afghanistan."

Beau looked over at his Chief of Staff, Terry Melancon, who was rubbing his eyes. "What's on your mind, Terry?"

He looked up. "Starting to look like a war, what with all these planes coming in. Pieces on a chessboard. I'm okay. It's just...worrisome."

"You talk to the Secretary of State?" Beau said.

"Yeah, she's on the phone with her counterpart in Beijing right now. We'll see. Man, we gotta defuse this thing."

Beau could see his buddy was tense. He knew Terry was thinking politically at the moment. He was a political animal. The fallout from this could affect the mid-term elections and ultimately Beau's re-election bid. If he capitulated to the Chinese in any way, there'd be hell to pay on the Hill and with the allies who were betting the U.S. would keep China's aggressive nature in check. He knew this date could go down in the history books as the date the U.S. stepped a little to stage-left in the world theater.

"Mr. President?" It was Mrs. Foster, his secretary. She had her head inside the door. "Mrs. Bergeron is on line one for you."

"Thanks, Mrs. Foster." He turned to the men in the room. "Can y'all give me a second?"

Terry led them out of the Oval Office and shut the door behind them.

"Hey, Baby," Beau said.

"Hey, Beau. You called? What's up?" Marissa said.

"This China thing is gonna get busy here. I just wanted to say hi before you got on your plane. Might be hard to talk later."

"That bad, huh?"

"Could be."

"Kids out on time this morning?" she said.

"Yeah, no problems there. They seem to be in their own world now. Guess that's better."

"The guys make it in?"

Beau laughed a little. "Oh yeah. They've got the run of the place. Got their boats out back. I think they went fishing today."

"Keep an eye on the silver," she said.

"Right."

"Everything else okay?"

Beau frowned. After 21 years of marriage, she could detect anything in his voice. Any subtle change that indicated stress, a change in mood, or guilt. "Umm. Yeah. Guess so. Maybe some things we can talk about tonight."

"Okaaayyy. Anything you want to talk about now?"

"Uh, no. Got people in the office right now. We can talk later."

"You sound funny," she finally said.

"I *am* funny," he replied. "Maybe a little crazy."

"That's for sure."

There was a bit of silence between them.

"Okay, Mr. President," she said. "See you this after-noon. Hopefully. Got a surprise for you."

He perked up. "Surprise? You mean like a gift I can unwrap?"

"No, more like *me* you can unwrap. I need an appoint-ment with President Johnson. Unless you want to spend the afternoon with the Chinese."

"Fuck the Chinese," he said.

"Good boy. See you later."

Beau hung up. His heart was pumping a little more. And all that blood was headed south, too. *God, I love that woman.*

He looked over to the sofas. Fillmore and Cleveland were still there. Fillmore said, "You need to watch this shit," he said, pointing to the map on the easel.

"No shit," Beau replied.

"No, we mean *really* watch this shit," Grover Cleveland said. He walked over to the map. "There's something else going on here."

"Like what?"

Fillmore joined Cleveland next to the map. He pointed to the island of Taiwan. "If I'd been studying my world events over the last 50 years – and I have – I'd know just how im-portant Taiwan is to the Chinese. They want it, and bad."

"Not gonna happen," Beau said. "We're committed to Taiwan's independence. Have been since long before I got here."

"Doesn't matter," Cleveland said.

"Why?"

"Because it's going to be China's in the next three days."

Chapter 12

A light breeze kissed the waters of the Potomac, and the bright sun was rapidly warming the cool spring morning. T-Ron threw a perfect cast along the riverbank. The plastic worm on the end sank slowly. He'd been working the submerged point for about 30 minutes, and had already pulled in a three-pound bass and a nice five-pounder. He figured a really big gnarly bass was lurking in the vicinity.

Jimmy Fontenot sat on the other end of the boat. He had earlier stowed his rod and was munching on some cheese and crackers. He was celebrating his last catch – a four-pounder he had just released. "Slow down, you're jerking that thing too fast," he said.

"You would know," T-Ron said.

Ten yards away, Big Mike Moreau sat alone in his bass boat. He was also working another part of the underwater point. "If you girls would shut up, I might catch something."

The three had driven south out of D.C on 95 and put in at the Hampton's Landing Marina in Woodbridge, Virginia. They had yukked it up with some locals there for a while, who enjoyed having some Cajuns up on their river. They had gotten some tips and info, and then headed south. They had heard that the fishing was excellent all the way to the 301 bridge, although they wouldn't be going that far. Top water action was excellent, deep stuff a little more challenging.

"We can win this thing," Big Mike said.

"Yeah, action's pretty good," Jimmy replied. "But the locals got the edge. They been fishin' here for years. Home-field advantage."

"We'll see," T-Ron said. He reeled the worm in and tossed out another perfect cast. "Got a few days to get our head 'round this river."

Big Mike said, "You think the Secret Service guys will call my boat 'Air Force One?' You know, cuz Beau'll be in it?"

"That's the stupidest thing I've ever heard," T-Ron said. "Why?"

"Because your boat can't fly, for one thing, asshole."

"He's almost right," Jimmy said. "I think they'll call it 'Navy One.'"

"Second stupidest thing I ever heard."

"I hope they don't put a Secret Service guy in the boat with me and Beau." Mike said. "That's gonna suck big time."

"For you, especially if you hook Beau. Unless the Secret Service guy will take a hook for the President," T-Ron said and laughed. "Bet they never trained for *that*."

"You take a bullet for Beau?" Big Mike asked his two friends.

"Fuck no," T-Ron said. "Bastard still owes me for that time he set me up with that chick for the Black Diamond Formal down in the Quarter. Junior year, I think."

"The lesbian?" Jimmy said.

"Among other things," T-Ron said

"I thought you bagged her that night?" Big Mike said.

"Well, I *did*. But it took some salesmanship."

They all howled at that one.

Jimmy said, "You noticed Beau looked a little...shitty? Acted funny, too."

"He's always been weird when he throws back the Scotch," Big Mike said.

"Maybe," T-Ron said. "But seeing ghosts in the White House? He was serious. It was freaking Terry out, too. And when Terry freaks out, it's a seriously freak-out moment."

"He was serious about thinking of something to do," Jimmy said. "Which is why I want to share a little plan I cooked up."

"Oh no," T-Ron said.

"No, listen up," he said. "Mike, get over here."

Big Mike finessed his trolling motor and eased his boat next to T-Ron and Jimmy. "What?"

"Okay. Beau thinks he's seeing ghosts. He always says he sees things. Always has."

"The *rougarou*," Big Mike added.

"Right," Jimmy said. "So we might need to fight some fire with fire. Help Beau get his head straight before he does something stupid. Or says something stupid to the wrong person."

"That *New York Times* chick," T-Ron said.

"Exactly," Jimmy continued. "So let's get an expert to take care of the ghosts."

"The *Ghostbusters?*" Big Mike said. "Right."

"No, asshole," Jimmy said. "I'm talking the real deal here. Somebody who knows this shit. Somebody that Beau knows *knows* this shit."

"No way."

"Yes. Miss Cecile."

There was a moment of silence among the three men. T-Ron stopped reeling in his line in mid thought. Then he said, "A voodoo priestess?"

Cecile Marie de Boissonet lived just outside of Houma on the bayou. She had been a voodoo priestess for as long as anyone could remember and was somewhat of a legend in the area for the last half century. Now in her seventies, the old woman still practiced the religion. The old Cajuns and blacks still believed, while the newer generations saw her as a fun novelty and part of the local lore for tourists. She was thought to be a *mambo,* a high priestess, but no one knew for sure and no one sure as hell was going to ask her about it.

"Why not? Let her do her thing," Jimmy explained. "Look, she can do her incantations or whatever the shit they're called, maybe get those ghosts out of there. Or at least convince Beau they're out of there."

Big Mike looked off toward the bank, and then back at Jimmy. "She can do that from Houma, or wherever the hell she is right now? You know, say some prayers or something?"

T-Ron just shook his head. "Uh, no. I don't think that's the plan, is it Jimmy?"

"Nope. We gotta get her here, inside the White House. Let her get a feel for what's going on. Then do her thing."

"At what point do we tell the Secret Service that we're bringing a voodoo priestess into the White House?" Big Mike said.

"Let that be Terry's problem," Jimmy said. "We'll need a cover story or something. Maybe we tell them she's my mother."

"She's black, dumbshit."

"Yeah, well. Maybe I take after my father."

T-Ron sighed deeply. "Can't we just use Boudreaux? He's the luckiest cock ever. Maybe he can bring some calm to Beau."

"Fuck that chicken," Big Mike said. "Jimmy's right. We gotta bring the big guns in. This'll be a blast. Sneaking a voodoo priestess into the White House! Now *that* would be epic."

"And how do you propose to make this happen?" T-Ron said.

Jimmy looked at Big Mike. "He'll call her. I'll have the jet pick her up in Houma and fly her here. No sweat."

Big Mike looked at Jimmy. "Me call her?' *You* call her. It's your idea."

"You know her better than me."

"That was over 20 years ago," Big Mike said. "And I was drunk."

"Close enough."

They all sat quietly in their boats for a moment, lost in thought. They each cast a line and slowly worked the action along the riverbank. Boudreaux, the Lucky Cock, took the moment to let out some steam. After he did so, T-Ron was surprised as a big bass hit his worm and took it for a ride. Big Mike and Jimmy watched him work it, all the while keeping an eye on their lines. In a few moments, T-Ron landed a nice seven-pounder. Boudreaux crowed again, proud of his handiwork.

"Look at dat, Boudreaux!" T-Ron yelled. "Yeah, baby."

No sooner had he said that than Big Mike and Jimmy each had big hits of their own.

Beau sat at the conference table in the Cabinet Room with all his cabinet secretaries. The morning sun filtered in behind him from the windows that overlooked the Rose Garden. The press had long since been ushered out, so all the bullshit smiles were over. The various Cabinet Secretaries were each getting their turn to talk about whatever made them looked great. Nobody mentioned the shit going on in their departments, of course. Everything was cheery and fantastic. On budget. Each one of them pissed perfection and crapped awesomeness. Bergeron tried to stay awake.

Currently, the Secretary of the Interior was droning on about national parks, and how he had been instrumental in upgrading hiking trails or some such shit. Beau sat with his chin resting in his hand, trying to stay focused. He was thinking about the First Lady, and he was going through her lingerie wardrobe, scrolling through all the potential outfits he might get to see tonight. Or maybe this afternoon. Or maybe both. Of course, in the little movie playing inside both of his heads, she was wearing each one of them. It was an endless parade of teddies, bustiers, stockings, garters and other bedroom sporting equipment he could not name but could certainly dream about.

His eyes wandered past the wonderful Secretary of the Interior toward his personal assistant, Cary Guidry, who sat along the wall, her ever-present iPad sitting in her lap. The cute little brunette was doing her best to stay focused, too. She made eye contact with him and gave him a warm smile. He gave her a little wink. Nothing suggestive, just an acknowledgement that he appreciated her staying awake. But then, the movie in his head did a nice match dissolve, and now the young Miss Guidry was sitting there in a red teddy thing, with red thigh-high stockings held up by a red garter belt. Of course, she had red stiletto heels on. Red was apparently the color of the day for Beau, for some reason. Somehow or another, her cute ponytail had morphed into a full wind-blown mane of dark hair. *Where did the wind come from?* Now her smile became a lot more suggestive. Might have been a swipe of her tongue across her full red lips, too. She gave her exposed cleavage a nice stroke with her red-tipped fingernails.

"You should definitely take full advantage of those, Mr. President."

Beau snapped out of his musings, and the movie ended abruptly like torn film in a movie projector. Cary now was dressed in her simple gray skirt and white sweater, ponytail back behind her head. He turned to his Secretary of the Interior. "What's that, Frank?"

"The new trails at Rocky Mountain National Park. Above the timberline. Pretty awesome views."

"Yeah, right. Gotta get the kids up there. Thanks, Frank."

Across the way, Terry Melancon tapped his watch and gave Beau a jerk of the head.

"Okay, ladies and gentlemen, thank you," Beau said. "We'll have to cut it short. You'll all be briefed on the situation with China as it develops. Thanks again."

Beau stood and noticed "President Johnson" had risen to the occasion in his pants, thanks to his recent daydreaming. He did an awkward pivot out of his chair and smoothed down his jacket. A quick glance around the table revealed no one had checked him out, including the three female cabinet secretaries and the multi-talented Cary Guidry.

Damn, I need to get laid, he thought.

"Woodshed," Terry whispered in his ear.

"Wood is exactly my problem," he said. "I need the distraction."

"What?"

"Never mind."

Beau began to walk out but scanned the room. Besides himself and "President Johnson," there were no other presidents in the room, living or dead.

"You see…them?" Terry said.

"No, they're not here."

"That's good."

Beau shook a few hands with his Cabinet Secretaries on the way out. Cary Guidry fell in line behind him, along with Terry and the ever-present Steve Olson, the Secret Service agent.

The Situation Room was bustling, with aides and military types at their stations, monitoring all the crap the world wanted to throw at the good ol' U. S. of A. Beau entered the conference room and found the usual suspects around the table: Secretary of Defense Severs, National Security Advisor Cassidy, assorted Navy brass, the CIA Director and Bergeron's Vice President, Wayne Lofton, who had just returned from a trip back to his home state of Pennsylvania. Lofton had been a second-term U.S. Senator when Bergeron tagged him as his running mate. He was a fast riser in the party, an excellent campaigner and moderate enough to keep most people happy. Lofton was a year younger than Bergeron, yet his full head of hair had more gray in it.

"Wayne, welcome back," Beau said.

"Wouldn't want to miss the fun," he replied, and shook the President's hand.

"Director," Beau said, and nodded to CIA Director Joe Cantoni.

"Mr. President," he said, and also shook hands with Beau.

Cantoni was a serious-looking dude, with dark, brooding eyes underneath gray stubble that covered his head. He was lean and hungry looking, and Beau thought he looked like a vampire. Those eyes didn't miss a thing. The old spook had been a field operative back at the end of the Cold War, and had seen some serious shit at postings all over the world. He was a legend over at Langley, worshipped by his people and feared around the world. A nice guy to have on your side.

Everyone sat and the floor went to Secretary of Defense Severs.

"Some new developments, Mr. President," he said, and turned to the big-screen TV. "Here are some satellite photos we took earlier along China's coast. What you're seeing are mobile missile launchers."

"Uh huh," Beau said. He was amazed at how sharp the images were, like they were taken from 100 feet away, when in fact, the satellite was hundreds of miles up in space.

"They're land-based ballistic missiles that can take out an entire ship."

"Like an aircraft carrier," Beau finished for him.

"Yes, sir. One missile has enough punch to sink the *Washington*."

"Is this a surprise?"

"No, we've known they had them. The new element is how quickly they moved them to the coast. The intent is obvious."

"Nukes?" the Vice President said.

Severs looked to Admiral Winston.

Winston said, "They're capable of being nuclear-tipped. But in this case, we don't think so. It would be overkill."

Beau looked at the vampire running the CIA. "Joe?"

"No, our assets over there tell us they're conventional loads. High probability."

"Still bad news," Beau said. "So how does this change our strategy? I don't want to turn the task force around and hightail it out of there. That's game-over for us and all our allies in the region."

"It's a chess move," Admiral Winston said. "So we match their aggressive move with one of our own."

"Which is?" Beau said.

"We can move the *U.S.S Lincoln* and her task force to the southern entrance to the South China Sea. It was on its way to the Persian Gulf, but we can let it hang around there for a while."

"Come up from behind the Chinese fleet?" Beau said.

Secretary of Defense Severs said, "Not yet. We can hold the *Lincoln* there for the time being, and save a move north into the South China Sea for later as an option. Give the Chinese something to think about."

Beau steepled his hands under his chin and thought for a second. It *was* a big chess board. Or a game of Battleship. They move their piece. We move ours. They do this. We do that. But one thing was clear, everyone was adding *more* pieces to the game board, not less. *Shit,* he thought. *We're boxing the Chinese in right in their own backyard. Somebody in Beijing is going to be pissed.* He looked back up at the flat screen, and when he did, his old presidential buddies winked into the room. Millard Fillmore. Grover Cleveland. And one other. This one he recognized.

Chapter 13

Beau's eyes went wide and his mouth hung open. Standing there in front of him was Andrew Jackson. "Old Hickory." The seventh president of the United States.

Fillmore and Cleveland found some empty chairs along the wall, but Jackson stayed standing near the flat screen, staring intently at all the pieces on the game board. Beau was transfixed on Jackson, a childhood hero of his due to Jackson's victory over the British in New Orleans in 1815. As a kid, he'd seen the movie *Buccaneer* with Charlton Heston as Jackson and Yul Brenner as the pirate/privateer Jean Lafitte. Later, he had read the Pulitzer-Prize winning biography about Jackson by John Meacham, *American Lion.*

Jackson wore a dark suit, circa 1830s, and his age seemed to reflect images of him as president, when he was in his sixties, with thick, flowing gray hair.

He was a badass of the first degree.

He had been born in 1767, and as a kid, he'd been a courier during the Revolutionary War. The war devastated his family, though. One brother was killed in battle by the British, another died from smallpox after he and Jackson had been captured. A British soldier had even taken a swipe at him with a sword when Jackson refused to clean the man's boots. It left a scar on his forehead. Then he was orphaned not long after when his mother died of cholera. Needless to say, he held the British responsible for a lot of his troubles as a young man. He would get some big-time payback later in life. He was a lawyer, a U.S Representative and a U.S. Senator. He was also a brawler, and frequently took offense when someone challenged his honor. He even killed a guy in a duel after the man made a slur about Jackson's wife. Jackson carried a bullet in his chest from that duel for the rest of his life. And, of course, Jackson served as a Major General during the War of 1812. This is where the payback came in. His defeat of crack British troops at New Orleans made him a national hero and propelled him into the White House in 1829.

Now he was standing 10 feet from Beau, engrossed in the coming conflict with the Chinese. Beau glanced at Fillmore.

Fillmore said, "Beats me. Wouldn't have been my first choice to join the party. They didn't call him 'Jackass Jackson' for nothing."

"I heard that," Jackson said, without turning back to address Fillmore.

Cleveland said to Bergeron. "That's why the Democrats have a donkey as their mascot. Got it from the General here. A little trivia."

"Uh huh." Bergeron had to stay focused on what his advisors were saying, while at the same time engaging his old dead buddies. He nodded at Admiral Winston, who was talking about submarines, while at the same time watching Jackson.

"Remember what I told you about Taiwan?" Cleveland said.

Beau nodded slightly. Cleveland had suggested that the Chinese would have possession of Taiwan in three days. He didn't understand what Cleveland was getting at, and now was definitely not the time to engage in a live conversation with a dead president.

"Okay, let's move the *Lincoln* into position," Beau said to Winston and his other advisors. "And what kind of defense do we have against those mobile missile launchers?"

"We've got some anti-missile missiles on our destroyers. But to be totally candid here, Mr. President, it's not a 100% defense. Something will get through."

Beau said, "Okay. But all it takes is one of those." He was glad that the old Admiral wasn't blowing smoke up his ass.

"We can also lay some cruise missiles in there to take those mobile launchers out," Secretary of Defense Severs said. "Again, not foolproof. We won't get all of them. They're not called 'mobile' for nothing."

Jeez, everybody is hedging their bets today, Beau thought. "Then we'd be attacking the Chinese mainland," he said. "That changes the stakes in the game, doesn't it?"

Everyone at the conference table agreed.

"Let's do the *Lincoln* thing and see how the Chinese react," Beau said. "And Frances, let's ramp up the chit chat with Beijing, and get the U.N. Secretary to make some public comment about open sea lanes. I want world opinion on our side of this thing."

Frances Gottlieb, the Secretary of State, gave Bergeron a slight nod, and she jotted something down in her notebook.

"Admiral Winston, let's keep the Chinese fleet busy. I want them watching frontways, backways and sideways. Surprise them a little. Remind them that the big dog is in their backyard and they need to watch their asses. Have a sub pop up in back of them or something." Beau stopped himself. "Okay, maybe not that, but you get the idea."

Winston said, "I understand what you mean, sir."

"Great," Beau said and stood up. "Let's stay cool, people. You're all doing a great job."

There were some 'thank you's' from around the table as everyone stood for the President. He and Terry walked out and headed back to the Oval Office. Presidents Fillmore, Cleveland and Jackson followed them out.

"What was that all about?" Terry said.

"What?"

"You're like Harrison Ford in the there playing the president. Tough, decisive, barking out orders. *In control.*"

"You got a problem with that?"

"No, no. I like it," Terry said.

Beau smiled. "Great. And move over a bit, Fillmore and Cleveland are right behind you. Andrew Jackson, too."

Terry couldn't help himself and turned to look that way. Of course, no one was there.

"C'mon, Beau. Cut that shit out," he said under his breath so Olson, the Secret Service guy, wouldn't hear.

"Yeah, Jackson just popped in. Did you know his nickname was 'Jackass Jackson?'"

"No."

"Learn something every day."

"So it seems."

"A lucky cock?" Carl Keegan said and chuckled to himself.

Dana Newton stood above him, arms folded, looking pleased with her investigative reporting skills. "You believe this shit?" she said. "And they were *serious.*"

"A man's lucky cock is not something to take lightly," Keegan added. He slapped his knee and laughed very hard, ending with a hacking cough. "I'm sorry. I'm sorry. Not very professional of me." He rubbed a tear out of his eye. "I've read our sexual harassment handbook, or whatever the hell it's called," he said. "I may be crossing the line here. Please don't report me." He laughed again.

Dana Newton just rolled her eyes. "Carl, the President is in the middle of an international crisis, and his friends are running around the White House with a lucky chicken."

"Has it actually been inside the White House?"

She shook her head. "I don't know for sure. They had it in their boat out back. Wouldn't be surprised."

"You got a picture of the President holding the lucky cock?" Keegan had to look away while he laughed some more.

"No. Not yet."

"Well, right now all you have is a funny human inter-est piece about some of the President's weird friends. You got pictures of the boat? Them?"

"Just like you asked me," she said.

"Okay, just push the story out on the Web like I said. You can add the cock thing if you want. It's just not some-thing that'll be above the fold in the paper. We need better than that. Like a shooting war in the Pacific."

"But all this bullshit is a distraction for the President," Newton pleaded.

Keegan shook his head. "No, it's not. Look, if he's got that lucky cock down in the Situation Room, *that's* a story. If he's praying to it, *that's* a story."

Newton sighed and looked up at the ceiling.

"What about that lead? Where the President might be seeing things? Even the excessive drinking?"

"Still working on it," she said. "I'm meeting my contact again later. We'll see about updates on that."

"Good," Keegan said. "I've got 15 minutes with Melancon later today. I'll sniff out anything our illustrious Chief of Staff might know. He and Bergeron are tight. I'll poke around a bit there and see if I can smoke anything out for you."

"Thanks," she said. "But remember, it's *my* story."

Keegan held up his hands to his aggressive young protégé. "Sure, sure. If the President is losing his mind, or is stumbling around drunk during all this shit, it's all yours."

She just stared at him.

"And keep your eye on that cock," Keegan said, and pointed a finger at her. He did it with a straight face. Or at least for a few seconds, before he lost it again.

Newton turned on her heels and stormed out.

Admiral Yang Jinping sat alone in his office just off the bridge of the Chinese aircraft carrier *Liaoning*. Outside, the moonless night was a velvet blanket over the fleet, and the waters of the South China Sea were nearly flat calm. He sipped a cup of strong tea as he held the phone to his ear. He nodded thoughtfully to the idiot on the other end of the line.

The idiot was technically his boss, the head of the Chinese military, on land, sea, air and space. Even cyber-warfare. He was also the de facto head of the Chinese government, during the "transition" time after Lu's death. *A general, for goodness sake, trying to tell me how to manage my beautiful, powerful fleet,* he thought.

"We've moved the mobile missiles closer to the coast, to cover your flank, Admiral," he said. "The Americans' satellites have no doubt already seen this. And we want them to. Let them know we have many assets at our disposal should they become...aggressive."

Yang nodded and rolled his eyes. "Thank you, sir. They will learn how well we can coordinate our forces on land, sea and air." He had no need of ballistic missiles covering his flank. His forces were well prepared to meet and defeat the American ships without any help from the mainland. The little stunt with the bombers earlier had also given the Americans pause, but Yang's own sea-based aircraft could do the job just fine.

"Admiral, any more contact with American planes?"

"By the hour, General Xu," he replied. "We're shadowing their fighters, meeting them at every opportunity."

"Remember, Yang," Xu said. "Demonstrate our pilots' skill and professionalism. Let them see our new planes. Show off some."

Yang put his empty teacup down on his desk. "Oh, we are showing off, General. Make no mistake."

"Just do not have them lock their radars onto the American fighters. This might be too provocative and could start something...unnecessary."

"Of course, General. My orders are to shadow only." This was a lie. Yang had issued no such orders. His fighters were lighting up the American fighters any chance they got. This was according to plan. A radar lock was a precursor to a missile launch. It would make the American pilots very nervous, right up until the Chinese pilots switched off those radars. After a while, the Americans would get used to the pattern and ignore it. So when the time came to really fire, they would be complacent.

"Our intelligence tells us the American fleet is still proceeding in your direction, Yang. However, they have slowed somewhat. This is good," Xu said.

"We have them thinking," Yang said. "They're buying time to consider their options. I think they will alter course." He didn't think that at all. In fact, he was counting on the Americans barreling his way. When one wrote the next chapter in naval warfare, one needed a war.

"That would be the optimal outcome," Xu said. "We want to intimidate, not humiliate," Xu said. "Their president is young and inexperienced, and no doubt he is being very cautious. The Pentagon is focused on their wars elsewhere, and their hunt for Al Qaeda in Africa and the Middle East. They have no time or interest in difficulties in the Pacific. We are counting on this," Xu added.

"True," said Yang. "But we will be prepared nonetheless."

"Understand your orders, Yang," Xu said. "If the American fleet runs your blockade, stand your ground, but do not fire. Even if their ships pass a single meter from yours. Stare them down, even as they come into our neighborhood. That will be enough to show our resolve. Our assertiveness will grow over time. They will fear that next time it will be even more dangerous for them."

"But the resources of the South China Sea, Xu," Yang said. "How long until we have them for ourselves?"

Xu sighed deeply. "We think two years minimum. Our strategy is slow and steady, but ultimately it will be ours."

"And if the Americans shoot?" Yang said.

"Then we will have to defend ourselves and our interests in the South China Sea...and elsewhere."

"Taiwan?" Yang said.

"As unwanted as a shooting war is to us, if it comes to that, this will present an opportunity for us to bring Taiwan back into the fold."

"So the Americans will play into our hands?"

"It would be one benefit of a shooting war." Xu said. "But let's hope it doesn't come to that,"

"Yes, let's hope not," Yang replied. He smiled broadly.

Chapter 14

Cecile Marie de Boissonet stood on her back porch and looked out onto the bayou. The foliage was lush with new spring growth, and the still water rippled in the sunlight with bream and bass feeding on bugs and small minnows. The damp, earthy aroma of the swamp filled her nostrils. Well, that and the acrid smoke of the blunt she was smoking. Her third of the day. She watched a large blue heron glide in and effortlessly land on a cypress branch near the water. It carried a small snake in its mouth. *An omen?* She hoped not. It was a beautiful day in southern Louisiana. And she was feeling no pain.

Cecile was 71 years old, but still a beautiful woman. Although her hair was gray, it had a healthy sheen to it, and she wore it long, to her shoulders. It accentuated her smooth, caramel skin and her large almond eyes. Her nose was long and thin, her cheekbones high and pronounced, more European than African, and it gave her face an overall delicate appearance. Her equally thin frame was perfectly proportioned, and at 5 feet, 10 inches, she towered over most women and some men.

She was a presence wherever she went. But it wasn't her physical appearance. She was a *mambo,* a voodoo priestess, and she carried a mysterious aura about her. Both her mother and her grandmother had carried that title, as would her daughter someday, and hopefully her granddaughter. It was a family business, and a powerful, successful one at that.

"Miss Cecile," as she preferred to be called, was quite the local celebrity. She was descended from slaves brought from Haiti, who brought much of their culture to Louisiana. This included voodoo, whose origins go back to Africa. The Haitian version was a weird mixture of voodoo and Catholicism, that, like most major religions, believed in one God, *Bondye,* similar to the one God of Christianity, Judaism and Islam. After, that, though, it started to get strange. There were also three groups of spiritual beings: the *Iwa,* which include spirits of family members and spirits of major forces of the universe; the *twins,* mysterious contradictory forces of good and evil, and finally, the *dead.* These were the souls of family members who have not been "reclaimed." Ignored dead family members were dangerous. Honored and remembered ones were good.

Cecile knew that most people around here and elsewhere looked upon her as an oddity, and eccentric old woman who did nothing more than magic tricks and could tell your fortune for a few dollars. But there were also the true believers, many of them African American whose parents and grandparents told them the stories and made them believe. But many of the local Cajuns also believed, because they had seen and experienced things they could not explain. Many of those things had been helpful, but for a few, the voodoo religion had been quite frightening, and deservedly so.

She closed her eyes and felt the world, felt the other spirits around her, the *Loa,* and her eyes opened again. She looked down her yard to the edge of the bayou and saw the spirit Ogou sitting on his horse. He was the Loa who presides over politics and war, among other things. Even stranger, hovering above the water, next to Ogou, was the spirit Agwe, the sovereign of the sea. Seeing the two together troubled Miss Cecile. She sucked a big hit off the blunt and held it longer than normal before exhaling. Her lungs emptied with a shudder.

Neither spirit spoke. The look in Ogou's eyes was dangerous. He did not look pleased, which fit his temperamental disposition. Agwe, on the other hand, never used words anyway. The only sounds that would come from his mouth were the sounds of the ocean.

Miss Cecile fell to her knees, bowed her head and prayed to Bondye. What did this vision mean? Minutes passed, and finally she opened her eyes and looked up to see that the two spirits had vanished. Her heart beat quickly as if it were going to burst. Sweat formed on her brow, and she felt clammy despite the pleasant spring day. She rose to her feet and smoothed her white dress over her thin hips. She took a deep breath and tried to calm herself. Another hit helped that endeavor. Over the many years since she had been a mambo, she had seen many visions and had come to rely on their power. Sometimes she understood their meaning, and at other times it took a while to grasp the message that was being sent to her by these spirits.

Miss Cecile sighed and rubbed her hands together as if to warm herself. She had no idea what these visions represented.

Then her phone rang and she damn-near jumped out of her skin.

Cary Guidry, the cute young assistant to the President, rapped her knuckles on the door to the Oval Office.

"Yes?" she heard from inside.

She popped her head in to see the President and Chief of Staff Melancon standing near the President's desk, talking in conspiratorial tones.

"Oh, hi, Cary," Beau said.

"Just wanted to let you know I sent that report on Fillmore and Cleveland to your iPad, sir."

Beau glanced at Terry, who gave him a 'WTF?' look that was obvious to the young aide. "Thanks, Cary. I'll check it out in a bit."

"Sure thing," she said. "Let me know if you need anything else."

"Will do."

Cary closed the door behind her.

Terry said, "Is she getting hotter or is just me?"

"It's just you."

"Boning up on your ghost buddies?" Terry said. "Why don't you just ask them about their histories?" He gestured toward the empty sofas.

Beau looked that way and nodded at Presidents Fillmore, Cleveland and Jackson. All three were enjoying cold beers. He had no idea when they had time to grab a beer on their way from the Situation Room. Jackson in particular was enjoying his. He read the back of the label studiously.

Of course, Terry still couldn't see them.

"They *are* there, Terry. I see them right now."

"And now Jackson is here, too?"

"Yep."

Terry just shook his head and looked at his watch. "I gotta go to my staff meeting. You eating in here or the Residence?"

"I'm gonna order up a sandwich and eat in here," Beau said.

Terry sighed and looked at the sofas. "Okay, knock yourself out. See you in a bit." He walked out and ran into Mrs. Foster, who was on her way in.

"Lunch, Mr. President?" she said.

"Yes, please," Beau said. "Can I get a fried shrimp po-boy and some fries. And some lemonade?"

"You want it in here?"

"Yep. Gotta read some stuff. I'll do it while I eat."

"Sure thing," she said, and closed the door behind her.

"Fine looking woman," Jackson said.

"A lot of fine looking women around here, Beau," Grover Cleveland added.

"We try," Beau said.

Fillmore just stared at Beau. "Fried shrimp po-boy? Never thought of frying shrimp and putting them on bread."

"You should try one," Beau said. "I'd order you one, but I get the feeling you guys are using a kitchen I don't have access to. But then again, somehow you're drinking my beer."

Jackson stared at his bottle. "Louisiana beer. Really good, too. We had some crappy beer back in '14 and '15 while I was down there. This beats the hell out of that."

"I would hope so," Beau said. He had a mental image of Jackson in some pub in New Orleans back in 1814, planning his defense of the city over some local brew. "So... President Jackson, what's your assessment of my situation with the Chinese?"

Jackson put his empty bottle down on the coffee table. He sat back and folded his arms. "Well, you're kind of screwed, I think," he said. "They're calling you out, testing your resolve. Except it's on their street, in front of their favorite saloon, so to speak. They're counting on you walking away, but you're not going to do that, are you?"

"Nope."

"Good boy," Jackson said. "They'll just keep challenging you, so you might as well just get this over with now."

"So why am I screwed?" Beau still had trouble with these ghosts using modern vernacular, but he was getting used to it.

"There's no clean way to end this," Jackson said. "Somebody is going to die. Probably a lot of somebodies. Sure, they want you to just sail away, but you're not going to do that. Which plays right into their hands. A limited shooting war just off their mainland, thousands of miles from your shores, is something to their advantage. They can throw a lot of things at you in a hurry."

"This I know," Beau said.

"But they'll use this as an opportunity to grab Taiwan," Jackson said. "That's their end game, I think."

"Told him that already," Cleveland said. "In three days...*pffffftttt,*" he said, and waggled his fingers.

"Then you're *really* screwed," Fillmore said. "A big piece of American foreign policy that's been on the books for decades will vanish."

"And with it, so will your presidency," Cleveland said.

Beau glanced over at the map of the South China Sea, which sat on an easel in the corner of the room. He got up from his desk and walked over to it.

"Fucking Taiwan," he said, and traced his finger over the island that had dominated America's Asia policy for a very long time. Would he be the president to lose it? And so what if he did? It's not like the Chinese would annihilate the place. They'd just use it to keep pumping out products the world needed. But then again, the opposition party would use it to pry him loose from the White House. But he'd lose the Senate long before that, too.

All three of the dead presidents got up and joined him at the easel. Jackson spoke for the group. "Your unofficial war council of Millard Fillmore, Grover Cleveland and Andrew Jackson has some advice for you, Beau." Jackson put his arm around him and gave his shoulder a strong squeeze.

Beau looked at the three ghosts. "What's that?"

Jackson nodded and then looked at the map. "Move the *Washington* battle group back to the north and surround Taiwan in a protective shield."

Beau looked at the map again. "But the Chinese will see us as backing down. They win the PR war."

Fillmore smiled and shook his head. "Remember the *Lincoln* battle group you just ordered to the southern entrance to the South China Sea?" He put his finger at the exact spot on the map.

Cleveland continued for Fillmore. "Don't just park those ships there. Barrel them north and come up from behind the Chinese fleet."

"Now *you* set the agenda," Jackson said. "Take them out of their plan and force them to figure out *yours*."

Beau stared at the map. "So we swap the *Lincoln* for the *Washington* as far as challenging their blockade?"

Jackson said, "Yes. Force them to spin around 180 degrees. Plus they're now in the wrong end of the South China Sea. Where before they were blocking the front door, you'll now be coming through the back. You'll be in their Sea long before they can sail down to stop you."

"A *fait accompli*," Fillmore said.

"Done and done," Cleveland added.

Jackson joined the other ghosts with accomplished looks on their faces. He arched his eyebrows and smiled in a *"whaddya think?"* expression.

Beau ignored them, looked back at the map and rubbed his face with his right hand. "Now *we're* blockading," he said. "Wonder how the Chinese will react to us surrounding Taiwan?"

"They're an ally," Cleveland said. "Say it's a training exercise or some other kind of bullshit." He took a pull off his beer.

"Their fleet will be out of position," Jackson said. "Plus it can't move with the *Lincoln* coming up from behind. They can't do shit."

Beau turned to Jackson and said, "You study naval tactics before? When did you get all this seafaring knowledge?"

"Ahhh," Jackson said with a wave of his hand. "Take away the water and it's land. Sailors are troops. Ships are artillery. Same thing as land warfare in my opinion. Just more fish involved."

"And what about you two?" Beau said to Fillmore and Cleveland.

"Makes sense to us," Fillmore said. "We've gotten smarter since we died." This brought a big laugh from both of them.

Beau just stared at the map. "Unbelievable."

"You really should tell your admirals to set this in motion," Jackson said.

"That should give them pause," Beau replied. "I was never in the military. The biggest boat I've ever sailed is a bass boat."

"Well, there you are," Jackson said with a wink. "They'll think you're a natural."

"I doubt it."

"Anyway, that's our advice," Cleveland said. "We assume we're here to help you. Nobody gave us directions. And the beer's good."

"You're welcome," Beau said. He looked around and paced a bit. "Okay, let me think about it. Got some reading to do while I eat. You three got some place to go?"

"We're going to take the tour," Fillmore said. "Starts in 15 minutes."

"You're kidding me, right?"

"No, no," Cleveland said. "Should be fun."

"Try not to scare anybody," Beau said.

"Oh, I think we're busy scaring *you,* apparently," Jackson said. "That's enough for us."

"Don't wait too long to tell your admirals," Fillmore said. "I've got a feeling your options are starting to vanish."

Chapter 15

Mrs. Foster brought a guy in from the kitchen who wheeled in a small table with Beau's fried shrimp po-boy, fries and fresh-squeezed lemonade.

"Thanks, Mrs. Foster," he said. "And thanks, Curtis. It's 'Curtis,' right?"

"Yes, sir," the young man said with a broad smile, happy that *The Man* knew his first name.

Beau tried his best to learn everyone's name around the White House. It had been challenging at first, but after a year, he was getting pretty good at it. Marissa was much better at it than he was, though.

"Give me about 30 minutes, if you can," he said to his secretary.

"Yes, sir," she said, and escorted the young man out.

Beau grabbed the food and brought it to his desk. He found his iPad in a drawer and powered it up, pulled up Cary's report on the dead presidents that she emailed him, and began reading while he wolfed down his food.

Millard Fillmore. Why are you here? Beau thought as he began to read.

Born January 7, 1800, in Summerhill, New York. Six months of grade school. Dirt poor. Crappy farm that couldn't support the family, so his father apprenticed him to a cloth-maker, which was a nice way of saying "slavery." Basically taught himself to read, worked his ass off, then borrowed

$30 to buy his freedom from the clothmaker. Headed back to the farm, worked his ass off again. But whenever he could, he'd read. The guy was a voracious reader, grabbing any book he could. Went back to school, where the 17-year-old was encouraged by his teacher, Abigail Powers. She was only 19, and apparently Millard was hot for his teacher, because he began dating her, and later they were married in 1826. *Nice,* Beau thought and smiled about that.

He became a lawyer, and later an unknown political party in New York, the Anti-Masonic Party, got him to run for New York's state assembly. *Why is everyone picking on the Masons?* Beau thought. *My father was a Mason.* He did three terms in the assembly and was later elected to the U.S. House of Representatives in 1832. *Hmm, Jackson was president at that time. There's a connection to the crazy shit going on here.*

Jackson was pretty much pissing everyone off as he aggressively expanded presidential powers like never before. Fillmore's Anti-Masonic Party merged with the Whigs. They opposed just about everything Jackson was doing. *Hmmm. They seem to be getting along better now that they're dead.* Anyway, Fillmore served four terms in Congress. This is around 1843. Tried to get on the ticket as Henry Clay's veep in 1844, but that didn't work out. Tried to run for governor that year but lost that. A few years later, his prospects improved after he was elected as New York's comptroller. *Huh. A money man,* thought Beau.

That kind of put old Millard back in the spotlight. In 1848, the Whig Party chose Zachary Taylor as their presidential nominee. Only problem was he was a slave owner who owned land all over the South, including Kentucky, Mississippi and Louisiana. That pissed off the abolitionist wing of the party, so they decided to balance the ticket with a Northerner. Enter Millard Fillmore.

They won the election, but they weren't what you called close. In fact, Fillmore didn't even meet Taylor until after the election. What's worse, they didn't like each other, and that put Millard on the outs with the White House from day one.

The shit started to hit the fan not long after that. Slavery was the big topic on the Hill. Henry Clay crafted a bill called the Compromise of 1850 that tried to make both North and South happy. Basically, it meant California would be admitted to the Union as a free state, which would upset the balance of power in the Senate among free and slave states. It also ended slave trade in Washington D.C. The bill set up territorial governments in Utah and New Mexico, letting them decide if they wanted to be free or slave, and it settled a boundary dispute between Texas and New Mexico. And one other thing that got everyone's attention: the Fugitive Slave Act that said any runaway slave caught anywhere in the U.S. had to be returned to his or her owner. *That really pissed off the abolitionists.*

Needless to say, Congress couldn't get a majority to pass it, and the fight continued throughout the summer of 1850. Taylor died in office in July, making Fillmore president. He was a big fan of the Compromise, and it finally passed and became law in September.

Both sides got something in the deal, but the North was really the victor, because they got the majority in the

Senate. The North never really enforced the Fugitive Slave Act, and that really got the Southerners stoked up. The country was well on its way to Civil War.

What a mess, Beau thought. *The country was going to split. No way in hell to make everyone happy. Slavery had to go and a lot of men were going to die to make that happen. There was no way around it.*

Back to Fillmore. He really believed the Compromise would save the Union. In fact, it had sealed its fate. The clock was ticking on the War Between the States.

Beau scanned the report. On the foreign front, Fillmore had the Navy open Japan to the West, and worked to keep Europe from controlling Hawaii. *Okay, there's a connection – the Pacific,* he thought. *Millard was looking across the ocean even then.* But Fillmore's presidency from then on was pretty miserable. Both the North and South hated him. He fought the South's attempts to invade Cuba and make it a southern slave territory. He angered the North by enforcing the Fugitive Slave Act. He didn't even want to run again, but friends urged him to do so. Then his own party refused to nominate him and chose Winfield Scott instead. Then Abigail died, followed by his daughter, Mary. He did try to run again for president in 1856, but failed, and that pretty much ended his political career. He died of a stroke in 1874.

And now he's back, Beau thought. *Drinking my beer and eating my potato chips. And quoting Jim Morrison.*

Beau looked up to see if old Millard had reappeared, but no one was there. He was alone in the Oval Office. The dead presidents must be on their tour of the White House by now.

He looked back down at the iPad and scrolled down to the section that gave the highlights of Grover Cleveland's life. *Okay, the 22ⁿᵈ and 24ᵗʰ president, Two terms, 1885 to 1889. Then 1893 to 1897.*

Born in 1837 in Caldwell, New Jersey. Fifth of nine children. Full name was actually Stephen Grover Cleveland. Nicknames included "Big Steve" and "Uncle Jumbo." Son of a poor Presbyterian minister. Had to quit school at 16 to support the family after his father died. Eventually worked in New York City as a clerk and part-time law student. Got admitted to the bar in 1858 when he was 22, although he never attended college.

Served as assistant D.A. in Erie County during the Civil War. Avoided serving by hiring a substitute for $300. *Whoa,* Beau thought. *Grover was a draft dodger? You could do that? Wonder if the substitute survived to later enjoy his $300?*

Went on to have a good career as a lawyer. Married Frances Folsom and would later have five children with her. Then elected sheriff of Erie County. Put on some weight. Put on a *lot* of weight. Got up to 250 pounds. Liked to eat, drink, play poker, hunt and fish. *That'll do it every time,* Beau thought. Later became a reformist mayor of Buffalo, then governor of New York. Fought corruption wherever he found it. Impressed the Democratic movers and shakers who saw him as a "fresh face," although quite a wide face, now topping out at 280 pounds.

He ran for president in 1884 against Republican James Blaine of Maine, and the campaign got weird when it became known that Grover had been fooling around on the side a few years back and had gotten some woman pregnant.

The boy was named Oscar Cleveland. The woman was later shipped off to an insane asylum and little Oscar given up for adoption. Despite the scandal, Cleveland won the election, if only by a hair.

Grover was a player, thought Beau. *And to think Clinton had gotten all the good press.*

He kept reading. A lot was pretty mundane stuff. But something did catch Beau's eye. Apparently, Cleveland took exception to how poorly Chinese immigrants were treated on the west coast. He figured it was so bad that America could never successfully absorb them into the general population. So he worked to limit Chinese immigration, mainly because he thought they were unwilling to assimilate into American society. *Okay, no big fan of the Chinese,* Beau thought.

Cleveland did have some foreign policy action in the Pacific. He wanted to put a Naval base on Samoa, but the Germans tried to install a puppet monarch. That riled Grover up, so he sent three warships there. They ended up with a tripartite protectorate over Samoa signed by Germany, Britain and the U.S. He hated the deal.

"Let's see what happened in that next election, Grover," Beau said out loud. The Republicans nominated Benjamin Harrison to run against Cleveland. Although Cleveland won the popular vote, he lost the electoral college and that was that. *Adios, amigo.* Then in 1892, there was a rematch between Harrison and Cleveland, and this time, he won back the presidency. *A lot of domestic issues, blah, blah, retired from politics in 1897. Did the private sector thing for a while. Died in 1908. Heart, kidney and gastro problems.*

Beau put down his iPad and sat back, rubbed his eyes and sighed deeply. Two fairly unremarkable presidents in the eyes of historians. Just a couple of jackasses like himself, trying to figure out what was going on, keep the thing in the middle of the road and try not to screw up the whole operation. Maybe leave the country in a little better shape than they had found it. *Good luck with that.*

They were the "D-List." Either through their own shortcomings, the machinations of Congress or the tide of history overwhelming them – Fillmore in particular – they had left little of their fingerprints on American history. *So why are they here?"* Beau had a sinking feeling that they were here to be with their own kind, namely *him.* Was he destined to be one of the D-List presidents? Mocked by historians, forgotten by time, trivia questions to school kids? *Name the only president from Louisiana?* Granted, he had only been in office for a year, but still, he felt like it had been a wasted year. Of course, the week wasn't over yet, and he could go down in history as the president who started World War III at the worst, or the president who lost the Pacific at the very least, who oversaw the sun setting on America's role as a superpower. Who caved to a belligerent Chinese government hell bent on controlling Asia and maybe even the world.

Hell, that would get you into the history books for sure. But not in a good way.

Beau picked at the rest of his food and gulped down the sweet lemonade. He'd like to chase it with a Scotch, but knew Marissa would be home soon, and he'd need to be in peak physical shape for that.

Which reminded him. He looked at his watch, did some math in his head and reached into his pocket. He pulled out a little blue pill, popped it into his mouth and washed it down with the last of the lemonade.

"President Johnson" would be at attention soon, ready for "Hail to the Chief." *Hell yeah.*

Chapter 16

The motorcade of black SUVs pulled into the North Portico of the White House. It was a smaller motorcade than the President's, with fewer cars, but the cargo was no less important: FLOTUS. First Lady Of The United States. Marissa Bergeron. Secret Service codename: *Skylark*.

As was customary, and safe, her Secret Service detail emerged from their vehicles first, took a quick look around, even though it was the White House, and only then opened her door.

A long tanned leg emerged and planted a Giuseppe Zanotti heel onto the pavement. As diligent as her Secret Service agent was, he was slightly distracted as her dress hiked up her leg to reveal a nice expanse of smooth thigh. He thought, *Oh hell yes I would take a bullet for this woman. I would probably take just about anything for this woman. Skylark is smoking hot.*

She emerged from the car and gave her detail a dazzling smile. The wind caught her flowing black hair, and she had to brush a few strands from her eyes. She wore a Carolina Herrera baroque-print stretch cotton dress that hugged her model's figure. Well, almost a model's figure. Her boobs were always too big for her to be a model, but they sure as hell got her stares from men since she was about 13. Her big dark eyes, delicate features and high cheekbones finished off her stunning natural beauty.

"Thanks, Jack," she said to her number-one agent. *Was he just checking out a little flash of leg?* she thought. She smiled at him. Nice-looking guy, maybe ten years younger than she was. Tall, blonde, broad shoulders, looked like an NFL quarterback. Nice view for her, too.

"Yes ma'am," he replied.

"Your office or the Residence?" a young man said as he emerged from the other side of the SUV. This was Kirk Guilbeau, Marissa's assistant. He was 31, handsome in a delicate, almost feminine way, with wavy brown hair and almond-colored eyes. He was originally from New Orleans, had been with Marissa since the governor's mansion, and unlike just about every man on the planet, was not dazzled by her beauty. But he did love those fabulous shoes. Not a big fan of the dress, though. He liked what Michael Kors was doing on the runway better.

Kirk was gay.

Which made the President happy. A good-looking young man spending so much time with his hot wife would have been unsettling.

"Residence,' Marissa said. "Gonna try to catch some quality time with the President, I hope."

"Good luck with that," Kirk said. "I hear things are getting a little tense around here."

Marissa bit her lip. "Yeah, I heard."

They proceeded up the steps, surrounded by her Secret Service contingent, and entered the Entrance Hall. The pink-and-white marble floor shone like glass. Ahead, in the Cross Hall, a public tour of the White House was in progress. Someone caught a glimpse of the First Lady and began to clap. The rest of the tour turned as one, and the whole group applauded. A few whistles were added to the excitement.

Marissa Bergeron stopped, smiled, and waved to everyone. She glanced at her Secret Service guy and nodded. He nodded back, knowing damn well what she was about to do. Since the tour group had been screened already before entering the White House, they were less of a threat.

Marissa walked into the crowd and welcomed everyone. She asked where people were from, shook some hands, posed for a few pictures, and generally worked the room like an old-school politician. A couple of the women commented on her shoes, or the dress. The men just smiled at getting so close to her. And they checked out her ass, and her boobs, and generally acted like teenagers near the prom queen.

A French couple was also in the group, and Marissa spoke to them fluently in their language. The Americans were duly impressed, and the men thought she was even hotter when she spoke French.

She said her goodbyes, gave one old man a kiss, which damn near sent him into cardiac arrest, and proceeded to the elevator for the ride up to the Residence.

The crowd continued on their tour, unaware that behind them were the ghosts of Millard Fillmore, Grover Cleveland and Andrew Jackson.

"*That* was the First Lady?" Jackson said.

"Wow," Fillmore said. "Beau is tapping *that*." Millard was always current with the vernacular of the times. He took some pride in this.

Cleveland put his hand to his chin. "Damn. I need to meet her."

Jackson and Fillmore just stared at him.

Beau Bergeron sat at the conference table of the Situation Room, waiting for his military and civilian advisors to reply. He noticed they were all a little dumbfounded.

Admiral Winston spoke first. "So...move the *Washington* and her group back around Taiwan, and shoot the *Lincoln* and her group north through the straight and into the South China Sea?"

"Yep," Beau said.

Terry Melancon, ever the friend and confidant, piled on. "At the very least, it could buy us some time. I like it, Mr. President."

Secretary of State Frances Gottlieb jotted something down. She was famous for her little black Moleskine notebooks, carried them everywhere and went through them like candy. She looked up and said, "The Taiwanese might be concerned that we're provoking the dragon. They may not want to be involved."

"They're always involved when we're dealing with the Chinese," Beau said.

National Security Advisor David Cassidy jumped in. "Interesting gambit. We're still going to run the blockade, only now it'll be from the south, not the north. A little reminder that we can change the pieces on the board more than they can."

"We've got more pieces," Beau added.

"Right."

Beau knew he'd have to convince Admiral Winston, no matter what anyone else said. The old sailor didn't like civilians messing with his ships and his people, even the President. Beau felt bad a little, because he was doing what he promised not to do – coach from the owner's box and tell his military people how to do their job. He was a damn oil-and-gas lawyer from Louisiana after all, with no military training. No skins on the wall. Yet here he was, acting like Hitler in World War II, telling his generals how to win the war. And that had not worked out so well for the Germans. Of course, Hitler didn't have the ghosts of his political ancestors advising him. Or maybe he did, and if so, he didn't listen to them.

"Admiral, I know I said I wouldn't armchair quarterback this thing, but I was in the Oval Office staring at that map you left in there," Beau said. "I like the idea of moving the *Lincoln* into the game. I just want to get them into it a little sooner. And I also like the idea of making the Chinese guess what we're going to do. Be a little unpredictable."

"I understand, Mr. President," Admiral Winston said. He was staring at the plot of all the planes and ships on the big-screen TV. Beau could tell he was working out the plan in his head, weighing options, risks and opportunities. Winston wasn't a "yes" man. He wouldn't just cave in. And that's why Beau respected the guy. But he was also a pretty astute politician, too, with natural political instincts. You couldn't be the head of the Joint Chiefs of Staff without knowing how to play the game a little bit. In truth, Beau wanted to see if his plan was a good one. Okay, it wasn't technically *his* plan – it was his dead president buddies' -- but still, he was hopeful Winston wouldn't poke holes in it.

While Winston thought it through, Secretary of Defense Severs weighed in. "Mr. President, I like that it tells the Taiwanese – and the world – that we care about our allies in the region, enough to put a big gray metal fence around them. My only concern, my number-one concern, is that we're now being the aggressor, putting that much firepower close to the Chinese coast, almost challenging them to take a shot at us. It will be tempting."

Beau looked at the Vampire, CIA Director Joe Cantoni. The scary old spook sat there like a sphinx with his arms folded. Cantoni made eye contact and said, "We'll get more eyes and ears on it. This will definitely get some chatter going in Beijing. I say go for it, but there is something worrying me. Something I just read before getting here."

"What's that?" Beau said, and sat up.

"The guy in command of the Chinese fleet, Admiral Yang Jinping. I ordered some background on him. Thought Admiral Winston and Admiral Lear could use some intel on their counterpart."

"Always," Winston said.

"Anyway, the guy could be trouble. No combat experience, but he's running the whole show. More of an academic than anything. It's like he read 'Naval Warfare for Dummies' and then got the job. Our psychologists and profilers worry he might do something stupid, and not a good stupid, either. He might be trying to prove himself to Beijing, make some hay out of all this. This is his one chance to really shine. I won't go into all of the psycho-babble, but bottom line, his personality, upbringing and shortcomings could cause us some trouble."

"Shit," Terry said. "You think he might go rogue or something, not follow Beijing's orders?"

"He fits the profile," Cantoni said. "There's one other thing. Purely conjecture, but Beijing might actually like that. If it goes to shit, they can blame him. Of course, if it goes their way..."

"Then all the better," Cassidy said.

"Absolutely," Secretary of State Gottlieb said.

Beau turned to Winston. "Admiral?"

Winston sighed, stood up and walked to the TV screen. He stuck his hands in his pockets. The room was very quiet, save for the rattling of a few sheets of paper by the Secretary of Defense.

"At first thought, the timing would have to be right," he said. He kept his eyes on the monitor. "Like a dance. We peel the *Washington* off and shoot her north with her group. But the *Lincoln* has to come into play almost immediately, way down here. I mean we have to get them hauling ass right into the southern entrance to the South China Sea. While the Chinese are slapping themselves on the back, thinking the *Washington* is chickening out, we've got to kick them in the ass while they've got their eyes on that. I don't mean literally kick them in the ass, but deliver a few surprises." He turned back to the President. "We can work on some options."

"Thank you, Admiral Winston," Beau said. "Anyone else?"

Everyone nodded their approval, glad this was Beau's idea to begin with. If this turned out to be a total goat fuck, and the movie was later made by some hotshot Hollywood director, they would all be off the hook. Of course, no one really objected, either, so there was that.

Beau thanked everyone, stood, and made a quick look around to see if his dead president war council had shown up to see their plan implemented by the living and breathing. No sign of them. Probably still on the tour. He felt a little alone without them when they weren't around. They were proving to be a valuable asset, *consigliores* of the highest order. Their advice had just paid off, swaying Beau's top military advisor. What other ideas did they have? He'd have to keep them close as things developed with China. It gave Beau a comfortable feeling, a little more confidence. Now the loneliest job in the world didn't feel that way as much. *This all might turn out okay,* he thought.

Terry Melancon checked his phone for a text message and leaned over to Beau. "Marissa is back, in the Queen's chamber, waiting for your highness." He gave his buddy a wink.

Beau checked his watch. "How much time do I have until the next thing? Half hour?"

"Right, but like I said before, you're only gonna need about four minutes, hot shot," Terry whispered.

Beau felt President Johnson awakening from his nap. He whispered, "Put a clock on it, dickweed. I'm going the distance."

"Good luck," Terry said, and they walked out of the Woodshed.

Chapter 17

T-Ron, Big Mike and Jimmy pulled their boats into the parking lot next to the White House. They had also pulled some strings to keep the spaces open that they needed for the boats. The morning fishing had been outstanding, and their confidence about the tournament was growing even more. They wanted to show up these East Coast fishermen in a big way, and maybe score some points for Beau in the process.

Of course, Boudreaux the Lucky Cock had a hand in it. Or claw, as it were.

"I need a beer," T-Ron said. He watched as Big Mike and Jimmy finished stowing their tackle.

"I need something stronger than that," Big Mike said. He looked a little fidgety.

"Relax," Jimmy said. "It's gonna work out."

Big Mike just shook his head. "I just had a very long, strange conversation with a voodoo priestess, who even now is packing her bags to come to Washington D.C. Then we're going to sneak her into the White House so she can do some kind of half-ass exorcism."

"I don't think she calls it an exorcism," T-Ron said. He jumped out of his boat and landed with a thud on the parking lot.

"Well, whatever the hell she calls it," Big Mike said.

Jimmy checked his watch. "The jet should be landing in Houma about now. She got a ride out to the airport?"

"She said she did," Mike said. "Maybe she'll just tele-port herself there."

"They don't do that, I think," T-Ron replied. "At least I don't think so."

"Save on gas," Jimmy said and cracked himself up.

The three finished getting the boats secure, and get-ting Boudreaux fed and watered before stowing his cage and covering it. They walked into the West Wing's west-side foyer, got the nod from security and then headed into the lobby. It was a small room with a low ceiling, like a normal house would have. It was more functional, almost a wait-ing room. Blue high-backed chairs and sofas sat along the walls and in a corner, with end tables and lamps. It could have been a lobby for a law office or doctor. They were on the ground floor, still a floor below where the Oval Office, the presidential advisors' offices, Cabinet Room and many of the other high-profile operational digs were located. But then again, they were on the same floor as the Situation Room, where all the real action was going on today. Well, at least till Beau and President Johnson made it up to the Residence to see the First Lady.

T-Ron, Big Mike and Jimmy heard a commotion to their right. There were people walking and talking in ur-gent tones. Some dudes in suits, some military types in their crisp uniforms and assorted aides were all headed down a hallway and coming their way. The contingent passed, but a moment later, Beau and Terry walked into the lobby.

"Hey, Beau," T-Ron said, and then caught himself. "Uh, Mr. President?"

Beau turned to see his buddies and stopped. He noticed their clothing – jeans, canvas shirts, tennis shoes and ball caps. "Boys. Y'all just getting in?"

Big Mike said, "Yeah, we busted 'em up on the Potomac. You shoulda been there."

"Decent?" Beau said.

"Four, five pounders," Jimmy said.

"T-Ron pulled in a seven pounder. Pretty nice," Big Mike added.

"Sweet," Beau said. There was a hint of regret in his voice that he hadn't been out there with them.

Terry tapped his watch. "Your *meeting*, Mr. President," he said.

"Chill out, Melancon," T-Ron said. "This is important shit we're talking about here."

"Right."

Beau looked around. "Sorry, Terry's right. Got a big meeting to attend." He looked at Terry and winked. "Probably a lot of screaming involved."

Terry just looked away and scratched his forehead.

"Y'all look like you could use a cold one," Beau said. "Why don't you go down to the Navy Mess Hall, back that way," he said, and pointed behind him. "Grab some grub, too. Food's pretty good."

Beau actually didn't want them following him up to the Residence. If they saw Marissa, it could derail the important screaming match with her and President Johnson.

"Hey, sounds good," Jimmy said. "We'll catch you later."

They started to move back toward the Navy Mess Hall, when Jimmy grabbed Terry's arm. "Hey, Terry, got a sec?"

"Yeah, what's up?"

"Look, I just found out my aunt's in town."

"Okay."

Jimmy leaned in and whispered, "How hard would it be to have her spend the night here?"

"Here? In the White House?" Melancon said.

"Yeah, in the Residence with us. Just for a couple of nights?"

"She got money for the next campaign? She ever in trouble with the law? Gun nut? Into weird shit?

Jimmy laughed, a little too loudly. "Yeah, right. Weird shit. She's just a sweet old lady from the bayou."

"Right. There are some scary old women from the bayou," Terry said. "Like my mother and most of my aunts."

"Nope. She's as normal as you or I."

"That's comforting."

"Anyway, whaddya say?"

"Fine by me. Just go by my office and tell my secretary. She'll take care of it. Gotta go." And with that, Terry hurried to catch up with Beau.

Jimmy hurried down the hall to the Navy Mess and found T-Ron and Big Mike. "We're a go."

"No shit?" Big Mike said.

"Yeah, Terry green lit it."

"Does he know?" T-Ron said.

Jimmy looked around and said, "Told him it was my aunt."

"Your *voodoo* aunt," Big Mike said. "You two better not stand by each other. The resemblance is a little iffy."

"Maybe I should hit a tanning booth," Jimmy said.

Big Mike sighed. "We are so going to jail."

Beau, Terry and the President's Secret Service escort headed to the Residence. Beau was moving pretty quickly up the stairs.

"Slow down, you'll need the energy," Terry said.

"Don't you have something to do?" Beau said.

"Hmmm, I wanted to say hi to Marissa."

"No you don't. You want to cut into my party time."

"Who, me?"

"I order you to vanish," Beau said. They made it to the Residence second floor center hall. Steve Olson, the Secret Service guy, hung back and took up a respectful if diligent position along the wall.

"All right, I'll go," Melancon said. "Be safe in there," He adjusted Beau's lapel. "You look great."

Beau shrugged him off. "Go."

Terry laughed and walked back toward the stairs. He stopped near Olson and said, "Nobody even knocks on that door until he comes out."

"Got it," Olson said with a nod.

Beau headed into the West Sitting Hall and hung a left into the Master Bedroom. He could have sworn his Secret Service guy said into his wrist mic: "Angler in Residence, about to put it to Skylark." Of course he didn't say that, but Beau thought it was something like that. The door to the bedroom was open. He closed it behind him and locked it. You never knew when kids, Secret Service agents, butlers or Chinese admirals would ruin a good session of afternoon sex.

"Honey, I'm home!" he yelled. And then did a double take to see Grover Cleveland, all 280 pounds of him, sitting in a chair in the corner of the bedroom. Fillmore and Jackson were nowhere to be seen.

"What are you doing here?" he said, a little under his breath.

"I live here," Marissa said, stepping into the bedroom from the adjoining dressing room.

Beau's jaw about hit the floor. His wife stood there in a sexy black bra and panties, garter belt and thigh-high black stockings, standing tall, still in her Giuseppe Zanotti's. She had one hip cocked to the left with her hand resting on it.

The leader of the free world gulped. President Johnson was trying his best to get a better view. And dead-president Grover Cleveland said, "Holy shit."

Beau glanced back that way and gave Cleveland a "get-the-hell-out-of-here" look. The big guy didn't even look at him. His eyes were wide and locked on to the First Lady.

"Something over there more interesting?" Marissa said in a seductive voice. She stepped over to Beau, pressed herself up against him and gave him a soft kiss, with a hint of tongue thrown in just because.

Beau couldn't help but put his arms around her. While she kissed him, he glanced back at Cleveland, and with one hand, gestured for him to get out or vanish or whatever ghosts did when they weren't wanted.

Marissa pulled her face away from Beau but still stayed pressed against him. She gave him a smile that would melt steel. "I missed you."

Beau cleared his throat. "Me, too. You look...great."

"Is that President Johnson making an appearance?" she said. She glanced toward the south.

"Uh...yeah," he said. "He missed you, too."

"I bet."

She reached down and shook Johnson's hand. Or head. Neck. Something. Beau didn't care.

"How long do you have?" she said in a deep, throaty voice.

"Long enough."

"Well, let's get to it, Mr. President."

She turned and walked slowly to the bed with an ex-aggerated sway to her hips. Beau and Cleveland were mes-merized. It gave Beau a chance to turn and look at the ghost and give him a "get-the-hell-out-of-here" scowl.

Cleveland let out a deep, loud sigh and then stood up. "Okay, okay," he said. "That is one stunning woman. Have fun." And with that, Cleveland just winked out. Gone. Beau looked around the room. He heard the bed covers being rus-tled and turned to see Marissa pulling the duvet back, bent over in a very inviting pose. She had pulled her long black hair to one side and gave him another heart-stopping – or heart-pounding – look.

He smiled at her and took his jacket off. He tossed it on the chair Cleveland had been in just seconds before, and took a moment to look into the living room.

"Beau, I'm in here, baby," Marissa said.

"I know, just checking to make sure the butler wasn't around."

"Is he?"

"No ma'am."

"Then get your cute ass over here, and leave your clothes over there."

And Beau did just that.

Some time later, definitely more than four minutes later, Beau and Marissa lay back in bed, both trying to catch their breath.

"Damn," she said. "Kind of missed me, didn't you?"

"A little," he said.

She reached over and gave him a playful slap across his chest. "Want to go again?"

"Yeah, just give me a second," he said.

"Obviously, the Chinese don't have you totally distracted."

"Well, yeah, you know. I've got my priorities straight."

Marissa turned and propped her head in her hand. "Seriously, everything okay? You sounded a little funny on the phone."

Beau sighed. He and Marissa had been together a long time and always had a healthy marriage. Mainly because they actually talked to each other. A lot. Issues were never allowed to fester. Cold shoulders weren't allowed, either. There was no such thing as "the silent treatment." If there was something going on, it was put on the table. He had never cheated on her, and he was certain she had been faithful as well. No doubt, men had and still were hitting on her. Even his jackass friends downstairs probably had some fantasies about Marissa. *Yeah, well, look who's naked in bed with the First MILF,* he thought. Should he tell her about his ghostly companions? If he didn't, would Terry? *Shit.*

"Well, Nina wants to have a party this weekend for her and some of her friends. Boys, too." Beau said.

"The regular crew?"

"Beats me. Who's the regular crew?" he said.

"You probably don't know them. There are four or five girls she hangs with a lot at school. There's also a bunch of boys that are part of that. They're all friends," Marissa said.

"Friends, right," Beau said. "I know what 16-year-old boys are thinking about."

Marissa smiled. "They're just boys."

"They're penises with legs," Beau said.

Marissa laughed in that deep, husky voice Beau loved. "Okay, let's change the subject. What else?"

"This crap with the Chinese could get out of hand," Beau said. "We've got to watch ourselves, but we also have to play it smart and firm, too. Kind of a balancing act."

"You got a plan?" she said.

He thought about *the plan,* although he couldn't take credit for it. Some dead guys had proposed it and he had set it in motion. Fantastic.

"Yep, we've got it in play right now. Waiting to see how the Chinese will react. We're kind of doing a rope-a-dope on them."

"A what?"

"Rope-a-dope. Muhammad Ali versus George Foreman. It's what Ali called his strategy in the boxing ring. He'd let Foreman get him on the ropes, then cover up and let Foreman punch away until he got tired. Let him think he had Ali on the defensive. Then Ali would counter-attack and win the fight, because Foreman was all tired out."

"Okay. Rope a dope. I get it."

"Anyway, we're going to move some ships around, sneak some in from behind. Make 'em nervous. Make 'em think we're backing up, covering up. See what happens."

"Uh huh. You also mentioned 'some things we can talk about later' on your call," she said. She reached over and traced her index finger across his chest.

"I said that?"

"You did."

"Huh. Might have been something about the kids. I can't remember."

"Sure?"

Damn, her wife-radar is locking on, he thought. He made eye contact with her. She was staring right at him, waiting for him to spill the beans. The sheet had slipped down, and he had a full view of the First Boobs.

"Yeah, I'm sure," he said and then let his eyes drift over her chest. He smiled and rolled over on top of her. "I'm sure, all right."

Marissa laughed and wrapped her arms and legs around her two favorite presidents.

Chapter 18

The tarmac at the Houma-Terrebonne Airport and Industrial Park was wet from an earlier shower, but the sun was now out, and the hot, wet asphalt left a pungent oily smell that filled the air.

Or maybe it was whatever the crazy old woman had in her bag.

The two pilots of Jimmy's Gulfstream IV stood off to the side of the sleek corporate jet, damn-near shoulder to shoulder in their generic black pants and white shirts with gold-and-black epaulets. The uniforms pilots seem to wear everywhere. One pilot was a little paunchy, in his late forties, with a receding hairline. The other, a slim blonde kid in his late twenties. As one, they both shuffled a little more away from the jet.

The gray-haired woman walked around the plane, carrying her bag around her shoulder, a live snake in one hand and a small pumpkin in the other. She was mumbling some kind of prayer, too. They couldn't tell what language it was. It sounded a lot like an African dialect, but there was some French in there as well. Maybe Latin. Who the hell knew? They were just a little freaked out about their passenger. Where the hell was the TSA when you needed them? Was she going to bring that thing on the plane?

She completed her walk around the jet and approached the two pilots.

"Oh, fuck," the older pilot said.

Miss Cecile stood within a few feet of the two men, held up the snake and said some more prayers. Then she reached into her bag, pulled her hand back out and tossed some kind of powder into the air. Both men held their breaths.

"Agwe will give us safe travels," she said and smiled at the men.

"Okay," the kid pilot said.

Miss Cecile closed her eyes and breathed deeply. When she opened them, she said, "Okay, let's go."

She put the snake in the bag.

"Is that thing coming with us?" the older pilot said.

"Of course," Cecile replied. She turned and walked toward the open door of the plane.

The baby pilot said, "I think I've seen this movie. *Snakes on a Plane."*

"Funny," the other said. "You know, I've flown some weird shit in my day, but this might be the weirdest."

"Mr. Fontenot said just bring her to Washington. And don't ask any questions."

Old pilot just shook his head. "She doesn't look like a Popeye's Chicken franchisee to me. Unless they're about to put snake on the menu."

They followed the old woman into the jet and took a look as she got situated in one of the large leather seats. The interior featured a galley and a bathroom, plus four big chairs in the rear that faced each other across a table. On one wall was a sofa, with a few more single chairs across from it. There was another quad-set of chairs around a second table in the front. That's where Miss Cecile sat. She put her bag on the table, reached down and buckled her seatbelt. One couldn't always count on Agwe, so she cinched the belt tight and gave the two men a pleasant smile.

"We'll keep you up to date once we're in the air," the older pilot said. "Just like on a big airliner."

"That would be nice, young man," Miss Cecile said.

The young pilot looked at the bag and then at the woman. "You might want to keep an eye on that thing," he said.

She gave him a scary squint of the eyes that all but chased him into the cockpit with his fellow pilot.

They locked the door behind them.

12,000 miles away, another group of pilots also prepared to take off. The squadron of Chinese fighters were catapulted off the deck of the carrier into the dark night, formed up and vectored their way toward the American fleet. The sky was filled with stars on this moonless evening, a beautiful sight to anyone on the water. But the Chinese pilots paid no mind of the celestial display. They were focused on their mission. It was a little ballsy, designed to provoke the Americans. It was a test of their ability to detect an approaching enemy, a way for the Chinese to learn something new about the Americans, and an adrenaline-pumping exercise for the group of young men who set off on their mission.

The sleek J-15 Flying Sharks, similar to the Americans' F-18 Hornets, were capable of carrying multi-type anti-ship, air-to-air and air-to-ground missiles. They could also carry precision-guided bombs. Tonight, they were loaded with the anti-ship variety, as well as a complement of air-to-air missiles, just in case they had to mix it up with the American pilots.

After the fighters formed up, the squadron leader gave the order, and the group of jets went nose-down for the deck. They leveled off at barely 100 feet above the waves of the South China Sea. Dangerous at any time, but especially so at night. The weather was fine, but there was no room for error.

The Chinese knew the "fence" around an American naval carrier task force was somewhere in the vicinity of 200 miles out from the carrier itself. The big ship's destroyers, cruisers and subs helped police that 200-mile limit, but it was the *Washington's* fighters that really kept aerial threats outside the fence. The stealth drone had gotten *way* inside the fence earlier, and that had pissed a lot of people off in the American Navy. But it was a small, slow aircraft carrying no weapons, unlike the J-15s, which streaked at wave-top level toward the American fleet.

The Chinese pilots' mission tonight was simple: get heavily armed aircraft inside the fence without being detected.

Admiral Yang Jinping tracked the progress of his fighters from the darkened bridge of the *Liaoning*. He was a little pissed off about his stealth drone, too. He wouldn't be getting it back. If the old men in Beijing knew he had lost it, they would be beside themselves. They didn't have many that were operational. And if all of them knew the

Americans had recovered most of the downed drone and were even now examining it, they would all be having heart attacks.

Yang strutted slowly around the bridge with his hands behind his back. There was no communications between the ship and the pilots, and right now, there was no communications among the pilots themselves. They were radio silent, lest the Americans hear their approach. The planes themselves weren't that stealthy, which was why he had ordered them to approach at an extremely low altitude. The Americans wouldn't see them in the radar clutter of the sea's surface. Or so he hoped. They would eventually. The trick was to see how far they could go inside the American fence, and what the response would be.

Yang had hand-chosen this group of pilots. They were the best on the ship, with proven dogfighting skills, cool nerves and an aggressive nature. The best of the best, really. He so wanted to down an American fighter. Not just with a missile from a ship, but in "hand-to-hand" dogfighting. Man against man. His best against the Americans' best. It would be characterized as a "mistake" if it happened, but it would be no such thing. It would be the precursor to something even more dramatic. The first big Pacific naval battle since World War II, with him becoming the victor.

This latest move could be the trigger that got things going. He had told his superiors in Beijing that tonight's flight was to be a simple reconnaissance mission, similar to others they had done over the last few days. He had conveniently left out *how* his pilots would be approaching the Americans. *Ooops, my bad,* he thought.

Time wore on through the evening, and Yang continually looked at his watch, until one of his bridge officers said, "Admiral, they should be there now."

Yang smiled.

Hundreds of miles away, the squadron leader also smiled as he checked his GPS coordinates to reveal they had reached "the fence."

Still no sign of American fighters or radar detection of any kind.

He looked left and right at the J-15s closest to him. He couldn't tell what his fellow pilots were doing, but he assumed they were smiling as well. They plowed ahead, the jets screaming across the sea's surface at nearly the speed of sound. They ate up mile after mile, getting closer and closer to the surface ships. They could only guess at this, though, since they had shut down their active radar so the Americans couldn't detect them.

Could it be that they could go in undetected and buzz right over the carrier? The squadron leader thought. *That would make them shit in their pants. What a story that would be!* He made sure his wing camera was on. He wanted to capture this on tape if he could.

The minutes went by, and now the Chinese flight leader was getting a little nervous. *Were the Americans leading them on, preparing some type of trick?* Despite this, he held his course and maintained radio silence. Whatever the hell was going to happen, it would be soon.

Not long after, he checked his position again. He should be right over the carrier, but all he could see out of his cockpit was the calm sea, faintly illuminated by the stars.

The American fleet was gone.

Rear Admiral Tony Lear felt it might be better for him to be outside the bridge on this beautiful night. He was fuming as he stared out over the ocean, and he didn't want to bite off the heads of any of his young officers if he didn't have to. After all, it wasn't their fault.

The big carrier seemed to shudder as she plowed through the water at her top speed of just over 30 knots. They were making hay toward Taiwan after being ordered to disengage from their impending showdown with the Chinese fleet and set up around the island nation.

And this is why Lear was about to explode. For one thing, he and his men were ready for their mission, and they were well prepared for whatever the Chinese had in mind. His aircrews had performed admirably during all the sorties they had flown out and back from the Chinese fleet. For Lear, though, it was especially galling. His whole career had been devoted to crises like these. He was cool, professional and deadly. Attributes the Navy admired and counted on. He was the guy you wanted on the front line, and now he was turning tail to his adversaries.

Son of a bitch. He tossed what was left of his Butera cigar into the roiling waters of the sea far below him. *Some asshole at the White House probably told the Joint Chiefs to pull this stunt. Nobody was telling him who came up with this boner of an idea. What the fuck were they going to do forming some kind of half-ass protective curtain around Taiwan? For what? The real action was south of here, with the Chinese fleet.*

Lear paced a bit as the wind whipped his hair. Now they had the *Lincoln* and her group sneaking up behind the Chinese to try and scare the shit out of them. In his war-tactics mind, it made some sense. But to pull him out of the fight – or the standoff – or whatever, just made no sense. He could see squeezing the Chinese fleet with America's superior numbers, but trading off one carrier battle group for another was just dumb.

"Sir?" It was Lear's XO, his Executive Officer.

Lear turned his way and tried to hide the dark thoughts going through his mind. "Yes?"

"Hawkeye picked up some Chinese fighters, flying right on the deck."

"Heading this way?"

The XO smiled and shook his head. "No, sir. Headed for *where we were.*"

"Huh. They picked us up yet?"

"Nope. I think they're probably scratching their heads at the moment, and running low on fuel."

"Who do we have out there?"

"Two Hornets, also down in the weeds. My guess is that the Chinese don't know they're there."

"Have 'em scare the shit out of those bastards and then head on home."

"Yes, sir," the XO said as he tried to suppress a smile.

The squadron leader of the Chinese fighters broke radio silence and ordered his planes to head back to the carrier.

He checked his fuel and knew they barely had enough to get back home. He hoped his guys got their deck landings right the first time. There wouldn't be a lot of fuel left for go-arounds.

The squadron formed up and headed toward the southwest and the *Liaoning*. *Where had the Americans gone?* he thought.

He heard the warbling alarm through his radio that told him an enemy fighter had just locked onto him. In seconds, his squadron mates were shouting that they, too, had been locked onto. They broke formation and got more altitude to give themselves some room to maneuver.

"American Hornets! At least two!" his wingman shouted.

Where the hell did they come from?" the flight lead thought, and banked sharply. He looked at his fuel gauge again. He figured he had one shot at this. And he was going to take it.

Chapter 19

Admiral Yang Jinping yelled at the young officer. "What do you mean, 'gone?'"

"Sir, our pilots report the Americans are just not there."

Yang looked around his bridge. "Can someone please tell me where you can hide an entire naval task force?"

No one spoke.

"Have them keep searching."

The Air Wing Commander, the head of the airborne wing on the carrier, piped in. "Sir, they're low on fuel as it is. They can't spend too much time out there."

Yang was about to read the young man the Chinese equivalent of the riot act, but one of the other officers interrupted. "Sir, two contacts closing on our fighters! Looks to be American F-18 Hornets. They are locking on with their weapons radars."

"Two against six? Yang said. "They must be crazy."

His Air Wing Commander said, "They're just doing what we've been doing. Getting a radar lock just to get our attention, and then disengaging. Ignore them."

Yang stood silent and contemplated his next words. His Air Boss was right. It was time to recover his aircraft and re-set. He had so wanted to shake up the Americans in one bold move, but now those plans had gone to shit. He would have to reload.

"Sir, one of our fighters is engaging the Americans. Now two. Must be his wingman. It's Captain Lua and Lieutenant Chang."

Yang looked at his Wing Commander. The man shook his head. "They've got maybe one minute to fool around out there and then they have to head back. If they're not careful, they'll burn too much fuel to make it home."

Yang was happy the pilots took matters into their own hands so he didn't have to give the order.

This should be interesting.

Captain Lua and his wingman shot up into the stars and went nearly vertical in an attempt to locate the Americans. Radar indicated they were still slightly above and east of his position. The warbling alarm cut in and out, then stayed off as the Americans lost weapons lock. Just what he wanted.

They leveled off and turned into the American fighters, who were now closing at supersonic speed. There was no sign the Americans were attempting to lock on, but Lua wasn't going to let that happen again. He'd give them something to think about for locking up his plane. Had he not done this bold maneuver, it was almost a certainty the Hornets would have locked on again and fired their Sidewinder air-to-air missiles at him.

They're not going to get that chance, he thought.

He peeled off to the right to get an angle on the lead American jet, which continued to maintain its course along with his wingman. In seconds, he had good position and locked up the American. And fired.

The 12-foot-long PL-12 air-to-air missile shrieked off the rail of Lua's J-15 fighter and in seconds was traveling at four times the speed of sound into the night.

"Motherfucker is shooting at me!" Lieutenant LaRonda "Gangsta" Jackson yelled. She jerked her F-18 to the right and peeled off her original heading in an attempt to evade the onrushing missile.

Laronda Jackson was the only female F-18 pilot on the *Washington,* and one of a small but growing number of women aviators in the Navy. And the only black one, of which her hometown of Atlanta was particularly proud. She'd grown up in a crappy neighborhood close to downtown, but was smart as a whip, as her grandmother used to say. And she was never afraid to take a swing at any of her four brothers when the situation called for it. She excelled at sports and in her grades, and got an appointment to Annapolis, where she gained the reputation of being a tough competitor. She was also a pretty good singer and dancer, and would liven up the dorm with her own hip-hop songs and moves. Which resulted in her official "call sign" as a Naval aviator: "Gangsta"

Gangsta was in some serious shit at the moment.

Her wingman, Jake "Jack Flash" Garvin, stayed with her as together they tried to avoid the oncoming missile.

"Missile tracking!" he said.

LaRonda keyed her radio and said, "I'm under attack! Permission to engage." Her urgency was apparent to the air controllers in the EC-2 Hawkeye aircraft that was tracking her flight. The *Washington* was also getting the play by play.

She heard a calm voice say, "Engage hostiles." She didn't know if that came from the Hawkeye or the carrier, and frankly, she didn't give a shit. She was first going to avoid being killed, and then she was going to kill the motherfucker who tried to kill her.

The American fighters jinked and juked, and LaRonda put her F-18 into a high-G turn that made her grunt as her pressure suit inflated around her legs and midsection, forcing blood that was draining out of her head back up there, lest she black out. She and Jack Flash also released chaff and flares in an attempt to fool the rapidly closing missile's radar, buying precious seconds to get away. And it worked. The missile passed 100 yards off LaRonda's starboard wing and vanished into the darkness.

"Okay, you motherfucker," she said. "Let's see what you got!"

She came around a few miles behind Captain Lua's J-15, locked on to it, and let loose an AIM-9 Sidewinder missile.

Lua was caught off guard at how quickly the American had gone from defensive mode to offensive, and was a few seconds too slow on the uptake. What he really didn't know was that he had a heavily armed, pissed-off black chick behind him. He tried to evade the missile but it was too late. He and his J-15 exploded in a bright fireball that lit up the dark sky for miles around.

"Splash one!" LaRonda shouted. She could hear her rapid breaths through her oxygen mask. "Asshole," she said.

Now, without their squadron leader, the five remaining Chinese fighters were a little confused as they sought to establish a new chain of command. Chang took over and rejoined the formation, whose fuel gauges were warning them they had to start back now or they would never make it home.

He cursed under his breath and ordered the squadron to do just that.

The little face-off between the Chinese and American fleets had just moved into a very deadly second act.

Admiral Yang slammed his fist down on the console. How had a simple plan to rattle the Americans' cage turn into a disaster like this? That fucking Lua had no order to take a shot at the American fighter. He convinced himself of this, although he secretly hoped the hotheaded pilot would do just that and take out one of the American jets. That would have been a nice trophy for the wall. The whole thing could have been presented as an unfortunate accident that had resulted in the downing of the American plane. The diplomats would cool the situation, but when all was said and done, it would be China 1, USA 0. That's what the world would remember. The People's Navy wasn't fucking around, and anyone would be well advised to keep a healthy distance.

But now, the opposite was true. Now he had to do some spin control. Who's to say the American didn't fire first? Well, maybe a few people around him, and Lua's wingman, but that could be managed. Yes, maybe he could use this to his advantage, giving him the opening he needed. In fact, it might be just the provocation he had wanted all along. He had originally thought it would be the ships themselves starting something up. But Lua's aggressions in his fighter turned out to be the spark Yang needed.

This might be a good thing after all, he thought.

Beau kissed Marissa goodbye, like any husband who snuck home for some afternoon delight and was rushing back to work. He straightened his tie and stepped out into the West Sitting Hall. Steve Olson, his Secret Service guy, stood up from his chair and said something into his wrist microphone. Beau figured it was something like, "Angler has finished banging Skylark's brains out, all clear" or maybe something like that. He looked for some sign of an "Atta Boy" from Olson, but all he got was a cool, professional demeanor from the agent. There was one point during he and Marissa's second go-around where the missus was getting a little aggressive. He half thought he might have to call Olson in and have him take a bullet for him. Well, take a very stoked-up First Lady, anyway.

"Sir, Mr. Melancon is on the way up," Olson said.

Beau said, "Thanks, Steve." He felt kind of awkward, like he was doing the "walk of shame" after a one-night stand. Some small talk might be in order. "How are the kids, Steve?"

"Good, sir, thanks for asking. Both into soccer right now."

"Great." Beau thought about Olson out watching his kids at a Saturday morning soccer game. He would be the dad in the suit, with sunglasses, an ear bud and a gun. Standing there like a stone. Pity the kid that knocked down one of his own.

Terry stepped out of the elevator and he didn't look good.

"What now?" Beau said. He and Terry walked out of the West Sitting Hall and into the Center hall, Olson trailing discreetly behind them.

"One of our fighters just shot down a Chinese fighter."

Beau dropped his head and let it roll from one shoulder to another. "Oh, man, that is just freaking fantastic," he said. He rubbed his eyes. "So much for my post-sex afterglow. Let's go."

They hurried down to the Woodshed and found the place crackling with energy. The group almost didn't notice when he came into the room. "Give it to me, Admiral," Beau said.

Admiral Winston broke up his conversation with a couple of aides and said, "Six Chinese carrier-based fighters, J-15s, were flying at wave-top level to where the *Washington* and her escorts had been. We had moved them to the north, as you had...suggested. Just so happened, we had a pair of Hornets in the vicinity that stumbled on the Chinese. Our pilots locked on their weapons radar, to rattle them a bit."

"Why'd we do that?" Terry said.

Admiral Winston gave him a quick look that said, *"Shut up, political punk, I'm talking to the President."* Winston, though, obliged. "They've been doing that to us for days now. We've been reciprocating. Just how the game is played. They lock us up, we try to evade. Then we do the same. In another time, it would be a friendly practice session. Think of it as a scrimmage. Testing each other's skills. Anyway, we locked one up, and then one of their guys broke formation and went aggressive. Locked one of our pilots up, then fired a missile."

"Shit," Beau said.

"Anyway, she takes evasive action and turns the tables on the Chinese."

"She?"

"Yes, sir." Winston looked down at his notes. "A Lieutenant LaRonda Jackson. Only female combat pilot on the *Washington*."

"Huh."

"Yes, sir. Pretty good, from what I hear. Anyway, she gets around on him and took the shot. Splash one J-15."

"The pilot?" Beau said.

"Don't think he got out. It was dark, and she and her wingman weren't sticking around. But they don't think he could have gotten out."

"That would have been better," Terry said.

"Well, at least for that pilot," Beau added.

"The remaining Chinese fighters headed back to their carrier," Winston said. "Probably low on fuel, so they couldn't hang round."

"Chinese response?" Beau said.

Winston sighed. "None yet. But here's the thing that everyone is ignoring right now. The Chinese were trying to come right at us in a radar-evading maneuver. I mean, they were being super aggressive, trying to get close. Not sure what they're intentions were, but Miss Jackson said the J-15 was carrying anti-ship missiles. Normally a pilot would cut those loose before dogfighting, but this guy didn't. Probably why he exploded like he did."

"You think this was a real attack?" Beau said. "Shit."

"Hard to say. Could have been a practice run. But very dangerous."

Beau rubbed the back of his neck. "Okay, Terry, get Cindy to get in front of the press ASAP."

"Uh, not Cindy," Terry said. "I'd get the Pentagon spokesman to handle this one. Keep us from looking like all that was run from here. Better."

Beau looked at Winston. "Admiral?"

"That's how we usually handle these things. He's right. Keeps you somewhat neutral. The diplomats love that."

Beau nodded. "Okay, but have Cindy prepare a statement. And get the Chinese ambassador on the line. Or get somebody on the line from Beijing. I don't want this to turn into a shit storm."

Admiral Winston looked at the flat-screen TV. "I'm afraid we may be too late for that, sir."

Chapter 20

New York Times reporter Dana Newton was making her rounds throughout the White House. Well, that's what she called it. It wasn't so much a walk around the building as it was a walk to find key people. It could be top-tier White House people down to aides, secretaries, doormen or butlers. Anyone who may have seen something, heard something or said something. Ironically, the loosest lips in the White House weren't the low-level guys. The secretaries and butlers were loyal and tight-lipped to a fault. It was the blowhards and egomaniacs who really ran the place, and the government, who were prone to saying something out of school.

These were the people she was looking for, but dammit, they tended to be really busy, too.

Her boss, Carl Keegan, was somewhere around here, but he was focused on the China thing. *But everyone was all over that*, Dana thought. Her official task of the day was to glean whatever she could about what was really going on down in the Situation Room. Very hard to do, unless you stumbled on the right person in the right frame of mind. All in all, she was doing Carl's grunt work, which is what she was supposed to be doing at this stage of her career. But she was also very much into *making* her career, with a story all her own. And the White House was about as rich of an environment for that as any. All she had to do was pick up the scent of something a little off, or out of the ordinary. A whispered word, or a leaked email, or a screen-grab of a text. The First Family was pretty enticing, what with those three teenagers getting into whatever mischief they could. The gorgeous First Couple was a great target, too, especially the First Lady. Dana really was a little too focused on Marissa Bergeron. There was something about the woman she just loathed. Rich, beautiful, intelligent and funny — pretty much everything Dana wasn't. She hated women like that. She'd love to get wind of the First Lady banging some of the help, or smoking weed up on the Truman Balcony, or doing a few lines of coke with the French ambassador after a state dinner. *If only,* Dana thought. She'd really like to know what the woman spent on clothes, shoes, her hair, makeup and everything else that made her so attractive. Probably could feed a family in Haiti for a couple of years.

Of course, a White House reporter didn't have to look too much farther than the First Family's extended family and friends. Just ask Jimmy Carter or Bill Clinton. There was always the wheels-off brother that made great copy. It's like so much went into making one brother the hot-shit president, that it pretty much sucked all the brains and common sense out of the other one.

President Bergeron had three of his crazy friends staying right here in the White House. *An interesting group. Millionaire good old boys worthy of their own story,* she thought. *With a lucky cock as the lead. You couldn't make this shit up.*

Dana wandered down the hall from the press briefing room, seeing what was up. Being on the same floor as the Oval Office could be a great advantage, not that she could just wander in there uninvited. But the press secretary's office was also down the hall, along with the offices of the National Security Advisor, the Vice President and the Chief of Staff, as well as other senior advisors. Basically, the varsity. She was pretty sure most of them were downstairs keeping an eye on the Chinese. But their aides might be about.

She nodded at a few folks she knew as she walked down the hall. Cindy Walker's door was closed. Probably working on the next press conference. She moved into the small lobby and ran into Felicia Smithers, Terry Melancon's secretary. Next to the president's secretary, Mrs. Foster, she was the most powerful secretary in the place. Smithers was short and a little chunky, with overly-teased brown hair and beady little eyes in a pudgy face. Dana had spoken to her many times while waiting for an interview with Melancon, so they knew each other enough to keep it cordial.

"Hey, Felicia. How's it going?" Dana said.

The woman stood in the corner of the room, flipping through some papers. She looked up. "Oh, hey, Dana."

"Busy day?"

"Pretty full agenda if you're looking for Terry."

Dana held up her hands. "No, no. I'm not about to ask for that interview. I'll let Carl try that."

"Yeah, well, he won't have any luck, either." She handed the papers to her assistant, a young blonde intern who looked to be an ex-SEC cheerleader type. "I have to run. Need anything in particular?"

Dana said, "No, just doing my rounds. Go ahead, I'm good."

Felicia gave her a nod and walked into the nearby hallway that led back to her office.

Dana smiled at the young blonde. "Intern, right?"

"Yes, ma'am," the cute thing said.

Bitch. Don't call me 'ma'am', Dana thought, but kept her smile. "Enjoying the job?"

The girl smiled broadly. "This is the best. It's like, soooooo amazing. And the people are soooooo nice."

Good grief, Dana thought.

"Yes, it is an amazing place. What are you working on now?"

"Uh, mostly scheduling. Keeping appointments straight. Making sure people are where they're supposed to be. There's a lot of that going on."

"I bet."

The girl looked down at the sheet in her hand. "Like, right now, I've got to get a visitor set up who'll be spending a few nights with us."

"A visitor?" Dana said.

"Yes. Kind of a last-minute thing. It's the aunt of one of the President's friends who's staying with us."

Dana said, "Really? Oh, you mean Jimmy, T-Ron and Big Mike?"

"You know them?"

"Sure, sure. I was out back talking to them about fishing. They've got some nice boats," Dana said. "And a chicken."

"A chicken?"

"Well actually, it's a...never mind."

"Okay."

"Which aunt?" Dana said. She didn't know why she asked, but it sounded like she knew the whole family.

"Hmmm. Let's see," the girl said. She looked through her paperwork. "Oh, here it is. Mr. Fontenot's Aunt Cecile. Cecile Marie de Boissonet."

"Wow. Very nice name," Dana said. "She's going to spend the night?"

"Looks like she'll be with us for two nights."

Dana thought the girl sounded like a clerk at a hotel booking a room. Which wasn't too far from the truth. "Oh, I'm sure Jimmy will be happy to have her here. Probably a big thing for an old woman to stay at the White House."

"I'm sure it is," the girl said.

"When does she get in?"

"Later this evening. Says she's arriving from Louisiana on a private jet."

"Huh," Dana said. "Jimmy flew her up here on his private jet? Must be a favorite aunt."

"Must be."

"Interesting," Dana said. She jotted something down in her notebook. "I can't wait to meet her."

Beau Bergeron was back in the Oval Office, signing shit people had put on his desk. There was a machine that could do this, but some things needed the real John Hancock. Mrs. Foster was giving him about 15 minutes alone to take care of this. Good thing, since his dead buddies had decided to show up.

Beau looked up at Grover Cleveland, Millard Fillmore and Andrew Jackson, and then returned to his signing. "How was the tour?"

"More room than I remember," Jackson said.

"And more people," said Cleveland. "It's like an office building."

"It *is* an office building," Beau said. He put the final signature on some proclamation or another and put the paperwork off to the side.

Fillmore said nothing. He had a bag of Doritos and was crunching away.

"My kids are going to want to know what happened to all the chips in the pantry," Beau said to him.

"This stuff is the bomb," Fillmore said.

"No one says that anymore," Cleveland said. "The 'bomb.' That's so nineties. Nineteen nineties. Not eighteen."

Fillmore ignored him. Jackson handed him a beer. Beau was starting to worry about his beer stash. "You guys didn't get much beer back in the day?"

"Not like this shit," Jackson said. "Amazing. And really cold."

'Uh huh," Beau said. "You three should've been down in the Situation Room. Seems your little strategy was put into motion with our ships. But we shot down one of their planes." He explained the recent dust-up in the South China Sea.

Jackson said, "I wish we had some of those fighters back in New Orleans. Would've put the Brits in a bad way, that's for sure." He and Cleveland did a fist bump.

Beau just watched them in action. The dead presidents' idea was pretty good. It just might buy him some time to settle things down out there without losing face, or more important, losing people and ships. But even with the new strategy, blood had been shed. His press secretary would be in next to review the statement she prepared, and what Beau's official response would be. The world would examine every word of it, to the point of finding hidden meaning when there wasn't any. And the Chinese would probably bring in their "American experts" to decipher what he said. They probably had a thick file on him, a psychological profile and how he liked his eggs in the morning. *Fuck them,* he thought.

The real issue would be the Chinese response. That would be his next big conference in a bit with his National Security Council. State, Defense, Intelligence. The whole power team.

And oh yeah, these three ghosts sitting in here, eating and drinking their way through my kitchen.

What an odd combination of presidents. A couple of so-so guys, and a badass military type. But damn if their idea wasn't a good one. Was that why they were here? Had past presidents been visited by their predecessors during a crisis? Had Washington visited Lincoln? Roosevelt visited Roosevelt? Had Jefferson hung out with Kennedy? Kennedy had been a big fan of his, after all. At least Kennedy had a keen sense of history. Beau thought JFK might have majored in history.

Anyway, whether these guys were for real or just a hallucination, Beau decided to keep them close and listen to their advice.

"Boys, I think the situation might become grave over the next day or so," he said. "You think you can stick around?"

The three dead presidents looked at each other, and Fillmore shrugged. "Sure. Love to."

"Great," Beau said. "I've got some top-notch advisors, and the best military in the world. But you three could be a game changer."

"Hell yeah," Jackson said. The three of them toasted with their beer bottles.

Beau had to smile. "Just stay close. I'm still not sure how to summon you, or call you, or whatever."

"Summon. Yes," Cleveland said, and slapped his fat knee and laughed.

"Yeah, and Grover, one other thing. Stay away from my wife."

After Cindy Walker spent a few minutes with Beau going over his statement, his top advisors shuffled into the Oval Office to get their heads around the unfolding developments in the South China Sea. A number of Beau's appointments had been either cancelled or re-scheduled, and this fact had been duly noted by the press.

Sitting around the Oval Office were the Secretaries of Defense and State, the president's National Security Advisor, the Vice President, The CIA Director, the Chairman of the

Joint Chiefs, Admiral Winston, and Terry Melancon, his Chief of Staff and confidant for over 25 years.

And Millard Fillmore, Grover Cleveland and Andrew Jackson. The Totally Dead Threesome.

"The Chinese fleet has begun to move north," Admiral Winston said. "They're looking for the *Washington* and her task force."

"Surprised they haven't spotted us yet," said Secretary of State Gottlieb. She sat on the sofa with her arms crossed.

"They will shortly," the Admiral said. "They've launched reconnaissance aircraft from the mainland. It won't be long now."

"What about the *Lincoln* and her group, coming up from the south?" Secretary of Defense Mark Severs said.

The *Lincoln* and her group of destroyers, cruisers, subs and support ships had high-tailed it north toward the southern entrance of the South China Sea. The movement of the *Washington* and the deadly dogfight had the Chinese looking in the wrong direction, which afforded the *Lincoln* the opportunity to sneak up behind the pre-occupied Chinese. This was the original plan, and it was working like a charm now. The shoot-down had helped matters greatly.

The old Admiral smiled. "Already in the South China Sea. No indication that the Chinese have seen them. No recon from the other side. Nothing."

The Vampire from the CIA, Joe Cantoni, nodded. "Nothing out of Beijing either. NSA hasn't picked up a thing, either. Everybody's looking north." The NSA - the National Security Agency -- were the fine people who liked to monitor other people's phone conversations, texts and emails.

Beau was half sitting on the front of his desk, arms folded. "Okay, what do we think the Chinese response will be? Are they going to attack one of our ships? Shoot one of our planes on sight?"

"They'll launch a lot of planes once they locate us," Admiral Winston said. "Both from the carriers and the mainland."

"I agree," said National Security Advisor Cassidy. "It's revenge time. Count on them going in hot against any of our fighters they encounter. As for ships, I don't think they'd want to escalate this thing to that level. Yet."

Everyone in the room nodded their agreement. Except the Vampire.

"What about this Yang guy? The Chinese admiral," Beau said. "You mentioned he might be a wild card."

The Vampire said, "Yeah, that guy." He paused for a moment to collect his thoughts. "I have to be honest with you, Mr. President," he continued. "Yang is going to be trouble, mark my words. He's probably not just pissed right now, but highly insulted. Borderline unhinged maybe. He might shoot first and then ask questions."

"I think he's done that already," Beau said.

"Right. I mean, the next time, he just might use a bigger gun."

Chapter 21

Jimmy, T-Ron and Big Mike sat in the small lounge of the FBO terminal at the south end of Reagan National Airport. Known as Hanger 7, it was where all general aviation flights arrived in Washington D.C., since it was only a few miles from the city's central business district. Jimmy had flown here a number of times, both for business, and to bring friends and family up to D.C. If he could have figured out a way to pull one of the bass boats behind it, he and the guys wouldn't have had to make the long drive.

"What if she turned my jet into a flying lizard?" Jimmy mused. He stared at his coffee cup.

"Can she do that?" T-Ron said.

Jimmy just shrugged and took a sip.

"Well, that would totally suck," Big Mike added. "Where would you park it?"

"You'd have to tie it up somewhere. And then you'd have to clean up the flying lizard shit," Jimmy said.

They all thought about that for a minute. Jimmy's jet was scheduled to land in the next few minutes, and they all wanted to be there when Miss Cecile got off the flying lizard. Or whatever she turned it into.

"Flying squirrel would be better," T-Ron muttered.

This got Big Mike laughing. "But it could only glide, and it could only fly at night. Flying squirrels are nocturnal."

"Bug eyes," Jimmy said.

This kind of intelligent patter had been going on for well over an hour, as the three highly educated, highly wealthy and highly idiotic friends of President Beau Bergeron passed the time.

Jimmy's phone vibrated in his pocket. He pulled it out, looked at the screen and said, "They just landed."

All three looked up and saw the sleek little white business jet roll down the runway and reduce its speed. No flying lizard. No flying squirrel.

Later they stood outside the secure area and watched as the two pilots let down the stairs, walked down out of the plane, and stand well away from the open door. Miss Cecile made her appearance. She wore a long, colorful African-style dress, which had an orange and blue pattern. Her near-white hair was done up and wrapped with an orange doo-rag/beret-looking thing. Long, red and brown rooster feathers hung from the back and blew in the wind. She carried a bag in one hand and a snake in the other.

"Well, this should be interesting when we walk into the White House," T-Ron said.

Big Mike and Jimmy just looked at each other, then out at Miss Cecile. Jimmy just said, "This is going to be so cool."

"Is that real?" Big Mike said.

Just then, the big snake coiled itself around Miss Cecile's arm and all doubts were laid to rest.

The younger pilot brought the woman's rollaway to the terminal as Miss Cecile walked regally behind him, like some kind of foreign queen arriving in the States.

Jimmy and the boys greeted her as she came into the lounge. She looked them over for an uncomfortable minute.

T-Ron was half afraid she would turn him into a turtle or something.

"Jimmy Fontenot, 'Big Mike" Moreau and T-Ron Guerin. I remember you three, especially you, Mike," she said and pointed a long, slender finger at him. "It's been a while, hasn't it?" She gave him a knowing smile.

"Uh, yes ma'am," he said. He looked away. For some reason, he was getting a little activity in his pants. Yep. Definitely some wood. *Weird.*

Jimmy and T-Ron shot him a look. As the story goes, they had gotten drunk one weekend when they were home from LSU for a little hunting. Beau and Terry had jointed them, too. The hunting had been crappy, so some booze had been flowing, and a little weed had been smoked, and then some bad decisions had been made. Well, not horrible decisions, like robbing a liquor store or stealing a cop car, but certainly mischief had been involved. First they had gone shining for bullfrogs, totally wasted, carrying 12-gauge shotguns, which hadn't worked out so well for the frogs. Then they thought about looking for some quality hookers, which was a bit problematic for Houma, Louisiana. Common sense prevailed on that idea, but it spurred some dares, though.

Like which one of them had the guts to go see Miss Cecile.

At the time, Cecile had been much younger, middle aged, and still kind of hot, mysterious, and well, just plain weird. She was already well known as a voodoo priestess, and rumors were rampant. For testosterone-fueled college boys, the best rumor was that there were all kinds of sexual rituals, orgies and other bacchanalian activities out at her house deep in the swamp. Rumor had it that if she liked you, she would say some incantations, have you drink some potion or another, which would get you so sexually stoked, you could go all day and night. Then in some kind of sexual trance, Miss Cecile and you would go at it in all kinds of crazy ways until you were exhausted but incredibly satisfied. The other rumor was that she would somehow mark you with a small tattoo down in your nether regions, as a sign of the night's adventures.

Or so the story went.

Anyway, the fearless crew journeyed out to Miss Cecile's that night, and they drew straws as to who would risk it all for a night with her. Mike had won.

The five had spent a few hours at her house, where she told stories and mesmerized them with her prayers and rituals. The signal was given, and Mike expressed a desire to stay and learn more when it was time for his friends to leave. Miss Cecile had given him an odd smile and invited him to stay as Jimmy, T-Ron, Beau and Terry left.

And that was the last they saw of Mike that weekend. In fact, they had driven back up to Baton Rouge Sunday night to be back in time for the fraternity's weekly chapter meeting, but without Mike. He had shown up at the frat house Monday afternoon. He couldn't remember how he got there.

For months, they had tried to get Mike to tell them what had happened, but his memory had been sketchy. Or so he said. He admitted to remembering being naked. He thought. And smoking something. And drinking something. And there were flashes of Miss Cecile being naked. And there might have been sex, because Big Mike never forgot a night of five or six good orgasms. Or so his story went. And there were other people he remembered being there. Or at least, he *thought* they had been people. There was something wild about them. And there was daylight, and another night, and maybe more sex. But maybe not.

Anyway, it was probably the biggest Lost Weekend of Big Mike Moreau's life, and to this day, it made him a little uncomfortable to talk about it. And as far as him being "marked" by Miss Cecile, Big Mike said there was no such mark, but no one at the house believed him. And no one had wanted to go exploring for it, either.

Jimmy spent a few minutes with the pilots, all talking in low tones, with occasional glances back at Miss Cecile. He gave the senior pilot a pat on the shoulder and handed him an envelope, then one to the younger pilot, and rejoined his compatriots.

"Okay, let's get going," he said and smiled broadly at Miss Cecile. They all piled into his truck and drove onto the George Washington Memorial Parkway and headed north back to town.

The guys kept staring at Miss Cecile's bag.

"That's never going to get through security," T-Ron said. "You know, the snake."

"What snake?" Miss Cecile said.

"The snake in your bag. The one you had in your hand," Big Mike said.

She reached down from the floor and pulled her big cloth bag up onto her lap. Then she dropped it on T-Ron's lap. He practically peed on himself.

"Shit!" he said.

She reached over, opened it and held it open for him and Big Mike. "What snake?"

They both looked inside, and although there were various toiletries, brushes and other bags of beauty products --- well, that's what they thought it all was. Chances were, there was dried toad, lizard lips and other weird shit in there, but there was no snake.

"Where's the snake, Miss Cecile?" T-Ron said. He had now caught his breath. Both he and Big Mike were looking all over the place for the reptile. Jimmy looked down at his feet to see if the thing was about to crawl out from under his seat.

The old woman just sat back and smiled.

T-Ron closed his eyes and said, "They're going to send us to Guantanamo for this, aren't they?"

"Probably," said Big Mike.

"Definitely," Jimmy added, and laughed so hard he almost ran the truck off the highway.

They fought the notorious D.C. traffic for 45 minutes before arriving at the White House. There was a check at the gate by the uniformed Secret Service guys, but all was cleared through by Terry's office, so they breezed in and parked near the two bass boats outside the West Wing.

"Remember, you're my Aunt Cecile," Jimmy said. "On my mother's side."

"I can see the resemblance," Miss Cecile said. But she didn't say it like a joke. She actually studied Jimmy's face for a moment.

Jimmy had a weird feeling they really might be related after he saw her look. There had been so much fooling around down in the swamps over the last couple of centuries, who knew?

"Jimmy was raised by mambos," T-Ron said. "Kind of like he was raised by wolves." He snorted.

"Okay, be serious here," Jimmy said. "Grab her rollaway and let's get her inside."

"You think they're going to put me in a cell down in Cuba with one of those Al Qaeda guys?"

"Hope so," Jimmy said.

He called Terry's office and spoke to some girl, letting her know that his aunt had arrived, and to make sure she could be processed through. The girl came down to greet them in the parking lot.

Miss SEC Cheerleader had a perfect smile and perfect hair, and she greeted them all with her perfect manners. With her help, they were able to get Miss Cecile checked-in to the hotel. Bags had been checked, and questions asked, but there was still no sign of the snake.

Miss Cheerleader led them up to the second floor of the residency and they put Miss Cecile in the West Bedroom. They all followed her in, and put her bag on the bed.

Then the weirdness started.

Miss Cecile stood very straight and very still. But her eyes darted from left to right, and T-Ron could see that she was trembling slightly. There was a low hum coming from her throat. They thought she was about to faint. Big Mike reached to steady her.

"Don't touch me!" she shouted, and Mike jumped back like he had been shocked.

Cheerleader was still smiling. This apparently was her only talent. "Anything I can get you, ma'am?"

Miss Cecile's eyes rolled back into her head for a moment. T-Ron, Jimmy and Big Mike froze, as did the young woman, still smiling. Finally, Miss Cecile's eyes rolled forward and focused. Her body relaxed and she let out a big sigh.

"Dis place," she said. "Dis room, bad things here."

Big Mike looked at Jimmy and T-Ron. He muttered, "Where'd the Haitian accent come from?"

"Who the fuck knows," Big Mike whispered. "Shut up."

Jimmy said, "Bad how, Aunt Cecile?"

Miss Cecile slowly looked around the room. It was as if she was seeing things no one else could see.

Jimmy looked at the young White House cheerleader. "Miss, I think we're good for now. Thanks for your help."

"Okay!" she said. She smiled broadly. Jimmy thought she was about to do a Herkie and wrap the moment up with a cheer. They were spared this experience and the young woman left them.

Jimmy turned back to Miss Cecile. T-Ron shut the bedroom door.

"Do you see any ghosts?" Big Mike said.

"No, there are no spirits here," she said. "But…there is sadness and grief in this room. The walls, the floor, everything reeks of it." The old woman shuddered.

The guys all looked around. The room seemed pleasant enough to them.

Miss Cecile turned to Jimmy. "Okay, maybe it's time you told me why you really want me here?"

Chapter 22

When Big Mike had called Miss Cecile at her home, he had told her that they were up visiting Beau, and that he wanted to see her. Yes, the President of the United States wanted to see *her*.

She had called bullshit on that pretty much right away.

Mike had tap danced around it for a bit, and then told her that they believed her services could help the President out of a jam. Problem was, he was too proud to ask for her help, so the guys wanted to arrange a trip to have her come to the White House and bring some good vibes to the place. But it had to be secret. So she would come as Jimmy's "aunt." A couple of days. In and out. And they'd send a jet to pick her up.

The old woman had been reluctant at first, but Big Mike had pleaded, she had acquiesced, and now she was in the West Bedroom in the White House.

Freaking out about something.

"There's some weird shit going on in this place," she said. The Haitian accent was gone now. Just your regular South Louisiana accent now.

"Like what?" T- Ron said.

"First, you tell me what I'm here for." She pointed that long finger at them again.

The boys looked at each other again, and Jimmy spoke. "This is in total confidence. Complete cone of silence, okay?"

"Yes."

Jimmy cleared his throat. "The President is seeing ghosts."

"Ghosts?"

T-Ron said. "The ghosts of dead presidents."

Miss Cecile just nodded. "Does he just *see* them, or do they communicate?"

"We think they talk to each other, and to him," Big Mike added.

"Uh huh," she said.

"At first he thought they were just hallucinations," Jimmy said. "But they kept showing up and talking to him. Started to freak Beau out a bit. Now, he's convinced they're real."

"And it's really a bad time," T-Ron said. "This conflict with the Chinese is really heating up. Beau's gotta be on his toes, to make good decisions. He needs a good night's sleep, too, I bet."

The guys all nodded. Miss Cecile just looked at one and then the others.

Jimmy said, "We thought this might be the *rougarou* or something. Beau always says he saw it outside of Houma when he was a kid. Beau's always seeing shit. Maybe it's the *rougarou*, doing that shape-shifting thing. Appearing as dead presidents?"

"That would be a first," Miss Cecile said. "The *rougarou* is real, but doing all this – that seems very odd."

"Well, it *is* Washington D.C.," Big Mike said.

"And maybe the *rougarou* and Beau have some kind of connection. Maybe he's back to harass Beau for seeing him in the swamp."

"What we need you to do, Miss Cecile, is exorcise these ghosts," T-Ron said. "Get them out of here. Or at least convince Beau they've gone."

"I will need access to the places where Beau goes," she said.

"I think we can make that happen," Jimmy said. *How the hell can I make that happen?* he thought.

"At some point, I will have to spend some time with Beau."

"What for?" T-Ron said.

Miss Cecile leveled a creepy gaze at him. Then she looked at her bag.

"Okay. Yeah. Sure," he said.

"But we have to be discreet, Miss Cecile," Jimmy said. "Not everyone in this building is a *believer.*"

"I'd say just about no one," Big Mike said. "We're going to have to keep a very low profile."

"Just be my aunt, like you're getting the tour, that kind of thing."

"All right," she said. She yawned and looked at the bed. "I am very tired. Can I rest for a while?"

"Sure, sure," Jimmy said. "We're just down the hall if you need us."

They left her and went outside into the wide hallway.

"Okay, we're good," Jimmy said. "'Operation Rougarou' is on."

"We're gonna have to tell Melancon at some point," Big Mike said.

T-Ron looked around and leaned into his two co-conspirators. "How the hell are we going to get her around this place? With that snake?"

"Apparently, the snake knows how to disappear when needed, so we'll leave that part to her," Jimmy said.

"You think that blonde chick will say anything?" Big Mike was whispering now.

"Really?" T-Ron said. "That girl is a full-on eight bags of stupid."

"Okay, okay," Jimmy said. "Listen. One of us has to always have eyes on Miss Cecile. She could just take matters into her own hands at anytime. I don't want her walking into the Oval Office carrying a chicken head, or some shit like that."

"Good point," T-Ron said. "We need to keep her away from Boudreaux, too. The Lucky Cock might not be so lucky when it comes to voodoo priestesses."

They all nodded at this important fact. Someone cutting the head off their Lucky Cock could be disastrous.

"Did you see the way she went into some crazy-ass trance in there?" T-Ron said. "Man, that was freaky. She said something bad happened in there. That gives me the creeps. Maybe this place really is haunted."

"Yeah, we gotta ask Beau or someone what happened in there."

Just then a door opened down the hall, and they all turned to see Marissa Bergeron walk out. She wore a tight, clingy maroon sweater and tighter designer jeans. She was *tight*.

"Hey, boys!" she said with a radiant smile. She put her arms out and walked over to them. She hugged each one of them. T-Ron might have held on just a beat too long.

"Okay, T-Ron," she said. "You can let go now. You've had plenty of boob smash. You're feelin' me up with your chest."

T-Ron pulled away. "Damn, Marissa. Why don't you leave that asshole and run away with me?"

"Because your wife is my friend and she'd kill me. And my husband has an army, and nukes, and spaceships, and all kinds of cool shit. You don't."

"I have a bass boat."

"Heard you got 'em out back," she said. "Y'all bring Boudreaux, too? We could use some luck around here."

"Hell, yeah," Big Mike said.

"Who's in the West Bedroom?" she said.

"What?" Jimmy said.

"I thought I heard y'all go in there. Sounded like a woman."

"Oh, *that* West Bedroom," T-Ron said. "That's... Jimmy's aunt."

Jimmy said, "Yeah, yeah. She heard we were here, and I invited her up. Terry said it was okay."

Marissa looked at the bedroom door. "Great, I'd like to meet her."

"She's taking a nap right now," Jimmy said. "Maybe later."

"Sure, sure."

Big Mike wanted to change the subject, and in a hurry. "Uh, do you know the history of the White House? You know, stuff that went on here?"

Marissa shrugged a little. "Some. Stuff I've heard about since we moved in. Why?"

"Oh, you know, just interested," he said. "Like, what's the history of the West Bedroom, for instance?" He gestured that way and smiled.

"Oh yeah. I know some," she said. "Sometimes it's called the Blue Bedroom. Little John-John Kennedy stayed in there. It was Amy Carter's room, too, I think. The Reagan's changed it into a small gym, but the first Bushes made it back into a bedroom."

"Oh, okay," Big Mike said. *JFK, Jr. might have heard about his Daddy's death while in was in there. Maybe that's what Miss Cecile was picking up.*

"Hmmm, let's see," Marissa said. She held her hand up to her chin. "Oh, shit. I almost forgot. And this is kind of sad, too. After Lincoln was assassinated, his wife, Mary Todd Lincoln, locked herself in there in total grief. She wouldn't even go into their regular suite."

The guys all looked at each other. Jimmy felt a little chill go up his spine.

"Does her...ghost...haunt the room?" T-Ron said.

"Beats me," Marissa said. "I haven't seen her. But they say this whole place is haunted. Who knows?"

They all laughed, a nervous kind of laugh that stayed buried in their throats."

"See any dead presidents?" Big Mike blurted out.

"Hmmmm, no," she said. "Unless you count the last time Beau passed out after he and I went after it."

She made a big face, pointed at them, and burst out laughing. Marissa was known for her ribald sense of humor among friends. Of course, the guys had been listening to her potty mouth for over 20 years now. She had the sense of humor of a 16-year-old boy.

"Good one," Big Mike said.

Marissa looked at her watch. "Y'all got plans for dinner? Maybe we can round Beau up and some of the kids. Get Terry, too. Have a big Looziana supper."

They all nodded. Jimmy said, "Sure, sounds great."

"And you can bring your aunt."

"Oh, yeah. Sure. I'll...see if she's made any plans herself."

"Okay, then there it is," she said. "I gotta run do some stuff. I'll let you know if we can put something together."

"Great," T-Ron said.

They watched as she walked down the hall on her way up to the third floor of the residence, where the kids had their rooms. They all paid careful attention to the sway of the First Ass. T-Ron yelled at her, "Can I have some fries with that shake?"

Without turning around, she exaggerated her walk a bit, like a model strutting down the catwalk, putting on a show, and gave them a little wave.

"Damn, that woman is still hot," Jimmy said.

"Okay, who's got first shift to keep an eye on Miss Cecile?" Big Mike said.

"I'll take it," T-Ron said.

"Don't screw this up," Jimmy said. "If she gets out and starts sneaking around, doing weird voodoo shit, we're screwed."

"Who me? Screw up?

Not far away, through the Yellow Oval Room across the hall and outside on the semi-circular Truman balcony, three other good buddies were yukking it up.

Millard Fillmore, Grover Cleveland and Andrew Jackson all sat in chairs along the ornate iron balcony. They were each into their third or fourth beers, with their feet up on the balcony, rocking back on their chairs. They were taking in probably the best view from the White House, looking toward the south.

Fillmore was checking out the Washington Monument in the distance. "I wish I had a monument," he said, and let out a loud burp. "Look at that thing. You can see it for miles."

"I think I got a plaque somewhere," Cleveland said. He chuckled and took another pull off his longneck. "Actually, there's a rest stop on the New Jersey Turnpike named after me. Between exists 11 and 12, going north."

"No shit?" Jackson said. "Very impressive."

"Yeah, brings a tear to my eye." He started laughing again. "People think of me when they need to stop and pee."

"Jackson, at least you have one," Fillmore said. "The one over in Lafayette Park. You're on the horse rearing up, with your hat in your hand, waving to your fans."

"Yeah, well, if you win a battle or two, they gotta put you on a horse," he said.

Cleveland looked at Fillmore. "You got that nice statue in Buffalo."

"My New York fans love me."

Cleveland looked off in the distance. "Jefferson. Lincoln. Washington. FDR's got one. Kennedy's over in Arlington Cemetery. Heck, even Buchanan's got one."

"The one in Memorial Hill Park?" Jackson said. "I've seen it. His statue has him sitting down. Kind of Lincoln-like."

"His niece paid for it," Cleveland said.

"The bachelor president," Fillmore said. "Wasn't he gay?"

"Rumor had it," Jackson said. "He lived with Senator Rufus King, from Alabama. I always called that guy 'Miss Nancy.'"

"Didn't y'all call them both 'the Buchanans?'"

Jackson laughed. "Oh yeah, I remember that. I was such an asshole then. Looking back, though, it wasn't uncommon for men to be roommates. Saved money. So...he probably wasn't gay."

"Well, at least he's got a monument," Cleveland said, and opened another beer.

The three ghosts sat in silence for a moment, watching as the last light of the day faded over Washington D.C. The sound of traffic could be heard in the distance, as well as the faint roar of a jet taking off from Reagan. Each of them had lived in this home, although none had the opportunity to sit on the balcony. It wasn't built until Harry Truman's time. Which probably explained how attracted they were to the spot. It really was a great view. In Jackson's time, the place was wide open. He was the first president to invite the public to the inaugural ball. Things had gotten a little out of hand, though. The crowd was so big that furniture and dishes were broken.

"Think young Beau will get himself a monument?" Fillmore said.

"He's got a hot wife, isn't that enough?" Cleveland replied.

Jackson nodded his agreement and they clinked beer bottles together.

Jackson said, "In a way, I hope not, for his sake. Usually a crisis is involved, and you need to resolve it really well. Like this thing with the Chinese. He took our advice and bought himself some time. We're going to have to stay close to Beau to help him through this. Four presidents are better than one, I always said."

"You never said that," Cleveland said.

"You know what I mean."

"Yeah, I could've used four presidents," Fillmore said. "I could have prevented the Civil War."

"No, you couldn't," Cleveland said. "The only people who could have prevented it were Washington and Jefferson. All of those guys. They should have dealt with slavery when they put the constitution together. It would have been politically painful, but they could have done it."

Jackson finished off his beer. "No way. They would have never been able to put the Union together unless they looked the other way and let the South have their slaves. It was political expediency. They were trying to start a country. The South would have told them to shove it. 'We ain't joining your United States of America.'"

"Yeah, well , maybe," Cleveland said.

"I hate politics," Fillmore said.

"It's total bullshit," Jackson added. "Let's talk about something else."

They were quiet for a moment, and then Cleveland said, "Why don't we have some fun?"

Fillmore and Jackson turned to him.

"Like, what kind of fun?" Fillmore said.

Cleveland just smiled and looked off into the distance. "Well, we *are* ghosts, aren't we?"

Chapter 23

The White House had made its statement about the shoot-down of the Chinese plane, and the apparent death of its pilot. Word had come first from the Pentagon, as planned. It was followed by President Bergeron's comment, in which he regretted the incident, but affirmed that the Chinese aircraft had indeed fired first on the Navy's jets, whose pilots had been authorized to defend themselves if attacked. Which they had done.

The White House geniuses then had a good idea to take the story off in another direction. They leaked, with the Pentagon's agreement, the story of LaRonda Jackson, the first female African-American fighter jock to shoot down another plane in a combat situation. The press went absolutely bat-shit crazy over that. Miss Jackson had become an instant hero. Or heroine. Especially when her call sign of "Gangsta" had also been released. She was a badass. In reality, once she landed back on the *Washington,* there had been a few high fives, but when she went back to her cabin, she had a big case of the shakes, put her face in her hands, and cried alone for ten minutes. She knew it could have easily been her splattered all over the South China Sea.

Of course, that wouldn't make the news crawl that night. Just the photo of her released by the Pentagon, where she sat in the cockpit of her F-18, looking *Gangsta.*

Admiral Yang Jinping got to watch the whole thing on his TV in his own room on board the *Liaoning*. He normally liked CNN. But not tonight. He didn't like anything American on this night. He had just got off the phone with his bosses back in Beijing. There were a couple of things they wanted to know. Like, "How did you lose an entire American carrier force?" And, "How did you lose a jet, even though they outnumbered the Americans six to two?"

Yang had placated the boys back in Beijing by reminding them of the obvious: the Americans had turned away from his fleet and retreated. He had accomplished his mission of keeping the Americans out of the South China Sea and establishing Chinese hegemony over the region. *Checkmate.* If the cost of that had been one pilot and one plane, it was a small investment for a huge return. He had also lied to them that it was the Americans who had fired first and caught his pilots off guard. That explained how the six-against-two scenario played out. The only reason his pilots didn't destroy the two American jets was because they were too low on fuel and had to get back to the ship. That, at least, was the truth.

Dawn was breaking over the South China Sea, and Yang felt the day would be momentous. He had his scout planes and drones out searching for the *Washington*. Beijing had tasked a satellite to look as well, but that took time. He had to find the Americans and punish them. If Beijing was happy about the current state of affairs, Yang was far from it. He still had dreams of a victorious naval battle playing through his head.

His phone rang.

"Yes?" he said.

"Admiral, you're needed on the bridge. We've found the *Washington.*"

"Excellent! Where?"

"She moved northeast, close to Taiwan."

"Really? I'll be right there."

Yang hung up the phone and sat back at his desk. *Interesting. Why would the Americans do that? Better if they had just headed back out into the Pacific.*

So they had not retreated per se, but had re-positioned themselves around their little pesky ally. But to what end? Had they sensed a move by China on the island? If so, they were right. A conflict in the region would have given China the opportunity to grab Taiwan once and for all. Now that the Americans had moved closer, this plan had become a bit more problematic. Were they positioning themselves for a fight? There had been no mention of this on CNN.

Yang hurried back to the bridge. As he did, various options flipped through his head. He could hold his current position and be satisfied that his original mission had succeeded. He could move closer, launch aircraft, and see if he could go round two and score an air victory of some kind to even the score. Or...*something else?*

He got to the bridge and ordered his fleet to steam north-northeast at best possible speed. He had his fighters prep for battle, some armed with air-to-air missiles exclusively and some with anti-ship missiles as well. He then got on the horn with Beijing and had them fuel up the mobile ballistic missiles arrayed along the Chinese coast, just in case. They had been somewhat reluctant at first, but when

Yang explained his plan, they had agreed. He had also ordered land-based fighter-bombers to be on stand by.

The sun hovered on the eastern horizon like a blob of red lava, casting a red sheen to the entire sky. What was the old saying? *Red sky at night, sailor's delight. Red sky at dawn, sailors be warned.*

Yang smiled. *Yes, the Americans should take heed of nature's warning. Yes, indeed.*

"They're moving north now, Admiral," the young captain said.

Admiral Winston sat at the conference table in the White House Situation Room and stared at the big-screen TV. *What are you up to, you little bastard?* he thought. He had predicted that the Chinese fleet would hold its position at the entrance to the South China Sea once it learned of the *Washington's* move north. But now, that prediction had proven very wrong. The Chinese were going after his task force.

"Get Admiral Lear on the line," he said to no one in particular. "And get me the *Lincoln*, too."

The place hustled to life as aides and assistants hit the phones and the keyboards.

"What's up, Admiral?" National Security Advisor Cassidy walked in with a fresh mug of coffee.

Winston explained the now-evolving state of affairs. Cassidy listened intently.

"What does it mean?"

Winston stood up and walked over to the screen. "My guess is they're going to try to flank us on the east, and pinch us between them and the mainland. If this were a shooting war, we'd be up shit creek for sure."

"What's your call?"

"I'm going to get Lear to move the *Washington* farther east. To here," he said, pointing at the screen. "Give us some room. Then I'm going to move the *Lincoln* in there behind them in a hurry. Get her planes up and get the Chinese's attention looking at their rear."

Cassidy squinted at the screen. "Man, it's gonna get tight in there. Lot of itchy trigger fingers."

"Yeah, well, I'm tired of this shit," Winston said. "After the *Lincoln* gets behind them on the south, I'm gonna tell Tony to put the pedal to the medal and drive the *Washington* right at them from the north."

"A big squeeze play," Cassidy said. "I like it."

"We'll see what kind of stones that Yang asshole has," Winston said.

Cassidy put his cup down on the conference table. "Right, but don't forget what CIA was saying about him. The guy might be a flake. Unpredictable. Maybe even rogue."

"I certainly hope so," Winston said.

"Hey, Mr. Moreau? Mr. Fontenot?" Dana Newton ran to catch up with Big Mike and Jimmy as they walked out of the West Wing to their parked boats. "Hold on a second."

The two men stopped and stood shuffling their feet outside in the dark parking lot. The air was fresh and cool, with the growing humidity of springtime in D.C. A couple of uniformed Secret Service guys walked by, patrolling the perimeter.

She caught up with them, clearly out of breath. "You talked to the President lately?"

Jimmy looked at Big Mike. "Some. Why?"

"I don't know. The Chinese thing is getting interesting. We shot down one of their jets today."

"Yeah, I heard," Big Mike said. "But Beau...the President...doesn't talk too much about that stuff with us. Fishing, yes. International crises, no."

"So how would you rate his performance during all this? You know, as friends, fraternity buddies. Fishing buddies. Guys from Louisiana?"

Jimmy said, "Is this for a story, you know, on the record?"

"Sure," she said.

"Well, I think he's doing a great job. He's not going in half-cocked or anything. Being smart and careful."

"Yeah, he was always like that," Big Mike added. "He was always fully cocked."

Jimmy stared at him.

"Fully cocked?" Dana said. "As in...?"

"Just...prepared. Ready to go," Big Mike said. "Fully cocked."

Uh huh," she said. She jotted something down in her notebook. She nodded toward one of the bass boats. "Does your cock over there have anything to do with the President being fully cocked?"

"You mean Boudreaux?" Jimmy said. "Hell, it couldn't hurt. That's one lucky chicken." He chuckled a bit at the thought.

"So the President has a distinct advantage over the Chinese, because of Boudreaux?

Big Mike thought for a second. "Sure, sure. I'd say that. Jimmy?"

"Oh, hell yeah."

"Uh huh," Dana said. "Did your aunt make it in today?"

Jimmy's eyebrows went up as he nodded. "My aunt? Oh sure, sure. She's tucked away upstairs. Can't wait to take the tour and maybe meet Beau."

"I bet," she said. "I'd love to talk to her. You know, get her perspective on things."

"Yeah, well, she's kind of shy," Jimmy said. "Probably not."

"Oh, hell," Dana said. "There won't be any cameras. Just she and I chatting."

"Chatting," Big Mike said.

"Right. The White House through her eyes, that kind of thing."

"Maybe not," Jimmy said.

"C'mon," Dana said. "I'll look for her tomorrow. She'll love it, being quoted in the *New York Times*. And so will you two. Got some great quotes from you for tomorrow's paper already."

They both looked at each other again. "What did we say?" Big Mike looked a little worried.

"Just how good a job the President is doing," she said with a smile.

Jimmy thought it looked more like a mean-ass cat baring its teeth.

Dana gave them a little wave and hurried back inside.

Big Mike and Jimmy just stood there in silence, watching as she stepped back into the West Wing.

"She's on to us," Big Mike said.

"Yeah, you think?"

"We gotta keep her away from Miss Cecile. How much access do those White House reporters have, anyway? Can she get up into the Residence?"

"I sure as hell hope not," Jimmy said. He rubbed his chin. "We may have to set up a diversion or something, especially when Miss Cecile starts checking out the place."

Big Mike scratched his head. "We're gonna need Melancon to run interference. You need to tell him she's here."

"He's gonna have a cow," Jimmy said.

"It won't be his first bovine delivery."

Beau looked at his watch. It was already past dinnertime, and he was hungry. The Scotch he held in his hand helped some, but he needed some food. He was finishing up some business in the Oval Office with Terry. His military and national security people had just left after briefing him on the latest developments with China.

"Are they around?" Terry said. He was throwing back some Jack Daniels.

"No. Haven't seen the guys for a while. I have no idea where they go."

Beau wasn't talking about Big Mike and the gang. He was talking about Big Grover and the gang.

"So that was their idea, the little naval maneuver we just pulled off?" Terry said. He sat back on the sofa and stared at the oval ceiling of the Oval Office. "I'm so glad you didn't share that tidbit with the Admiral. Or anyone else for that matter."

"It was a good idea, you have to admit."

"We'll see," Terry said. "This thing ain't over. It's just beginning."

Beau stretched his legs across the coffee table. "Yeah, well. I've got my Dead President's Society to help now. That Jackson's a military guy. He gets it. Millard and Grover are smart guys, too. Smarter than historians give them credit for, anyway. I like 'em."

"I'm not hearing this," Terry muttered.

"Why can't you believe it? Beau said. "You know I always worried I had some gift, or curse. I see things."

"I'm seeing a one-term presidency if this gets out. Maybe not even that."

Beau dismissed the thought with a wave of his hand. The freakiness of the ghostly visits had passed now. He had accepted them as fact, strange or not. Truth be told, he was feeling pretty good now. Better than he had in days. His confidence was up. He felt decisive. Having his long-dead hero Andrew Jackson around to lend some advice was admittedly very cool. Again, he wondered if other presidents had been visited by some of their dead predecessors. A sobering thought then rushed through his head. Would *he* be someone's ghost-advisor some day in the distant future? He took another sip of the vintage Macallan and savored the smooth texture. That wouldn't be a bad gig. Run around the place, dispensing wisdom. Apparently allowed to go through the White House booze closet. Eat potato chips.

"Beau, you with me?" Terry said.

"Huh? Yeah. Just thinking I might make a good dead president some day."

"That's just a fabulous thought. We'll see what your legacy will be. You're only one year into your first term. Plenty of time to fuck things up."

"That's true."

"I need to drink more," Terry said, and finished off his whiskey.

"Relax," Beau said. "What could go wrong?"

Chapter 24

The next morning, Terry walked into the White House's West Wing, his head down, lost in thought. He usually rolled in about 7:30 to get a jump on the day, which of course, never ended. Just periods of light and dark filled with stress, bullshit, compromise and then more stress. He loved it.

He and Beau had officially met the night they rushed FIJI at LSU. They and 26 of their other newly pledged brothers had gotten pretty wasted, ran over to Sorority Row over by the lakes, absconded with various lingerie from as many sororities as they could approach, and later crashed at the house. They had become fast friends immediately, eventually serving as officers in the fraternity. Beau had run for and won Student Body President for the university his senior year, no thanks to a brilliantly run campaign by Terry – his first real foray into politics. After that both he and Beau were hooked. It led to a state senate seat, a term as lieutenant governor, then the mansion, and then the White House. Not a bad run. Of course, the next stop was down. Way down.

But not yet, he thought. Not if he could help it. And he could.

Normally the White House is relatively quiet, not like the bustling and hustling one sees in Hollywood movies or TV shows. And at 7:30 in the morning, it's downright serene. But for some reason, the place seemed buzzed this morning, despite his distraction as he walked in. People were milling about, talking in whispers and murmurs. A couple of aides were standing around looking at something on the floor, next to the wall.

He made it up to his office on the first floor and was greeted by his secretary, who sat on her desk with her arms folded, looking perplexed.

"Morning, Mr. Melancon," she said.

"Felicia. What's up?"

"You didn't notice?"

"What?" He looked around.

"Come on," she said, and grabbed him by the arm.

She led him down the hall, and then left into the Roosevelt Room. A big conference table dominated the empty room. She pointed to a life-sized portrait leaning against the mantle, in front of the fireplace. "See that?"

"What?" Terry said.

"That's a portrait of Martha Washington," she said.

"Okay. So?"

"This is the Roosevelt Room," she said. She folded her arms across her chest. "There's supposed to be a portrait of Teddy Roosevelt on his horse hanging right there over the mantle. His Rough Rider days."

"Makes sense," he said. "What, did somebody steal it?" He looked at his watch.

"No, no one stole it. It's over in the East Room, where this portrait of Martha is supposed to be. It was here yesterday when I left. Saw it when I was walking out last night.

And I got here this morning at seven and they had been switched."

He shrugged his shoulders and gave her a perplexed look that said, *and this is important why?*

"No one ordered a portrait moved," she said.

Terry felt like he was having one of those marital conversations with his wife. When something fairly trivial was important to her, but not him. But he knew better not to be dismissive. Or she'd hand him his head. So would Mrs. Smithers.

"Okay, you want me to check with someone about it?" That was about as accommodating of an answer he could think of.

She laughed a bit and it caught him off guard. "Probably, but you should wait to hear the whole story."

"Shoot," he said.

She took a deep breath and seemed to compose herself. Then she looked him straight in the eye. "Every portrait in the White House has been moved and switched around. Every one of them. Even the ones in the Oval Office."

Terry squinted at her. "When did this happen?"

"Last night, apparently."

"That's a lot of artwork to move around," he said. "Didn't anyone see anything?

"We're checking, but so far, no one saw a thing."

Terry started to get that jicky feeling. Part panic. Part disassociation from reality. Part freak out. He held it together. "There's got to be dozens, hundreds of paintings all over this place." He swallowed a big gulp of air.

"Yes, sir. Who could have done this?"

Terry just shook his head. "Who the hell knows? First, let's get an inventory done. Make sure nothing is missing. Who would know that?"

"That would be the Office of the Curator. Down on the first floor of the Residence. Mr. Carswell."

The position of Curator of the White House was begun during the Kennedy administration, when Jackie had begun a big restoration. Today that office consisted of a staff of five, and they were charged with the conservation and study of all the fine art, furniture and other important knick knacks around the place.

"Okay, get him on it. Make sure Cindy Walker knows. This will get out before my second cup of coffee." He looked down at the floor. "How the hell do you spin this without looking like a total idiot?"

She ignored the question and just stared at the portrait of Martha, late of the East Room. The full-length, eight-by-five-foot oil painting of the old girl was done in 1878 by Eliphalet Andrews. He based it on a head-and-bust sketch from life by Gilbert Stuart. Mrs. Smithers thought Martha's serene face now looked downright confused. As in, *What the hell am I doing in this meeting room?*

"And get someone from security," Terry said. "This whole place is wired with cameras and God knows what else."

"On it," she said.

"And have you seen or heard from the President yet?"

"No, sir."

"Okay, get Cary Guidry or Mrs. Foster to get in touch with him. I'll need a minute with him the moment he gets vertical." He looked at the painting of Martha Washington. "I'll be right back."

Terry headed over to the ground floor of the Residence and went straight to the Foyer. A couple of uniformed Secret Service guys were talking to a young woman he didn't recognize. When he walked in, they all turned to him.

"Morning, Mr. Melancon," the woman said. She looked to be in her early thirties, bookish, with stylish glasses and a short brunette 'do. "Can we help you?"

"Sure, sure," he said. He looked at the walls, where there was a haphazard display of portraits hanging. Some small, some rather large. Most were crooked. There were scenes of battles, portraits of First Ladies, a few Presidents, some other shit he didn't recognize. It looked like he had hung them and arranged them. In other words, a pretty crappy attempt.

"Is this where the portrait of Millard Fillmore was hanging?" he said.

The woman made a slight coughing sound. "Uh, yes, sir. It used to be right there. But someone moved it last night."

"Looks like someone moved every painting last night," he said.

The woman looked downright apoplectic now. "We know. We don't know what happened. By the way, I'm Laney White. With the Curator's Office."

"Sure, sure, Laney." He shook her hand. "What happened?" He looked at the two Secret Service guys. They appeared serious and just as confused.

"We were on duty last night," one said. "Didn't see anything."

"Where are the video monitors?"

The two men stared at each other, waiting for one or the other to answer the question.

"Yeah, that," the other one said. "Hard to explain. You'll just have to see if for yourself."

"Let's go, then," Terry said.

They all hurried to a room filled with monitoring screens from security cameras all over the White House and its grounds. One of the agents hit some keys on a computer keyboard and brought up a live image of the Foyer. He tapped a few more keys and said, "Okay, here's the Foyer last night at 1:22 a.m. You see Fillmore's painting on that wall right there. Okay, I'm going to let the video roll for a minute or so."

Terry, Laney White and the two agents stared intently at the screen. There was no movement in the empty foyer at that time of night. The scene was kind of creepy, especially for Terry, who had been hearing ghost stories from Beau for the last few days. He half expected Fillmore to jump down out of his portrait. What happened next was just a freaky.

There was a slight glitch in the image. Not a cutaway. The image on the screen never disappeared. It was like a video hiccup. But in that nanosecond, the portrait of Fillmore was instantly gone, and in its place were three smaller portraits, one hanging slightly askew.

"Whoa," Terry said. "Back that up."

The agent rewound the video and played it again. Same result.

"Somebody edited that?" he said.

The agent shook his head. "No, sir. Look at the time stamp. It's continuous. We didn't lose a second."

Terry had the agent rewind the video again and again, with the same result. It was like a very tight edit, or special effect seen in a movie. The portrait of Fillmore was there, and then it was instantly replaced with three smaller paintings. *Snap.*

"Somebody must have doctored the tape and put it back in there," Laney said. "Figured out how to make it look like the time code didn't change."

The other Secret Service agent said, "There's no tape. It's all digital on a hard drive."

"Plus, we had people here all night," the other one said. "No way anyone could have messed with this, unless it was one of us, and that just didn't happen."

"How many cameras do we have inside the White House?" Terry said.

"With the exception of the family rooms, every room in the place is covered," the first agent said.

"Is it like this on all of them?" Terry said.

"Yes, sir."

"Anyone have a theory?"

Everyone just shook their heads.

"Okay, let's keep this quiet until we figure it out," he said. "Any press queries, run them through Cindy Walker. Everyone clear?"

They all nodded. Terry walked out and spent the next 15 minutes taking a tour of the White House. He hadn't really taken much notice of all the artwork. He was just too damn busy to appreciate it. And there was a lot. Now, he took the time to look at each one he saw, many obviously in the wrong location because the wall area was too small or too large for the art, or the paintings were all crooked, mismatched, or poorly arranged. Some of the bigger ones were just leaning against walls, like Martha Washington's in the Roosevelt Room. Now alone, Terry allowed himself to let the full-on willies take over his psyche.

He finally made it back to the first floor of the West Wing. As he walked down the hall past the Cabinet Room, he saw his secretary, Mrs. Smithers, talking to Mrs. Foster, the President's secretary. They both turned when he approached them.

"The President is on his way, and I told him you needed to see him," Mrs. Foster said.

"Thanks, I'll just wait in the Office."

"Coffee's already in there," she said.

"Anything stronger?"

She gave him a look.

"Never mind, never mind," he said with a wave of his hand. He walked into the Oval Office and noticed it right away. Portraits of Millard Fillmore, Grover Cleveland and Andrew Jackson were all hanging on the walls. They looked too big for the walls, but they were all up. Terry tried to remember what paintings were there before, but he was drawing a blank. *Shit, I've been here hundreds of times and I can't remember that. Man, I gotta stop and smell the roses,* he thought.

He poured himself a cup of coffee and stood there looking at the portraits.

"I hate it when you're in here waiting for me first thing," Beau said.

Terry turned.

"We're not at war yet?"

"Not yet," he said.

"What the...? Beau stopped at his desk without sitting. "Who put those in here?" He nodded at the portraits.

"Good question," Terry said, and proceeded to describe the Great White House Art Switcheroo to the President.

Beau slowly sat down. "Son of a bitch," he said. "That's really weird."

"This coming from a guy who's been talking to these three guys for the last few days," Terry said. "What paintings were there before?"

"Washington, Lincoln, and Jefferson." Beau sat back and a smile slowly formed on his face. "Those crazy old bastards," he said.

"Who?"

"Fillmore, Cleveland and Jackson, who else?" Beau got up and walked over to the portrait of Fillmore, looked up and laughed out loud.

"Your ghosts did all this?" Terry said with a wave of an arm.

"Hell, yeah. Looks like they had themselves a little party last night. I've just been punked by three dead presidents!"

Terry thought of the weird video he had seen earlier. The switch was instant. Or *appeared* to be instant. He would have figured the paintings would have been floating on their own as they moved around the White House during the wee hours. If ghosts had done that. *Ridiculous.*

He ignored Beau's theory. "I'm going to put this on the Curator's office. Tell them if anybody asks, it was their idea. Make up some bullshit about doing a little inventory, or rethinking the art, or whatever. We don't have time for this bullshit."

There was a tap on the door. Mrs. Foster stuck her head in. "Sir, do you have a moment?" Before she could announce why, David Cassidy, the National Security Advisor, squeezed inside.

"Sir, you're needed down in the Situation Room."

"Why?"

"The Chinese are on the move."

Chapter 25

Beau walked into the Situation Room and found the place already bustling. Of course, it was always bustling, especially when two fleets were on a collision course. The conference room was filled mostly with military types at the moment, save Cassidy and his two aides.

And standing in the corner, near the big TV, were Fillmore, Cleveland and Jackson. They were laughing as Beau entered, and then tried to compose themselves.

Cleveland made a silly face and used his two hands to form a frame around it. Fillmore and Jackson did the same. Then it was knee-slapping laughter time again.

Beau tried hard not to react to the presidential pranksters. All he could do was direct a quick glance that way with just a hint of a smile. He took a seat and everyone reciprocated.

"Go ahead," he said to Cassidy.

"Well, we've drawn them out towards us, this way," he said as he pointed at the screen. "We had to move the *Washington* farther east, per Admiral Winston's order, to give us some breathing room."

"They could have bottled us up in there if we didn't, sir," Winston said. He picked up the briefing after a nod to Cassidy. "The *Lincoln's* group has moved well north, into the South China Sea. Here. Still no indication the Chinese have picked them up."

"That's a relief," Terry said.

"It is," Winston continued. "Won't be long, though, before some patrol boat or random plane sees them."

"So what's the problem?" Beau said.

Winston sighed and looked down at his notes. "Admiral Yang – that's the guy running their show – is really hauling ass towards us. We thought he might just stay put after we moved. Now he's launched fighters and picked up some extra help from the mainland. They're sending aircraft, too. We're worried he might do something...rash."

"Looking for some payback?" Beau said.

"We think so."

"He wants it to look like he's chasing us back into the Pacific," Cassidy said. "They've leaked some of this to the world press already. We're going to have to get the *Washington* into the South China Sea as we originally planned. Anything short of that is a retreat."

Beau stared at the screen again. The *Lincoln's* ships were now moving north, through the South China Sea. They had been holding their position, per the plan, but now were racing to get behind the Chinese fleet.

"So we'll squeeze them?" he said.

"Right," Admiral Winston said. "In a bit, we'll launch fighters from the *Lincoln*, as soon as it gets a little closer. I would love to see the look on the faces of those Chinese radar guys when they see a squadron of F-18's heading for them from behind. That'll make them crap their pants."

Beau looked to the dead presidents, who were listening intently. They kept glancing at the screen and whispering among themselves, as if anyone could hear them. Well, except for Beau. He was hoping they might weigh in with a comment.

"The good thing to come out of this is that the Chinese fleet is now technically out of the South China Sea," Cassidy said. "They're in the Philippine Sea."

"Good, how?" Beau sat back and folded his arms.

"Well, they were sitting in their so-called territory before, to make a statement, a claim to the South China Sea," he continued. "Now, they're out of there, and *really* in international waters."

Winston chimed in. "Make no mistake. The South China Sea is international waters, Mr. President, but you see our point. They're losing their story."

Beau nodded, and glanced again at the dead guys. Their plan was still working.

"Your suggestion, once again, sir, was a good one," Admiral Winston said. "You sure you weren't in the Navy?" He gave the president a slight smile.

"Thanks, Admiral. It *was* just a suggestion. If it had been a stupid idea, you wouldn't have blessed it."

"True," Winston replied. This got some nervous laughter around the room. They knew Beau was a pretty laid-back guy, not prone to outbursts. Not prone to being a total asshole, either.

"So, how are we going to get the *Washington* past them and into the South China Sea?" Beau said.

"We'll let the Chinese know we're behind them first," Admiral Winston replied. "While they're trying to get their heads around that, chatting back and forth with Beijing, we'll make our move, right at them. Just like before."

"And what about the *Lincoln's* task force?" Beau said. "We link up with them and sail south, or what?" He looked around the room.

Winston and Cassidy looked at each other. Winston ceded to Cassidy, because what they had in mind was as much political as military.

"One idea we're proposing, and the Navy's still working it out, and it's only one option, sir..." Cassidy began.

Beau sat up and put his elbows on the table.

Cassidy continued. "Is...we let both task forces stay in the South China Sea for an extended period. To make a statement."

"That's some statement," Beau said. "The big 'F-You.'"

"Pretty much."

Terry, who had sat quietly during the whole exchange, turned to Beau. "Yeah, and now *we're* the assholes. It'll look like we're picking a fight. Poking a stick at them. Before, we were just sailing along, minding our own business, just passing through. Now we're setting up shop in the neighborhood. Maybe buying a house."

Beau nodded to Terry's observation. "Good point."

"We did say it had political implications," Cassidy said.

"I'll say," Terry added. As Chief of Staff, all this was pretty much out of his jurisdiction. But for many decades now, it was understood that the White House Chief of Staff did more than run the operations of the White House. He was the guy who had the President's ear. His top advisor. His *consigliore*. Often, the President's best friend.

"Your call, Mr. President," Admiral Winston said. "And we don't need to have your answer right this second."

"Okay, I'll consider it," Beau said. "Just make sure you guys have some contingencies if we decide to do that. I'll want to be flexible. There's a big difference between standing up for our rights in international waters and being downright provocative. We're going to have to deal with the Chinese for a long time. I'd rather talk to them than do this every few months." He waved his hand around the room. "When they finally get their leadership sorted out, we're going to have to sit down and get to know each other. I don't want to embarrass them, just make our point."

"Understood, Mr. President," Winston said.

"Good. I'll let you know my decision before the end of the day."

Beau got the feeling Winston and the Navy wanted to embarrass the Chinese. He got that. He kind of wanted to do that, too. But he had to put his big-boy pants on and be diplomatic about these things and not overplay his hand.

He looked over at Fillmore, Cleveland and Jackson. They were all giving him the thumbs up.

"Mr. President?" David Cassidy said. "Just one more thing. We think if this Admiral Yang guy is going to do anything, it'll be today."

"Like what?"

"He'll want to take out one of our planes at the very least. My guess, he's sending his best guys out there and telling them to make something good happen. Which is bad for us, of course."

"They're down one to zero," Winston said. "The world press is making them look bad. They'll want to even that score somehow."

"They fired on us first," Terry said. "They got what they deserved."

"Right," Beau said. "Nothing's changed. We have a right to defend ourselves."

Winston nodded and looked directly at Beau. "And I'm sure we'll have to exercise that right today."

Beau and Terry retreated back to the Oval Office for some morning appointments with staff and other affairs of state that didn't include the word "Chinese." Marissa stopped by for some late coffee and a kiss. She had her own full day ahead, and urged her husband to try to be home for dinner. It was their running joke, since he was technically *always* home for dinner. He just missed dinner a lot, or had it too late. Which was bad for his health and his waistline.

By 10:30, Terry excused himself for another meeting and left Beau in the Oval Office by himself for more paperwork and a review of that morning's intelligence briefing. The CIA sent him the hot sheet every day, with a summary of good and bad shit that was happening, or about to happen, all over the world. Beau was fascinated by each day's report. He had always loved spy thrillers, but this shit was pure gold. And *real*. There were moles the CIA had in places all over the world, some very high up in world governments – both friend and foe. They were running covert ops all over the place. And they were working with Special Forces teams to kick down doors in the middle of the night and waste terrorist ass by the truckload. Most of which never made the paper. They were also squeezing information out of captured terrorists and spies. Beau knew "squeezing" was now a more accurate word for what they were doing to those guys. He had no problem with "enhanced interrogation" techniques. If it meant a bunch of innocent civilians would live, then so be it. This had earned him a lot of support from Langley, who saw him as a big fan of the spy agency. Any intelligence on the Chinese crisis was in a separate report, but most of this he already knew from his live meetings down in the Situation Room.

"You have spies everywhere," a voice said.

Beau jumped a bit and looked up to see Andrew Jackson standing right in front of his desk. Millard Fillmore and Grover Cleveland were sitting on the edges of the sofas. Cleveland was chowing down on a cream-filled donut. He had a cup of coffee in the other.

Beau looked down at his report and then up at Jackson. "Yeah, I do. Not enough sometimes, it seems."

Jackson folded his arms and thought for a second. "You know, back in New Orleans, we had spies, too. I had some in the city, hanging out at bars, getting a feel for what the citizens were thinking."

"As I recall from your biography, they were none too happy with you," Beau said.

"Whatever," Jackson said. "Had to have martial law in place, what with a British army camped five miles from town. And the Brits had their spies, too, so we were always trying to do some counterintelligence."

"Good point."

"Had a few spies in the British camp, too. Those bastards were conscripting escaped slaves to fight for them, or at least to do a lot of the manual labor. I had a couple planted there. Got a few pieces of info that were valuable."

Fillmore snorted. "I could have used a few more spies in Congress."

"Heard that," Cleveland mumbled through his donut.

"How's your spying on the Chinese?" Jackson asked.

"Not bad," Beau said. "Could be better. We need more high-level people in their government, according to the CIA. Of course, we've got satellites. We eavesdrop on their phone calls whenever we can. Always trying to crack their codes. That's a hit or miss thing. Plus cyber warfare stuff. You know, the web."

Jackson began to pace a bit. "I was paying attention down in the Situation Room. Our little chess moves are looking good at the moment. But I worry a bit about that Chinese fleet. They're spoiling for a fight. I get the sense that their admiral is aggressive. Maybe too much so."

Beau smiled and said, "You should know."

Years earlier, he had read everything he could about Jackson, and among other things, he was a very aggressive commander. When he learned that an advance part of the British army had camped south of New Orleans back in December of 1814, Jackson didn't hesitate to attack. And he did it at night, too. He used land and naval forces that surprised the British. The thing had turned into hand-to-hand fighting in the dark, with the lines so confused, no one knew what the hell was going on. The night had ended in pretty much a draw, but the attack really freaked out the British commanders, and from then on out, they were a little shaken and back on their heels. They knew they weren't dealing with some cautious American who played by the rules.

Jackson smiled back at Beau. "You know me well. Which is why you need to pay attention to this guy. He's up to something, mark my words. He's inexperienced and aggressive, and that makes him unpredictable and extremely dangerous. Certainly to his own forces, and especially to us."

"Okay."

"You need some real-time intel on this guy," Cleveland said from behind Jackson.

"The best," added Fillmore.

"No shit," Beau said.

Jackson winked at him. "We think we can help with that."

Chapter 26

Jimmy tapped on the door a few times. "Uh, Aunt Cecile? You ready?"

There was no reply.

Big Mike also gave a few more hits to the door, this time a little heavier and louder. "Miss Cecile? Time for the White House tour!"

"Oh man, I bet that fucking snake killed her or something," T-Ron said. He had his hand to his face.

"Shut up," Jimmy said. "It was a king snake, you idiot. It eats mice and shit. Not poisonous." He knocked some more.

"Yeah, well, it had stripes like a coral snake," T-Ron said. "What is that saying, 'red touch yellow, kill a fellow. Red touch black, he's okay, Jack?'"

"It's the other way around," Big Mike said. "I think."

Jimmy ignored them and put his ear to the door. "Shit." He opened it a crack and looked in. "Aunt Cecile?"

They all eased into the room but didn't see Miss Cecile. The bed had been made up, either by her or the White House maids. The rollaway was in a corner and empty of any clothing. Jimmy checked the bathroom and saw that the old woman had put a few toiletries on the counter.

"Crap, she's gone," Big Mike said.

"We should've checked on her earlier," T-Ron said. He kept looking at the floor and on top of the dresser. Under chairs and the bed. "Anybody see her bag?"

The others looked around. "You mean the snake?" Big Mike said.

"Yeah."

"Man, she's walking around the White House," Jimmy said. He rubbed his hand through his curly brown hair.

"With a fucking snake," T-Ron added.

"Oh, man." Big Mike paced a bit. "You don't think she's doing her thing now, do you? You know. All that mumbo jumbo shit?"

"Okay, let's go," Jimmy said. "We gotta find her."

They did a quick search of the second floor of the Residence, where they, Beau and Marissa had their bedrooms. There were a few butlers and maids around, doing morning chores. Beau and Marissa had gone off to work – he to the Oval Office in the West Wing, she to her office over on the second floor of the East Wing. They checked the dining room, where a butler was preparing the table for a lunch. They looked in the Yellow Oval Room that led out onto the Truman Balcony. No sign of her. She wasn't in the Treaty Room or either of the sitting rooms at the far end of the hall.

"Can we go upstairs?" Big Mike said. Upstairs, the third floor of the Residence, was where the kids had their bedrooms.

"Hell if I know," Jimmy said. "Let's go."

They bounded up the stairs and into the large Central Hall. There were more rooms up here. Bedrooms. Sitting rooms. A music room. A solarium. Offices. Storerooms. A game room. An exercise room. Even an outside promenade. Besides cleaning staff, there was no sign of Miss Cecile.

T-Ron walked up to a maid who was about to switch on a vacuum cleaner. The woman looked to be middle aged and Hispanic. "Excuse me, ma'am. Did you see a tall black woman up here?" *With a snake in her hands. You couldn't miss her,* he wanted to say.

"Oh, yes. Cecile. I saw her downstairs earlier. She was on her way to look around."

"On her way *where?*" Jimmy said.

"She didn't say. Just look around, you know? Nice lady. Your aunt, I understand?" She looked Jimmy up and down.

"Uh, right," he said. "Let's go, guys."

They headed down to the first floor where they finally found her in the big East Room, gazing at a portrait of Dolly Madison. Standing next to her was Dana Newton, White House reporter for the *New York Times.*

"Oh, shit," Big Mike said.

"Stay cool," said Jimmy

Miss Cecile looked like she just stepped off the boat from Haiti. She wore a floor-length madras bandana skirt with a frilly white blouse that puffed out high on the arms, and a matching madras bandana in her hair. Her chest was covered with colored, beaded necklaces, some with strange figurines and amulets hanging on them. Gold bangles adorned her wrists, and just about every finger had a ring of some sort on it. And slung from her shoulder was her bag. And whatever the hell she kept in it.

"Hey, good morning," Jimmy said, maybe with just a little bit too much cheer in his voice.

Miss Cecile and Dana Newton turned.

"Who's that?" Jimmy said. He looked up at the portrait.

"Dolly Madison," Miss Cecile said. "A good woman. She saved a portrait of George Washington just before the British burned the White House down in the War of 1812. Did you know that, Jimmy?"

"Sure, sure," he said.

"Your aunt is a lovely woman," Dana said. "I ran into her just a while ago. Wow, what an interesting lady she is."

Jimmy didn't like the knowing look on Dana Newton's face. He figured it was time to ratchet up the bullshit quotient. T-Ron and Big Mike just hung back.

"That she is," he said. "What all she been telling you?"

"Just a little, so far," she said. "Her little home on the bayou. Your family history." Dana smiled. Maybe too broadly.

"Oh, wow. Our family history! Man, hope you didn't tell her *everything,* Aunt Cecile."

The old woman gave Jimmy a glance, like a mom with an annoying son underfoot. "Just that our family has a very *colorful* background. Mixed race and all that."

"Ha! Yes." Jimmy needed to get ahold of this conversation in a hurry. "Oh, yes. You should see our family reunions. A regular United Nations convocation. Very colorful."

"I bet," Dana said. She turned back to the Madison portrait. "There seems to be a bit of a mystery this morning here at the White House. Looks like someone moved all the paintings around last night."

The guys looked around at the walls. T-Ron said, "I hadn't noticed."

"Yeah, well. That should make for a great story," Dana said. "All kinds of interesting stories busting out around here today. And I haven't even got to the Chinese crisis yet."

"Yeah, that," Big Mike said. "You might want to pay more attention to the Chinese thing. Scary."

"That I will," Dana said. She turned to Miss Cecile. "Ma'am, what was that interesting prayer you were saying a minute ago?"

"I was speaking to the *Loa*," she said. "The spirits who exist in that realm between *Bondye* and all of us mortal humans."

"Bondye?" Dana said. She was jotting all this down in a small notebook.

"Yes, the Creator. God," Miss Cecile said.

Jimmy was sure he was going to crap in his pants. Then maybe faint.

"These Loa, they're here, in the White House?" Dana said.

"They are everywhere, but you must call on them. Some are very kind. Others not so much. I really need to speak to the *Ghede Loa*, especially."

"And he is..." Dana said, still writing furiously.

"They are the spirits of the dead. This place, it is filled with them," Miss Cecile said with a wave of her arm. "Sometimes they mount people."

"Ohhhhkaaaaayyyy, Aunt Cecile," Jimmy said. He reached for her elbow. "I think we're late for the tour."

"Mount?" Dana said. She stopped writing.

"Oh, yes," Miss Cecile said in somewhat of a whisper. The Haitian accent was slowly being dialed up. "They go inside people."

"You mean, like, a possession?" Dana said.

"Yes."

"You think these Ghede Loa had something to do with all the paintings being moved around?" Dana said.

"They *can* be mischievous," Miss Cecile said. "But there is something else going on here. Something…more powerful. Not evil. But…strong." She looked up at the ceiling and closed her eyes.

T-Ron and Big Mike looked up with her. Jimmy was now officially catatonic. Dana also looked up, but then at Miss Cecile.

"These Loa, the things you're talking about? What is all that?"

Miss Cecile opened her eyes and looked at the reporter. "It is *Vodu.* The old religion."

"*Vodu?* You mean, like, voodoo?" Dana said.

"As it is known here," Miss Cecile said. "But it is very ancient, back to Africa, when the Earth was new."

Dana turned back to Jimmy. He made a turning circle with his index finger next to his head and gave her a wink.

Dana cleared her throat "I see. Interesting." She gestured to Miss Cecile's bag, which seemed to be moving of its own accord. "What's in the bag?"

Jimmy prayed, *Oh, dear Lord. Please don't let her pull out that snake.*

T-Ron and Big Mike held their breath.

Miss Cecile reached into her bag. She pulled out what looked like a homemade rattle created from a small gourd. "This is the *ason,*" she said. "The magic rattle of the mambo."

"What's a mambo?" Dana asked. She had stopped writing.

"I am a mambo. A voodoo priestess."

"Aunt Cecile likes to tell fortunes, stuff like that," Jimmy said. "The kids love it when she does it."

Miss Cecile cast a withering look at Jimmy. Next, she showed a necklace with elaborate, colorful beads. An odd human-shaped talisman hung from it. She let that drop back into the bag and rummaged around some more.

Jimmy gulped.

Miss Cecile pulled out the dried head of some small animal. It had shrunk to a size slightly bigger than an egg. It was hard to tell what it was, and no one was asking for any more details.

Dana gasped and leaned back slightly. "What's that used for?"

"It is for the ritual. It has certain powers."

Dana said, "Are you going to do some kind of ritual here in the White House?"

Miss Cecile looked around and closed her eyes again. She opened them and placed both of her hands on the wall below the painting of Dolly Madison. "If it is called for," she said. "There is much spirit life here. Much good. Some bad."

"Is this something I can watch?" Dana said.

Miss Cecile ignored her and walked down the hall, mumbling a prayer.

They all watched her for a moment, and then Dana turned to the guys.

"You've got to be kidding me?"

"Yes, we are," Jimmy said.

"Absolutely," Big Mike said.

"Hell, yes," T-Ron added.

She looked at all three of them. "That's not your aunt, is it?"

Jimmy looked down. "Uh, she's my common-law aunt."

"What the hell is that supposed to mean?"

"Well, she's been close to our family for years. She's like an aunt to me. For all practical purposes, she's my aunt."

"Common law," Big Mike said for emphasis.

"Look, all that voodoo stuff is just her putting on an act for you," Jimmy said. "She's always done these parlor tricks to entertain people. It's just for fun."

"Fun."

"Uh huh."

'You three are up to something." Dana said.

"Just fishing," T-Ron said. "And visiting an old friend."

"Does the President know her?"

"Yeah, sure. Everybody who grew up in Houma knows Miss Cecile. *Aunt* Cecile," Jimmy said.

"Is she going to see him while she's here?"

"Ha!" Jimmy said, and slapped his thigh. "Like *that's* gonna happen. Sheesh."

T-Ron and Big Mike just shook their heads.

"Unbelievable," Dana said. She dropped her notebook into the small bag she wore around her shoulder. "Is she going to do anything with your lucky cock?"

"I sure hope not," T-Ron said.

Dana just shook her head. "I'll be in touch."

She walked away in the other direction. They thought they heard her say something along the lines of *unfuckingbelievable.* Or that was the gist of it.

Big Mike just stared at her as she walked away. "Why do I get the feeling I'm going to be in tomorrow's edition of the *New York Times?*"

"We're fucked," T-Ron said.

"Oh, shit," Jimmy said.

"What?"

"Where the hell did she go?"

Miss Cecile had vanished. Again.

Dana pulled out her cell phone and hit speed dial. After about five rings, she got through.

"Keegan."

"Carl, you're not going to believe this shit," she said.

"I've worked in this town for forty years. I've seen every piece of shit imaginable, dear."

"Uh huh. When's the last time you saw a voodoo priestess casting spells inside the White House?"

"Okay, that's a new one."

Dana went on to describe her earlier encounter with Miss Cecile and the President's friends. Keegan didn't say a word as she went through every detail she could remember.

"And Bergeron's friends got her inside?" he said. "As their aunt? Why the hell would they do that?"

"They claim the President knows her," she replied. "I'm going to make some calls down in Houma and see what else I can find out about her, and if there's any past connections with the Bergerons."

"Amusing," was all he could say. "Nice sideshow to what's going on in the Situation Room. Now, if you can make a connection between *her* and the crisis with the Chinese, now *that* would be a story."

"Oh, yes," Dana said. "And if Marissa Bergeron might be involved, even better. Maybe she thinks her husband needs to put a spell on the Chinese."

Keegan laughed. "Reminds me of when Nancy Reagan had her Hollywood astrologer in the White House. Reagan's spin masters about had a shit fit with that one."

"That seems normal compared to what I saw today. The woman had the head of some kind of animal in her purse."

"Okay," Keegan said. "Run it down and see if you can connect it to the China crisis."

"Right, but I want to break it tomorrow morning. Tie it in with Bergeron's three bubba friends and their stupid lucky rooster. And the crazy mystery about the paintings. This is just too rich," she said and chuckled a bit.

"You have my blessings, my child," Keegan said, and hung up.

Dana Newton held her cell phone to her chest and smiled.

"Lucky rooster, my ass," she said to herself.

Chapter 27

Admiral Yang continued to stare at the plot that indicated the position of the American fleet. The *Washington* and her support ships had moved east much faster than he thought they would. He had hoped to get around them and block them from moving out into the Philippine Sea, but no such luck. It was just as well. He had a little surprise waiting for them out that way. The Chinese attack submarine, *Lóng*, or "Dragon," a brand-new, very stealthy nuclear-powered sub, had been sitting quietly to the east. Yang had sent his old, noisy diesel subs out to the American fleet, knowing damn well the Americans would hear those derelicts from a hundred miles away. They would serve as a suitable decoy, while his powerful new nuclear sub would wait in ambush like a wolf, or dragon, as it were. *Did dragons wait in ambush?*

The *Lóng* carried torpedoes, cruise missiles, anti-ship missiles, anti-submarine missiles and even mines. *Quite an impressive armament,* he thought. There had been a time when he thought he wanted to command a sub like that, or maybe one of the new "boomers," the ballistic missile subs that could send nuclear weapons to Washington D.C. from half a world away. But the prospect of not seeing the sun for weeks or months at a time made him nauseous. Plus, the lure of the big new carriers was just too great.

Anyway, he had laid his trap, and he wanted to see if the Americans would step into it.

His second-in-command, a captain, stood over him and looked at the map. "They don't even know it's there," he said.

Yang smiled. "Yes, and once we send our fighters over their ships, we'll see what they do. We'll buzz this destroyer, here," he said, pointing at one of the *Washington's* escorts at the far eastern edge of the fleet. "If they so much as spit at one of our planes, they will be in for the shock of their lives. Their very *short* lives," he said. "They won't be expecting a submarine to respond so quickly to their aggression."

The young captain nodded his head slowly in understanding. "And while they tend to the rescue of that sinking ship, we'll close on them, chasing them out into the Pacific while the politicians and diplomats work out the details."

"Precisely," Yang said. "The American's won't risk a retaliatory strike so close to our mainland. We could sink their whole fleet in minutes."

"A bold move, sir," the young man said.

"It is time for boldness," the old Admiral said. "Time for us to assert our power."

One other old bold soldier stood next to Yang and looked over the plot of ships, carefully noting the positions of the opposing forces, especially the deadly Chinese sub lying in wait to the east of the *Washington.*

Andrew Jackson had looked at hundreds of battle maps in his career, and could spot a disaster in the making better than anyone. Sea or land, it was always the same: surprise, speed and aggression. He had served up plenty of that to his British opponents back in the day. Now he faced a new opponent, on the sea this time. Well, maybe *he* didn't face them. His successor, President Beau Bergeron did. But he was still part of this fight, and he damn well wasn't going to let America lose this battle.

Whether he was dead or not.

"I think this is going to blow over," Terry said. He and Beau had spent another hour in the Situation Room, monitoring the fleets, the aircraft and the sailors who did their deadly dance in, under and over the seas.

Beau ignored his naval-tactics-impaired buddy and glanced over at Admiral Winston, who had been making notes on a pad. He ripped the paper off and handed it to an aide, who scampered out of the room. Winston, sharp as ever, looked up at the Beau.

"All these aircraft in the skies have me a little concerned," he said. "There's a fifty-fifty chance there'll be a shoot-down. If we can keep that to just dogfighting, we can manage it. If our ships come into play and start shooting down their planes, then that might change everything."

"How so?" Beau asked.

"We don't like planes getting close to our ships," the Admiral said. "Especially the carrier. Technically, a plane can fly over us, but it really makes us a bit jumpy. The Russians used to do that all that time. And we did it to them. It was tense, but everybody knew it was part of the game. This situation, though, is different, especially since they've already lost a fighter."

"One twitchy pilot could set off a bad sequence of events," Terry said. He was already on his fifth cup of coffee this morning, and Beau noticed he was getting a bit twitchy himself.

Seated at the other end of the table were Grover Cleveland and Millard Fillmore. They were sharing a bag of Cheetos and listening intently. Andrew Jackson was MIA. Beau turned around to see if Jackson was standing behind him, but no one, living or dead, was there.

And then he was there. He just winked in, and stood next to the big-screen monitor. There was no sound, no rush of wind, no tinkle of a bell. He just *appeared.* It was so startling, it made Beau blink several times, just to confirm that it had happened. Everyone at the table turned to the monitor, as if the President had seen something there that he couldn't believe. The military types assessed the situation, but nothing had really changed, so they turned back to Beau.

"Any questions, sir?" Admiral Winston said.

"Not really. You've laid it all out very well, Admiral."

Jackson pointed at Bergeron, then at himself, then at Millard and Grover and finally pointed up in the air. Or maybe he meant upstairs. Beau wasn't sure.

"Okay, I'm headed back to the office," he announced and stood. Everyone did likewise. He had yet to get used to this bit of deference, but he understood it was as much directed at the Office of the President as it was to Beau Bergeron. Jackson nodded and smiled. He and his dead buddies walked out behind Beau and Terry and followed them up to the Oval Office. Beau kept turning around to see if they were still behind him.

"Your dead guys behind us?" Terry said. He was getting more and more used to the madness.

"Yeah. All of them. But Jackson wasn't there the whole time. He popped in towards the end. I think he wants to have a meeting in the Oval Office."

"Hmmm, I wonder if he's on the calendar," Terry said and looked at his smart phone.

They made their way past Mrs. Foster, who announced a couple of upcoming appointments for the President. He asked for a few minutes alone with his Chief of Staff. And the dead guys.

They all sat at the sofas. Grover Cleveland was licking the cheetle off his fingers from the Cheetos.

"Who am I sitting next to?" Terry said, as he looked to his right.

"No one. They're all sitting on the other sofa."

"Great." He turned and looked at the empty sofa across the coffee table.

"What's up?" Beau said to Jackson.

"Well, you said you needed some good intel," Jackson said. "And I've got it." He proceeded to fill the President in on what he had learned while he was visiting the Chinese carrier.

"Wait, wait," Beau said. "You popped in on the Chinese ship? Right there with their admiral?"

Jackson nodded.

"Holy shit," Beau said. "And they've got a secret sub about to ambush us?" He was saying this more for Terry's benefit than anything else.

"Yes. Get some paper and write down these coordinates."

Beau jumped up and ran to his desk. "Shoot," he said, pen over paper.

Jackson gave him the precise coordinates of the sub.

"You might want to give that to Admiral Winston right away," Jackson said.

"Right."

Terry just watched his buddy and listened to the one-sided conversation. If Beau was hallucinating, it was very real.

"Good stuff," Fillmore said. "I told you we were on it."

Grover Cleveland nodded his approval. "Old Jackass comes through."

"It's *Old Hickory*," Jackson said.

"Whatever."

Beau stared down at the precise GPS coordinates he had written on his note pad. He rubbed his forehead and then looked up. "Of course, the Admiral's going to want to know how I know this."

"Know what?" Terry said.

Beau caught him up on what Jackson had just given him.

Terry got up and walked around the desk and looked down at the coordinates the President had written down.

Beau sat back and looked up at him. "How am I going to do this?"

Terry shook his head and walked back to the sofa. This time he just lay down. He put his arm over his eyes. "Beau, really? C'mon!"

"Damn it, Terry! This is as real as you and I."

Terry glanced up and rolled his eyes. "I'm feeling very *unreal* at the moment."

Beau put his face in his hands and thought a moment. "Okay, okay, I know how you feel. But listen. Let me get this info to the Navy. If there's no Chinese sub at those coordinates, you'll never hear me speak of Fillmore, Jackson or Cleveland again." He looked up at the newly placed portraits of them, and then turned to the dead presidents themselves. "But if it's there, you're totally on board with this. Deal?"

Terry sat back up and folded his arms. He stared down at the floor. "All right. I'll go with that deal."

"So how are we going to tee this up to the Admiral? Where in the hell would I get this kind of information?"

"You could say the CIA or one of the other agencies."

Beau shook his head. "No way, they talk to each other too much. And I don't want to piss off the Vampire. That dude scares me."

Terry thought a moment. "Okay, what about this? You got a tip from another foreign leader. We won't say who it is. Maybe *their* intelligence people picked it up, passed it on to their leader, who called you. But they want to remain unidentified."

"You mean, like, the Russians? Or Britain? Some NATO ally?"

"Yeah, but we won't say who. Presidential secret. Keeping your source anonymous."

Beau thought for a second, and then nodded his head slightly. He looked at his dead president buddies.

"That'll work," Jackson said.

Cleveland and Fillmore looked at each other. Fillmore said, "Yeah, sounds like some good bullshit. Go for it."

"Okay, that's what we'll do," Beau said. He looked at his watch. "Let's get the Admiral up here and tell him in private. And it's best that you not be in here," Beau said to his friend. "That way it'll seem like it was a hotline kind of call, something only I would know about. I can get Mrs. Foster to play along in case somebody asks her anything."

Terry chewed on his lower his lip. "Yeah, okay. But if someone really wanted to investigate this, you know, pull phone records, that kind of thing, they'll know this is bullshit."

"Probably."

"The damn NSA records every call in the world, or some shit like that."

"We gotta chance it," Beau said. "It's all we have."

Terry took a deep breath and stood up. "Okay, I'm out of here. I don't know if I want you to be right or wrong about this sub."

Beau smiled at him and put up his arms. "Either way, you win."

Five minutes later, Admiral Winston sat across the desk from Beau. Jackson, Fillmore and Cleveland stood behind him, which slightly unnerved Beau, but he tried to ignore them.

The Admiral looked down at the slip of paper in his hands and back up at the Beau. "Are you serious?"

He nodded. "I'm as surprised as you. Of course, you understand I can't say who gave us this information. Let's just say it's someone who doesn't want this to get out of control. Their agenda is the same as ours."

"I understand," the Admiral said. He ran through possible sources. He also went right to the Russians, who still had a decent blue-water fleet and enough subs around to have maybe spotted the Chinese sub. Maybe a NATO friend. That would have to be Britain or France. But it could also be someone in the Chinese government who was secretly trying to defuse the situation, or trip up a rival.

"How soon can you confirm this is all true?" Beau said.

"We'll have to see what assets we have close to this position," the Admiral said. "I'll probably have one of our new P-8 Poseidon sub-hunter jets get out there and take a look. Give me an hour."

"Please, hurry," Beau said.

Chapter 28

The six J-15 Flying Sharks had picked up the American destroyer *U.S.S. Stethem,* an Arleigh Burke-class guided missile destroyer, five minutes earlier, and were vectored straight at the ship. The *Stethem* was part of the *Washington's* task force, and was situated due east of the big carrier, protecting her from any threats from that direction.

The Chinese pilots knew this was an extremely risky move. Any hostile aircraft approaching an American guided missile destroyer was flying right into the belly of the beast. The *Stethem* was armed to the teeth, with anti-aircraft missiles and guns, anti-submarine missiles, Tomahawk cruise missiles and Harpoon anti-ship missiles. The pilots' orders were very specific: fly right at the ship in a simulated attack run to see what response they'd get from the Americans. They were expecting to get picked up by American fighters as well, who were also in the vicinity.

The pilots were a little more vigilante today, after the loss of one of their own in a disputed dogfight yesterday. Rumors were rampant, but everyone was buying into the spin that the Americans fired first.

The *Stethem* had picked up the fighters on its radar earlier, but not as early as the fleet's airborne early warning radar plane, the E2-C Hawkeye. It had seen them the moment they formed up over their carrier. That's also when the Hawkeye had vectored six F-18 Hornets towards the oncoming Flying Sharks.

So in a matter of minutes, there were Sharks and Hornets converging on each other. There was a Hawkeye, and a Poseidon flying around, too, not to mention a Dragon, which *should* be flying, as its name inferred, but was actually lurking under the ocean. Boys loved to name their toys, and the playground was filled with them at the moment in the dark skies of the Philippine Sea. Very deadly toys. But still driven by boys. And a few girls, too, for that matter.

The Chinese Sharks had gone supersonic and were closing fast on the *Stethem.* The Hornets were going to be a few minutes late to the party, but they were on the way. The *Stethem* went immediately to general quarters.

The captain of the *Stethem,* Frank Hargrove, stood at the bridge window, night-vision binoculars to his face, trying to pick up the oncoming fighters. The redheaded, lanky Texan was furiously working a wad of bubble gum. Even if he couldn't see them yet, his radar did, and his bridge crew read off the numbers as the Sharks approached.

"Paint 'em," Hargrove said, without taking his eyes off the horizon.

The *Stethem's* weapons radar locked onto the jets, hitting them with so much microwave energy they could pop popcorn inside the cockpits. Well, not really, but it was a nice thought.

Simultaneously, the flight of American Hornets had started to lock *their* weapons' radar on the Chinese fighters from behind. For the Flying Sharks, this was the proverbial rock and a hard place. A phrase they were not familiar with, but understood completely.

The lead pilot for the Chinese, a very green lieutenant whose father was a big deal in the Chinese government, was a bit jumpy. His threat warning systems inside his cockpit were screaming to him that he and his very fast jet were on the verge of being blown out of the sky. *From two directions.* The Americans had yet to launch a missile, but they were a push-button away from doing that.

And that's when the kid kind of panicked.

Instead of manning up and staying cool, his sphincter took over all rational thought from his brain, and decided to take over his mouth. Which turned it and him, of course, into an asshole.

"We are under attack! We are under attack!" he yelled into his radio. "Evasion action!"

The formation of Flying Sharks split left and right, some going for the surface, others peeling off and heading for the stars. The American jets matched them move for move, and everyone had a dance partner. But as of yet, no one had fired a missile.

Of course, on the bridge of the *Liaoning*, Admiral Yang and his bridge officers had heard only one thing: their fighters were under attack from the American destroyer.

Yang smiled and turned to his communications officer. "Alert the *Lóng*. Sink the American destroyer."

The captain of the Chinese attack submarine *Lóng* – the "Dragon," was handed the order his communications officer had just received from Yang. His heart raced, but he tried not to show any emotion. He was about to sink an American ship, but he wanted to portray an air of calm professionalism for his crew. They had all been trained to believe that the Pacific would someday become the domain of the new, powerful Chinese navy. It was inevitable. He just didn't think he would be the one to hasten that inevitability.

For weeks, they had stayed silent and deep, barely moving lest they be discovered by the American Navy. What submariners the world over called "becoming a hole in the water."

Now the hole was going to unleash a dragon.

He ordered his weapons officer to get a firing solution on the ship, which was five kilometers to their northwest. Torpedoes were loaded into two of their tubes and prepared for firing. One was enough to sink the relatively small destroyer, but two would be more spectacular.

"Open outer doors. Stand by," he ordered.

And that's when everyone on the bridge jumped. The sub was lashed by a piercing sound that echoed throughout the ship. It was an active sonar wave, a pulse of sound that shot through the water, hit the sub and bounced back to the surface. But the waves were continuous, over and over, signaling one clear message.

They had been discovered.

"What is that!?" the captain yelled. "Another sub?"

"No, sir. Sonobuoys. Multiple ones. Probably from the air. All around us!"

The captain slammed his fist down on the console. "Helmsman, get us out of here! Close outer doors. Stand down the torpedoes."

High above that spot in the Philippine Sea, the American P-8 Poseidon banked slightly to begin its orbit over the Chinese sub. The big jet, basically a reconfigured Boeing 737, was outfitted with a full load of weaponry to take out subs and even surface ships. Its crew of nine airmen – and women – had tagged the sub the moment the first sonobuoy had been dropped from the plane into the water. They were right on top of it.

"And that's how we do *that*," the technician said to her fellow crewmen. She had a big smile on her face. "Looks like we scared the shit out of them. Getting screw turns, and I mean *wide open*."

"Copy that, Kate," the plane's pilot said. "Get the *Stethem* on the horn and let 'em know they've got a bad guy in the backyard." He turned to his co-pilot. "Of course, it helps when somebody gives us the *exact* location. Some spook somewhere earned his pay today."

"It was one of their new fast-attack subs, similar to our *Los Angeles* class boats," Admiral Winston said. He sat in a chair in front of the President's desk. "Nuclear powered. Pretty sophisticated, too, at least for them. We've been tracking a few of their old diesel subs around their fleet, hoping to tag this one. But it just never showed up. Now we know where it was."

Beau tried to suppress a smile. To the Admiral's left sat Bergeron's buddy, Terry Melancon, who looked a little pale. Terry kept looking around the room, as if someone was behind him. Actually, there *was* someone behind him. Andrew Jackson was doing a few celebratory fist pumps, like Tiger Woods draining a 25-foot birdie putt on the 18th at the Masters. The old boy had a beer in his hand, too. Millard Fillmore and Grover Cleveland also were pounding down a few next to him.

"Just glad we got the tip in time," Beau said.

"Yes, indeed," the Admiral said. "We don't know for sure yet, but it looked like that Chinese sub had a bead on one of our destroyers. We heard their outer doors opening, a prelude to firing torpedoes. Might have jumped them just in time."

"Wow," Beau said.

"You should call your contact back and thank him, or her, Mr. President," the Admiral said. "Whoever that is, we owe them a big one. Put them on your Christmas card list."

"Definitely," Beau said.

Winston glanced at his watch. "Okay, I need to get back. We're about to shock the crap out of that Chinese carrier. He's about to get a surprise visit from the south. Some of the *Lincoln's* planes are going to come out of nowhere and buzz him. Pretty sure it's going to ruin his day."

"Better him than us, Admiral. Thanks," Beau said.

Winston stood and left the Oval Office. Terry just looked down and strummed his fingers against the arm of his chair. Finally, he looked up at Beau.

"Are they in here now?"

"Behind you. They seem very proud of themselves."

Terry turned around slowly, but still didn't see anyone. "Gentlemen," he said to nothing but air, or so it seemed.

"They're real, Terry. They're here," Beau said. "I don't know how, but Jackson was standing on the bridge of the Chinese carrier and saw and heard everything."

"Jackson speaks Chinese?"

Beau looked over at Andrew Jackson. Jackson shrugged and said, "I understood what they were saying. I don't speak Chinese, though, but somehow I just *understood.* Must be another benefit of being dead."

Beau glanced back at his Chief of Staff. "No, but he somehow understood, is what he's saying."

"Okay, okay, I'm in," Terry said. "We gotta get these guys back out there again. This may be the biggest intelligence coup since we cracked the German code back in World War II."

"Better. This is real time. Primo stuff."

Fillmore raised his hand. "I'm going next. Millard Fillmore, super spy. James Bond, 007." He smiled broadly. "Fillmore. *Millard* Fillmore," he said, in a fairly decent British accent. "License to kill." Grover Cleveland and Andrew Jackson cracked up.

Beau joined in laughing at Fillmore's performance.

"What?" Terry said.

"Apparently they get to watch James Bond movies in heaven."

Terry sighed. "When can I get to see them myself?"

The three dead presidents just shrugged. Cleveland said, "Not our call. But who knows?"

"They don't know," Beau said.

"Were they the ones who moved all the paintings around?"

The three presidents smiled and pointed at each other.

Beau said, "Oh, yes. It seems our super spies are also quite the practical jokers."

"Fantastic," Terry said. "Maybe they should turn their attention back to the Chinese, instead."

Beau thought a moment. "That might not be a bad idea."

"How did they find it?" Admiral Yang said. He paced around the bridge of the *Liaoning*.

His senior officers stood at attention. They had no clue, but one managed to say, "I think they just got lucky, sir. Sometimes it happens."

Yang gave him a hard stare. "I don't believe in coincidences like that."

"Yes, sir."

"And is there *any* confirmation the American ship or planes fired on our aircraft?" This was the proverbial trick question, asked for the benefit of his senior officers and the official ship's log. It appeared no shots were fired, but that idiot pilot had yelled like a little girl that he was under attack, prompting Yang to give the order to sink the American destroyer. He might have just dodged a bullet. If he had sunk the destroyer without provocation, there'd be hell to pay. Now, no one would be the wiser. The Americans – and Yang – had gotten lucky. So had his sub, the *Lòng*. That advanced American sub-hunting plane would have probably destroyed her if it had dropped its anti-sub torpedoes.

Yang stared out into the night. *How the hell did they get so lucky?* He had a sick feeling that someone in the chain had tipped off the Americans. Some enemy of his in the government, perhaps? *No,* he thought. *I'm not that powerful –yet.* No, all signs were that the American's had smelled a rat and then found it. At least they didn't kill it.

"What is the *Washington* doing now?" he asked.

"She and her escorts are now moving south, sir. Coming right for us. It looks like they are back on their original heading toward the South China Sea."

Yang thought a moment. *An attack?* He discarded that notion almost immediately. They were testing him. The little maneuver to Taiwan was just a little dance on their part. They were back on track to run his little blockade.

"Take us back to just east of the Paracels," Yang ordered. "Our original position."

"Yes, sir," the helmsman said. His communications officer began to alert the rest of the fleet. He then stopped abruptly, as an incoming message surprised him.

"Uh, sir. One of our destroyers to the south of us has picked up something unusual."

Yang just rolled his eyes. *Why did these young people have to start with the drama? Couldn't they just say what "unusual" was?*

"What is it?" he said.

"Numerous high-speed aircraft, coming this way from the south. They appear to be at least two dozen American F-18 fighters."

"From the south? Where did they come from?" If there were any American planes heading his way, they'd be coming from the north, from the *Washington.* Or maybe from the east, if they launched any from the Philippines.

"Launch aircraft!" Yang ordered. "Let's see where our visitors are coming from."

Another carrier? Yang thought. *This could get interesting.*

Chapter 29

Big Mike, Jimmy and T-Ron finally caught up with Miss Cecile on the ground floor of the Residence in the huge Diplomatic Reception Room. The big oval-shaped room is the main entrance to the White House from the south grounds, and it's where ambassadors typically present their credentials to the President. The room was especially known for its panoramic wallpaper called "Views of North America." It was installed by Jackie Kennedy in 1961. The images were of North American scenes based on engravings from the 1820's. There was the Natural Bridge of Virginia, Niagara Falls, New York Bay, West Point and Boston Harbor. Normally, there was a portrait of George Washington over the mantle. Now Chester Arthur was getting his moment of glory, thanks to Millard Fillmore, Grover Cleveland and Andrew Jackson and their sense of humor.

Miss Cecile was standing near the image of Niagara Falls, pounding on a little drum and singing or chanting a song. A maid stood off to one side, mouth agape, stopped in mid-dusting of the mantle.

"We've got this, miss, thanks," Jimmy said, and shooed the maid out of the room. T-Ron and Jimmy shut the doors.

The movement broke Miss Cecile's concentration, and she looked back at the men. "Much work to do," she said.

"Why's that?" Big Mike said.

"The *Loa* are everywhere here," she said. "The spirits. There is an energy around. Good, bad, joy and sadness."

"Well, that just about sums up the last 240 years of American history," T-Ron said. "What about ghosts of dead presidents?"

"They are here," she said.

"Which ones?" He knew which ones, but he wasn't saying. This was her chance to prove her skills, and his chance to get a serious case of the heebie jeebies if she guessed right.

Miss Cecile put her little drum back into her bag and looked at the men. "Fillmore, Cleveland and Jackson," she said. She didn't hesitate or concentrate. It was more matter of fact.

T-Ron gulped and turned a shade paler. He glanced at Jimmy and Big Mike.

"That all?" Big Mike said.

"For now," Miss Cecile said. "They are particularly strong. Almost alive, they are."

Jimmy wondered when Miss Cecile started speaking like Yoda, if Yoda had a Haitian accent. The woman had a tendency to drop in and out of whatever dialect or word choice suited her.

"Look, you're going to have to stay with one of us," Jimmy said. "You can't just roam around by yourself. That reporter back there could be trouble. We think she's working on a story about you, and us. Probably Boudreaux, too. Might be in tomorrow's paper."

"This doesn't concern me," she said.

"We understand," Jimmy said. "But we don't want it to hurt Beau, you know?"

"I am here to help, not hurt. It's these spirits who could be trouble."

"How so?" Big Mike said.

"They are meddlers, I think. They may cloud the mind of the living. President Bergeron, in particular."

"Which is why they need to go," T-Ron said.

"Okay, Miss Cecile," Jimmy said. "What else do you have to do?"

"There are prayers, rituals and such I must attend to. At some point I must confront these spirits. That's why I have to move freely around the house."

It was the "freely" part that freaked Jimmy out. He figured they had the rest of the day and night to have Miss Cecile do what she had to do. Once the story broke tomorrow, and he had no doubt that it would, Terry Melancon would have a heart attack and Miss Cecile would have to be escorted out of the place. Probably he, Big Mike and T-Ron as well. So much for the fishing tournament, too. That would really suck.

"Okay, but we're going to take turns staying with you, okay?"

"As you wish."

"I'll stay with her for now," he said to T-Ron and Big Mike. He turned back to Miss Cecile. "Where do you want to go next?"

"To the Oval Office," she said.

Jimmy's eyes went wide. Big Mike cleared his throat. "Okay, good luck with that. We gotta go." And with that, he and T-Ron escaped from the room.

Jimmy said, "Uh, why do you need to go to the Oval Office?"

"I must speak to the President," she said.

Jimmy led Miss Cecile up to the first floor of the West Wing, trying his best to figure out how he was going to get her in to see the President, and exactly what he was going to tell Beau. They passed a number of different people, all looking serious and focused. A few gave Miss Cecile an extra glance. He guessed they figured she was some dignitary or something.

Hmmm, there's an idea, he thought.

They made their way to Mrs. Foster's office, Beau's secretary. She was seated at her desk, on the phone. She glanced up at him and he gave her a little wave. She hung up.

"Jimmy, how are you?" she said.

"Mrs. Foster, good to see you." He shook her hand. "Uh, this is...Marie d'hemecourt, the assistant ambassador for cultural affairs...and domestic policy...research... things...from...Haiti," he said. He figured that all sounded pretty official.

Mrs. Foster stood and greeted her. "Ambassador," she said. "Welcome." She looked down at her computer screen and tapped a few keys. "Were you scheduled for the President today?" She looked at Jimmy. "And how did you two meet?"

Jimmy smiled. "Me and the guys were just doing a walk through downstairs when we ran into her. A very nice lady."

Miss Cecile surprised him by playing along and saying, "I was just taking a tour. I'm not scheduled to see the President."

"Oh, I see," Mrs. Foster said. "That's just as well. The President isn't in the office right now."

"Oh, darn," Jimmy said, and slapped his hip.

"Is there any chance I could see the Oval Office?" Miss Cecile said.

Mrs. Foster looked from her to Jimmy. Judging by his face, and reputation, and her experience teaching high school boys and raising a few of her own, he was up to something. But he *was* the President's friend, and he *was* staying a few nights here at the White House.

"Okay, I'm sure you can take a quick peek," she said. "Come this way."

She led Jimmy and Miss Cecile to the Oval Office and ushered them in. Without a meeting going on, and totally empty of people, it looked like a museum, not a functioning executive's office. Mrs. Foster gave Jimmy the high- school teacher look and said, "Don't touch anything."

"Yes, ma'am," he said.

"I'll be out here if you need me," she told him, and walked out the door. She didn't shut it.

"Please don't take the snake out," Jimmy said, and glanced at her bag.

She ignored him and walked around the room. She did pull something out of her bag. It was some kind of small amulet or statue that fit in the palm of her hand. Jimmy couldn't see what it was, but Miss Cecile squeezed it and rolled it in her hand, all the while mumbling something in Haitian.

Miss Cecile, for her part, was feeling a little jumpy. Her heart was racing, and beads of sweat were forming at her hairline. In all her years of voodoo practice, she had never felt such a palpable sense of the dead around her. There was a *whooshing* noise in her ears that at first sounded like wind through pines. But in a moment, she could make out words, not from one person, but from many, all running together. Men and women. Some talking. Some shouting. Some laughing. It was like a huge cocktail party.

She tried to pick up some of the conversations, but it was too difficult because they overlapped so much. She continued to pray, and shut her eyes to concentrate. The voices swirled like a pool at the bottom of a waterfall, but the more she concentrated and the more she prayed, she began to pick up specific threads of conversation. Now just men. One, then two. Maybe more. The words became more distinct, and she thought she heard a voice call the President by name – Beau Bergeron.

She opened her eyes and dropped the amulet from her hand.

There in front of her were Millard Fillmore, Grover Cleveland and Andrew Jackson. They were drinking beers and laughing, sharing a good story. They all turned to her.

Miss Cecile stepped back with a fright as the three apparitions locked their gazes upon her.

"Hey, good looking," Grover Cleveland said. "What's your name?"

Miss Cecile gulped, took another step back and looked at Jimmy. She reached down and picked up her small amulet from the carpeted floor and put it back in her bag. She then pulled out the shrunken head of the dead thing and said something to the three dead presidents.

Andrew Jackson looked at the dead thing and back at Miss Cecile.

"Boo!" he said, and raised his arms in a menacing way. He spilled some beer on the carpet.

"Ahhhh!" she yelled. She turned to Jimmy. "Let's go. Now!"

They nearly ran over Mrs. Foster as they hurried out of the Oval Office.

"What just happened?" Jimmy said as he escorted Miss Cecile down the hall. Her caramel skin was much lighter. She now had Jimmy's complexion, so they were really starting to look like they might be related.

Miss Cecile looked back in the direction from which they had come. "I saw them," she said. "The ghost presidents."

Jimmy also turned to see if ghosts were chasing them. Just a couple of cute interns were behind them engrossed in some conversation.

"I need to sit down," she said, clearly out of breath.

They had made it as far as the hallway just outside Terry Melancon's office. Miss Cecile plopped down in a chair along the wall. She used her hand as a fan to try to cool herself. Some color was returning to her face.

Jimmy looked around and waited as an aide walked by. "You really saw ghosts?"

She nodded quickly. "Three of them. Just like you said."

Jimmy was a little freaked out. This was Miss Cecile. The mysterious Miss Cecile. Voodoo priestess. *Mambo.* He figured she saw weird shit all the time. Hell, she *was* weird shit.

"Can you get rid of them?"

She looked up at him. "I believe so. But they are very strong. It will take all of my strength to remove them."

"What do you need?" he said.

"Like I said. I need to move about freely. I need to confront these spirits and send them on their way before they can do the President harm."

"They're trying to hurt Beau?"

"Not physically," she said. "But...other ways. I'm not sure. And there are other forces at work in this place."

Jimmy didn't like the look she just gave him. That last bit of info gave him the serious shit-fits. He leaned in closer to her. "What do you mean, 'other forces'?"

"The *Petro Loa.* The aggressive ones. *Carrefour. Ogoun. Marinette. Ezili Dantor.*"

"Uh huh." Jimmy didn't know if he should write any of this down. "They're, like, evil spirits? Demons? The Devil?"

She shook her head. "There is no Satan in *Vodu.*"

"Good to know."

"But the *Petro Loa* can cause lots of trouble."

"So we have to get rid of them, too?"

"Hah. You do not *get rid* of them." Miss Cecile closed her eyes again and her lips began to twitch, but soon she formed silent words with them.

Jimmy stood straight and looked around to make sure no one was in ear shot of all this. And that's when Terry Melancon walked out of his office.

"Yo, Jimmy. What's up?" Terry said. He glanced down at his phone to check a text and kept talking. "What you boys up to today?"

Jimmy looked down at Miss Cecile and moved slightly in front of her, to block Terry's view. "Oh, you know. See some more sights. Stuff like that."

Terry looked up. "Sounds great." He looked around Jimmy at Miss Cecile. Jimmy tried to block his view, but to no avail.

"Jimmy, is that Miss Cecile?"

Jimmy moved out of the way and turned to look at the old woman. "Why, yes it is."

"What is she doing here? And tell me this isn't your aunt?"

"My aunt? Funny. She's just taking the tour, you know, seeing the White House."

"And is she praying or something?" Terry looked closely at Miss Cecile, who now looked like she was in a trance. "Is she okay?"

"Sure, sure," Jimmy said. "She's fine."

"I don't even want to know what's in that bag, do I?"

"Probably not."

"T-Ron's cock's not in there?"

"Nope."

"Shush, Terry Melancon," Miss Cecile said. Then she opened one eye.

Terry shushed.

"I need to see the President," she said.

"That's not going to happen." He looked at his watch. "He's in a meeting with some senators from the Hill."

"Much trouble here," she said.

"It's a troubling place."

Terry, of course, knew Miss Cecile from way back. Even as a kid when he and Beau would sneak around her house to see ghosts or zombies or whatever kind of weird shit two boys' imaginations might conjure about a voodoo priestess who lived down the bayou.

He glanced at Jimmy. "Anybody else around here know about her?"

Jimmy laughed. "Me and the guys. You. I think that's all. She was kind of walking around by herself there earlier, though."

"By herself?" Terry said. "Dear God." He pulled Jimmy aside. "You gotta get her out of here. The last thing I need is a story about a voodoo priestess at the White House breaking in tomorrow's paper."

"Yeah, that would be bad," Jimmy said, and looked away.

Chapter 30

"Sir, the *Lincoln's* Hornets are approaching the *Liaoning*," the radar officer said to Rear Admiral Tony Lear. "They see them, too."

Lear had his arms folded and leaned against his chair on the bridge of the *Washington.* He had his task force hauling ass right at the Chinese fleet from the northeast, while the *Lincoln* and her group were approaching from the south.

"What they got in the air?"

"Looks like a squadron of Sharks, a radar plane, a sub hunter and a rescue chopper loitering around."

"Good. Anything from the mainland?"

"No, sir. That last flight of fighter bombers is landing now. Nothing else up from that direction. But a lot of radar pinging us from the coast."

"Intel on those mobile missiles?"

"Still there, fueled up and ready to rock," the young officer said.

Lear sighed. "Comforting."

"The Chinese are now at their original position in the South China Sea. Holding station there."

"Back to square one, where we were a few days ago," Lear said. He stood and paced around the bridge. A waxing moon cast a silver glow across the slate-black sea, giving the whole scene an unearthly pall. Lear wasn't a superstitious man, but his gut was telling him that this whole dance was going to end tomorrow, one way or the other. For him to plow through the Chinese blockade successfully, a number of fortuitous things would have to happen. First, his crew had to be focused and disciplined, including his air crew. *No problem there,* he thought. The *Lincoln's* crew would have to be the same. Also, not a concern. Then, the Chinese would have to remain calm and not do anything stupid and just let the American fleet sail on by. Having the *Lincoln* back behind them should force the Chinese to chill out. But then again, it could provoke them into doing something very, very rash.

Like that stunt they just pulled with the *Stethem. Pretty stupid,* Lear thought. Running right at a destroyer, with a bunch of Hornets on your tail? *It was like they were daring us to take a shot at them.* Then that tip about their sub hiding out there. The intel guys were on their game today, for sure. How the hell they found out exactly where that sub was located was still unknown to him. Probably would be for a long time, too. It calmed his nerves a bit to know the U.S. had that kind of intelligence asset in place. *Probably reading their mail. Cracked their code, maybe?* That would be the proverbial ace he would need to get out of this bullshit unscathed and to have American Asia-Pacific foreign policy intact.

Daring us to shoot at them. That thought wouldn't leave Lear's head. The more he played back the *Stethem* incident, the more it looked like the Chinese had been running a play. *We shoot at their jets, their sub takes a shot at us.*

"We still tracking that sub?"

"*Stethem's* still got her, sir, as does the Poseidon from the air. The sub's course is paralleling ours. It can't shake our guys."

"Good," Lear said.

"What about their diesels?"

"All tagged. They're sitting right in front of their fleet. We're gonna run right over them if they don't move."

If this had been real war, Lear would have taken out all the subs and be done with them. They could ruin your day in a hurry, and they were a distraction of the highest order. His Aegis cruisers could protect him from the ballistic missiles on the coast, but they might not be able to shoot down all of them. The Air Force guys would have to get most of those before they launched. The cruisers would take care of the ones that lit off.

Lear also knew the guys back at the ranch in Washington would use this whole experience to create a simulated naval battle, based on everything happening now. Just to see how it would play out for real. They had so many scenarios already in place that they loved the chance to think up something new. Watching the Chinese go through their paces was a lot of fun for them. Not so much fun for him.

His own internal radar knew the Chinese would have another trap set up for him soon. He just needed to figure it out before it was too late.

Beau picked through a chicken salad while he thought about a bowl of seafood gumbo and some French bread, which is what he really wanted for lunch. He had promised

Marissa that he would eat at least one salad for lunch each week, and today was that salad day.

He had just returned from briefing some of the Senate assholes about the Chinese fun and games. He had been careful not to say too much, because they would all be in front of the cameras within the hour, acting like they had this whole thing under control, and looking very *foreign-policy savvy* for their constituents back in bum-fuck wherever.

Beau, of course, had everything under control for real. He had failed to mention to them that his best spy, Andrew Jackson, had delivered some juicy intelligence on a Chinese sub, averting a possible naval clash and the loss of one of America's destroyers and her crew. And now that his ghostly pals had stepped up their game a bit, the President was feeling pretty good about things.

He had decided to have lunch with Marissa, but that had proven to be a bust. By the time he made it up to the family dining room, she had already grabbed a quick bite and hurried on to her next meeting. Actually, he had hoped to grab another nooner like he had yesterday. That had really mellowed him out for the rest of the day. Maybe he could get Mrs. Foster to schedule one a few times a week. *Maybe not.*

"That looks boring."

Beau nearly jumped out of his skin. "Holy shit!"

Millard Fillmore was now sitting next to him at his right. Cleveland was at the far end. Andrew Jackson sat to his left, eyeing the salad.

"You've got to be kidding," Jackson said. "What *is* that shit?"

Beau looked down at the salad and then pushed it away. "Yeah, you can say that again."

Cleveland smiled. "You can order up anything you want, and you asked for *that?*"

"A nice steak would be nice," Fillmore added.

Beau ignored the comment. "Can't y'all appear with a little warning? Maybe a chime or something. Crap. Where you boys been?"

"Here and there," Jackson said.

"You been back to the Chinese fleet?"

"Not yet."

Cleveland chimed in. "I'm hoping to make the journey, too. See some action, you know?"

"How about you, Millard?" Beau said.

"I'm in, too. Pretty exciting stuff."

"And nobody over there can see you? Like here?"

"Guess not," Jackson said. "We'd stand out in more ways than one on a Chinese ship."

Beau glanced at his watch. "You might want to think about getting over there. My advisors tell me this thing is about to come to a head."

"We're on it," Fillmore said. "Your spy team will deliver the goods." He saluted Beau.

"You worried?" Jackson said.

Beau nodded. "My guys think the Chinese might get antsy and do something stupid."

"They already have," Jackson said. "Bastards tried to take command of the high seas."

Beau had considered withdrawing the *Lincoln* in order to give the Chinese a back door if they chose not to engage the *Washington.* But his military advisors didn't want to lose the chance to teach the Chinese a lesson. Plus, they had praised Beau for his early calls and the intelligence coup he had delivered to them. He was feeling pretty naval at the moment. He was a badass.

Who saw ghosts.

Jackson walked to the window and looked out onto the White House north lawn. The day was sunny, and a lone groundskeeper mowed the vast expanse of green.

Beau turned around to watch him. "You know about something else?" he said.

Jackson just shook his head. "Nothing new. But that Chinese admiral is a scheming little bastard. I get the feeling he's out of his league, but he wants to show off to his bosses. Or the world. Who knows? Now that you've got him surrounded, he's running out of options to impress them."

"That's good. Right?"

"Maybe," Jackson said. "Maybe not.

Admiral Yang stood on the noisy deck of his carrier, the *Liaonong.* His young crew was prepping for another launch of fighters, but first they had to retrieve the latest flight, which was low on fuel. His carrier didn't have a refueling tanker, nor was he able to get one from the mainland. This had hindered his flight operations somewhat, but it was becoming less and less of an issue as the area of conflict had grown increasingly smaller. The two American fleets were closing on him from two different directions, so soon they would all be in a relatively confined space in the South China Sea.

His superiors from Beijing had counseled for caution. The arrival of the *Lincoln* had changed things dramatically. They wanted Yang to stand firm, show some resolve, but keep a cool head.

Yang had assured them he would. But of course, they weren't out here, where things could get tense, and a mistake by the Americans could set off a naval battle of epic proportions. Yang sure hoped so.

After spending time in his room, thinking of options, he had come to the conclusion that being surrounded by American naval might was an opportunity for him. This was a chance to prove his tactical genius, to show how he could turn a disadvantage into an advantage. *Surrounded on all sides, Yang proved his mettle and showed the superior American fleet how the new Chinese Navy could act.* Yang was writing the news reports in his head now, seeing how his countrymen would devour the stories of his bravery and decisive action.

To make his move, he was counting on the fog of war, what strategists and military men had known for centuries. That sometimes the unexpected happened, usually caused by confusion at an inopportune time. *Confusion,* Yang thought. The origins of the word "war" had at its core the idea "to bring confusion." The two words were etymologically linked. *Just as well.*

For Yang's week to end on a high note, he knew he had to hit one of the American ships. A cruiser or destroyer. A carrier would be even better, but not necessary. He had to draw blood, even if it meant he lost some, too. Well, maybe not his exactly, but some of his sailors. Acceptable, under the circumstances.

He knew he would not have this opportunity again in his career. If he were to make his mark on history, and propel himself into the upper echelons of the Party, he had to act now.

His best asset, the mobile ballistic missiles on the coast, could surely take out a ship, but those missiles were not directly under his control. No, it would have to be something from the fleet. He had many weapons to choose from. Ship-to-ship missiles, air-launched anti-ship missiles, torpedoes, sub-launched cruise missiles. His only problem was he had to make it look like he was fired upon first. That would cover his ass after everything settled down. So how to get the Americans to fire on him first? He knew the Americans were professionals, not prone to rash acts, unless provoked. Could he supply that provocation?

So much out of my control, though, he thought. *But what if that provocation was under my control?*

A plan began to form in his head.

Chapter 31

"Terry knows," Jimmy said.

He, T-Ron and Big Mike were out back of the White House, enjoying the pleasant day and checking on Boudreaux. The rooster was in good spirits. Always a good sign. Jimmy had deposited Miss Cecile in her room, with strict orders not to come out until one of them came for her.

"What'd that asshole say?" Big Mike said.

"Just to get her out of here, he didn't need that kind of distraction right now. That kind of thing."

"I hope he doesn't read the paper tomorrow morning," T-Ron said.

"Yeah, that, too," Jimmy said. "He's going to go ape shit over that. You think there's any way she's not going to run that story tomorrow?"

"Only if World War III starts before then," Big Mike said. "Short of that – no."

"Beau's gonna have us shot," T-Ron said. "What are we gonna do?"

"Get her out of there, that's what," Big Mike said.

Jimmy smiled as some political types walked past them in the parking lot. An older man and a younger woman. Typical Washington pairing. When they had passed, he turned to his co-conspirators. "First, we need to see Beau. Today. Tell him what we did and why. Then we get her out.

The jet's not here, though. I gotta get those guys on the horn and have them fly back up."

T-Ron nodded. "I got another idea. I'm gonna track down that *New York Times* chick and mess with her head a bit. Maybe I can trick her into pulling the story. Those papers usually don't go to press till late, right? Might have a shot."

"Good luck with that," Big Mike said.

Boudreaux let out a pretty loud cockle doodle do. The three men turned toward the Lucky Cock.

"Boudreaux's on board," T-Ron said.

Mrs. Foster, the President's secretary, stared at the three men who stood just outside the Oval Office. T-Ron, Jimmy and Big Mike just smiled, trying to turn on the charm. The older woman wasn't having any of it. Cary Guidry, the President's young assistant, she of the imaginary red teddy, also stood nearby, a sheepish expression on her face. The guys had cornered her earlier in an effort to catch a quick five minutes with Beau. Cary had checked her ever-present iPad, figured she could squeeze them in for a minute between appointments, and herded them over to the Oval Office. Mrs. Foster wasn't amused, but they were the President's friends, and the Chief of Staff's, so she grudgingly went along.

Big Mike was checking out Cary's ass when the door to the Oval Office opened. The guys recognized the vice president but not the two men with him. They nodded respectfully as Wayne Lofton, the V.P. walked by. Cary saw her opening and scooted inside. A few seconds later, she peeked out and waved the guys in. Mrs. Foster gave her a stern look and pointed at her wristwatch. Cary gave her a thumbs up and let the guys in. She closed the door after they went in and waited outside with Mrs. Foster.

Beau had a phone to his ear and nodded a few times. He looked up at his friends, smiled and pointed toward the sofas. The men dropped into them and looked around. They noticed the paintings in the room had changed since the last time they were in there.

Beau hung up and walked around his desk. "You assholes still drinking my beer and eating my food?"

"Hell, yes," Big Mike said.

"Paid for by taxpayers' dollars. My dollars," Jimmy replied, and pointed to his chest.

T-Ron laughed at that one. "That's right. I never thought of it that way. We're paying your grocery bill."

Beau sat down. "Hey, watch it, or I'll have some black helicopters pay you a visit one night. They'll never find your bodies."

T-Ron cocked his head and looked at Beau. "You really got black helicopters?"

"All colors," he said. "It's the black ones you gotta worry about, though. Fly you straight to Area 51 and that's the end of the line for you."

"Yeah, right. Whatever."

Beau looked at his watch. "Gotta make it quick or those women out there will have my head. What's up?"

The three men looked down at their laps, and then at each other. Jimmy took point.

"Remember Miss Cecile?"

"Sure. How do you forget someone who can change you into a squirrel?" He laughed. The guys didn't.

Jimmy made a clucking sound with his tongue. "She's here."

"Here?"

"In the White House," Big Mike said.

"No shit?" Beau said, curious now. He sat up straight. "How'd she get here?"

"You still seeing the ghosts? The dead presidents?" T-Ron said.

"What? Yeah, I am as a matter of fact."

Big Mike jumped in to the conversation. "Well, that had us worried."

Beau sat back and listened.

"We thought she could come up here and do her voo-doo thing, maybe talk to these ghosts, see what they were up to," Jimmy said. "That sort of thing." He was lying, of course. He wanted Miss Cecile to get rid of the ghosts.

"I know what they're up to," Beau said. "I'm *already* talking to them. I don't need some medium or voodoo priestess to help with that. It's not like I need a séance or anything. Jeez."

"We know, we know." Big Mike said. "We just thought it might help, you know, with all the strain you're under from the Chinese thing."

"I'm fine," Beau said. "She can do her prayers or what-ever, but let's get her out by tomorrow, okay? That shit's gonna freak Terry out, and my press secretary will have some trouble spinning this story if it leaks."

Jimmy, T-Ron and Big Mike all looked away. No one made eye contact.

"What?" Beau said.

T-Ron smiled sheepishly. "You get the *New York Times* here by any chance?"

Cecile Marie de Boissonet, voodoo priestess and *mambo,* sat on her bed in the West Bedroom of the Residence. She looked around the room where little John Kennedy, Jr. used to stay. Where Amy Carter lived. Where Abraham Lincoln's son Willie used to sleep. Where his grieving widow, Mary Todd, lay in shock, refusing to go into her own bedroom.

Cecile could feel all of them. She could hear the whispers, the crying. And yes, some laughter. She always had that gift, or curse. It was part of her heritage. Her daughter and her granddaughter had it, too. But they were not why she was here. Jimmy, T-Ron and Big Mike had brought her here to rid the place of the mischievous spirits of the dead presidents. She had been somewhat leery, until she saw them for herself. They had frightened her. They had looked so real, so *corporeal.* She had seen spirits of the dead before, although rarely. Normally she sensed them, but these had been both visual and *strong.*

She felt they were a distraction to the President, and that was why she was brought here. To bring the White House and the President some peace.

She stood up, grabbed her bag and said a silent prayer. She knew Jimmy and the others had told her to stay put, but she had work to do. There was a growing sense of *endings,* that an unfolding story was about to be concluded. But Cecile felt that the story's end had yet to be written, that it could go different ways, and that she would be the one who could write it.

She looked down at her bag and watched it move. Yes, she would need all of her skills for this to succeed. She took a deep breath and walked out of the West Bedroom.

Dana Newton pretty much had her story written by three o'clock that afternoon. She read it again, and it still made her smile. Sure, it was a fluff piece, more character-driven than pure journalism. And she did feel a little guilty doing it, what with a real crisis going on in the White House. But her boss, Carl Keegan, would take the lead on that. She had just been shagging interviews for him, gathering facts, checking facts and otherwise contributing to the big story. She hadn't dared push him to include her name on the byline, but she was hopeful. He was a dick, after all, but not a complete dick. She might get lucky.

But *this* story was all hers. It would be perfect if she could sell it to *Vanity Fair.* They loved this kind of shit. Maybe in a few months, after everything calmed down. She could expand it, do more interviews, and really do an in-depth and highly amusing feature on Bergeron, his strange friends and what could be his personal voodoo priestess. *Man, you just couldn't make this shit up.* The only way it could be better is if she could bring Marissa Bergeron into all this. That would be awesome.

Dana logged out of her computer and pushed away from her small desk in the White House Press Room.

Keegan was out somewhere, probably having a drink with his buddies at the Town and Country Bar over in the Mayflower Hotel.

Hmmm. Marissa Bergeron, Dana thought.

She grabbed her notepad and headed for the East Wing, where the First Lady had her office. Marissa Bergeron's schedule was well known to the press corps, who usually ignored it. The First Lady wasn't out making policy after all, or confronting the Chinese. Most of her day was staged photo ops with kids, dogs, charities and the occasional women's group. Pretty boring stuff.

Dana checked her watch. The First Lady was scheduled to make a visit over to a meeting of military wives pushing for better care at the VA hospitals. It was over at Walter Reed National Military Medical Center. She would be leaving in just a few minutes. Dana high-tailed it to the wood-paneled first-floor lobby of the East Wing. Marissa Bergeron would be coming down this way from her second floor office. It would be a perfect place for an ambush.

She hurried in and positioned herself near the small elevator just off the lobby down a short hall. She did a quick check to make sure Marissa Bergeron hadn't left yet. Her car was still waiting outside at the East Wing entrance. She could see the black SUV and some Secret Service guys milling about waiting for her.

The hum of the elevator caught her attention and she turned to wait for the doors to open. *I'll only have a minute or two. I need to do this right,* she thought.

The doors opened on the small elevator. Inside were the First Lady and her ever-present assistant, Kirk Guilbeau.

They were in mid-conversation and not paying attention to what awaited them.

"Mrs. Bergeron?" Dana said.

The First Lady turned from her assistant and smiled at Dana. She was *on*. She stepped out of the elevator and turned right to head to the lobby, but she maintained eye contact with Dana. "Hi," she said.

"Dana Newton with the *New York Times*."

"Yes, Dana, I remember you from last month's state dinner. Good to see you again."

Dana had to give her credit. She had chatted with the First Lady for a few minutes at a state dinner for the British Prime Minister. The woman was good with names and faces. *Southern sorority girl bullshit manners, probably.*

"I know you're in a hurry to Walter Reed, ma'am, but I had a couple of questions while you walked out."

Marissa Bergeron glanced at her assistant, and then back to Dana. "Sure."

"I'm working on a story and needed some background from you. Do you know Cecile de Boissonet?"

The First Lady slowed her walk and cocked her head slightly. "Cecile de Boissonet?" She pronounced the last name with a flawless French accent. "Miss Cecile?"

"Yes, I believe she's called that."

"Sure, she lives outside of Houma, Louisiana," the First Lady said.

Dana detected a slight hesitancy in her voice.

"Is she a voodoo priestess?" Dana said. She felt ridiculous even saying that.

Marissa Bergeron stopped walking and stood in the middle of the East Wing lobby. "The locals say that, yes. I believe the proper term is *mambo.* She's kind of a legend down there. Part of Louisiana's rich culture."

Spare me, Dana thought, and then smiled. "Did you know she's staying here at the White House?"

Marissa lowered her head and stared down at Dana. "She's here *now?*"

"Yes, I believe she's staying in the West Bedroom."

The First Lady looked at her assistant. Kirk Guilbeau just shrugged his shoulders. She said to Dana, "Wow, I didn't know that."

Dana could see and hear the wheels turning in Marissa Bergeron's head. "Is she a guest of the President?" she said.

Marissa smiled again. "Well, if she is, he hasn't told me yet. But as you might guess, he's pretty busy. But I kind of doubt it. I can have Kirk here check for you, though."

Dana nodded. "Great. Could she be a guest of the President's friends that are staying here?" She looked down at her notes. "Jimmy, Big Mike and T-Ron."

The First Lady thought about that for a second. "Huh. It's possible, but you'd have to ask them."

Kirk cocked his head towards the waiting SUVs.

Dana continued. "Do you think she, or they, had anything to do with all the White House artwork being moved around last night?"

"I was told that was *our* people doing that," Marissa said. "Some kind of inventory thing. Kirk, you hear anything more about that?"

"Uh, no ma'am. I heard the same thing."

Dana quickly changed the subject with a pointed question designed to catch them off guard. "Is she doing voodoo rituals inside the White House?"

Marissa suppressed a laugh. "Voodoo rituals? Here? Not heard anything about that. You might want to ask Miss Cecile. Or Jimmy and the guys."

What the hell, Dana thought. "Do you practice voodoo? Or use voodoo rituals, or have people do them for you?"

The First Lady looked slightly offended. "I'm Roman Catholic, Dana. That's my religion. Voodoo is also a religion, a mix of African ritual and some Catholicism mixed in. So, no, I don't *practice* voodoo."

Dana jotted something down in her notebook. *Did the First Lady actually answer my question? She doesn't practice it, but does she let others do it for her?* She smiled and nodded at the First Lady. "Of course not, I just had to ask."

"Gotta go," Kirk said.

"If you'll excuse us, Dana." The First Lady turned and started walking.

"Sure, sure," she said. "Thanks for the time." *Perfect.* She smiled and went back to the press room.

Chapter 32

A spring storm rolled through Washington that night as Beau and Marissa had dinner together in the family dining room. They had earlier been blessed with the appearance of all three of their children, and for the first time in weeks, the entire family ate together. The kids caught them up on their lives, the unusual, the mundane and the outright hilarious. Typical family dinner conversation. There had been some talk about the Chinese crisis, and the artwork crisis, with abundant theories about how all the paintings had been moved around. Beau assured everyone nothing supernatural was going on. He did this with his best poker-politician-lawyer face. They had seen that face before.

One by one, the kids excused themselves for homework. Even Nina, but Beau and Marissa knew she wouldn't be opening a textbook. More like a text-a-thon with her friends. Or a tweet-a-thon, or some such shit. After all, she was planning a party this weekend at the White House.

Beau had noticed that Marissa wasn't making as much eye contact with him as she usually did. She had that distracted look, like something was on her mind. Something that would be discussed in private, after the kids vanished. He really hated that look.

She was doing it now, as they sat alone finishing dinner. The room was regularly illuminated by lightning flashes, and the deep thunder rattled the old house. The effect gave the place a truly haunted feel. Which was appropriate under the circumstances of the past few days.

Beau tried to make some headway. "The Walter Reed thing go okay?"

Marissa took a last bite of sherbet, licked the spoon and put it down in the bowl. "Yeah. You gotta make sure the VA system is funded well. Got a lot of hurt people in that system. Physically and mentally. Their government is responsible for them being that way. And their government is responsible for making them better." She stared at her husband. By government, she meant *him.*

Beau said, "Every president since Dubya has been ratcheting up the support for the Veteran's Administration, me included. I think we increased spending for them substantially this last budget."

"Keep it up," she said. "And it wouldn't hurt for you to make a visit to a few of those hospitals, you know. Give the patients and the docs some support."

"Right."

Marissa played with the spoon in the bowl. "Did you know Miss Cecile is sleeping here in the White House?"

That caught him off guard a moment. *Hell, did everyone know this?* "Yeah, the guys told me earlier. Jimmy got her in here."

"And why the hell did he do that?"

Beau looked away and sighed deeply. "You're going to think I'm crazy."

"I already know that. That's why I married you," she said. "What normal guy would want to be President?"

"Point taken."

"Where on the crazy scale is this going?" she said.

"Nine. Maybe a ten. Okay, a ten."

She said nothing.

"They wanted her to come in and say a few prayers or whatever she does. Bring some peace to the White House. We could use some, especially now." He looked at his watch. He was supposed to get an update from the South China Sea right after dinner.

"You know that the *New York Times* knows she's here, right? Pretty sure the world will know about it in the morning."

"Yeah, that," he said. "The guys 'fessed up about that, too. I'm talking to Cindy later tonight so we're prepared for that in the morning. And the artwork switcheroo thing."

"Miss Cecile have something to do with that?" Marissa said.

"Oh, hell no," Beau said with a wave of the hand. "Seriously?" He laughed weakly.

"So far, you're only about a five on the crazy scale," Marissa said. "Let's take this to a nine or ten."

Beau sat back and collected his thoughts. He smiled and scratched his chin, stalling for time. *What the hell.* "You know that I've...seen things...in the past. The ghost at the FIJI house. The rougarou when I was a kid."

"Uh huh," she said.

"Well...I've been seeing...some things over the last few days."

"Oh shit," she said.

"This is really nuts, but I swear to you it's real. You ready?" He paused to work through what he was about to say. "Millard Fillmore, Grover Cleveland and Andrew Jackson have appeared to me. I've seen them. Talked to them."

"Oh, Beau," she said, like a mother who just learned her son had just taken a crap in the bathtub. Or had some weed hidden under his bed. More disappointment than anything.

He put up his hand. "I know what you're thinking. But I have proof, sort of." He explained Jackson's intelligence coup about the sub, and how the Navy was forewarned, and how they found the Chinese sub exactly where Jackson said it would be. For her part, Marissa listened without a word. The occasional flashes of lightning added a nice dramatic flair to Beau's discourse. "And Terry's on board with this thing."

"He's seen them?" she said.

"No, not yet. But he bought into it after the sub thing."

"So how does Miss Cecile fit into all this?"

"The guys were worried about the ghosts. They thought Miss Cecile could come up here and talk to them, confirm they were real. Hell, I don't know." He rubbed his hand through his hair.

Marissa just stared at him without blinking. Beau didn't like the look she was giving him. It appeared she was partly mad, partly afraid. Like she just discovered her husband was psychotic. Like the wife in *The Shining*, when she found out that her novelist husband typed "all work and no play makes Jack a dull boy" about a million times on the manuscript he had been working on. *Psychotic. Oh wait, that's what was actually happening here,* he thought. He remembered when he told her about seeing the ghost of the dead pledge at the FIJI house. They had only been dating for a couple of semesters, and although they were already deeply in love, they weren't completely settled into a full-time *trust* mode. For months, she had thought he was messing with her, but when she spent some time talking to his frat brothers, mainly Terry, Big Mike, T-Ron and Jimmy, she learned just how serious Beau had been. That's also when she learned that he had claimed to see the legendary rougarou when he was a kid. She knew Beau was special, but she didn't know he was *that* special. So from then on out, she believed that Beau believed he saw dead people. It added to his mystique, she had said. But when he started to run for public office, she had advised him to hide that mystique way, way back up in his closet.

Man, he didn't like the look on her face. He was regretting telling her about this. She looked like a wife who had come to the conclusion that she didn't really know her husband. That everything had been a lie. That he was a mass murderer or something.

"Baby, you gotta believe me," he pleaded. "I saw them."

She paused for a bit, and then softly said, "I do believe you."

"You do?" *That was easy.* "What convinced you?"

"They're standing right behind you."

The White House has over 55,000 square feet of living space. "House" may not be an accurate term. The place was huge. For a mambo on a mission, the task was daunting. Miss Cecile had spent the better part of four hours moving around the White House. Surprisingly, she had access to most of it. Some places were off limits to guests, even "aunts" of guests. Those were usually associated with the President, of course, or national security, but otherwise she had managed to practice her craft at will. The place was a creepfest, though, filled with the good and bad energy of presidents past. There was certainly a presence to the White House, and in every room she entered, she felt an invisible hand tugging and pushing her, probing her psyche and testing her resolve. She had expected to run into a ghost on every floor, but so far she had seen none. Well, except for Fillmore, Cleveland and Jackson earlier. That had been eye opening. But so far, she had seen nothing else. So she moved about, saying her prayers and performing rituals in the hope that those restless spirits would end their mischief and move on.

What really creeped her out were all those paintings of people. They were everywhere, their eyes watching her. Just about all of them had lived in the White House at one time or another, and she felt like they were not happy she was there. Presidents and First Ladies, generals and other heroes of the Republic – they all cast their gaze upon her. She had learned earlier that someone had moved all the paintings around, and she watched as people worked to put them back where they belonged. This was more work of the mischievous spirits, an example of how they could affect the mortal world. They were able to move physical objects, a powerful thing for a spirit, and something that troubled Miss Cecile.

She thought back on her original vision back in Houma. Of the *Loa* spirit *Ogua,* who presides over politics and war. And of *Agwe,* the sovereign of the sea. Why had they appeared? What was their message? She had hoped to see them again, to see if they had specific instructions for her. But so far, there had been nothing. *What role were they to play?* she thought.

She didn't pay much attention to the news. Just so much human foolishness, she often said. So she was unaware of the events happening on the other side of the world. What was important was the here and now, and that constituted three unruly spirits who somehow were a distraction to the current president. She knew Beau Bergeron from long ago back in Houma, when he was just a boy. She recalled the first time he and his friend had come by her place. There was something about him that day, something she rarely saw. He was one of the few who often saw the things she saw, the sort of person who had a connection to the other world. Beau was a bright boy who was sensitive to things. Miss Cecile had no idea he would grow up to be president, or that even his friend that day, Terry Melancon, would remain at his side until this day. But there had been a *specialness* about the boy, and she had smiled the day he had been inaugurated President of the United States.

And now fate, or more precisely, Jimmy Fontenot, had brought her to Beau Bergeron once again. Strange how life always wanted to complete circles. It was time for her to return to her room and complete the ritual. She was close now.

The low morning sun gave the South China Sea a golden hue. Admiral Yang felt it was a good sign. Today would be momentous, for both he and the People's Republic of China. He stood on the bridge of his ship and looked down at the tactical plot of the area, and the positions of all the players in today's little game. His fleet sat in the northern part of the South China Sea. To his northeast were the *U.S.S George Washington* and her contingent of support ships barreling his way. To his south, the *U.S.S. Abraham Lincoln* and her ships, slowly drifting his way as well. His orders were clear: stand your ground and make the Americans either slow down, alter their course or turn around. Let them know this was your sea. Harass, yes. Intimidate, certainly. *But by no means engage their fleet.* Those orders had come in before dawn, no big change from yesterday's orders, but the fact they had come again spoke volumes. For all their bluster, the senior military leaders who now ran China were not prepared for a hot war with the United States. That notion had been a fun theoretical for them to discuss over dinner and at their private villas around the country. But when faced with the actual opportunity to truly make a statement, they had flinched.

I will not, Yang thought.

He so desperately wanted the Americans to fire on his ships first, so he could defend the honor of his fleet and his country. *His* honor. But he was pretty sure they would not. So they would need some help from him. But very discreet help.

He had a plan, and he was 90% sure it would work. It was bold, highly suspect and downright sneaky. And he was reasonably sure he could cover his tracks, so that when the shooting was done, there'd be no evidence of his deceit.

Or so he hoped. Of course, there was always the chance he might not live through it, but all great leaders faced their trial by fire. This would be his. And if he could take out an American aircraft carrier in the process, so be it.

Yang turned to his air wing commander and ordered him to follow him into his office.

Once inside, Yang sat down. The younger officer stood at attention in front of his desk.

"Please, sit down," Yang said. "I have a mission for you to implement today, and it will require your utmost discretion."

"Yes, sir."

The young officer was Yang's protégé, who owed his rank and position to the admiral. And, of course, his complete loyalty.

"With the Americans headed this way, and their other fleet behind us, I'm concerned our men aren't ready for what may lie ahead. I hope nothing happens, so I want to make sure these young men are prepared."

The air wing commander nodded his agreement.

Yang continued. "So I want to run a little drill in the next few hours, to test our skill at handling an unprovoked attack. But I don't want any of my bridge crew to know about it. I want to see how they will react."

"Very smart, sir. It would be wise to make sure they're prepared," the younger man said.

"Yes, it would. So here is what I want you to do…"

Chapter 33

Beau, Marissa, Millard Fillmore, Grover Cleveland and Andrew Jackson all sat around the table in the family dining room. Beau sat back in his chair, sipping a glass of Scotch, with one leg crossed over another. He was watching his wife. Marissa's eyes darted from one dead president to another, then back to the living one.

"This is freaking me out," she said, with a bit of a girlish laugh, as if she were a tweener sitting down for lunch with the Biebs.

"Yeah, welcome to my world," he said. Beau especially kept an eye on ol' Grover, who looked like a wolf about to devour a little lamb. He could swear the big guy was licking his lips as he stared at Marissa. *Horndog.*

"Madam, no need to be freaked out," Jackson said.

Old Hickory looked relaxed, and smiled warmly at the First Lady. He was putting on the charm. Beau remembered from his biography how much Jackson liked to entertain the ladies. He genuinely enjoyed their company.

"So what did you guys do to make yourselves visible to my wife?" he said.

Fillmore shrugged and looked at his dearly departed buddies. "We didn't do anything. The ability to be seen by the living is out of our control. We don't understand it either."

Marissa reached over and touched Grover Cleveland's arm. He bowed slightly, took her hand, and kissed it. "Very real, my dear."

The old bastard actually winked at her. Jeez, a dead guy is hitting on my wife, Beau thought. He remembered a Rolling Stones song, *Start Me Up.* Something about a woman who could make a dead man...

"So you all have been helping my husband, I hear," Marissa said.

"Well, we do what we can," Fillmore said. "Beau here seems to be in a bit of a jam with the Chinese."

She looked at Jackson. "And you actually were standing next to the Chinese admiral, listening in on his plans?"

"Sure was. Proved to be some valuable intelligence." Jackson said. He looked quite proud of himself. "Good to see some action again after all these years."

Marissa put her face in her hands for a few seconds. Beau and the rest of the presidents waited patiently. After a moment, she looked up, but her eyes were still closed. Slowly she opened them.

"You're still here," she said to all of them.

"Well, *I'm* not going anywhere, that's for sure," Beau said.

"I think we'll be leaving soon," Fillmore said. "We've got a sense that something's up with that Chinese fleet. Apparently our job is to find out what that is and report back to your husband. We're the Dead President's Spy Club. Named it myself." He winked at Cleveland, who was still ogling the First Lady.

Beau smiled. "I gotta tell you, they got the CIA beat. I mean, they put us dead-on that Chinese sub. Think about it. I can get a spy *on the bridge of the Chinese flagship.* I'll know exactly what they're saying and doing." He looked at his watch. "In 12 hours or so, our fleet will be right on top of theirs. But I'll be reading their playbook, so our guys will know what to do. Pretty awesome."

"Wish I had that kind of help back in the day," Cleveland said. "Not that I had any kind of crisis like this, but maybe to spy on my opponents."

"Hell yes," Jackson said. "Would have kept Mr. John Quincy Adams from stealing that election from me in 1824. I got more of the popular vote than him, you know."

No one could remember exactly. Beau thought for a second about it and remembered from Jackson's biography. In his first try at the presidency, Jackson *did* get more popular votes *and* more electoral college votes, but not a majority. The election got kicked to the House, where Henry Clay, Adams' ally, used his influence to win Adams the election. But Jackson would have his revenge four years later during a vicious campaign. He trounced Adams and took the presidency.

"Old news," Fillmore said. "Anyway, we've got some..."

He sat up straight, eyes wide open. Cleveland and Jackson did the same thing. The three dead presidents looked at one another.

"Uh oh," Fillmore said.

All three of them disappeared. Just winked out. They were there. Then they were gone.

Beau and Marissa sat speechless for a moment. Then she said, "They just disappear like that? They *are* gone, right? You don't see them?"

He looked around. "Well, they usually just vanish that way, although that was pretty abrupt, even for them. Like mid-sentence, you know?"

"What happened?" she said.

Beau sat back and thought a second. "Something's up with the Chinese, I bet. Shit, wonder what's about to happen?" He looked at his watch again. "Gotta get down to the Situation Room. Pretty sure our late great presidents are on the bridge of the Chinese carrier right now. If I'm right, they'll be back in a bit with a full report." He got up and kissed his wife. "I'm outta here. Pretty weird stuff, right?"

Marissa just sat there, slowly shaking her head. She glanced at the empty chairs where the ghosts of three American presidents had just sat. "Yeah, pretty weird."

T-Ron, Jimmy and Big Mike high-tailed it up to their rooms in the Residence. They had dinner out in another of Washington's finest eateries, a steak place filled with politicians and hot young interns. After dinner, they had hit a couple of watering holes and ended up at some bar filled with foreign embassy types, where they regaled their international friends with stories of the bayou.

Now, fully fed and still buzzed from drink and feeling no pain, they checked in on Miss Cecile. She had been safely ensconced in her room when they left, and she had assured them she wouldn't wander. Which of course was a lie, but they had bought it nonetheless.

T-Ron tapped on the door. "Miss Cecile? You in there?"

"You *and* the snake," Big Mike said. He was currently in the lead as far as inebriation was concerned. He laughed. Jimmy elbowed him.

The door opened, and Miss Cecile stood there in some kind of floral silk robe. Her eyes were wide and darted from one man to another. In her hand was, indeed, the snake. She held it up at them.

"Shit!" Big Mike said, and stumbled backwards.

"Whatchoo want?" she said. She sounded a little pissed.

Jimmy held up his hands. "Is that snake loaded?" This got the three of them howling.

"You're the one who is loaded. Hush your mouth, Jimmy Fontenot," she said. "It has been a very long day. I'm tired."

"Sorry, sorry," he said.

"Have you been doing...that voodoo...that you do?" T-Ron said. He suppressed another laugh. Miss Cecile just glared at him and then the other two.

"Yes, I have spent hours performing the rituals and prayers. This place is crazy. Very crazy. Spirits everywhere. Some you see, some you don't."

"And?" Big Mike said.

"They are gone," she said. She stroked the snake's head and looked both satisfied and proud of her work.

"The ghosts of the three presidents?" Jimmy said.

"Of course they are gone," she replied. "I can't say that the whole house has been cleansed, but that's not why you brought me here, correct?"

"Right, right. Just the three that were bugging Beau. Or so he says."

"How do you know they're gone?" T-Ron said.

She just stared at him as if he were a child. "I am a mambo. I am in touch with the spirits, the *Loa*. Trust me, they are gone."

"Okay, then," he replied. T-Ron looked at Jimmy and Big Mike. "Then our work, *your* work is done. Jimmy, how soon can you get her back to Louisiana?"

"I can have her wheels up by 10 tomorrow morning."

T-Ron turned to her. "Okay, we'll take you to the airport then."

Miss Cecile stepped back into her room and placed the snake into her bag. She returned with something in her hand, but they couldn't see what it was. She tossed a powder of some kind into the air toward them. It had a reddish tint and hung in the air like cigar smoke before the air conditioning fan dispersed it into the hall. T-Ron, Jimmy and Big Mike waved at the air and coughed.

"What the fuck was that?" T-Ron yelled. "Shit!" He coughed again.

"It will help you sleep tonight," she said. "And keep you from being bothered by troublesome spirits."

Big Mike said, "The only troublesome spirits I've seen is that bottle of Ketel One I threw back tonight. I hope that was a hangover cure. Or preventer." This cracked him up.

Miss Cecile smiled. A knowing, sly look on her face. "We shall see what it does for *you*, Big Mike."

"Okay, great," Jimmy said. "I'm feeling better already. Thanks, Miss Cecile. We'll see you in the morning."

If only that would turn out to be true.

As Washington D.C. began to wind down for the night, as politicians and lobbyists downed their last martinis of the day, as young interns climbed into bed with very old bosses, and foreign embassies sent their last encrypted messages back to their home countries, half a world away, the blazing sun lit up the blue waters of the South China Sea like giant Klieg lights on a movie set. The sky was completely clear, and the sea was relatively calm. A great day to be on the water.

Unless, of course, this was your day to die on the water.

Odds were someone would not see the end of the day. How many "someones" depended on the actions of thousands of sailors and airmen – and women – who either wore the uniform of the People's Republic of China or the United States of America.

Below decks of the Chinese aircraft carrier *Liaoning,* the Flying Shark fighter of Captain Zhang Yunshan, Admiral Yang's air wing commander, was being loaded with what appeared to be a dummy warhead version of the C-704 anti-ship missile. The dummy version was used to train crews and airmen on how to load and drop the missile, and how their aircraft would handle with the added weight of the missile. Its bright orange warhead indicated that there was nothing in it that would blow up. If there had been it would carry 130 kilos of high explosives – able to cause significant damage to a ship at sea. The weapons crewman handled the missile with casual care. It was only natural to relax when you weren't handling a live weapon. So the young men went about their business loading the missile under the fighter, but without the usual tension. They had wondered why Zhang's fighter carried live air-to-air missiles, but a dummy air-to-ship missile. It seemed a little strange, but it wasn't any of their business. Orders were orders.

What they didn't know was that although the missile looked like a dummy, it was far from it. The warhead was live and fully loaded for...war. Someone in the ordnance group had painted a live warhead orange, and made certain it was designated for Zhang's aircraft. There were no witnesses to the act, so no one could ever be blamed for the switch. All was in order. That way, when the smoke cleared, literally, no one could trace how the whole sequence of events started. They would know the *what* but not the *how.*

Officially, the day would start normally for the Chinese fleet. Aircraft would be launched, patrols established, contact with the Americans initiated. But what most of the crew didn't know was that today they would be part of a surprise pop quiz from the Admiral. He had wanted to see just how they would respond to a missile attack from the American fleet, a missile attack against one of their own ships.

The best way to do that was to arm one of his fighters with a dummy missile, fire it at one of their ships, and see how well the crew performed in either evading the missile or bringing it down. For this little test to work, very few people were to know. In fact, only two knew: the Admiral himself, and the wing commander, Zhang, who had personally altered the dummy warhead to be a live one. The ordnance crew would never know the dummy was very, very smart and very, very lethal.

Admiral Yang was fairly confident the crew of the destroyer that would be the target of the "test" would fail. But this time, instead of a failing grade, they would receive a death sentence. Their ineptitude would result in the destruction of their ship.

Zhang was well aware he would be sinking one of his own ships, but the young captain was ambitious and would follow Yang's orders to the letter. Big things would be in store for him.

After the destroyer was hit, the initial blame would be on the American fleet, and Yang would launch a massive counterattack. He had been fired on first, and had to avenge the destroyer. It was the opening he needed. After the battle, the American government would say that it didn't fire first, but there would be no way to substantiate that claim. Yang would have his victory.

If for some reason none of this came to pass, the whole thing would be written off as a training accident. That some fool ordnance man loaded a live missile on Zhang's plane instead of the dummy, turning the exercise into a tragic mistake. Yang and Zhang would be in the clear.

But Yang knew it wouldn't come to that. Once his destroyer had been hit by the missile, he would attack the Americans.

His goal in response: sink the *Washington.*

Chapter 34

Big Mike Moreau was in deep doo doo. Earlier in the night, he had been led out of his room in the Residence by the ghosts of Richard Nixon, Teddy Roosevelt and John Adams. Not his kid, John Quincy Adams, but the father, just plain old John Adams. This was an important point that the third president made to Big Mike.

The hallway had been quiet, and although Big Mike wanted to awaken his buddies to introduce them to his new presidential podnuhs, he had no such luck. The ghosts demanded he stay quiet.

At first, this had been kind of fun. He had wondered what the ghosts had wanted with him. He had even felt a little honored. Then things started to head south a little bit. It had started when they took him to a secret elevator, one he had never seen before. It was tucked away in a small closet. Big Mike had figured it was some kind of secret escape elevator for the first family. He was cool with that. But it had been a tight squeeze. Big Mike was, well, big. And Teddy Roosevelt was packing a spare tire. And although John Adams was a little guy, at just 5 foot 7 inches, he lived up to his nickname – His Rotundity – very well. And Dick Nixon wasn't exactly svelte, either.

Nixon hit the "down" button and away they went. It took way too long, as far as Mike was concerned. They should've hit the bottom floor a lot sooner, but the elevator kept going farther and farther down. He figured they were going down to the bunker. The *real* bunker, the one capable of surviving a nuclear strike on Washington. He kind of wanted to see *that*.

Finally, the elevator stopped, and when the doors opened, what he found wasn't some high-tech bunker, but a dank, dark room that smelled of fetid water and wet concrete. He could hear a dripping sound echoing off the walls.

"Hey, fellas, what the hell is this place?" Big Mike had said. Then, *bam,* he bumped his head on something, maybe a pipe. Or he *thought* he had bumped his head on something. *Somebody didn't hit me, did they?* he had thought before slipping into darkness.

When he awoke, he was strapped to a table, with the head end down somewhat. A lone light bulb hung from a wire in the ceiling. The room was small, and the cinderblock walls were glistening with moisture.

"Hey, what the hell is going on?" Big Mike said. He tried in vain to get out of the straps that held his feet and arms to the table.

Richard Nixon loomed out of the darkness. He wore a blue suit and red tie that seemed out of place for the room. His dark eyes and jowly cheeks were accentuated by the weak light in the room.

"Hey, buddddyyyy," Nixon said in that deep gravelly voice of his. "You and your friends have been up to no good around here, haven't you?"

"What?" Big Mike said. He didn't like the sound of his own voice. It sounded like a 12-year-old girl.

Little Johnny Adams appeared next, from the other side of the table. "You assholes have no idea what you've done, have you?" Adams popped his open hand on top of Big Mike's forehead.

"What? You mean Miss Cecile? We were just trying to help!"

"Well, bully for you, you fucking idiot." Teddy Roosevelt now stood at the end of the table. Big Mike had to look kind of up towards his feet to see him. Old Teddy was wearing his Rough Riders uniform. *Was he wearing that in the elevator?* Big Mike had thought. *No, he had been in a suit.*

"C'mon, guys. Beau didn't need all the distractions with the ghosts. They *were* ghosts, weren't they? Fillmore, Cleveland and Jackson?"

"What the hell do you think *I* am?" Nixon said. "The ghost of Christmas past or something?" He laughed, but to Big Mike, there was nothing gleeful about it.

"Tell us where Miss Cecile is," Adams said.

"She's in her room, I guess," Big Mike said.

"Wrong, dickweed," said Roosevelt. He nodded to Nixon, who disappeared into the darkness for a moment and returned with a large white towel.

Nixon said, "You like watersports, Mikey?"

"Ummm, I guess," he said. His head turned right and left quickly as he tried to figure out what the hell was about to happen.

"Good, then this'll be fun," Nixon said. He folded the towel a couple of times and then placed it over Big Mike's face.

Adams grabbed a bucket of water and began to slowly pour the water onto the towel over Big Mike's face.

"Hey, what the fuck!" Big Mike mumbled, but his voice caught in his throat as the sense of drowning took over his brain's focus. All he could do was grunt and squirm and gasp for air. He had the distinct feeling he was dying.

Yes, he was in some serious shit.

Nixon yanked the wet towel off Big Mike's face. "Well? Where's Miss Cecile?"

"She's gotta be in her room!" he said. He blew water out of his mouth and nose. "Go see! Shit, I don't know."

Nixon nodded at Adams and placed the heavy wet towel over Big Mike's face again. The water really started to flow this time.

In all his years on the water -- hunting, fishing or water skiing, he had never thought he would die drowning. He'd been a good swimmer, despite his size. Hell, half the bayous and swamps he'd been in were shallow enough for him to stand up in. Now he was going to drown in the basement of the White House. *Unbelievable.*

He tried to hold his breath for as long as he could, but the panic coursing through his lizard brain was too strong. He couldn't help himself and took in a big gulp of air. But instead of air, all he got was water. He sensed his lungs were filling up, precious air being replaced by deadly liquid.

Adios, mofos.

"Hey, shithead, wake up!"

Big Mike ignored Teddy Roosevelt's order. He kept his eyes shut and hoped his death would come soon.

This time, Teddy slapped him on the cheek. "Hey, wake up!"

Big Mike didn't feel the water on his face anymore, and wonderful air was filling his lungs. He opened his eyes.

T-Ron stood over him. Jimmy Fontenot was behind him.

"Dude, you're having a bad dream."

Big Mike sat up with a start. He looked at his wrists and ankles. There were no straps holding him down. He was in his bed in the Queen's Room.

"Fuuuuckkkkkk!" he said, and shook his head.

"You alright?" T-Ron said. "You're sweating like you got a fever or something." He laid his hand across Big Mike's forehead. It was clammy, but there was no fever.

Big Mike rubbed his eyes and looked at his two friends. "That was the worst fucking dream ever. Richard Nixon, Teddy Roosevelt and John Adams had me strapped down to a table, and they were *waterboarding* me, man. It was so real!"

"Waterboarding?" Jimmy said. "Why?"

"They wanted to know where Miss Cecile was. They wanted her for some reason."

"Tricky Dick was torturing you?" T-Ron said. "That's awesome."

"No, it wasn't."

Jimmy said, "Follow me." He led them out into the hallway and down to Miss Cecile's room in the West Bedroom. They didn't have to knock this time. The door was open.

Jimmy peered in. The room was empty. The bed had even been made up. He checked the bathroom and still there was no Miss Cecile.

"Aw, shit," he said. "She's gone again."

Big Mike froze in his place. "That *was* a dream, right?"

President Beau Bergeron stood at the podium in the Brady Press Room and squinted slightly at the lights. It was bad form to squint, his advisors had told him once. It made him looked pained, they had said. *Pained.* Yeah, that felt about right.

When the *New York Times* had hit the front porch this morning, the above-the-fold headline sounded ominous. *American, Chinese Fleets Poised for Battle.* If that bored you, the below-the-fold headline said, *Voodoo, Lucky Rooster, Friends All Help President.*

For the last half-hour, Bergeron dealt with questions about the above-the-fold headline. He had tried to explain what was happening in the South China Sea. Or what was about to happen. The fleets were now just about on top of each other. The American fleets were on the move, and the Chinese were holding their ground. Or water. Or whatever the appropriate expression was.

"Sir, it's night time there," one reporter from CNN said. "Was it our plan all along to make this passage at night? Do we have some tactical advantage over the Chinese fleet at night?"

Bergeron wished Admiral Winston were here to answer those questions. Winston and his people were down in the Situation Room, watching the game, so to speak. It was the fourth quarter, and the home team was driving down the field.

"Our fleet, our sailors and aviators are equally capable, day or night," he said. "But no, there was no plan that it be dark as our fleet approaches the Chinese. It's just the way it is at the moment."

Beau looked away from that reporter and found another hand. It was the Associated Press guy. "George?"

AP George said, "Is the *Lincoln's* task force moving through the South China Sea, or did you order it to stay there?"

"The *Lincoln* is performing some routine flight operations," Beau lied.

AP George continued, "But their orders were changed. To move into the South China Sea."

"And...your question is?"

"That doesn't sound routine. Was the change in orders a direct result of the Chinese fleet's aggressive actions earlier in the week?"

"Duh," Beau wanted to say. He gave the room one of his classic shit-eating grins. Sly and knowing. He nodded his head. "It seemed like a prudent move, under the circumstances. Next?"

The CBS guy. "Ryan?"

"What are the *Washington's* orders?"

Beau looked down at his notes and cleared his throat. "Well, we won't broadcast operational orders, but I can say that our intent is the peaceful transit through international waters. As it has been all along."

And so it went for another 15 minutes. Pretty much everyone was asking the same question without really asking it. "Are we going to get into a shooting war with the Chinese?"

Then Beau made his first mistake, and it was a good one. He didn't know Dana Newton from the *New York Times*. Never met her before, so when he called on her and she stood, he wished Scotty would immediately beam him up. But it was too late.

"Dana Newton. *New York Times.* Mr. President, why is there a voodoo priestess staying at the White House?"

Beau had already read the article this morning. It was quite detailed and very accurate. It starred his three buddies, T-Ron, Big Mike and Jimmy. As well as Boudreaux, the Lucky Cock, and headlining the whole thing was Miss Cecile. Newton had even called her by her proper title, *Mambo.*

In the nanoseconds before he responded, he went through all the advice that his Chief of Staff, Terry Melancon, had given him. As well as some talking points that his press secretary, Cindy Walker, had shared. All solid suggestions.

Beau went for it, though. "What, you don't have a voodoo priestess at your house, Dana?"

This got the tense room laughing a bit. It bought Beau some time, turned the tables on Dana Newton and set the tone that this was a frivolous line of questioning in light of what was going on – without actually having to say that.

"No, I don't, Mr. President. Perhaps you could shed some light on why I should?"

If this had been high school, the whole class would have said, *Ooooooooooooo, she got you on that one, Beau.*

Beau smiled. *Okay, so that's how this is going to be. Personal.* He had learned over the years to answer media questions in a measured way. To pause a moment, even it was for just a few seconds, to give his brain time to process a decent response. Early on, he didn't do that, and some of his press conferences as governor, especially in his first term, had been, well, a bit interesting. But he had learned. Sometimes, though, he just wanted to hammer these bastards.

"The woman you're referring to is a wonderful lady who accompanied friends of mine from Louisiana. Although she's not a *personal* friend of mine or the First Lady's, we do know her from our years living in Houma. And yes, down there she is known as a *mambo,* a voodoo priestess. It's her religion, a mixture of Catholicism and African beliefs. I do respect her faith, although it isn't part of my belief system. The ability to practice your faith is every American's right and privilege. Including hers. I hope you don't have a problem with a woman's right to worship in her own way, Miss Newton?"

Twice now, Beau had violated one of the unwritten rules he and his people had set down. *Never ask a reporter a question.* But Beau was an attorney, and he knew better than to ask a witness a question unless he already knew the answer. In this case, he knew how she would respond. *All he needed was a...*

"Uh...of course not," she said.

Pause.

"But..."

He jumped on her weak response.

"So to your original question as to why a voodoo priestess is here in the White House, my answer is quite dramatic: I believe she wanted to take the tour." More chuckles in the room.

"But she was saying some ritualistic prayers and…"

"Good. There are a few people running around here who *should* be turned into zombies."

Big laughs now.

Beau smiled as if he was enjoying himself now. He had watched virtually every press conference JFK had done, and had tried to copy Kennedy's charm and wit whenever he could. The guy was smooth.

"Next question. Frank?"

Beau knew old Frank Lawrence from Fox would get everyone back on topic. Frank said, "Mr. President, how is the Secretary of State trying to diffuse the situation in the South China Sea?"

Thank God, Beau thought.

Dana Newton fumed in her chair. Her face was flushed and her jaw worked like she was grinding corn in her mouth. She was far from done with this thing. Far from done.

Chapter 35

Beau took his chair at the conference table in the Situation Room. The place was electric with activity, but he felt relatively calm. He was in post-game mode after the morning press conference, mentally exhausted from the effort, and because of it, somewhat physically drained, too. An aide placed a big cup of black coffee in front of him. He took a sip and looked up at the big screen.

"Admiral, is it just me or does the monitor look more complicated than I've ever seen it?"

"It's show time, sir," Admiral Winston said. "You've got three task forces occupying the same piece of ocean at the same time. And that's just on the surface. Aloft, you've got aircraft from three different carriers, plus some land-based planes from the Chinese mainland and a few of our long-distance B-2s. Below, we're tracking three of our attack subs, plus seven of theirs. And lest I forget, we've moved three of our satellites over the area, and they've got one of theirs in position. So we're stacked up pretty good."

"My tax dollars at work," Beau said. He looked around the room, hoping to see Fillmore, Cleveland and Jackson pop in. They hadn't been in the room when he entered, so he supposed they were still looking over the shoulder of the Chinese admiral and would return shortly with some key intelligence. So far, though, everyone in the room had a pulse.

"They're ignoring the *Lincoln* behind them," Secretary of Defense Mark Severs said. "They've got everything pointed at the *Washington*."

"How close?"

"Some of our picket ships are in sight of theirs. Rock-throwing distance."

"Some rocks," Beau said under his breath. Then, "How fast are we moving toward them?"

"About 15 knots," the Admiral said. "A nice clip, but not flat out."

"So this is going to take a while until the *Washington* and the *Lincoln* link up?"

"Yes sir. Over most of the day here. Night there."

"Anybody got any theories on what the Chinese play will be?"

"Well, they're not getting out of the way," National Security Advisor Cassidy said. "We'll walk right past them, like you would ignore a bully. My guess is they'll lean their shoulder into us to remind us they're there. Like a bully."

"What does that mean?" Beau said. He took another gulp of the fresh coffee. His nerves were beginning to settle a bit, but he had a bad feeling they were about to be ratcheted up again.

"My guess, another dogfight," Cassidy said.

"More like a knife fight," Admiral Winston said. "When aircraft are that close to each other in a dogfight, it gets pretty intimate. The aviators call it a 'knife fight.'"

Beau thought about the movie *Top Gun,* when old Maverick had knocked some bad guys out of the sky. He liked that movie. It ended well.

"Pretty dumb, with all the hardware we've got up there," he said.

"This Admiral Yang isn't the most...experienced... commander in the world," Winston said. "He's got plenty of opportunities to do something dumb."

"Well, that just makes me feel all tingly inside," Beau said. "Anything else?"

Secretary of Defense Severs just shrugged. "We just have to wait and see."

Beau looked back up at the monitor. There were triangles and squares and round circles all over it, many either right next to or on top of one another. Other icons designated ships, and they, too, were dangerously close to each other. It looked like a huge traffic jam at rush hour. With heavily armed drivers. *Nice.*

"And that's all in darkness, right?" he said.

"Yes, sir," Winston replied.

"Seems like a perfect scenario for a mistake to happen. Or confusion."

Admiral Winston just nodded and glanced over at the Secretary of Defense. "That's what we're most afraid of, sir."

Beau sighed and looked around the room. *Where the hell are those guys?"* he thought.

Captain Zhang Yunshan banked his J-15 Flying Shark slightly to port, to change his flight path and maintain his more-or-less circular orbit around the *Washington's* task force. He glanced out of the cockpit into the pitch darkness in an effort to see anything of the outside world, but it was pointless. Despite all the military assets in the air and on the sea, he couldn't see a thing. He turned back inside his cockpit to look at his radar. It told the true story. The sky and sea were filled with aircraft and naval vessels.

There was only one that he was interested in at the moment, and it wasn't the American ships that were training their radar on him and his colleagues. He was looking for a Chinese destroyer, one of their new Type 052D ships, similar to the American Arleigh-Burke-class guided-missile destroyers. It was the *Lanzhou*. Or the newer version of her. The sleek, gray ship was out there protecting the carrier, just as the American destroyers were doing for their mother ship. If his calculations were correct, he'd have her in contact in just a few minutes. He wondered if her sailors were ready for what was about to happen. A live-fire test of their skill and courage. Yang didn't think they were up to it, and guessed the missile would get through and sink the ship. Zhang wasn't so sure. He thought – hoped – that they would survive. He didn't like the prospect of killing his own countrymen, but he was ambitious enough, and had rationalized the reasons enough, to use this opportunity to light a match to get this battle started. Both he and Yang knew their careers could be catapulted by the end results, like his fighter being thrown off the deck of his carrier by the ship's catapult system. Like a rocket.

Up till now, he and his squadron had flown a predictable flight pattern around the American task force. Nevertheless, American fighters had shadowed them constantly. This time, there had been none of the foolish radar locks of the last few days. Everyone was keeping their missile radars quiet, behaving like good boys and girls. *Yes, the Americans had women pilots. Interesting. One had even killed one of my pilots.* In a nation where having a female baby was frowned upon, the idea of women being productive members of any society was hard to get his head around. It was one of the things the Chinese and the Muslims agreed upon.

Zhang checked his radar once again and noted the position of his fighters in relation to eight American fighters at his two o'clock position. For his and Yang's plan to work, he would have to create some confusion, timed perfectly and hidden under the cover of darkness.

That time was *now.*

He ordered his men to follow him as he "frightened" the Americans right out of their aircraft. He hit the afterburners and climbed to his right. The rest of his squadron followed suit.

Immediately, an American AWACS radar plane detected the course change by the Chinese aircraft and relayed the information to the flight of eight F-18s. The American pilots were not to be intimidated, and rolled into the rising flight of Chinese Flying Sharks.

Hornets versus Sharks. Game on.

Half a world away in the Situation Room of the White House, Admiral Winston was handed a phone. He listened without saying a word, thanked the person on the other end of the line and handed the phone back to an aide.

"Chinese fighters just changed course to engage one of our F-18 squadrons." He stood up and walked to the big flat-screen. He stared at it a moment and pointed to one section. "Here."

Beau stood up and joined the Admiral. "Are they shooting?"

"Not yet. We're going to have to watch this, though."

Beau watched as circles and triangles moved towards each other and turned into one big blob. He looked around the room again. All eyes were on the screen, and the volume in the room had dropped considerably. He turned back to the screen and muttered, "Knife fight."

Zhang found one particular F-18 of interest and locked it up on his missile radar. He knew the American pilot was probably shitting in his pants at the moment, trying to lose his adversary and praying to his God that he would survive the next few minutes. Zhang's other pilots were now doing the same, scattering the flight of F-18s as the Americans tried to avoid getting shot down. Or so they thought. The Chinese were alternately switching their fire control radars on and off, confusing the Americans who didn't know if this was just more Chinese bullshit or the real thing. One second of miscalculation on their part would result in death. Or the start of a huge naval battle.

Zhang was having fun. He loved to fly, and he felt in total control as he rolled his fighter this way and that, diving and twisting, then hitting the afterburners and climbing for the stars. His and the American fighters were so close now that he had to be careful he didn't run into one of them – either theirs or his.

But while all eyes were on each other's fighters, Zhang had one eye on the position of the Chinese destroyer *Lanzhou*. He was carefully maneuvering his Flying Shark in such a way as to give him a maximum look-down angle on the ship. The American F-18 he had been behind had performed a very nice high-g barrel roll to escape Zhang's pursuit. As expected, Zhang overshot the Hornet -- the intended effect of the American's maneuver -- but instead of trying to re-engage, Zhang turned his full attention to the *Langzou*. He locked his radar on the ship and fired his C-704 anti-ship "dummy" missile. The weapon flew away from under his wing, and the bright exhaust lit up the night sky all around Zhang's fighter. In seconds, the missile was gone, angling down towards the surface of the South China Sea. It had found its target and was tracking true.

The bridge crew of the *Langzou* had been watching the aerial dance of the Chinese Flying Sharks and the America F-18 Hornets with some interest. They used the opportunity to hone their skills in distinguishing friend from foe on the radars, all the while staying alert if the Americans decided to go after any of the ships in the Chinese fleet. The young men were on edge, knowing that just over the horizon were the American fleet and all of its firepower and technology. Right now, though, their full attention was on the skies. Had this been war, those fighters would be shooting at each other in an attempt to protect their respective fleets. But right now, all they were doing was pretending to be in aerial combat.

All of that changed in an instant.

"Missile launch, Captain!" The young radar operator's voice was strained.

The *Langzou's* captain stepped closer. "What? Where?"

"There, sir!" he said. He pointed at his radar plot.

"They're shooting at each other?" The captain tried to get precise information from the child who sat in front of the radar.

"No, sir. That's a big one. Anti-ship and it's locked onto *us*!"

"What the hell?" the captain said. "General quarters. Alert the *Liaoning*."

"Was that a missile launch?" Laronda "Gangsta" Jackson said into her mike. She turned her head back to her left and her right in the cockpit, trying to put her eyes on what she thought was a missile in the air.

"Copy that, Gangsta," her wingman said over the radio. "Big one, tracking to the southeast."

Laronda thought his normally calm voice was a tad higher. "Anybody hit?"

One by one, the rest of the squadron's aviators checked in that they were alive and well.

Their eye in the sky aboard the high-flying EC-2 Hawkeye radar plane chimed in. "Confirm missile launch, heading two-one-zero. Who fired that thing?"

Like a bunch of schoolkids busted for doing something wrong, each of the Hornets responded with various versions of "Not me!"

But the proof was right there, in the sky, flying at high speed. The radar operator aboard the Hawkeye said, "Well somebody did, and it's heading right for that Chinese destroyer."

The C-704 anti-ship missile flew at wave-top level now, honing in on the *Langzou.*

"They fired on us, sir! The Americans are shooting at us!" the young radar operator said. "Missile closing fast!"

The Chinese captain resorted to his training for such situations. Of course, he had never experienced anything like this in real life. Only in simulations. He knew there was no way his ship, although fast, could get out of the way of the missile. Its electronics were deadly and very responsive to any course changes the destroyer could do.

"Countermeasures," he ordered. Immediately, a high dose of electronic noise pulsed out from the ship, directed right at the incoming missile. It was designed to confuse the tracking radar on the deadly weapon, to effectively blind it so it would lose contact with the ship it was trying to sink.

Despite their apparent fear for their lives, the young bridge crew acted professionally, and the captain was duly impressed. He hoped he got the chance to commend them later. The countermeasures were activated, and now they had to see if they worked.

"Missile still tracking, sir," the kid said again.

The captain stood straighter. "Engage the close-in guns." The H/PJ12 Close-In Weapons System was a big seven-barreled Gatling gun mounted on the ship that could fire 5,400 rounds per minute. It could lock onto an incoming anti-ship missile and shoot it down from as far away as three kilometers. It spit out a deadly wall of flying metal that could shred a missile. If it could lock on in time. It was the ship's last line of defense. The crew's last hope of going home to wives and girlfriends standing up, instead of in a box.

"Weapons engaged," someone on the bridge said. "Stand by." All eyes looked out into the dark sky. Death was on its way and they couldn't even see it.

Chapter 36

Admiral Tony Lear on the *Washington* wanted answers fast. "Who the hell fired that missile?" he said. He was pacing around the bridge, moving from one station to another.

"Not ours," was the immediate response. "All our fighters report weapons accounted for."

The controller on the Hawkeye was on the horn. "Definitely an anti-ship missile, sir," she said through the loudspeaker. "Tracking to one of the Chinese destroyers. Estimating impact in 60 seconds."

"Son of a bitch," Lear said. "You sure that's not ours?"

"Pretty sure," she said. "That signature is not a Harpoon. "It's something else."

"General quarters," he said to his second in command. Immediately, the *Washington* and her entire task force were at maximum preparedness. The *Lincoln's* group was also locking things down.

"Shit. Get the White House link up," he said.

"Put it on speaker," Admiral Winston said from within the White House Situation Room.

Tony Lear's voice filled the room. The visual on the screen switched to Lear's image as well. He turned to face the group. He could see them as well from his viewpoint on the bridge of the carrier. He laid it out for them as much as he could in the few seconds remaining before the missile impacted the Chinese destroyer.

"We'll know in just a few seconds," he said. "Stand by."

Everyone in the Situation Room went silent immediately. Beau looked over at his friend and Chief of Staff, Terry Melancon. Terry gave him the same "oh fuck" look he'd been giving Beau since they were kids, whether they had just been caught lifting a pack of gum from Gaudin's Grocery Store, busted for a bottle of Jack in their rooms when they were teens, or surprised by LSU campus security down by the lakes with a couple of half-nekkid coeds in the back of Terry's old Ford van. One of which may have been the future First Lady.

While everyone was staring at the big screen, watching the game, Beau took a moment to scan the room again. Everyone he could see was alive and from this century. Fillmore, Cleveland and Jackson were still nowhere to be found.

Terry Melancon, sitting next to Beau, leaned in and whispered, "They here?"

Beau just shook his head. "Don't see 'em."

"You think they're out there?" Terry said, nodding to the big screen.

"I guess so. But they need to get their dead asses back here, and I mean now. We could use some fresh intel here."

Beau turned his head back to the screen. He couldn't tell what was going on with all the icons all over the TV. In the movies, he would be seeing a small image of a missile heading to a graphic representation of a ship. But that visual wasn't up at the moment.

"Any second now," Admiral Winston said.

"Are we sure that's not our missile?" Beau said to the room.

"Not ours, Mr. President."

Terry leaned back close to Beau's ear. "Doesn't really matter at this point. A sinking Chinese naval vessel will have our fingerprints all over it."

On board the destroyer *Langzou,* the bridge crew wasn't breathing. They were still alive, but just not breathing. All of them were looking out into the darkness, counting the seconds down.

The night lit up with light and noise. The big close-in Gatling gun opened up on the incoming missile, spewing hot metal out into sky, laying down a protective curtain the crew hoped the missile would run into and be destroyed. The 5,400-rounds-per-minute leaving the seven barrels sounded like a giant weed-whacker. *Rrrrraaappppppppp.* In a way, that's exactly what it was.

About two kilometers out from the ship, the crew saw the light of an explosion illuminate the waves of the South China Sea. A few seconds later, the sound and concussion hit the ship like thunder as the C-704 anti-ship missile was destroyed.

The bridge crew let out a yell of relief, satisfaction and joy. They were still alive. The captain began to speak, but something caught in his throat and he cleared it. Then he said, "Any more missiles, lieutenant?"

"No...sir," the young man said. He, too, had cleared his throat, or found some saliva for his bone-dry mouth. "Nothing out there."

"Stay alert. And get me Admiral Yang. We need to know how we are to respond to this attack."

"Aye, sir."

Everyone in the Situation Room glanced at each other. Something should have happened by now. An image of Admiral Tony Lear aboard the *Washington* popped back on the screen.

"No impact," he said to the room half a world away. "One of our drones picked up an explosion, but it wasn't the ship. Looks like they knocked it down with some of their close-in systems."

Admiral Winston turned to the President. "The Chinese ship shot it down."

Beau sighed and shook his head. "Thank God."

Terry Melancon now asked the obvious question no one had time to consider in all the excitement. "So whose missile was that if it wasn't ours?"

Admiral Winston scratched the back of his head. "Tony, you hear that one?"

Lear looked down from the TV screen onto the assembled heavyweights around the conference room table. "I'm recalling all of our aircraft now. We'll do a plane-by-plane assessment of everyone who was up there. Most of the Hornets were carrying Harpoons."

"Our anti-ship missiles carried by our fighters," Winston said to Beau.

Lear continued. "None of the *Lincoln's* aircraft were in the vicinity, so if it was one of ours, it was from our flight, not theirs. But it wasn't one of ours."

"You getting more planes up?" Winston said.

"We will as soon as we recover this bunch. *"Lincoln's* picking up the slack till then."

"Are we sure that missile came from a plane?" This was Secretary of Defense Severs. Pretty much everyone's boss in the room, except for the President. Who was *his* boss.

Beau didn't understand the meaning and looked at Severs.

"The Harpoon missile can be launched from a plane, a ship or a submarine, right, Admiral?" Severs said.

"Correct. Tony, what's your thought?"

Lear shook his head. "It was a plane. One of our Hornet pilots saw it light off somebody's wing. We're looking at the data now. We think we can ID whose it was. Chinese fighters were mixing it up a bit with our guys before this happened."

Beau leaned forward. "Whoa, wait a minute. Are you saying there's a possibility that the Chinese accidently fired a missile at one of their own ships?"

"That is a distinct possibility, Mr. President," Admiral Lear said. "You get some kid up there, getting all excited with all these American fighters all around him, and he pulls some boneheaded move like that. What's worse, he probably thought he was going to fire his air-to-air missile and hit the air-to-ship one instead."

"What's really worse is he had the damn thing pointed at one of his own ships," Admiral Winston added.

"Can we prove that, and I mean in a hurry?" Beau said.

The men at the table and on the screen glanced at each other. "Not in a hurry," Admiral Lear said from the bridge of the *Washington.*

"We gotta get Frances on the horn with Beijing," Terry said to Beau. "This shit is gonna blow up, and I'm not talking rhetorically."

"Agreed," Beau said. "Where is the Secretary of State?"

"At her office, Mr. President," someone said.

"Let's get her on the line," he said. "And now."

Admirals Lear and Winston exchanged looks across 12,000 miles of land and ocean. Winston said to the President, "I wouldn't waste any time, sir."

"Why's that?"

"The next shot is theirs."

Those lucky bastards, Admiral Yang thought. He had his head down, hand on his chin as if in deep, leadership mode. He wanted to look like he was planning his next three moves to his men on the bridge of the *Liaoning.* His destroyer was still floating out there. It would have been better if the damn thing were sinking. More dramatic that way, his entire fleet filled with righteous anger and focused on revenge. True, he had the next best thing, the apparent firing of a missile by the Americans at one of his ships. He'd have to make some hay with that. But he didn't like his tactical situation at the moment, with an American carrier in front of him and one behind him, their planes filling the skies and their ships arrayed from one horizon to another. Trying anything now would be suicide, but his men expected some response.

This is how legends are born, he thought. *How the clever Admiral Yang Jinping turned the tables on the Americans, despite being surrounded.* Yang let that little movie starring him play out in his own mind. What he needed right now was something the American fleet didn't have close at hand. A land-based ballistic missile that was so close the American carriers would have little or no time to defend themselves from the huge, deadly missiles. The problem was, he didn't have operational control of them. His army comrades controlled them, and Beijing controlled *them.* If he could light off one of those babies, he could sink one or both of the American carriers, forcing their fleets to withdraw. Game over. The only problem with that was that he wouldn't get credit for the victory. It would look like he was saved by land-based forces. No, if he were to come out of this as the new Chinese naval hero, he would have to use the assets he had under his command. Ship against ship. Now, he *could* have the army move those missiles around and distract the Americans. That could help. But ultimately, he would have to take things into his own hands. But first, he had to get Beijing stirred up. And float a little idea by them.

"Get me headquarters," he said and looked over at his radio operator. "In my office."

Yang left to go to his office for the call. The connection was already established when he got there. He explained the situation in very clear language.

"We are under attack," he said. He allowed his voice to be calm and strong. Knowing the Americans weren't actually attacking him helped matters immensely, but the idiots in Beijing didn't know that.

"Unprovoked?" was the only response he got.

"Of course," Yang replied.

"Are they firing again?"

"Not yet, but I expect a missile barrage at any minute."

Yang heard other voices at the other end of the line. The bastards were debating their next move. He didn't have time for that. Finally, they came back on.

"Maintain defensive status only."

"What?" Yang said. "The only real way to defend myself is to attack."

"We are talking to the Americans at this very moment," the man said. "Stand by. We'll get back to you."

"I may not be here when you call back!" Yang said. He put some real aggression into his voice. When this story was written, whoever played him in the movie would have to get this scene just right.

"I understand. Do what you have to do to defend yourself and the lives of your crew. Just as a last resort."

"We got lucky the last time, due to the skill of the *Langzou's* crew," Yang said. "I can't count on that again. That missile for all intents and purposes was aimed at me, at the carrier. We have to launch a counterattack."

"What are your plans?"

"Well, I'm glad you asked," Yang said. "Listen carefully. The Americans will never know what hit them."

Beau and Terry went back to the Oval Office to get Secretary of State Gottlieb's take on her call with the Chinese. Admiral Winston had cautioned the President to "not go far." Shorthand for this whole thing can go to shit at any time.

Gottlieb had insisted to her Chinese counterpart over the phone that the missile was *not* American. She was assured by the Chinese that *they* didn't fire on their own ship, so it had to be the Americans. That was their stance on the whole thing. They just weren't buying what she was selling. She tried to get them to understand that American forces were not in an offensive mode, and that the Chinese should also take a more defensive attitude. They called bullshit on that one, too. A missile coming right at you tended to get your attention. And so it had gone, with no progress made, but at least the two sides were talking at the moment. The call had ended with only an assurance that both sides would answer the phone if it rang.

After they hung up with the Secretary of State, Beau and Terry sat staring off into different parts of the room.

Beau said, "Think they'll hold off launching an attack on us?"

Terry turned to him. "Maybe. We've got them in a shit sandwich between the *Washington* and the *Lincoln*. It'd be crazy if they tried anything. Problem is, mainland China is *right there.* It's like a giant aircraft carrier of its own, filled with missiles, men and planes. They could attack from there and take us out."

"Thanks for reassuring me," Beau said. He got up from his desk and looked out the window into the garden outside. "Where the hell did those guys go?" He turned around and looked up. "Millard? Grover? General Jackson?" he said loudly.

Terry winced and put his hands out, palm down, patting the air. "Shhhh. Keep that shit down! Mrs. Foster will hear you."

"I'm *trying* to wake the dead."

"Well, just don't wake the White House press corps, okay?"

"I got a bad feeling they're gone for good," Beau said. "It's like the connection is gone. Why now? Right when I really need them."

Terry didn't say anything as a thought washed over him. Beau could tell his friend was on to something. "What?"

"Miss Cecile."

"What about her?"

"You think she had something to do with this? The guys brought her here to help."

"Yeah, they told me. I said I was fine and didn't need any help from Miss Cecile."

"But what if she...did something? You know, something to make the ghosts stay away?"

"Then I would be fucked at the moment. Which I am," Beau said. "You think she did some kind of exorcism or some such shit?"

"I don't know, but I can find out," Terry said. He picked up the phone on Beau's desk. "Mrs. Foster? Terry. Can you find T-Ron, Big Mike and Jimmy and get them in here? Right away? Great. Thanks."

"I need a drink," Beau said. "What time is it?"

"Too early. Have some coffee."

Chapter 37

Beau sat on the sofa, sipping fresh coffee. The coffee had been a better idea than the Scotch. But not by much. "I need to know what that Chinese admiral is up to. I can't let this thing get out of hand."

"It's already out of hand," Terry said.

"Great, so I'm out of options now? My next move is to keep the conflict confined to the South China Sea? Their back yard?"

"We gotta do what we gotta do *fast*," Terry said. "Sink their carrier, take out most of their fleet and then get the hell out of there. Get the diplomats to settle things down. They won't mess with us again."

"Thank you, Dick Cheney."

"You're welcome."

They sat in silence for a few moments, and then Terry switched on the TV to catch CNN. They were already reporting the attack on the Chinese destroyer. Undoubtedly, the Chinese had released that information to take the high ground in the propaganda war. *U.S. fires first on Chinese ship, but missile is downed by the destroyer's defensive systems.* The talking heads were chattering about the whole thing. There were ex-admirals, ex-politicians, ex-ambassadors to China. Pretty mush every ex out there. Might have been a few ex-wives, too, just for good measure.

There was a knock on the door. Mrs. Foster opened it and stuck her head in. "Got 'em."

Beau said, "Send them in, thanks."

T-Ron, Big Mike and Jimmy ambled in. Gone was all the frat-boy goofiness and banter.

Terry didn't waste any time. "Did Miss Cecile do some voodoo shit and make Beau's dead presidents disappear?"

The guys sat down on the sofas and glanced at each other. Big Mike said, "Yeah, she did something. We didn't see anything, but she told us later that they were gone. That she'd been successful."

Beau's head dropped like it had been cut off. Without looking up he said, "Can we please get them back?"

The guys looked around, avoiding eye contact with Terry and Beau. Jimmy coughed once. "Uh, I guess so. We'd have to ask her."

No one spoke for a bit. Finally, Terry said, "Okay, so...let's get on that right away."

Beau looked up. "Look guys, I know this all sounds like bullshit. But I really did see those guys. But, the important thing is, they're acting like spies for us right now with the Chinese. Jackson actually went to their carrier and overheard some good shit that turned out to be very useful."

Terry nodded. "He's right. I didn't believe it either, but this info we got from Jackson was effing gold, man. Seriously."

"And now I need him back over there," Beau added. "It's nut-cuttin' time."

T-Ron rubbed his forehead. "Okay, okay, but there's just one little problem with Miss Cecile. We can't find her. She's gone. Jimmy was going to put her on the plane this morning, but when we went to her room, she had cleared out."

"Gone where?" Beau said. "Like...just walked out of the White House? She's running around D.C.?"

Big Mike shrugged. "We guess. Unless she caught her own flight back to Houma."

"But why would she do that?" Jimmy said. "I had my jet fueled up and ready to go. For free."

Terry just shook his head. "Unbelievable. We gotta find her. You jackasses gotta find her."

"Can't you just get the FBI or Secret Service to find her?" Jimmy said.

"Oh, yeah. Right," Terry said. "Let me make *that* call." He pretended to pick up a phone. "Oh, hi. Director? Yeah, could you find a lost voodoo priestess for us? We need her to bring some dead presidents back."

Beau cut in. "Maybe we could do just *that*. Not to the FBI, but maybe discreetly ask D.C. Metro to keep an eye open. Say she's Jimmy's aunt and she might have some mild dementia or early Alzheimer's or something."

Terry's eyes went wide. "You gotta be shitting me."

"No, Jimmy can do that. Talk to the cops. Keep us out of it," Beau said.

"Sure, I could do that."

"We'll take the truck," T-Ron said.

"Leave the boat," Terry said.

"Of course."

"But take Boudreaux," Terry added. "This is important."

Bergeron stood up. "Yes. By all means, take the fucking chicken."

T-Ron, Big Mike, Jimmy and Boudreaux rode in the front of Big Mike's Big Pickup. Mike was driving. Jimmy was navigating. T-Ron was checking the sidewalks. Boudreaux was acting like a Lucky Cock.

They were all *focused*.

"Anybody know what she was wearing?" Big Mike said.

"A snake?" said Jimmy.

"Funny. But probably true."

T-Ron chuckled a bit. "This is like a Tom Clancy novel or movie. The world on the brink of war. The president up against the wall. All that stands in the way of Armageddon are three patriots, their lucky cock and their trusty pick up truck. Roaming the streets of Washington, and the clock is ticking."

"You're an idiot," Big Mike said.

T-Ron started making some dramatic movie theme music noises with his mouth. *"Dunh, dunh. Dunh, dunh, dunh."*

Jimmy just shook his head and finished the voice-over for the movie trailer. "Looking for a voodoo priestess, who has to perform a ritual to return the ghosts of three dead presidents back to the White House in time to save the world."

"I wouldn't pay to see that movie," Big Mike said. "Sounds ridiculous." He looked at his two buddies and the rooster. "Then again…"

"Hey, there's a cop. Pull over," Jimmy said.

Big Mike eased the truck over to a curb, where a D.C. cop was talking to a few people at a bus shelter. Jimmy rolled down his window on the passenger side. "Officer?"

The cop walked over. The truck had "lost tourist" written all over it and he made a bored face. He looked inside to see three middle-aged men, one holding a nasty-looking rooster. *This ought to be good,* he thought.

Jimmy smiled. "Uh, wonder if you could help us with something? My aunt has gone missing. She was staying with us over at the...at the hotel...but we think she went for a walk. Problem is, she might have some early Alzheimer's. She may be lost."

The cop took out a notepad and asked for a description. This is when things got a little iffy. Jimmy said, "Name is Cecile Marie de Boissonet." He spelled it for him. "Tall, thin, African American. Early seventies, maybe. Gray hair. Might be wearing some African or Haitian long, colorful dress. She might have a snake with her."

The cop glanced up. "Whoa, wait a sec. She's black?" He eyed Jimmy.

"Long story. I was adopted."

"Okay. And she's got a snake?"

"A pet. I think his name is...Rufus."

T-Ron and Mike had to look away.

The cop stared at Jimmy and then the others. "You boys been drinking?"

"No, officer. Too early for that. This is serious."

Boudreaux the Lucky Cock crowed so loudly the cop jumped back.

"Shit!"

"Sorry. He does that sometimes."

"Uh huh."

Jimmy handed the cop his business card. "My cell is on this. If you guys see her, give me a call."

The cop looked at the card. "Popeye's Fried Chicken."

"That's me."

"Does your pet there know what line of business you're in?"

Jimmy shook his head "no" very quickly and looked at Boudreaux. He whispered, "He can't read."

"What a relief," the cop said. "Okay, we'll keep an eye open." He walked away.

Mike said, "Well, that will get us nowhere, except a great story he'll tell his buddies when his shift ends."

"Keep driving," T-Ron said. "I think Boudreaux senses something."

"Yeah, that he's in the hands of three complete idiots," Big Mike said.

"Relax. You're still tense from your nightmare."

"I'm telling you, man, I think that really happened. I was soaking wet when I woke up."

"Sweat."

"Fucking Nixon," Big Mike muttered, and drove back out into traffic.

The clock – and the cock – was ticking.

Admiral Yang of the Chinese navy had not been having much luck with some of his tactical decisions over the last few days. Nor much luck with his strategic decisions either. It seemed the Americans were charmed. No matter what he did, he couldn't start the conflagration he needed to give his career a needed boost.

Well, that was going to change, he thought. *He'd had enough failure for one week.*

He stood below decks of his aircraft carrier, on the hangar deck. The huge area was filled with all manner of aircraft. Mostly Flying Shark fighter-bombers. A few reconnaissance planes. And the sleek, 21st-century stealth drone that stood before him. The thing looked like something out of a science fiction movie. Black and evil. Like a giant manta ray. It was a flying wing, patterned after the big American B-2 stealth bomber, just not as large. And no pilots, of course. At least none that would be in it. The pilot would be safely seated here on the carrier, flying the thing remotely. The Americans were way ahead of the Chinese when it came to drone aircraft. They had honed their skills in Iraq and Afghanistan, and then took what they learned to the high seas. They had been launching drones off their carrier decks for years, but it was somewhat of a recent thing for the Chinese. He suspected – no, he *knew* – the Americans were at least one generation ahead of the Chinese in such technology. But still, his drones were pretty good. He had gotten one very close to the American carrier a few days ago. And he was prepared to do it again. Only this time, he would be upping the stakes. A lot.

The first time, he used a drone like this just for reconnaissance. Now he would use it for something a little more deadly. For the Americans, anyway.

He watched as his weapons crew wheeled the big anti-ship missile under the drone. It was a prototype missile, far bigger than the regular anti-ship missiles his traditional fighters carried. Bigger payload. Bigger punch. Made to sink big cruisers, and possibly an aircraft carrier, if you hit it the right way at the right time. Like if that carrier happened to have fueled-up planes on the deck carrying tons of weapons. That would set off a chain reaction of explosions that would sink her. Yang figured that's how it was on the *U.S.S. Washington* right now. A very ripe target indeed.

The crew carefully jacked the thing up until it was inside the belly of the aircraft. The men carefully attached the weapon to the drone's bomb bay, careful to make sure all connections were secure. When completed, the belly doors of the drone would be closed with the missile hidden inside. If it had been carried under and outside the plane, it would have defeated all of the stealth technology. That's why it had to be inside.

Yang sensed someone behind him and turned. It was Lieutenant Chen Yi, a bright young man in his twenties. He was somewhat tall for a Chinese man, almost six feet, with a slim build. He wore stylish silver-framed glasses, and was dressed in a green aviators flight suit.

"Admiral, sir," he said and saluted smartly.

"Yi. Are you ready for this mission?" Yang knew the kid's father from the academy, and had often visited their home. He had known Yi since the boy was a child.

"Yes, sir. She is a beautiful craft, is she not?"

"Quite so. And now very deadly. Your years of video-game experience will now be put to some good use, yes?"

Yi smiled and looked down, somewhat embarrassed. Despite the flight suit, he was not a pilot. He was a drone pilot who sat in the safety of a room far from the action and flew the plane into combat. Like the Americans, many of these "pilots" were exceptional gamers with incredible skills with a mouse and a joystick. They could sit for hours "flying" the aircraft. All they needed was a Red Bull and junk food. "My father can now at least see I had not wasted all of my teenage years in front of a computer monitor."

Yang laughed. "That is true. Tonight, you will earn a medal that he will be proud for you to have. You will honor him, your family and the nation."

"Thank you, sir."

The crew chief gave a thumbs up to the Admiral and to Yi. He brought two controllers over to Yi. The young drone pilot slipped his right and left hands into each of the devices, giving his arms the look of a robot with odd buttons, joysticks and toggles in each metal hand. He flexed his fingers inside the special gloves.

"Time to fly," Yi said.

The weapons crew and Admiral Yang stepped back and watched as the drone was hooked to a small airplane truck. It was towed to the waiting elevator, joined by its young pilot. They were all lifted to the flight deck. The control surfaces on the flying wing went up and down as Yi manipulated them remotely with his hands to make sure he'd be able to control the thing once it lifted off. The drone would next be hooked to the ship's catapult system, which would shoot it off the deck into the night sky.

And to its appointment with the *U.S.S. Washington.*

The clock was ticking.

Chapter 38

Dana Newton had been staked out in the parking lot of the White House since early that morning. She had gone into the press room, tracked down a couple of early-risers who worked in the West Wing for any updates from Asia, and pretended to do some work. About 8:00, she went back out to her car and parked herself inside and watched the door. Who left was as important as who was arriving, in her opinion.

It started a little after 8:30, when Miss Cecile walked out carrying her bag. The woman looked like she just stepped out of a voodoo movie. She wore an embroidered short-sleeved blouse, a long orange, red and white ankle-length skirt, and her head was wrapped in an orange scarf. He neck was adorned with beads and necklaces. Huge, hooped earrings framed her long, delicate neck.

Dana had almost followed the old woman out the gates. She had watched as the voodoo priestess hailed a cab and disappeared into morning rush hour traffic. She figured Miss Cecile was headed for a city tour. No story there. The real story was still inside. Besides, Dana had to attend the presidential press conference and bask in the glory of her morning story. Maybe get a few digs in to the President. But when that ended, and she and the President had sparred, and that asshole had gotten a few good jabs in to *her*, Dana had returned outside for her surveillance. She wanted to know what Bergeron's Buddies were up to today. So here she was.

She thought about Big Mike, T-Ron and Jimmy. They had turned out to be a great source of information. She had been very pleased with her story, but she sensed it wasn't over yet.

Her hunch turned out to be valid. The guys had come out later in the morning, grabbed that stupid lucky rooster or cock or whatever, and took off in one of their pickups. They looked like they were in a hurry. And a little worried, too.

So now she watched from a discreet distance as they stopped and talked to a cop. *Wonder what that's about?* she thought. After a few minutes, the guys drove off. Judging by where they were going, and how their heads turned this way and that, they were either sightseeing or looking for someone. And judging by where they were driving, they weren't checking out the sights. They drove in and out of some of D.C.'s worst neighborhoods, and then into more fashionable sections of Georgetown.

Maybe they weren't looking for *something*. Maybe they were looking for *someone*.

Miss Cecile?

The woman didn't leave with her luggage, so she hadn't gone to the airport, Dana figured. So had she gone rogue? Was she going to do more of her voodoo rituals somewhere else? Dana had her camera with her, and she'd love to get some shots of *that*. Good for the follow-up story. She was going to nail Bergeron and all these idiots if it was the last thing she did.

She stayed a few cars back from the pickup and settled into traffic.

"This is pointless," Big Mike said. They had driven around D.C. for the better part of an hour and were now stopped at a light, not far from the White House. "We're never going to find her. You tried her cell again?"

"Nothing," Jimmy said.

"Where the hell would she go? She doesn't strike me as the type who would spend a day at the Smithsonian or something," T-Ron said. Boudreaux made a half-ass crowing sound, as if to announce his agreement. "Where you think she went, Boudreaux?" he said. He stuck his fingers into the small cage and rubbed the rooster's wing.

"She's a voodoo priestess," Jimmy continued. "What would interest her? Is there a voodoo museum somewhere? Or a voodoo union hall? Maybe she's checking in with the local chapter."

"Ridiculous," Big Mike said. "It's not like there's a voodoo sorority or club."

Jimmy stared out the window at a pack of Japanese tourists walking down the sidewalk. "Right. If there was a local chapter, that would be perfect. We could call over and have them send one of their ghost specialists. It's not like we *have* to get Miss Cecile, right? You think only the mambo who did the spell can undo it? You know, like Jeannie in *I Dream of Jeannie?*"

"She was a genie, idiot," T-Ron said. "They have different rules."

Big Mike just shook his head. "We need a specialist in the *dead*, as in 'bringing them back.'"

Boudreaux crowed loudly.

T-Ron patted the bird. "Damn, that'll wake up the dead."

Big Mike sat up and looked straight ahead. The light turned green, but he didn't move. A horn sounded from behind them. Mike eased forward, a slight smile on his face. "Damn."

"What?" Jimmy said.

"I know where she is. I think."

"Where?"

"Just hang on."

They left the city and took the Roosevelt Bridge over the Potomac and headed south down the Jefferson Davis Highway. You really had to know your presidents driving around Washington D.C. Even presidents of short-lived breakaway confederations. Every major road bore somebody's name.

Big Mike turned into the parking lot of Arlington National Cemetery. He found a spot, turned off the truck and looked over at the guys.

"Dead people."

T-Ron and Jimmy looked around.

Jimmy said, "You think she's *here?*"

"Got a hunch," Big Mike said, and undid his seatbelt. "Let's go."

Only family members could drive into the cemetery. Everyone else had to hoof it, and it was a long hoof. The cemetery covered 642 acres and had over 300,000 graves, from the lowliest private right up to generals and two presidents: Taft and Kennedy. Death tended to be the ultimate democratic concept. It didn't care much for rank.

Big Mike, T-Ron, Jimmy and Boudreaux walked into the huge cemetery and stopped. The expanse of white headstones was sobering.

"Where do we look?" T-Ron said.

Big Mike scanned the cemetery in all directions. "Keep walking. If she's here, she couldn't have walked far. She's old."

For 15 minutes they walked the hallowed ground. In the distance, they could hear taps being played as another soldier was laid to rest. It could have been an elderly warrior from wars past, or some kid from today's conflicts.

They came up on a slight hill and stopped. Down on the other side they saw a dazzling splash of color – a woman dressed in a red and orange dress. It seemed out of place in the predominantly white and green color motif of the cemetery.

"There she is!" Big Mike said.

They practically ran down the hill until they reached Miss Cecile. When they got close, they could see she was in some kind of trance. Her head was tilted back, her eyes were closed and she had her arms outstretched. Her lips were moving, but they couldn't hear what she was saying. They knew better than to speak until she was done.

No one saw the snake. But her bag was sitting at her feet.

Slowly, her head titled forward and her eyes opened. She dropped her arms and sighed deeply. There was a slight smile on her face.

"Dis place. It is full of peace."

"Miss Cecile?" Jimmy said.

She ignored him and continued. "They were connected by such violence in life. But now, there is so much peace for them. They are happy. *Bondye* has brought them home. Much happiness."

The guys looked around, as if they would see the spirits of dead soldiers. They could certainly feel them but they couldn't see them.

Big Mike said, "Miss Cecile, we need you to come with us back to the White House."

She reached down to pick up her bag. "What for? My work is done there."

"Umm, well," he said. "Long story, but we kind of need to get those ghosts back. You know, the one's you ran off."

"Fillmore, Cleveland and Jackson," T-Ron said. "The President kind of needs them to come back."

The old woman squinted her eyes at them. "Come back? I've never been asked to bring spirits like that *back*."

"We know it sounds kind of strange," Jimmy said. "Can you do that?"

Miss Cecile didn't speak for a full minute. Her face looked like she was deep in thought, her brow furrowed, as if she were speaking with the spirits at that moment. The guys just stood there. Even Boudreaux shut up.

"I do not know if I can do such a thing," she said. "I want to go home."

"Just come back to the White House with us and try," Big Mike pleaded. "It's a national emergency."

"The people there make fun of me," she said. "You saw the newspaper this morning? That young girl disrespects *vodu*."

"Yes ma'am," Big Mike said. "None of us came out looking good from that one. Even Beau. Uh, the President. He could use the help."

Miss Cecile looked all around her, as if saying goodbye to the 300,000 new friends she had just made. She turned to Jimmy. "And after this, I can go home?"

"Absolutely. Got the jet waiting for you."

"Then let's go," she said.

Big Mike turned to Jimmy. "Call Melancon. Tell him we have the package and to have the gates to the castle open."

T-Ron smiled and they began to walk back. "Just like a Tom Clancy novel. This is so cool!"

A hundred yards away, Dana Newton stood behind a large oak tree. She clicked one final shot from her camera, the long telephoto lenses perfect for her purposes. "Now we're talking," she said out loud. She turned and hurried back to her car.

She had a hunch they were headed back to the White House. If they were taking Miss Cecile to the airport, the story was over anyway. No, they were on the way back to 1600 Pennsylvania Avenue.

Dana practically ran back to her car, no small feat, even in her low heels. She sped out of the Arlington parking lot and high-tailed it back across the river into town. She kept looking in her rearview mirror to make sure the guys in the pickup weren't getting ahead of her. So far, she seemed to be in the lead.

She flashed her press credentials and was waved into the small lot outside the West Wing's west side. She sat in the car for a few minutes, checking the power in her big Nikon digital camera. She was nearly fully charged. She *and* the camera. She aimed it at the entrance to the lot and swung it back to the door leading into the West Wing.

She thought for a second. *Shoot them from here, or get positioned by the door?* No, she wanted to follow them inside as far as she could go. That meant she had to position herself by the door. She grabbed the camera and hurried to the entrance, under the small, white porte cochere that extended over the sidewalk. A few guys she recognized as low-level White House aides were standing off to one side, engrossed in something on one of their phones. Other than that, she owned the space. No other reporters were around.

Dana made sure she had a good line of sight for any car coming into the lot. Good thing, because seconds later, the big pickup rolled in. She started to click away, watching it as it parked. Big Mike, T-Ron – holding the stupid Lucky Cock, Boudreaux – Jimmy and Miss Cecile all piled out. *What a great shot,* Dana thought. The whole whacked-out Cajun Crew in a single frame. She could almost see the cutline under the photo in tomorrow's paper. *President*

Bergeron's Cajun Advisors arrive, including his voodoo priestess and lucky rooster. Just too good to be true.

They still hadn't seen her as they approached the door. She took a couple of more quick shots, retreated inside and switched to a shorter lens for the interior stuff. She hid behind a big plant so she could get the money shot.

And here it came. The doors opened and they were all inside. They were even bringing the rooster. *Perfect.*

"Hey, Miss Cecile!" Dana yelled.

They all turned in the direction of her voice. She stepped out and fired away, hitting them with the flash in rapid succession. Their eyes were all wide in surprise. Even the rooster was looking directly at the camera, as if to say, *Please, no photos. I'm just your average Lucky Cock.*

She brought the camera down from her face. "Hey guys, where ya headed?" she said. She sported a slightly evil smile.

The guys stumbled for an answer. Finally, Big Mike said, "Uh, just back from a little sight seeing. Gonna head back to our rooms."

Miss Cecile scowled at Dana.

"I have some questions, if you don't mind?" the young reporter said.

"Sure, sure," Miss Cecile said. She had now matched Dana's evil little smile with her own.

"Are you here to do any more rituals?" she asked.

The guys looked like they wanted to run.

Miss Cecile just continued her smile. "Why yes, young lady. I am."

Dana looked like she had just won the lottery.

"What for?"

"Well, the ghosts of Millard Fillmore, Grover Cleveland and Andrew Jackson are needed by the president. They were here earlier in the week, helping him out with all this China nonsense. I removed them, but the president wants them back."

Dana's jaw went slack. T-Ron let out a sound that was very similar to the gulping sound a dog makes before it pukes.

"I'm going to do it right now, if you care to watch," Miss Cecile said.

Chapter 39

Jimmy said, "Miss Cecile, we really need to go. Stop telling jokes to this nice young woman. *Please.*" He had a stupid look on his face. The kind a baby makes when it was passing gas.

"No, no. She really should see this, so her story is *accurate*," Miss Cecile said. She reached into her bag and pulled out the shrunken head of the nondescript animal she kept in there. "Hold this." She handed it to Dana.

Dana gently accepted the grotesque head in the palm of her hand. She winced slightly and looked back at Miss Cecile.

The old woman's smile grew larger. "Don't move." She reached back into her bag and rummaged around a bit. She hummed a little tune while she did it. The guys were frozen in place. "Ah, here it is." She held out her hand. It held a reddish powder.

Miss Cecile looked up at the ceiling and said some little prayer in her patois French. After a moment, she held her palm up to her mouth, and with the flick of her wrist, threw the powder into the air. The reddish substance now turned into a cloud that engulfed Dana.

The young woman's gag reflex kicked in, but not before she inhaled a large amount of the stuff. She began to cough. Miss Cecile snatched the animal head from her hand.

Dana staggered back a bit, a little unsteady on her feet. "Shit!" she said. She backed up and sat in a chair along the wall. She shook her head and put her hand over her eyes. "What...what *was* that?" she said. "I feel dizzy."

"Just sit there, my dear. Sometimes the effect can be a little unsettling." She turned and looked at Jimmy. "Let's go."

Jimmy wasted no time. He grabbed Miss Cecile's elbow and led her away. T-Ron and Big Mike just looked down at Dana Newton. The young woman's eyes looked a little glazed over. She blinked them opened and closed. She also opened her mouth wide and snapped it just, over and over again, like she was trying to taste something horrible on her tongue.

"Was that really the ritual?" asked Jimmy.

"No," Miss Cecile said.

"Is she going to be all right?"

She glanced back. "Doubtful."

Admiral Yang looked down at the flight deck from his perch on the carrier's bridge. The big ship had turned into the wind to launch aircraft. His Flying Sharks were now lining up for takeoff. They had to wait until the stealth drone had taken off. That launch had happened earlier, and the sleek flying wing was now flying low over the water, heading for its final bomb run on the American carrier *U.S.S. Washington.* It had been a flawless takeoff, young Yi doing a professional job taking control of the aircraft after it had been catapulted off the deck. Now Yi was below decks, in his secure flight operations room, "flying" the drone while sitting safely and comfortably in front of a bank of computer monitors and TV screens. Next to him were an engineering officer who monitored the drone's systems, and another man who kept a watchful eye on threats from American aircraft, if by some lucky chance they spotted the drone. *Highly unlikely,* Yang thought. Their radar couldn't detect it, and in fact, the only reason they had lost this drone's sister aircraft earlier in the week was because a high-flying American pilot had visually spotted it, enabling the Americans to shoot it down. Not so, tonight. There was no way it could be spotted by the human eye.

Yang called down to the young man. "Yi, status report."

"Everything is fine, Admiral," Yi said. "She is flying very well. I'm so low, the fish have to jump out of the way."

Yang smiled. *Arrogant little bastard.* "I already have submarines, Lieutenant. I need an undetectable aircraft."

"Understood, sir, I'll keep her dry. I'm at 10 meters. No lower."

"Very well. We want to get very close. I don't want the Americans to have any time to activate their defense systems."

"I promise they will be very surprised."

Yang knew that as long as the big anti-ship missile was inside the drone's belly, the aircraft was virtually invisible to the Americans. But once those bomb-bay doors opened to release the missile, the plane's stealthy radar signal would be lost until the doors were shut again. If Yi released too far from the American carrier, it would be detected, as would the inbound missile. It could be shot down by the ship's close-in defensive guns, or the missile's tracking radar could be jammed, causing it to fly off course and crash. The missile also had its own systems to defeat anything the Americans threw at it, but it wasn't worth the risk for a long shot. To kill the *Washington,* he would have to take the shot at point-blank range.

There was a roar below him. He looked down to see another of his fighters launch from the deck. He would fill the sky with these conventional planes to give the Americans something to focus on, less they detect his stealthy drone by accident. He didn't want to take any chances. He had also put his defensive ring of ships on notice, in case the Americans counter-attacked after their carrier was hit.

This was where things could get tricky. The *Lincoln* and her group of ships were still behind him. They could attack him with ease. What he was counting on was confusion. The explosion on the *Washington* would happen so quickly, there was a good chance they would think something had gone wrong on the deck, like one of their own missiles detonated by mistake. Things like that happened on carriers. He knew the Americans had nearly lost the *U.S.S. Enterprise* that way back in the sixties. The snap shot from the drone would be so close, it was very likely that's what they would initially think. This would buy him time to move his fleet closer to the Chinese mainland, under the protection of coastal forces and the big ballistic missiles the American admirals feared. That, at least, was the plan.

He figured it would work. He'd trade one lost aircraft for one lost American aircraft carrier. A very good trade.

"Yi, notify me the moment you begin your final attack run."

"Aye, Admiral."

Marissa got the call from Terry and raced over to the West Wing to meet the guys and Miss Cecile. She caught up with them in the Navy Mess Hall dining room. At this time of the afternoon, the place was empty.

"Any trouble getting in?" she said. She was out of breath.

"Not us," Big Mike said. "Can't say the same for that reporter back there."

Marissa looked back to the door. "Reporter? Shit."

"I wouldn't worry about her anymore," Miss Cecile said.

Marissa shook the old woman's hand. "Miss Cecile, good to see you again. I'm Marissa Bergeron. It's been a long time since I saw you last."

"I remember, dear. Your husband was running for governor. You had asked me for some...prayers, I believe?"

The guys looked at Marissa.

She smiled sheepishly. "What? Thought it couldn't hurt." She looked down at Boudreaux in his cage. "And I'm not the one carrying around a Lucky Cock. So there."

"Hey, be nice," T-Ron said.

"Anyway, Miss Cecile, my husband said to help you anyway I can. Is there someplace you need to be to, you know, perform your ritual or whatever? I've got access to pretty much the whole place."

"Where is the President now?" she asked.

"He's in the Situation Room with his advisors, monitoring the events over in Asia."

"Then that's where I need to be."

"What?" Marissa had gone a little pale.

"I need to be with the President."

Marissa looked at the guys and then back at Miss Cecile. "I don't think you can go in there. I can go get him, maybe. He's just right next door. How's that?"

Miss Cecile just shook her head. "There is much confusion here. It is best I be there, in the middle of it all."

"Oh boy. Wait a minute."

It was a short walk over to the Situation Room. Marissa jogged down the hall and looked into the Briefing Room. It was a small conference room off the main watch center. There was an aide in there, placing documents on the table. She figured Beau and the rest of the team were in the bigger video conference room on the other side of the watch room.

"Damn."

She walked into the watch room, which looked and sounded like Mission Control in Houston. Men and women, some in military uniforms, some civilian clothing, sat at computer stations. As First Lady, her security clearance was pretty good, but technically, her clearance was based on the fact she got to see the President naked. Which had to count for something. She smiled at a young man, who greeted her politely.

"The President is in there, ma'am," he said, pointing toward a door that led into the big video conference room. "Want me to get him?"

"No, no. Thank you. I've got it."

She half tiptoed through the room, trying not to make a scene. She opened the door and looked in. There must have been 10 men and women in there. Big brass. Top advisors. The big kahunas. Her guy was the biggest kahuna. He sat at the head of the table near the door. He turned when she stuck her head in.

"Oh, Marissa," he said. "What's up?"

Everyone in the room turned her way and nodded. Terry had a nervous look on his face. She gave him a wink to let him know Miss Cecile was in the building.

She half-whispered. "I know this is a bad time, but can you step over into the briefing room for a sec?"

Beau turned to his admirals, generals and intelligence leaders. Admiral Winston looked a little tense. He tapped his wristwatch and nodded in the affirmative. In other words, *"Sure, but for just a minute. If World War Three starts, you might want to be in here."*

Beau nodded and followed Marissa out. Everyone in the watch room stood as he walked through and into the briefing room. The aide had left and the small conference room was empty. She shut both doors.

"She here?" he said.

"In the Navy Mess."

"She doing her thing?"

"Not yet. She wants to do it in the Situation Room. Here. With you."

"Are you fucking kidding me?" he said. "I got the game on here." He pointed out the door toward the watch room. "The whole national security council is in there."

"We don't have to go in there. We can do it here."

Beau looked around the empty room. He rubbed his forehead. "Man, I really need to get another job."

"The guys are here, too. And Boudreaux."

"Oh, hell. Why not?" He looked around and threw up his arms. "Go get 'em. Just make sure no one sees 'em. Especially the chicken."

Marissa stuck her head out the door of the briefing room that led into a short hall that opened to where the Navy Mess was located. No one was in there. She hurried in and waved to the guys and Miss Cecile to follow. By her cautionary look, they knew this was on the down low. Way down low.

"This way," she whispered.

They hurried with her and entered the briefing room. The President was standing there with his arms folded.

"Miss Cecile," he said. "Good to see you. Thanks for coming."

"Mr. President," she said, and extended her hand.

T-Ron put his Lucky Cock on the table.

Beau looked down at the rooster. "Is he on his game?"

"Yeah. Good mojo," T-Ron said.

"Okay, let's do this," Beau said. Miss Cecile was already pulling weird shit out of her bag and putting it all on the table. The dead head. A cruet of water. Some small leather bags filled with unknown substances. A small gourd rattle. Some talisman-looking things that looked like African idols. Or maybe they were St. Peter and St. Paul. It was hard to tell. And last but not least, the snake.

Marissa gasped and stepped back.

Beau was now praying to God no one walked into the room.

"Mike, Jimmy? You mind watching the doors, please?" His voice sounded a little strained.

The guys took up positions with their backs to the doors and folded their arms.

Miss Cecile picked up the snake and a rattle and began shaking it. The rattle. Not the snake. She recited a prayer or incantation. Beau didn't know the difference and frankly could care less. She walked around the room once and put the snake back in the bag, much to everyone's joy. Then she poured some powder into one hand, and another one into her other hand. She mixed them together by rubbing her hands together. Next she walked around the room again, sprinkling the powder here and there until it was all gone.

She closed her eyes and put her hands together in prayer and nodded her head three times. Next, she picked up the cruet of water and sprinkled some around the room. She put a little on her fingers and made the sign of the cross on Beau's forehead. He figured this was the Catholicism part of voodoo he had heard so much about. A little blessing of holy water.

There was a knock on the door. Everyone jumped, except Miss Cecile.

"Yes? Bergeron said in his most authoritative presidential voice.

"Sir? Admiral Winston asks that you return to the video room."

"Thank you. On my way. Give me a second."

The aide walked away, wondering if the President and the missus were getting in a little action on the conference room table. She was sure as hell hot enough to distract anyone from World War Three.

That's when he heard a rooster crow. Everyone in the watch room stopped and turned around.

Inside the conference room, Bergeron put both hands to his face and mumbled through them, "Shut that fucking chicken up."

T-Ron stepped over from the door, picked up the cage and began to stroke Boudreaux's head.

Miss Cecile was now kneeling on the floor, praying loudly. Beau hoped there were no cameras or listening devices in the room. This would be gold to anyone who hated him. Or was looking for a book deal.

She stood up. "I have done all I can do."

Beau looked around. No sign of his dead presidential buddies.

It didn't work.

Chapter 40

Beau left the conference room first and hurried through the watch room and into the room where all the top brass was gathered. After he had left, Marissa led the guys and Miss Cecile out and back to the Residence.

Terry gave him a look that asked only one question. Bergeron shook his head slightly. He looked around the room in the hope he'd see Fillmore, Cleveland or Jackson. Any dead president would be fine at this point.

"What's up now, Admiral?"

"They're launching fighters again. Lots of them."

"Anything else?"

"There's some activity with their onshore mobile ballistic missiles again. More movement. More fueling."

"Great." Beau eased into his chair. "Our response?"

"We've had our people up for a while now. Adding more," the Admiral said. "Our B-2's are still in the vicinity. And we're detecting a slight change in the Chinese fleet's course. Moving due east, but not very fast. We're not sure what that's about. Maybe getting out of our way, if we're lucky."

"That's encouraging."

The Admiral nodded. "Yes, it is. If so, we may be about to dodge a bullet here."

Lieutenant Yi took another sip from his Diet Pepsi and put the can down on the console. He checked his altitude and airspeed. Still holding at 10 meters, and moving at 400 knots, skimming the surface of the South China Sea. Speed wasn't a big plus for these drones, but when you were invisible, you didn't have to be fast.

Why be fast when you could be invisible?

He liked that thought. Maybe he could get T-shirts made for his "crew" who flew the drones. He knew a guy in Hong Kong who did good work and would print them cheap.

Although he was technically flying the stealth drone, it was really the onboard computer that kept the craft in the air. No human could fly the unstable thing alone. It took too many data inputs to maintain its position in the air. Even the American pilots of the stealthy B-2 bomber needed big-time computers to help.

Yi turned the craft slightly to port and glanced at his video display. The high-powered optics in the night vision camera picked up the signature of the *U.S.S. Washington* in the distance. The unmistakable profile of the aircraft carrier was hard to miss. The ship looked closer than it actually was, thanks to the telephoto lens mounted in the nose of the drone.

"Admiral Yang, sir," he said into his headset radio.

"Yang here," the Admiral replied.

"Making my final run, sir."

"Outstanding, Yi."

Rear Admiral Tony Lear paced around the bridge of the *Washington,* now bathed in red light so as not to hamper the men's night vision. He kept scratching the back of his neck, a nervous habit he picked up at the Naval Academy before finals each year.

"Contacts bearing 1-9-0 and climbing past 15,000 feet, sir," his radar guy said. "Vectoring the Hornets their way."

"Very good. Anything else?"

"No, sir. Nothing here. All ships report clear."

"Hawkeye?"

"Reports the same. Eyes on the Sharks."

Lear sighted deeply. "Okay, stay sharp, everyone."

Yi could see through another camera on board the drone and spotted an American destroyer off to his starboard. The drone would fly right past it at five kilometers distance. They wouldn't see him either. But they would get to live. So there was some consolation for them, anyway.

Yi smiled and took another sip of his Diet Pepsi. He was about to sink an American aircraft carrier. *Cool.*

"Mr. President, Secretary of State Gottlieb is on the line," an aide said from behind Beau. He had stepped in from the watch room. "You can take it here or in the other conference room."

"I'll take it in there," he said and excused himself from the table. He walked through the watch room again and back to the smaller conference room. For a moment, he had a feeling that when he walked in, the dead presidents would be there. But the room was empty. He stepped in and the aide shut the door behind him.

Beau picked up the phone. "Frances?"

"Yes, Mr. President. Sorry to bother you."

"No, you're probably the one person who can bring me some good news right now."

"Right. I've just spoken to the Chinese Foreign Minister. He's taking a pretty hard stance about the fleet. Now that we have two of our carrier groups in the South China Sea, they see that as highly provocative. A contradiction of your statement earlier in the week."

"Yeah. Okay."

"Anyway, they're taking a 'whatever happens is our fault' stance on this thing. They've shown great restraint, despite our firing a missile at one of their ships."

'We didn't fire any missile at them."

"They're not buying it. I get the sense they're leaving it up to their military to respond as they see fit. Their guy out there is green lit to do whatever he has to do."

"What did you tell them?" Beau sat down and rubbed his eyes.

"The same. We're just passing through, and for them to just get out of the way and we'll be gone."

"And their response?"

She sighed over the phone. "Well, I just learned how to say, 'bullshit' in Chinese."

"Anything else?"

"No. The guy pretty much hung up on me."

"That's not a good sign."

"No, it's not. The military is running the show over there. They were probably standing over his shoulder. My advice is to tell our guys to watch it. They're gonna do something."

"Yeah, that's what we're thinking. Thanks."

Beau hung up and leaned back in his chair for a moment. When the diplomats stopped talking, soldiers generally started shooting. This thing was now officially going to shit. And him with it.

He got up and walked back to join the others. His knees felt a little weak as he entered the room. It was quiet now, and the vibe was about as tense as he had ever seen it. Terry got up from his chair and sat next to Beau.

He said, "Winston thinks we'll be shooting in the next 30 minutes. We can't stop it. Our best course of action will be how fast we can slow the thing down after it starts, and then stop it. Cut losses and get the diplomats talking."

Beau thought back to his conversation with his Secretary of State. "I think the diplomats have dropped their pens and picked up their rifles."

"That's pretty dark."

"Yep."

Beau looked across the conference table. A bag of potato chips was just out of reach. He had the nervous munchies. "Pass me those chips," he said.

Terry turned and looked down the table. "What chips?"

"There," Beau said. He stood up and started to reach over for the bag of chips. When he did, he saw there were three bottles of Abita Amber Ale sitting behind the big bag. Unopened. "Do you see the beers?"

Terry looked again and shook his head. "No chips. No beer."

Beau slowly sat back down in his chair, a big grin forming on his face.

"What?" Terry said.

Beau's smile grew wider. "Son of a bitch," he said. "I think our dead presidents are back."

"Here?"

"No, not here," he said. "I think they're *there*." He pointed at the big TV screen.

Yi sat up straight in his chair. The screen of the video monitor in front of him was now filled with the image of the *U.S.S. Washington.* He was closing on the ship very fast. He toggled the joystick a bit and the stealth drone rose slightly in altitude, from just 10 meters over the wave tops to 30. He had to gain some altitude to drop the anti-ship missile, lest it hit a wave before its engine lit off. The extra altitude would solve that problem, and it wouldn't compromise his radar invisibility either.

This maneuver would be critical. Once he opened the bomb bay doors and dropped the missile, he would have to do a hard turn to prevent the drone from crashing into the side of the aircraft carrier. He would be that close when he released. Of course, if it did hit the ship, he would be safe and sound in this little room. He just didn't want to lose another drone. The damn things were expensive, and the Chinese Navy didn't have many. Besides, this one would end up in a naval museum one day, as the craft that sunk the *Washington*. His picture would probably be in the display, too. *Cool.*

"Stand by for release," he said into his mike. The two other men in the room acknowledged him. Admiral Yang was the last to chime in.

"You are cleared to launch," Yang said.

"Roger."

Yi took a deep breath, closed his eyes for just a moment to settle himself and...

"Hey, kid, be careful with that!"

Yi jumped at the sound of the booming voice. Sitting on the console was a big fat man. A Westerner. But he spoke fluent Chinese. His huge girth blocked the TV monitor.

Grover Cleveland. The 22nd and 24th president of the United States.

"Hey, we're talking to *you*!"

Yi pushed back from the keyboard and his chair rolled backward. He looked to his left and another Westerner sat there. A smaller man with a stern expression.

"Who are you?!" Yi yelled.

Millard Fillmore thumped the kid in the head with his finger.

"Oww!!"

The two other officers in the room looked at him. One said, "What's wrong?"

"Call security and get these men out of here!" Yi said. He reached for the joystick and tried to look at the monitor. The stick fell from the console and hung by its cord, but not before it hit the hard floor. Yi stood up and watched in horror as the stealth drone reacted to the jarring movement of the joystick. The image wavered right and left and the plane wobbled. Yi reached down and finally got his hand on the joystick. Cleveland slid off the console and kneed the kid in the groin.

"Ohhh. Sorry about that," Cleveland said.

Yi howled in pain and hunched over. That was not a good thing for a pilot to do.

The stealth drone's right wing tip dipped and the plane lost altitude as it banked to starboard. The wing tip caught a wave and then good old-fashioned physics took over. The drone hit the water hard, pin-wheeled and broke into pieces in a large fireball that dragged across the dark sea.

"No!!!" Yi yelled.

"Yessss!!!" Fillmore and Cleveland yelled back.

On the bridge, Yang held the night-vision goggles to his eyes. He looked out into the distance where the *Washington* was just over the horizon. He should be seeing the flash just about...

"Hey, asshole," a voice said from behind him.

Yang dropped the binoculars from his eyes and turned. Standing there was a tall Westerner. He had a shock of thick gray hair, piercing eyes, and he wore an old military uniform from centuries past. It was a blue wool frock coat, with gold-colored buttons on the front and the sleeves. There was gold trim at the high-collared neck and the cuffs, with epaulets. A curved sword in its scabbard hung from his belt.

"That ship out there is named after a friend of mine, you piece of shit," he said in perfect Mandarin Chinese.

General Andrew Jackson, seventh president of the United States, was reporting for duty. He still fit in his uniform from the Battle of New Orleans, he was pleased to note. Death had been good for his figure.

Yang let out a tight yelp of surprise and he looked up at the odd, imposing figure. His entire bridge crew turned to him.

"Who is this?" Yang cried out. "Get him out of here!"

One of his men rushed over. "Who, sir?"

"This Westerner, you fool. Get him out of here and lock him up!"

The young man looked all around, and then at his comrades. He turned to Yang. "Sir, there is no one here."

"You're the only one getting out of here, Yang," Jackson said. "As you can see, your little surprise attack on the *Washington* failed. Time for you to go."

Yang backed up slightly. "You don't see him?"

Another bridge officer stood up. "No, sir. Who?"

"Quit your bawlin', Yang," Jackson said. He pulled his curved sword out of its scabbard and put the tip under Yang's chin. "I'm gonna slice you up, you little shit."

Yang moved around and backed toward the door that led out of the bridge. Jackson held the sword up and sliced it through the air. Yang gulped, backed into one of his men and yelled, "Help me!"

All of his men now stood and looked confused. They shot glances at each other and then at Yang.

Jackson poked the tip of the sword into Yang's chest, and the Chinese admiral felt the pressure and the sharp pain. This was no hallucination. It was real. He turned and ran from the bridge, with Jackson in hot pursuit.

Yang took the stairs down the tall island of the carrier. He stole quick glances behind him as Jackson continued the chase. The sword clanged against the gray steel of the structure as Jackson swung it for effect. Yang cried out in fear. He missed one step and fell three feet to a landing. He winced, got to his feet and kept running down the next set of stairs.

Finally, he made his way to the fight deck level, opened the hatchway and ran out into the night. The deck was bustling with activity as more of his Flying Sharks prepared for takeoff. The noise was near deafening.

Yang stopped, caught his breath and looked back. The Westerner was no longer there. Yang turned and got the shock of his life. The Westerner was now in front of him, seated on a horse, his sword held high in the air.

"Prepare to die, scoundrel!" Jackson said, and swung the sword.

Yang screamed like a little girl and took off running. He could hear the hoof beats of the horse on the deck behind him. The crazed Westerner was screaming, too, as if he were leading a cavalry charge. *How did he get a horse on his ship!*

Yang tried to grasp what he was seeing. And why no one else was seeing it. He couldn't figure it out. He just ran. Right in front of a fighter being taxied for takeoff. Yang avoided being hit by the nose wheel. He backed up slightly, turned to see the horseman chasing him, and took one step to his right.

It was his last.

The powerful air intake of the jet's port engine sucked the little man right off his feet and into the engine. There was a flash of flame as the engine swallowed Yang. What came out the back wasn't really Yang anymore.

Chapter 41

Rear Admiral Tony Lear's face appeared on the TV monitor. He was talking to another man off camera on the bridge of the *Washington*.

"You guys hear me?" he said to the room.

"Loud and clear, Admiral," Beau said. He stood up and walked close to the monitor in anticipation. Something had happened.

"Something exploded and crashed about a kilometer out from us," Lear said.

"A boat?" someone said.

"No, it was airborne, but very low. There was nothing there, then *bam*, it exploded and we caught it on radar."

"Ours or theirs?" Beau said.

"Theirs. I'm thinking another drone. Probably flying too low, hit the surface. But there was something about the explosion. Too big to be just the fuel on that thing. I think it might have been carrying a bomb or a missile."

"Heading straight for you, too," Admiral Winston said. "That was close. Another few seconds and..."

"Yeah," Lear said. "We got lucky." Lear turned to someone else that was talking to him off camera. "Stand by a second," he said, and held up his index finger.

"Okay, here's something interesting. You know their fleet was moving east very slowly? Our airborne reconnaissance reports they've picked up speed. The *Liaoning* has doubled her speed and is taking her task force with her."

"What happened, Admiral?" Beau said. He had a pretty good idea *who* happened.

"Not sure. Might have had something to do with that thing blowing up out there. And it looks like their fighters are pulling back, too. We'll keep you posted."

There was an audible exhalation of relief in the room. Not a cheer. No high-fiving. Just a moment of broken tension. Terry stared right at Beau, a slight smile forming on his lips. "Did they...?"

Beau shrugged. "I don't know."

The whole team sat in the room for the next hour, gathering as much information as they could on the turn of events. Beau listened intently to the exchange between the admirals as more and more intel came in. He asked a few questions, but was content to just watch the crisis seemingly resolve itself. He also stayed there hoping Fillmore, Cleveland and Jackson would pop back in for their own little report.

The door to the room opened slightly, and Cary Guidry, Beau's personal assistant and sometimes chief fantasy girl, stuck her head in the room. "Mr. President? It's Mrs. Bergeron. She needs you up in the Residence right away."

Beau and Terry followed Cary up to the Residence. Steve Olson, ever-present Secret Service guy, followed behind.

"They're in the living room," she said, and pointed to the door. "I'll be out here if you need me." She made a little worried frown face.

"Thanks, Cary. Who's all in there?"

"Ummm. The First Lady. T-Ron, Jimmy and Big Mike. The voodoo lady. And the chicken."

The two men exchanged glances and walked in. Terry shut the door behind them.

Cary had missed a couple of guests. Three, actually. Millard Fillmore, Grover Cleveland and Andrew Jackson stood over by the windows. Each had a beer in hand, looking like three guys who just shot a great round at the club. They were chill.

"Guys!" Beau walked over to them and shook their hands. "I'm glad to have you back."

"I bet you are," Fillmore said.

Marissa cleared her throat and said, "The guys can't see them, Beau."

"Neither can I," Terry said.

Beau turned to his living buddies. "Say hi to the best dead presidents ever," he said, and introduced them.

Big Mike, T-Ron and Jimmy just stared blankly at the area by the window. Of course, no one was there.

"Uh, hello," T-Ron said.

Big Mike gave a slight wave.

Jimmy just stared at Beau.

Miss Cecile got up and walked over to the dead presidents. She eyed them carefully, and then placed her hand on Andrew Jackson's chest.

"Madam," he said, and gave her a slight bow. He was still in his battle uniform.

Beau clapped his hands together once. "Okay. So just Terry and the guys can't see you. Not sure about the Lucky Cock. I wonder why?"

Fillmore shrugged. "Beats me."

"Miss Cecile, thanks for your help getting these guys back," Beau said.

The old woman nodded and returned to her chair. She looked a little shaken.

Beau turned to Cleveland, Fillmore and Jackson. "So what happened? What did you do?"

The three presidents clinked their beer bottles together. "Well, let's just say it was a coordinated attack on our part," Cleveland said.

Jackson went on to explain the details.

"Holy shit," Beau said when he heard about Admiral Yang's close encounter with the jet. He turned back to Terry and the guys and filled them in on what Jackson had said.

"He rode a ghost horse across the deck of a Chinese aircraft carrier?" Big Mike said.

"That's so cool," T-Ron said. "Ghost horse. Awesome."

"And the drone *did* have a bomb in it," Beau said. "They say it was pretty close to the *Washington* when it crashed and blew up."

"I don't think the young man flying that thing will be the same," Fillmore said. "He ran out of that room screaming like a girl."

"At least he didn't run into a jet," Jackson said. "Or should I say run *inside* a jet."

"I kneed him in the nuts," Cleveland replied and chuckled. "I've got big knees, too."

Marissa had been repeating this exchange to Terry and the guys, like a translator giving both sides of a conversation.

Jimmy stood up. "Beau, look, we're sorry about getting Miss Cecile to run these guys off. We thought, well, we thought that's what you needed."

Beau turned back to his friends. "That's okay. You didn't know. Hell, none of us knew. Kind of a strange few days for everyone."

"You said it," Fillmore replied. "Very weird couple of days for us, too."

"At least the beer was cold," said Cleveland.

"The best I ever had," Jackson added.

"So what now?" Beau said. "You staying? Going? What?"

"I think our time here is over," Fillmore said. "At any moment, too. You mind if we have a few minutes with you? Alone?" He gestured to the rest of the living in the living room.

Marissa, who had heard this, stood up and said, "Sure. Let's go guys. Get Boudreaux, too." She led everyone out, including Miss Cecile.

When they had left, Beau got a little misty eyed. "Look, I don't know how to thank you. Once again, you've served your country well."

Fillmore looked out the window. Cleveland and Jackson just stood there, stone faced. Finally, Fillmore turned and said, "We all served. Continue to serve. We tried our best. Sometimes things worked out. Most of the time, they didn't. Like I said, our picture's not on any money."

Jackson coughed.

"Okay. *Me and Grover's* pictures aren't on any money. But the point is, this job is ridiculous. No one's going to get it right. All you can hope for is not to permanently screw the whole thing up. What happened over the last few days could have turned out to be very bad. For you, the country, maybe the whole world."

"Thanks to you three, it didn't," Beau said.

"True, you got some help," Cleveland said. "Not sure how you warranted special treatment. I sure as hell never did. But you got it, and it turned out to make the difference."

"I really didn't do anything."

"But you *did*. You used every asset you had at your disposal," said Fillmore. "You listened to your advisors. You deployed your people. Even if some of those people were dead. An asset is an asset. Bottom line, you were *in charge*."

"Learn the lesson," Jackson said. "You're not as smart as you think you are. Not as dumb, either. Avoid the stupid compromises. Listen to your trusted friends, but in the end, listen to your own voice. Then make the decision. Don't worry about pissing people off."

Beau just nodded.

"We're all just men," Fillmore said. "Some of us were great presidents, with spectacular achievements and the monuments to go with them. Many of us, not so much. Some of us were complete duds in public office. Maybe not in our private lives, though. But still, we love our country.

It works, despite its occasional failings. Or maybe it doesn't fail as much as *we* fail." He pointed to his two dead buddies.

Beau just stared at them. "Why me? Why did I get this kind of help?"

Fillmore smiled. "Don't flatter yourself, kid. It's not the first time a living president got any help from the other side."

"What?"

Cleveland said, "We kind of failed to mention that this sort of thing happens from time to time. You weren't the first. Or the last."

"Seriously? I thought you said you didn't know why you were here."

Jackson said, "In case you hadn't noticed, Beau, we're politicians. We're born liars."

"Who got help?" Beau said.

"Well, let's see," Fillmore said. "That Cuban Missile Crisis back in 1962 almost got out of hand. You can thank Harrison, Coolidge and Jefferson for that not turning into a major cluster."

Bergeron was speechless. "That wasn't all Kennedy?"

All three of the dead presidents shook their heads in unison.

"Where is all this going?" Beau said. "What are you trying to tell me?"

Jackson stepped closer to Beau and stuck a finger in his chest. "Just have fun. Be a jackass sometimes. Just don't screw it up." He stepped back and disappeared.

Cleveland looked at his empty beer bottle, placed it on a nearby table and burped loudly. "Just keep the thing

out of the ditch. When all else fails, you've got a hot wife."
Then he also disappeared.

That left just Millard Fillmore.

Beau said, "I feel like I'm in that scene at the end of
The Wizard of Oz. I want to say, 'I think I'll miss you most
of all.'"

Fillmore slapped Beau on the shoulder. "It was a good
time, wasn't it?" He looked around the room. "I wanted to
thank you."

"Me?"

"Yes. My presidency was just one of the final steps
to a horrible war. Over 500,000 men dead. A country torn
apart. The whole thing. History hasn't been too kind to
me. But this little adventure? Finally, I feel like I really did
something good. Thanks to you."

Beau smiled. "You sure the *real* Commander in Chief
didn't have something to do with that?"

Fillmore looked up and returned the smile. "Maybe.
Probably."

"Thanks, Mr. President," Beau said, and shook the
ghost's hand.

"Until we see each other again," Fillmore replied.

"Hopefully not any time soon."

"Of course not. You've got a country to run, Beau. Do
it well."

And with that, Millard Fillmore disappeared and
stepped out of history again. Maybe with something new to
put on his resume.

Chapter 42

Things kind of returned to normal after that. Well, as normal as Washington D.C. could return to. The Chinese fleet headed back to port, its gambit to bully its way into controlling the South China Sea a complete failure. Lieutenant Chen Yi, having lost two high-priced stealth drones, was dismissed from service and became the assistant manager of a video game store in Beijing.

Admiral Yang Jinping was memorialized by a few friends back in China, but in the halls of government, he forever more became known as "Admiral Puree." A fitting tribute if there ever was one.

Dana Newton, late of the *New York Times,* was found later that day after her encounter with Miss Cecile, dancing in the Rose Garden, butt naked, singing every song from *The Sound of Music.* When they took her away, she was babbling something about shrunken animal heads, zombies and lucky cocks. Last anyone heard, she was writing organic gardening stories for a small paper in upstate New York.

The guys, including Beau, managed to get out to the fishing tournament that weekend. They did pretty good as a group, although they didn't win the thing. It was assumed that Boudreaux, the Lucky Cock, had been tapped out in the luck department after the week's events. Had it not been for those Chinese assholes, they figured, Boudreaux would have been at maximum power, and they would have won. And much to Big Mike's delight, for a few hours that Saturday, his bass boat, carrying the President, had been designated "Navy One" by the Secret Service. So there was that.

Six months later, President Beau Bergeron found himself listening intently as his Secretary of State, Frances Gottlieb, gave a full report to the rest of the Cabinet about her recent trip to China. She had cleared the way for Beau to visit Beijing in the next month. Rather than gloating over his success in what was now called "The South China Sea Showdown," Beau had reached out to China's new government – a *civilian* government that had come to power just after the Chinese military's poor handling of the crisis. *Thank you, Admiral Puree.*

"Thanks, Frances," he said when she was done. "I know that took some doing over the last months. Nice job."

Everyone clapped for the Secretary of State. She was last on the agenda, so the meeting was over. Beau thanked everyone and rose. This time, the clapping was for him. After 18 months on the job, Beau's approval ratings were through the roof. The best for any president a year-and-a-half into a first term. He now had some legitimate foreign-policy street cred, and some of his domestic policies got a lift in Congress after the successful outcome of the international incident

There were a few short, private conversations and congratulations as everyone shuffled out of the Cabinet Room. Terry Melancon leaned in and whispered in Beau's ear. "It's here."

He turned and stared at Terry like a kid who just got told his birthday present was on the kitchen table. "No shit?"

"No shit."

"Let's go. Oval Office?"

"Yep."

The two men hurried down the hall and walked into the most famous office in the world. Waiting for them were three people. Two were from the White House Curator's Office – the director, Stu Carswell, and an assistant, Laney White. Standing next to them was a thirty-something guy in a poor- fitting suede coat with an open collar. He was short, stocky, with beefy arms and shaggy brown hair. He looked like a blacksmith, which wasn't too far from the truth.

Carswell introduced the young man to the President. His name was Garvin Gates.

"Garvin. Glad to finally meet you," Beau said.

Gates smiled and said, "You ready to see it?"

"Absolutely."

He gestured to the coffee table, on which something large sat, covered with a sheet.

"Before I show it, I just wanted to say I like your thinking, Mr. President. It's bold. Unexpected. Maybe even risky. You'd make a fine sculptor."

Beau constantly had pixie dust shoved up his ass, but he actually liked this flattery. "I'll see how this job works out. If not, I might come apprentice with you."

"Deal."

Gates pulled the sheet off and revealed a bronze sculpture. It was Andrew Jackson, astride a horse, his sword raised to the air. Standing on one side of the horse was Grover Cleveland with a big smile on his face, looking up at Jackson. On the other side was Millard Fillmore, holding the reins in one hand. He was leaning against the horse, with a jaunty smile on his face, too. The three of them stood on a limestone base.

Beau carefully touched the sculpture. "Wow. That is just awesome work. Great detail on the faces, too. They look like they all knew each other."

"Just as you requested," Gates said.

"Perfect. It'll look great in here."

"It's to scale," Gates said. "If you ever decide to actually build it, the real thing will be double life size."

"Who knows?" Beau said. "It could happen. I've got three millionaires from Louisiana who would throw in some money." He winked at Terry, who just rolled his eyes. "It would have to be totally paid for by private donations."

"If we do, we'll have to find some land somewhere in town," Terry said. "That's gonna take some wrangling from Congress. They'll laugh at us. As will the press."

"As long as it's in D.C. proper. On the tour," Beau replied. He was still admiring the craftsmanship. "Prime time."

Terry said, "Oh, sure. We'll put it right next to the Lincoln Memorial. That'll be interesting."

Beau ignored his snarky buddy and eyed the sculpture closely. "Outstanding."

Carswell, the director of the White House Curator's Office, carefully broached the obvious subject. "If you do, it will be…unusual, controversial, even for this town. Certainly a conversation piece for years to come. A monument to…"

Beau finished his sentence. "To *all* presidents, great and small. Having Jackson, an obvious choice for greatness, right in the middle, is key. Having Fillmore and Cleveland next to him, kind of lends credence to this exclusive fraternity thing. All the presidents, just by serving, have done their duty during their lifetime."

Terry mumbled under his breath, "And even beyond that." No one heard him, he hoped.

"It's a reminder of the duty to serve, no matter what. That alone deserves respect." Beau was practicing a future speech.

"Where do you want us to put it, Mr. President?" Laney White said.

"Leave it right there," he said.

Terry excused himself for a meeting, and the Curator people took the sculptor on a quick tour of the White House. Beau went back to his desk and sat down. He looked up at the paintings of Fillmore, Cleveland and Jackson that now adorned the Oval Office wall. He never had them taken down after the big artwork switcheroo six months earlier. He had no idea where they put Washington, Jefferson and Lincoln. He was very happy with the current arrangement.

He gave the three paintings a salute and smiled. He grabbed the phone and called his secretary.

"Mrs. Foster? Could you have a butler bring something for me?"

"Yes, sir," she said. "What do you need?"

"How about a bag of potato chips and a cold Abita Amber?"

"Right away, sir."

Author's Note

Once again, thank you for reading the book. It's the first ghost story I've ever written, but I've told many to my kids. I think we all love a good one. I've always been a big history buff, too, so to mix in some presidential history in the process is just that much more fun. If you get a chance, grab a biography of any of your favorite presidents. Maybe even your not-so-favorite presidents. It's always interesting to see how men (to date) have tried to wrestle with that job. As I mention in the book, a few do it well. Most struggle. But they're all human. I liked *American Lion,* the great biography of Andrew Jackson by Jon Meacham, which I also mention in the book. Jackson is credited with defining the modern-day presidency and giving it real power. As far as accuracy in this book, the White House is always changing as one president moves in after another. I tried to be as true to the 'People's House" as possible. And for all the ships, planes and other military technology that's in the book, it's all real – or about to be real. Anything wrong is all on me. Big thanks also to all my early readers. My wife, Debra; Rosalind Tuminello; Jim and Audrey Shanks and Pat Butler. Thanks also to Bryan Foux, designer extraordinaire, for another great cover. And a huge shout-out to the staff at Duke Street Press. To Sam and Kelly: thanks for the inspiration. Can I borrow the rooster sometimes? And to all my FIJI brothers, you really can't make this shit up.

Or maybe you can.

About the Author

Louis Tridico grew up in Louisiana's bayou and plantation country, listening to all the strange stories, legends and folklore his father and uncles told. After graduating from LSU with a journalism degree, he started his career in advertising, PR and political consulting. He also served as media spokesman for the East Baton Rouge Parish Sheriff's Department. He currently lives in Texas as a Louisiana expatriate with his wife, two kids, two dogs and one box turtle. They make regular pilgrimages back to the swamps.

Visit him at his author website: www.LouisTridico.com or his Facebook author page

Look for Louis Tridico's new thriller, *Redcoat,* in early 2014.

Emma Eaton, historian and restoration architect, is tasked with resurrecting a run-down plantation no one believes is worth saving. But before she can get started, the FBI and Scotland Yard enlist her services to help solve the murder of a British diplomat in the French Quarter. The sword-wielding killer was dressed as a British redcoat, and the killing doesn't end with the diplomat. As the body count increases, Emma begins to connect the dots to the

1815 Battle of New Orleans. She suspects the killer is trying to bury a long-lost secret with connections to the present. But as she gets closer to the truth, the Redcoat gets closer to her. Will he bury her as well?

Also by Louis Tridico

Fort St. Jesus Bait & Tackle

Doug Malone e-book novellas:

Draken's Fire

Viper

36172211R00235

Made in the USA
San Bernardino, CA
14 July 2016